Who's

that

Girl?

Mhairi was born in Scotland in 1976 and her unnecessarily confusing name is pronounced Vah-Ree.

After some efforts at journalism, she started writing novels. *Who's That Girl?* is her fourth. She lives in Nottingham with a man and a cat.

BY THE SAME AUTHOR

You Had Me At Hello
Here's Looking At You
It's Not Me, It's You

Who's
that
Girl?

MHAIRI McFARLANE

HarperCollins*Publishers*

HarperCollins*Publishers*
1 London Bridge Street
London SE1 9GF

www.harpercollins.co.uk

Published by HarperCollins*Publishers* 2016
1

A catalogue record for this book
is available from the British Library

ISBN: 978-0-00-818479-7

This novel is entirely a work of fiction.
The names, characters and incidents portrayed in it are
the work of the author's imagination. Any resemblance to
actual persons, living or dead, events or localities is
entirely coincidental.

Typeset by Palimpsest Book Production Ltd, Falkirk, Stirlingshire

Printed and bound in the United States of America by
RR Donnelley

Find out more about HarperCollins and the environment at
www.harpercollins.co.uk/green

For Natalie, Paula & Serena
My favourite mix tape

1

Life through a phone is a lie. Edie imagined the process like a diagram from physics lessons, the one on that Pink Floyd album cover – a beam of white light refracted in a prism, splintering and fanning out as a rainbow.

I mean, how much artifice, she wondered, was crammed into this one appealing photograph? She gazed at its seductive fictions in the slightly greasy, warm slab of screen in her palm as she queued at the hotel bar.

Activity in the room whirled around her, messy unkempt sweaty reality, soundtracked by The Supremes 'Where Did Our Love Go?' In this still life, everything was forever image managed and perfect.

Untruth number one: she and Louis looked like they adored each other's company. In order to squeeze into the frame, Edie had rested her head against his shoulder. She was coquettish, wearing a mysterious smile. He was doing the self-satisfied, slightly 007 quirk of the lip that conveyed *hey life is great, no big deal*. It really wasn't a big deal.

They'd spent five hours as platonic plus ones – the wedding

planner had demanded pairs, like Noah's Ark – and now they were grating on each other, in heat and booze and wedding clothes with waistbands that had got tighter and tighter, as if inflating a blood pressure cuff.

Edie's heels had, like those high enough for special occasions, moved from 'wobbly and pinchy, but borderline tolerable' to stabbing at her viciously like some mythic pain where she'd given up her mermaid tail for size 4s and the love of a prince.

Falsehood number two, the composition. Twinkling-happy party girl Edie, looking up through roadsweeper-brush-sized false lashes. You could glimpse the top half of her red dress, with nicely hoisted pale bosom, stomach carefully held in. Louis's cheekbones were even more 'killer in a Bret Easton Ellis' sharp than usual, chin angled downwards.

This was because they'd held the lens at arm's length above their heads and discarded five less flattering images, bartering over who liked which one. Edie had eye bags, Louis objected he looked gaunt, the expressions were slightly too studied, the shadows had not fallen in their favour. *OK, another, another! Pose, click, flash.* Half a dozen was the charm: they both looked good, but not too much like they'd *tried* to look good.

('Why does everyone do that expression now, like you're sucking on a sour plum?' Edie's dad asked, last time she was home. 'To make yourself look thin and pouty, I suppose. But you don't look like that face you pull, in real life. How strange.')

Louis, an Instagram professional and very sour plum, fiddled with the brightness and contrast settings. 'Now to filter ourselves to fuck.'

He selected 'Amaro', bathing them in a fairytale cloud of lemonade fog. Complexions were perfected. The mood was filmic and dreamy, you'd think it captured a perfect moment. *You had to (not) be there.*

And then there was the caption. The biggest deception of all. Louis tapped it out and hit 'post.' *'Congratulations Jack & Charlotte! Amazing day! So happy for you guys <3 #perfectcouple living their #bestlife.'*

This was mostly for the benefit of the rest of the Ad Hoc agency, who'd all found elegant excuses not to travel from London to Harrogate. Nothing tested popularity like several hundred miles of motorway.

Like after admiring Like rolled in. 'Sigh. You two are another #perfectcouple!' 'Shame I'm a bender!' Louis replied. *That'd be the least of our problems*, Edie thought. They'd all done the arithmetic with Louis, that if he slagged off everyone else to you, he slagged you off, too.

And of course, Louis had not stopped grousing under his breath about the 'amazing' wedding. Edie thought criticising someone's big day was like making fun of the way they ate, or the size of their ankles. Good people instinctively understood it was not fair game.

I really thought Charlotte would go for something more clean, minimal. Like Carolyn Bessette marrying JFK Jnr. The crystal beading on that gown's a bit Pronuptia, isn't it? Even women with taste seems to lose the plot and go Disney disaster in a bridal salon. I am so over those rose bouquets with pearl studs and white ribbon round the stems, like a bandaged stump! Once a WAG has done something, it is DONE. And sorry, but I find a tanned bride vulgar.

Ugh, two sips of that Buck's Fizz and it was into a plant pot. I can't bear orange juice used to hide cheap champagne. Look at the DJ, he's about fifty in a blouson leather jacket, where did he get that from, 1983? He looks like he should be on Top Gear. *It'll be rocking out to Kings Of Leon's 'Sex On Fire' and Toni Braxton for the erection section. Why can't weddings be more MODERN?*

The Old Swan in Harrogate was not, as the name suggested, modern. It had the exciting association of being the place Agatha Christie disappeared to during her 'missing days' in the 1920s, even though there was probably nothing exciting about being in a confused fugue state.

Edie loved it here. She wouldn't mind absconding from her life into one of its rooms with four-poster canopied beds. Everything about The Swan was comforting. The ivy-clad frontage, the solid square portico entrance, the way it smelled like cooked breakfasts and plushy comfort.

It had been a blistering high summer day – *Haven't they been lucky with the weather* becoming the go-to banal conversation opener – and the French doors in the bar opened on to the honey-lit rolling gardens. Children in shiny waistcoats were zooming around playing aeroplanes, high on Coca Cola and the novelty of being up this late.

Nevertheless, this was, for none of the reasons Louis described, the worst wedding Edie had ever been to.

Giving her order at the bar, she found herself next to a group of women in their seventies and possibly eighties, dressed as flappers. Edie guessed they were here for a Murder Mystery weekend; she'd seen a coach from Scarborough pull up earlier.

There was a 'suspect' with no legs, sitting in a wheelchair.

She was wearing a feather headband, long knotted beads and draped in a white feather boa. She was sipping a mini bottle of Prosecco through a straw. Edie wanted to give her a cuddle, and/or cheer.

'Don't you look lovely,' one of the group said to Edie, and Edie smiled and said, 'Thank you! You do too.'

'You remind me of someone. Norma! Who does this lovely young lady look like?'

Edie did the fixed embarrassed smile of someone who was being closely inspected by a gaggle of tipsy senior citizens.

'Clara Bow!' one exclaimed.

'That's it!' they chorused. 'Ahh. Clara Bow.'

It wasn't the first time Edie had been given a compliment like this. Her dad said she had 'an old-fashioned face.' 'You look like you should be in a cloche hat and gloves at a train station, in a talkie film,' he always said. 'Which is appropriate.'

(Edie didn't think she talked *that* much, it was more that her father and sister were quieter.)

She had shoulder-length, inky hair and thick dark brows. Their geometry had to be aggressively maintained with threading, so they stayed something more starlet than beetling. They sat above large soulful eyes, in a heart-shaped face with small mouth.

A cruel yet articulate boy at a house party told her she looked like 'A Victorian doll reanimated by the occult.' She told herself it was because she was going through her teenage Goth phase but she knew it was still applicable now, if she hadn't had enough sleep and caught herself glowering.

Louis once said, as if he wasn't talking about her when

they both knew he was: 'Baby faces don't age well, which is why it's a tragedy it was Lennon shot instead of McCartney.'

'Are you here with your husband?' another woman asked, as Edie picked up her white wine and V&T.

'No, no husband. Single,' Edie said, to lots more staring and curious delighted *ooohs*.

'Plenty of time for that. Having your fun first, eh?' said another of the flappers, and Edie smiled and nearly said, 'I'm thirty-five and having very little fun,' and thought better of it and said 'Yes, haha!' instead.

'Are you from Yorkshire?' another asked.

'No. I live in London. The bride's family are from—'

Louis emerged from the restaurant, gesturing for her to join him with an urgent circling motion of the hand, hissing:

'*Edie!*'

'Edie! What a beautiful name!' the women chorused, looking upon her with renewed adoration. Edie was touched and slightly baffled by her sudden celebrity status. That was Prosecco drunk through a straw for you.

'Are you this young lady's gentleman?' they asked Louis, as he joined them.

'No, darlings, I like cock,' he said, taking his drink from Edie while she cringed.

'He likes who?' said one of the women. 'Who's "Cock"?'

'No. Cock.' Louis made a flexing bicep gesture that Edie didn't think made it much clearer.

'Oh, he likes *men*, Norma. He's a Jolly Roger,' said one, casually.

Attention shifted to Louis, the not-that-jolly Roger.

'I prefer a game of Bananagrams and a hot bath, these days,' another offered. 'Barbara still likes a bit of cock, well enough.'

'Which one of you did it, then?' Louis said, eyeing their costumes. 'Who's the prime suspect?'

'There's not been a crime yet,' one said. 'Rumour has it there's going to be a body found on the third floor.'

'Well you can probably rule her out then,' Louis said, tapping his nose, gesturing at the woman in the wheelchair.

'*Louis!*' Edie gasped.

Fortunately, it caused a cackle eruption.

'Sheila used to dig her corns out with safety pins. You don't mess with Sheila.'

'Looks like she overdid it.'

Edie gasped again and the old ladies fell about, howling. She couldn't believe it: Louis had found his audience.

'Great meeting you, girls,' Louis said, and they almost applauded him. Edie was forgotten; chopped liver.

'Come back to the table. It's all kicking off big style in the main tent,' Louis said to her. 'The speeches are starting.'

With a heavy heart, Edie excused herself. The moment she dreaded.

An Audience With The Hashtag Perfect Couple, Living Their Hashtag Best Life.

2

'Was that free?' barked the sixty-something man with the hearing aid, dressed as a posh country squire, eyes fixed on the glass in Edie's hand. Edie and Louis had been put on the odds and sods, 'hard work, nothing in common' table. The others had immediately abandoned the hard work and scattered, in the longueur between meal and disco. This sod remained, with his timid-looking, equally tweedy wife.

'Er, no? I can get you something if you like?'

'No, don't bother. You come to these bloody interminable things and they fleece you like sheep. As if the gift list wasn't brass neck enough. Four hundred pounds for some bloody ugly blue cake whisk, the silly clots. Oh hush, Deirdre, you know I'm right.'

Edie plopped down in her banqueting chair and tried not to laugh, because she thought the KitchenAid was a rinse, too.

She swigged the acidic white wine and thanked the Lord for the gift of alcohol to get through this. The top table passed the microphone down the line to the groom, Jack. He tapped his glass with a fork and coughed into a curled fist. His sleeve was tugged by his new mother-in-law. He put a palm up to indicate, 'Sorry, in a second, folks.'

'What's this crackpot notion of wearing brown shoes with a blue suit and a pink tie, nowadays?' said hearing aid man, of the groom's attire. 'Anyone would think this was a lavender liaison.'

Edie thought Jack's tall, narrow frame in head-to-toe spring-summer Paul Smith looked pretty great but she wasn't about to defend him.

'What's a lavender liaison?' Louis said.

'A marriage of convenience, to conceal one's true nature. When one's interests *lie elsewhere*.'

'Oh, I see. We're having one of those,' he grinned, clasping Edie to him.

'Forgive me if I don't scrabble for my inhaler in shock,' he said, looking at Louis's quiffed hair. 'I had you down as someone who likes to *smell the flowers*.'

Edie had heard more inventive euphemisms for 'homosexual' than she expected today.

'Think you'll ever bother with marriage?' Louis said, under his breath.

'I think it's more whether marriage will ever bother with me,' Edie said.

'Babe. *Loads* of people would marry you. You're so "wife". I look at you and think "WIFE ME".'

Edie laughed, hollowly. 'Surprised they're not making this known to me then.'

'You're an enigma, you know . . .' Louis said, prodding the bottom of his glass with the plastic stirrer. Edie's stomach tensed, because meandering, whimsical trains of thought with Louis were always headed to the station of *I Can't Believe You Said That*.

'Hah. Not really.'

'I mean, you're never short of fans. You're the life and soul. But you're always on your own.'

'I think that's because *being a fan* doesn't necessarily equal *wanting a relationship*,' Edie said neutrally, casting her eyes over the hubbub in the room and hoping they'd snag on something else they could talk about.

'Do you think you're the commitmentphobe? Or are they?' Louis said, moving the stirrer to one side as he drank.

'Oh, I repel them with a kind of centrifugal force, I think,' Edie said. 'Or is it centripetal?'

'*Seriously?*' Louis said. 'I'm being serious here.'

Edie sighed. 'I've liked people and people have liked me. I've never liked someone who's liked me as much as I like them, at the same time. It's that simple.'

'Maybe they don't know you're interested? You're quite hard to read.'

'Maybe,' Edie said, thinking agreeing would end this subject sooner.

'So no one's ever promised you a lifetime of happiness? You haven't broken hearts?'

'Hah. Nope.'

'Then you're a paradox, gorgeous Edie Thompson. *The girl who everyone wanted . . . and nobody chose.*'

Edie spluttered, and Louis had the reaction he'd been angling for.

'"Nobody chose"! Bloody hell, Louis! Thanks.'

'Babe, no! I'm no different, no wedding for loveless Louis any time soon. I'm thirty-four, that's dead in gay years.'

This was nonsense, of course. Louis no more wanted a wedding than an invasive cancer. He spent all his time hunting for meaningless hook-ups on Grindr, the latest with a wealthy, hirsute man he called Chewbacca to his 'Princess Louis'. It was just a way of claiming the latitude to take the mickey out of Edie.

'I did say gorgeous, you diva,' Louis pouted, as if Edie had been the aggressor. You had to admire the choreography of Louis's cruelty – a series of carefully worked out, highly nimble steps, executed flawlessly.

'Ladies and gentleman, sorry about the delay. . .' said the groom into the microphone at last.

Jack's slightly anaemic speech ticked off the things it was supposed to do, according to the internet cheat sheets. He said how beautiful the bridesmaids looked and thanked everyone for being there. He read out cards from absent relatives. He thanked the hotel for the hospitality and both sets of parents for their support.

When he finished with the pledge: 'I don't know what I did to deserve you, Charlotte. I will spend the rest of my life trying to make sure you don't regret your decision today,' Edie almost knocked back the flute of toasting champagne in one go.

The best man Craig's speech was amusing in as much as it was horribly misjudged, with gag after gag about the varying successes of Jack's sexploits at university. He seemed to think these tales were suitable because 'We were all at it!'

and they were, 'A bloody good bunch of chaps.' (Jack went to Durham.) At the mention of a rugby game called 'Pig Gamble,' Jack snapped, 'Perhaps leave that one out, eh?' and Craig cut straight to, 'Jack and Charlotte, everyone!'

The bride had a nervous fixed grin and her mum had a face like an arse operation.

Charlotte's chief bridesmaid, Lucie, was passed the microphone.

Edie had heard much of the legend of Lucie Maguire, from Charlotte's awed anecdotes in the office. She was a ruthlessly successful estate agent ('She could sell you an outdoor toilet!'), mother of challenging twins who were expelled from pre-school ('they're extremely spirited') and a Quidditch champion. ('A game from a kid's book,' Jack had said to Edie. 'What next, pro Pooh Sticks?')

She 'spoke as she found' (trans: rude); 'didn't suffer fools gladly' (rude to peoples' faces) and 'didn't stand for nonsense' (very rude to people's faces).

Edie thought Lucie was someone you wouldn't choose as your best friend unless there'd been a global pandemic extinction event, and probably not even then.

'Hello, everyone,' she said, in her confident, cut-glass tones, one hand on her salmon silk draped hip: 'I'm Lucie. I'm the chief bridesmaid and Charlotte's best friend since our St Andrews days.'

Edie half expected her to finish this sentence: 'BSc Hons, accredited by the NAEA.'

'I've got a bit of a cheeky little surprise for the happy couple now.'

Edie sat up straighter and thought *really? A wedding day surprise with no power of veto? Oof . . .*

'I wanted to do something really special for my best friend today and decided on this. Congratulations, Jack and Charlotte. This is for you. Oh, and to make the song scan, I've had to Brangelina you as "Charlack", hope that's OK, guys.'

Song? Every pair of buttocks in the room clenched.

'So, on one, two, THREE . . .'

The other two – blushing, literally – bridesmaids simulta-neously produced handbells and started shaking them in sync. They wore the expressions of people who had come to terms with their fate a while ago, yet the moment was no less powerfully awful for it.

Lucie began singing. She had a good enough voice for a cappella, but it was still the shock of a cappella that was sending the whole room into a straight-backed, pop-eyed rictus of English embarrassment. To the tune of Julie Andrews' 'My Favourite Things', she belted out:

> *Basset hounds and daffodils and red Hunter wellies*
> *Clarins and Clooney films on big HD tellies*
> *Land Rover Explorers all covered in mud*
> *These are a few of Charlack's totes fave things!*

Edie found it hard to comprehend that someone thought this fell into the category of a good idea. That there'd been no shred of doubt during the conceptual process. Also, 'Charlack' sounded like a *Doctor Who* baddie. A squirty one.

Cotswolds and cream teas and scrummy brunches
Meribel and Formula One and long liquid lunches
These are a few of Charlack's totes fave things!

Fresh paint and dim sum and brow dyes and lashes
Rugger and Wimbledon and also The Ashes
These are a few of Charlack's totes fave things!

Edie couldn't risk her composure by glancing at Louis, who she knew would be almost combusting with delight. The top table simply stared.

. . . When the work bites!
When the phone rings!
When they're feeling totes emosh
They can simply remember these totes fave things
and then they won't feel so grooosssssss

Edie held her expression steady as Lucie fog-horned the last word, arm extended, and hoped very hard this horror was over. But, no – Lucie was counting herself into the next verse.

In the brief lull, the hearing-aid man could be heard speaking to his wife.

'What *IS* this dreadful folly? Who told this woman she could sing? My God, what an abysmal din.'

Lucie carried on with the next verse but now the room was transfixed by the entirely audible commentary offered by hearing-aid man. He apparently didn't realise that he was shouting. Desperate shushing from the wife could also be heard, to no avail.

'Good grief, whatever next. I came to a wedding, not an amateur night revue show. I feel like Prince Philip when he's forced to look at a native display of bare behinds. Oh nonsense, Deirdre, it's bad taste, is what it is.'

The spittle-flecked *shhhhhhhh!* of the spousal shushing reached a constrained hysteria, while laughter rippled nervously around the room.

Edie could feel that Louis had corpsed, his whole body convulsing and shaking next to her.

Ad land and glad hand and smashing your goals
Jet planes and chow mein with crispy spring rolls
Tiffany boxes all tied up with ribbon
These are a few of Charlack's totes fave thiiiinggssssss

'. . .Will this ordeal ever end? No wonder this country's in such a mess if this sort of vulgar display of your shortcomings is considered suitable entertainment. What? Well I doubt anyone can hear me over the iron lung yodellings of Kiri Te Canary. This is the sort of story which ends with the words, "Before Turning The Gun On Himself."'

Edie didn't know where to look. Having the heckler on her table made her feel implicated, as if she might be throwing her voice or feeding him lines.

Edie's eyes were inexorably drawn to Jack, who was staring right back at her, palm clamped over mouth. His eyes were dancing with: *what's happening, this is insane?!*

She might've known – he not only found this funny, he singled Edie out to be his co-conspirator. Edie almost smiled in reflex, then caught herself and quickly looked away. Oh no you don't. Not today, of all days.

Just nipping to the loo, Edie muttered, and fled the scene.

3

While she washed her hands, Edie pondered the mounting conviction that she shouldn't have accepted her invite today. She'd rehearsed all the reasons for and against, and ignored the most important one: that she would hate it.

When the 'Save the Date' dropped into her email, the struggle had begun. It would be easy enough to have a holiday. She needed to say so quickly, though – a break booked immediately after she'd received it could look suspicious.

Though like anyone up to their necks in something they shouldn't be, she found it very hard to judge how much she was giving away. Perhaps her absence would barely register, or perhaps there'd metaphorically be a huge flashing game show arrow over her seat saying HMMMM NO EDIE EH, I WONDER WHY.

So she uhmmed and ahhhed, until Charlotte said: 'Edie, you're coming, aren't you? To the wedding? I haven't had your RSVP?' while they were standing at the lukewarm-water in-crackly-cup dispenser. In the background, Jack's head snapped up.

Edie smiled tightly and said: 'OhyesofcourseI'mreallylookingforwardtoitthanks.'

Once her fate was sealed by her stupid mouth, she promised herself that attending wouldn't just be politically astute, it'd be *good for her*. As if approaching social occasions like they were a Tough Mudder corporate team package had ever been a good idea.

As the happy couple exchanged vows, and rings, Edie predicted she'd not feel a thing. Her feelings would float away like a balloon and it'd draw a line under the whole sorry confusion. Hah. *Right*. And if her auntie had a dick she'd be her uncle.

Instead she felt numb, tense, and out of place. And then as the alcohol flowed, it was as if there was a weight of misery sitting on her chest, compressing it.

Edie removed her hands from underneath the wind turbine of a hot-air drier. One of her false eyelashes had come unstuck and she pressed it back down, between finger and thumb.

If she was honest, the reason she was here was her pride. Avoiding it would've been one giant I Can't Cope red flag. To herself, as well as others.

There was something about seeing herself in a bathroom mirror – the 'Amaro' magic cloud gone, make-up melting, eyeballs raspberry-rippled by booze – that made Edie feel very contemptuous of herself. What was wrong with her? How did she get here? No one sensible would feel like this.

She took a deep breath as she yanked the toilet door open and told herself, *only a few hours until bedtime*. With any luck, Lucie would have stopped singing.

As she headed back through the bar, instead of braving the restaurant, she was drawn to the sounds from the garden, and the still-warm fresh air.

Edie could do with some solitude, but was conscious that drifting around the gardens, appearing melancholy, wasn't the look she was aiming for.

Aha, the mobile as useful decoy – on the pretext of taking a panoramic of the hotel, Edie could wander the grounds. No one noticed that someone was on their own, if they were fiddling with their phone.

She picked her way delicately across the grass in her violent footwear. Lucie's jihadist mission appeared to be over, Sade's 'By Your Side' was floating from the open doors to the restaurant-disco.

A few of the Murder Mystery pensioners were having a sneaky fag on the benches. It was quite a lovely scene, and she wished she could enjoy it. She wished other peoples' happiness today wasn't like a scouring pad on her soul. This is the beginning of getting better, she told herself.

Edie was far enough away from the hotel to feel apart from it all now, watching the wedding as a spectator. The distance helped calm her. She turned her phone on its side and held it up in both hands, to capture the hotel at dusk. As she played with the flash and studied the results, cursing her shaky hands and trying for another shot, she saw a figure moving purposefully across the grass. She lowered the phone.

It was Jack. She should've spotted it was him sooner. Was the groom really tasked with herding everyone inside to watch the first dance? Edie had hoped to *whoops-a-daisy* accidentally miss that treat.

Reaching her, Jack thrust his hands inside his suit pockets.

'Hello, Edie.'

'. . . Hello?'

'What are you doing over here? There are toilets inside if you need to go.'

Edie nearly laughed and stopped herself.

'Just taking a photo of the hotel. It looks so pretty, lit up.'

Jack glanced over his shoulder, as if checking the truth of what she said.

'I came to say hi and couldn't find you anywhere. I wondered if you'd disappeared off with someone.'

'Who?'

'I didn't know. Instead you're skulking around on your own, being weird.'

He smiled, in that way that always felt so adoring. Edie had thought 'made you feel like the only person in the room' was a figure of speech, until she met Jack.

'I'm not being weird!' Edie said, sharply. She felt her blood heat at this.

'We need to discuss the elephant,' Jack said, and Edie's heart caught in her throat.

'What . . .?'

'The Pearl Harbor-sized atrocity that was committed back there.'

Edie relaxed from her spike of shock, and in relief, laughed despite herself. He had her.

'You left before she got the bridesmaids jazz scatting. Oh

God, it was the worst thing to ever happen in the whole world, Edie. And I once walked in on my dad with a copy of *Knave*.'

Edie gurgled some more. 'What did Charlotte think of it?'

'Amazingly, she's more worried her Uncle Morris upset Lucie with the comments about her singing. Apparently he's got "reduced inhibitions" due to early stage dementia. That didn't make anything he said inaccurate, to be fair. Maybe he's not the one with dementia.'

'Oh no. Poor Uncle Morris. And poor Charlotte.'

'Don't waste too much sympathy on her. Uncle Morris is tolerated because he's absolutely nosebleed rich and everyone's hanging in there for a slice of the pie when he dies.'

Edie said, 'Ah,' and thought, not for the first time, that she was not among her people. She had thought there was at least one of 'her people' here, and yet apparently, he was one of their people. Forever, now.

'It's bizarre, this whole thing,' Jack said, waving back at the hubbub from the yellow glow of the hotel. '*Married*. Me.'

Edie felt irritated at being expected to join in with rueful, wistful reflection on this score. Jack had stopped copying her into his decision-making processes a long time ago. In fact, she was never in them.

'That's what you turned up for today, Jack. Were you expecting a hog roast? A cat's birthday? Circumcision?'

'Haha. You will never lose your ability to shock, E.T.'

This annoyed Edie, too. Unwed Jack never found her 'shocking'. He found her interesting and funny. Now she was some filthy-mouthed unmarriageable outrageous oddball. Who nobody chose.

'Anyway,' Edie said, sweetly but briskly. 'Time we went back inside. You can't miss the most expensive party you'll ever throw.'

'Oh, Edie. C'mon.'

'What?'

Edie was tense again, wondering why they were stood in the gloaming here together, wondering what this was about. She folded her arms.

'I'm so glad you came, today. You don't know how much. I'm happier to see you than pretty much anyone else.'

Apart from your bride? Edie thought, though she didn't say it.

'. . .Thank you.'

What else could she say?

'Please don't act as if we can't be good mates now. Nothing's changed.'

Edie had no idea what he meant. If they were always just good mates, then obviously marriage changed nothing. It struck her that she'd never understood Jack, and this was a problem.

While she hesitated over her response, Jack said: 'I get it, you know. You think I'm a coward.'

'What?

'I go along with things that aren't entirely me.'

' . . . How do you mean?'

Edie knew this wasn't the right thing to ask. This conversation was disloyal. Everything about this was grim. Jack had married someone else. He shouldn't be saying treacherous things to a woman he worked with, by some shrubbery. There was nothing, and no one, here of value to be salvaged. She'd known for some time now he was a bad person, or at least a very weak one, and this behaviour only proved it.

But Jack was dangling the temptation of talking about things she'd wanted to talk about for so long.

'Sometimes you don't know what to do. You know?' Jack shook his head and exhaled and scuffed the toe of a Paul Smith brogue on the grass.

'Not really. Marrying is a pretty straightforward yes or no. They put it in the vows.'

'I didn't mean . . . that, exactly. Charlie's great, obviously. I mean. All of this. Fuss. Oh, I don't know.'

Edie sensed he was several degrees drunker than she'd first realised.

'What do you want me to say?' Edie said, with as little emotion as possible.

'*Edie*. Stop being like this. I'm trying to tell you that you matter to me. I don't think you know that.'

Edie had no reply to this and in the space where her answer should be, Jack murmured, 'Oh, God,' stepped forward, leaned down, and kissed her.

4

She almost reeled with the surprise, feeling the soft brush of his freshly shaven jaw against hers and the pressure of his warm, beer-wet lips on hers. The 'Jack kissing her' information was so huge, it didn't get through to her central cortex in one go. Full comprehension had to be delivered in stages.

1. Jack is kissing you. On his wedding day. This does not seem possible?! Yet early reports are it is DEFINITELY HAPPENING.
2. Is this going to last longer than a peck? Was it a mistake? Was he aiming for your cheek and missed?
3. OK no, this is definitely a KISS-kiss, what the hell? *What the hell is he doing?*
4. What the hell are YOU doing? You now appear to be responding. Is this definitely something you want to do? Please advise.
5. ADVISE. Urgent.

Seconds lasted an age. They'd kissed. Edie finally had a grasp of the magnitude of the situation, and her part in it, and pulled back.

There was movement to her right and she saw Charlotte behind them, her white dress glowing like exposed bone in the encroaching darkness. Jack turned, and saw her too. They made a bizarre tableau, for a split second, looking at each other. Like seeing the lightning crack and only hearing the thunder roll a second later.

'Charlotte . . .' Jack said. He was interrupted by screaming or, more accurately, a kind of low howling, emanating from the new Mrs Marshall. 'Oh, Charlotte, we're not . . .'

'You fucking bastard! You utter fucking bastard!' Charlotte screamed at Jack. 'How could you do this to me? How could you fucking do this to me?! I hate you! You fuck—' Charlotte sprang at him and began hitting and slapping him, while Jack tried to grab her wrists and stop her.

Edie watched blankly with a sudden, intense desire to vomit.

Earlier in the day, Louis had described his abhorrence at brides involved in procedural admin of any kind on their big day. They should float on stardust, and anything like work was earthbound and tawdry. 'You shouldn't see the ballet dancer sweat.' Edie had thought he sounded like he'd swallowed a copy of *The Lady*.

However, there was something particularly aberrant about seeing someone in such glamorous, feminine attire having a full-tilt barney. There was Charlotte, hair in French roll, shimmering collarbones, princess skirt rustling like tissue, lamping her new husband with manicured hands, one of them bearing the giant sparkling engagement ring and fresh white-gold wedding band.

'It wasn't what it looked like!' Edie said, hearing her voice say those words, as if listening to a stranger. It looked like what it was.

Charlotte paused momentarily in her grappling with Jack and snarled, her subtly made-up, lovely face contorted with rage: 'Go to fucking hell you fucking bitch.' There was no comma or exclamation mark in that statement, only certainty.

Edie wasn't sure she'd heard Charlotte swear before. Edie realised she'd not moved from her position because of a strange conviction it'd make her 'look guilty' and she should stay and explain.

Having realised the lunacy of this idea, Edie finally moved. As she charged back towards the hotel, the first few people were looking over in curiosity and confusion as the voices drifted across the lawn.

OK, first things first, Edie was definitely going to be sick. Not in the general toilets; too conspicuous. She'd have to get to her room.

Edie dug the hotel key with the metal fob out of her bag with shaking hands as she did a quick swerve towards the main entrance. Fewer people to pass, that way.

Her only object right now was making sure she boaked the chicken dinner that was on its way back into the world into an appropriate receptacle. She knew after that a horrible, terrible, bleak immediate future would open up. One thing at a time.

As she bolted up flights of stairs, and along the quiet hotel corridors, it seemed impossible to Edie that time was still stubbornly linear, and that this alternative universe was in fact implacable reality. That there was no breaking a magic stop-watch open, twirling the hands and stopping this whole lurid saga from unfolding.

That Edie couldn't un-decide her choice to walk out into the gardens. She couldn't scroll back, like rewinding old video tape, and say something different to Jack, stalking away as soon as he started uttering gnomic, meaningful things. Or simply have stood somewhere that she could see Charlotte walking toward them, wedding gown draped over one arm, wondering why Jack was gossiping with Edie, wanting to tell him it was time to cut the cake.

No. Edie was the woman who kissed the groom on his wedding day, and there was no way of changing history. Right at that moment, if she had a Tardis, there was no way that Hitler was getting assassinated as a first item of business.

She burst into her deserted hotel room, its disarray reminding her it was so recently the scene of innocuous hair-straightening and full-length-mirror-checking and tea-with-UHT-milk-making. She locked the door and pulled at the handle, rattling it to make sure she was safe, kicking off her shoes.

Edie made it to the loo, held her hair out of the way and retched, once, twice, three times, and sat back up, wiping her mouth. When she came face to face with her reflection, arms braced on the sink, and could barely stand looking at herself.

The bargaining began.

Charlotte knew Jack had followed *her*, though? That *he'd* kissed *her*? But she couldn't make that case. It was up to Jack to explain.

Edie thought about what was going to be said. She had to leave. Now. She made herself steady and check her watch: 9.14 p.m. Too late to get a train? Could she get a taxi? To London? At no notice? That would be insane money. Still, she'd pay it. Only she considered she'd have to pass through reception with her luggage when it arrived, a walk of shame if ever there was one.

There was only one option left: going to ground. Staying barricaded in here.

The size of what had occurred kept roaring up, fresh waves breaking against her. The disco reverberated below, the tinny squeals and squelches of Madonna's 'Hung Up' mocking her predicament. *Time goes by, so slowly.*

This was now a horror film, where the arterial splatters and screams are ironically juxtaposed with the sitcom laughter track of whatever show the unwitting victim had been watching.

Edie wrung her hands and ground her teeth and paced the room and vacillated about going back down and facing people down, shouting, 'It was him!' while knowing nothing could dissolve the Dark Mark now upon her.

When she risked peeping out of the window, the gardens were spookily empty.

It was impossible not to look online, as much as she didn't want to, with every fibre of her being. On her four-poster bed, she sat staring grimly at the moon glow of her phone.

Every time she clicked, she thought she might be sick again. So far, nothing.

The calm before the storm. Tagged photos of the aisle walk, or smiling, signing the register, a status from Charlotte saying, 'Champagne for my nerves!' with scores of Likes. What would people say? What was happening downstairs?

'Edie? Edie!' a sudden hammering of a fist at the door had her fear-pulsing heart stretching right out of her chest, like a Looney Tunes cartoon.

'Edie, it's Louis. You better let me in.'

It was only then that Edie realised the music had stopped.

5

Louis's unusually twitchy demeanour did nothing to make Edie less panicked. She hoped against hope he'd sail in and say, *It's blown over, what are you doing up here?*

She let him pass, walking on weak, pipe cleaner legs and re-locked the door behind him, as if there really was a murderer loose in The Swan. Louis surveyed her as if suddenly in the presence of a notorious individual. He put his hands on his hips, under his suit jacket.

'Er. So. What the HELL happened?'

'Oh God, what's everyone saying happened?!' Edie wailed.

'Jack and Charlotte,' Louis paused, unable to keep himself from the stagey pause, as if he was announcing the winner on a talent show, 'they've split up.'

Edie gasped and sat back down on the edge of the bed, to steady herself. She was trembling, almost juddering. She knew she'd ruined their wedding day. But to cause them to separate, during it? It didn't seem feasible. It wasn't a thing that could happen.

'This can't be real,' she mumbled.

'Charlotte's gone back to her parents' house,' Louis said, enjoying himself now. 'And Jack's somewhere here I think, holed up with a bottle of whisky and his stag-do lads. There was a screaming match, total hysteria. It was chaos. Charlotte threw her wedding ring at him.'

Edie closed her eyes and held on to a bed post with a clammy palm, as the room swam and shifted. 'What are they saying about me?'

'That Charlotte caught you together. That you've been having an affair.'

'We haven't been having an affair!'

'What happened then?' Louis said.

It was the first time Edie had recounted it out loud and she hesitated.

'I went into the garden and . . . he kissed me. Just for a moment.'

'Wait, are you saying you weren't shagging?'

Edie's jaw fell open. 'Shagging? No?! Of course not! How could we have been . . . Are you winding me up?'

'Some people are saying you were, you know. At it. Or on the way to being at it.'

Edie knew Louis was prone to exaggeration and amping up drama but she had no way of telling if this was what he was doing. She could well imagine the Chinese whispers were out of control. As if the truth wasn't terrible enough.

'We were only a few yards from the hotel!'

'Yeah, I did think that's more the sort of encounter that happens on a car bonnet, after midnight. And usually, y'know. Not with the groom. So he kissed you?'

Edie nodded.

'But you are having an affair, yeah?'

'No!'

Oh God, this was agony. Everyone thinking the last thing she'd want them to think, ever. If she could be granted the option of being forced to streak, instead of this kind of exposure, she might just take it.

'Erm, OK, darl. So out of the blue, Jack was like, "Are you enjoying my wedding day oh and also my tongue"?'

'He started saying I meant a lot as a friend, he was very pissed I think, and the next minute he's kissing me.'

'And you didn't kiss him back?'

'No! Hardly. I mean, I was shocked.'

'Mmm. Kind of odd you were hanging around out there alone? How did he find you? Sure you hadn't texted him?'

'I'd gone to take a photo. I can show you the photo!' Edie waved her phone at him. 'Also, no texts on here!' As if there'd be a court case, and she could put her phone in a Ziploc evidence bag. It was the court of public opinion. She'd do much better from the former kind of trial.

'Louis, think about it,' Edie pleaded. 'Why today, of all days, would I try to get off with him?'

'Why would he try something like this, out of nowhere? You're leaving something out, Edie. You must be.'

'We messaged at work. Chatted. That was all. We were friends. Nothing more.'

'You flirted?'

'A bit. I suppose.'

She couldn't give Louis nothing and get his vote, she

knew that. He chewed his bottom lip, weighing things up.

'. . . I believe you. I think you're going to have a problem getting anyone else to believe you, though. The rumours are halfway around Harrogate and the truth doesn't have its boots on. Also . . .'

Louis's pause made Edie's eyes bulge. 'What?!'

He lowered his voice.

'There's only two people who are going to be blamed here: you and Jack. He's the kind of guy who falls into a pit of shit and comes out wearing a gold watch. Not to sound cold, but you need a PR strategy. You have to let people know it was him who did this, not you.'

'How do I do that?'

'I'll do what I can,' Louis said, magnanimously. 'You should think about that though. We work in advertising. Do crisis management for your brand.'

Edie nodded. She had to put aside everything she knew about Louis and trust him. A friend in need was a friend you couldn't afford to doubt.

'Do you think Jack and Charlotte are over, really over?' Edie said, voice wavering.

Louis lifted his shoulders and let them drop.

'Not sure I'd forgive a wedding day like this. The shame of it. Could you?'

Edie shook her head, miserably. She hadn't thought of that until now. She'd focused on her own survival. Look at what Charlotte would have to face, the fact everyone would know about this carnage.

There was a clomp-clomp and a banging at the door, a

thud as if a slavering wild animal had suddenly thrown itself at it. Both she and Louis jumped out of their skins.

'EVIE THOMPSON! This is Lucie Maguire! I am the chief bridesmaid! Open the door THIS INSTANT!'

Edie and Louis boggled at each other.

'EVIE! I KNOW YOU'RE IN THERE, YOU LITTLE COW. FACE THE MUSIC.'

'Tell her it's your room!' Edie hissed to Louis.

'What? What if she goes off to my room instead?'

'You're not in that room.'

'I will be later.'

'Then tell her that's your room, too.'

'Then she'll know I lied about this room.'

'Louis!' Edie said, near-feral in desperation. '*Tell her.*'

He grimaced and said, loudly: 'Hi, Lucie, this is Louis. Not Edie.'

'Where's Evie? This is her room! The man on reception told me! Do not toy with me, I am in a VERY AGGRESSIVE STATE.'

Louis made a middle-finger gesture with both hands at the door and sing-songed: 'No, my room. Little Louis in here.'

'. . . Let me in. You know this girl? You can tell me where to find her.'

'I'd rather not. I'm naked.'

'Put some clothes on, then.'

'I'm naked, with someone else who is also naked. Get it?'

'Is it her?'

'No, it's a man, *man*. Now if you don't mind, we'd like to get on.'

A pause.

'Do you know where this slut is?'

'No, I thought we'd established I'm otherwise engaged.'

'Well if you do see her, tell her I'm going to be wearing her tits like they're ear muffs.'

'Will do!'

Edie winced.

Pause. 'Also, can I just say I think it's very bad taste to be having sex while a woman's life is in ruins? We're trying to help. And meanwhile you're up here, naked.'

'That's me. Always naked in a crisis. It's when I do my best work.'

There was tutting and Lucie's fearsome clomping stride retreated. In the depths of the despair, Louis and Edie couldn't help small, stifled laughter.

'How am I going to get out of here in one piece?'

'Mmm. There may be scenes of a harridan nature. I'd check out early.'

Edie had already formed this plan. The reception was staffed 24 hours, she could escape at dawn. She reasoned that even the very angriest were unlikely to be prowling around, fired up by fury, at half five. Although with Lucie, who knew.

'Look on the bright side. No music Lucie can get you to face can be worse than the music she already made you face.'

Edie laughed weakly and thought how that experience, where someone else was the centre of attention for the wrong reasons, seemed an era ago.

'I think it's safe for me to leave, now,' Louis said.

At the prospect of being alone again, Edie felt desolate.

'Louis,' Edie said, in a quiet, broken voice, 'I know what I did was wrong but I'd never want any of this. I feel terrible. Everyone will hate me.'

'They won't hate you,' Louis said, unconvincingly, 'Just let them know Jack jumped you, not vice versa.'

They both knew that a) it wouldn't be possible to let everyone know this and b) no one was going to be inclined to absolve Edie and thus lose a key player in such compelling You'll Never Guess What gossip. The narrative needed a vixen.

'We're still friends, aren't we? I feel like I'll have no friends.'

'Babe,' Louis squeezed her in a quick, hard, brusque hug, 'Course we are.'

After re-locking the door after him, Edie sank back down on the bed. Every bump or scuffle in the hotel startled her. She imagined a procession of people queuing up, Lucie Maguire having rejoined at the back, waiting to scream and rant at her and do horrible things to her tits.

When she could bear it, she looked online. Again, nothing but a chilly calm. She couldn't see any comments alluding to what had gone on, she hadn't been unfriended on Facebook (though that was coming, obviously).

And yet . . . as time ticked by, suddenly, an ugly, worrying notion gripped a panicky Edie. She wrestled with it. She was being paranoid. She didn't need to check. Of course she was wrong.

OK, Edie had to look. Just to reassure herself she *was* being paranoid. She fumbled with hot fingers on the touch screen.

Oh, God. *No.* She blinked back tears and hit refresh and refresh again and willed herself to have made a mistake. But she hadn't.

Louis had deleted the picture of them together.

6

Edie never wanted to be this woman. The Other Woman. Who would? Who in their right mind wanted the heartache, the unsympathetic misery of playing that part? No one was the villain of their own story in their own mind, wasn't that screenwriting law?

Edie had a feeling for some time that her life had wandered badly off course, and she had to face facts now: it might never come back.

It wasn't always like this. After a romantically chaotic youth gadding about the capital in the post-university years, she'd settled down by her mid-twenties with her picture perfect soulmate: a difficult, intense, complicated young northern poet and Alain Delon lookalike, called Matt.

He was the glorious culmination of a reinvention, where messy Edith became Edie, pretty, funny writer girl who was taking life in her stride and London by the scruff.

Edie had tried to make the relationship as great on the inside as it looked on the outside. They matched. People envied them. She fantasised the wedding, even babies, but increasingly when faced with Matt's moods, it was obvious to Edie that it was best kept as fantasy.

After three years of wrestling with difficult, intense and complicated, Edie was thoroughly knackered with the effort of trying to work him out and cheer him up.

They split, and while Edie was very sad, she was also twenty-nine. She wasn't short of men hovering at the edges of the fall-out, willing to help pick up her pieces. She assumed that Mr Right was a few dalliances away, over the other side of the horizon of thirty, holding a bunch of flowers.

Yet somehow, he never happened. Single went from a temporary glitch to a permanent state. There was no one worth falling for. Until Jack. Who she absolutely shouldn't have fallen for.

Do we ever choose who we fall for? Edie had many a long lonely evening in with only Netflix for company to contemplate that one.

Edie often cast her mind back to that first meeting with Jack, at the advertising firm where she was a copywriter. Charlotte was an ambitious account executive and had successfully talked their boss, Richard, into hiring Jack, despite a strict No Partners rule.

Edie hadn't given the arrival of Jack Marshall much thought, beyond assuming he'd be another gym-before-work super over-achiever, like Charlotte.

'Edie, this is my boyfriend!' she had called across the table, late last summer, in the Italian wine bar they piled into every Friday. 'You'll love Edie, she's the office clown.' A mixed compliment, but Edie took it as one and smiled.

Over the table, awkwardly pitched half on the pavement and half inside the restaurant, she stood up to shake the tips of Jack's fingers in lieu of his hand. She'd later marvel at her total indifference at the time. Jack looked prima facie Charlotte business, with his sharp suit, sandy hair and slim build, and Edie returned to her conversation.

In the weeks afterwards, Edie caught Jack throwing the odd stray glance her way, and assumed he was simply getting the measure of his new workplace. Charlotte was a willowy goddess of the southern counties, it seemed unlikely he was admiring a Midlander who covered her greys with L'Oreal Liquorice and dressed like Velma from *Scooby Doo*.

One lunchtime, she was reading a Jon Ronson book and eating an apple at her desk and she caught Jack staring at her. She would've blushed, but Jack said quickly: 'You frown really hard when you read, did you know that?'

'Elvis used to slap Priscilla Presley when she frowned,' Edie said.

'What? Seriously?'

'Yeah. He didn't want her getting lines.'

'Wow. What an arsehole. I'm giving away my copy of *Live in Vegas* now. You don't need to worry, though.'

'You're not going to slap me?' Edie grinned.

'Hahahaha! No. No lines.'

Edie nodded and mumbled thanks and went back to her book. Had she been flirted with? She doubted it. But not long after, a passing client, Olly the wine merchant, had paid Edie particular attention, and again, she felt Jack's gaze.

'My little Edie! How are you?' Olly said, clearly kippered

by the lunchtime intake. 'What a delightful blouse. You remind me terribly of my daughter, you know. Doesn't she? Richard? The image of Vanessa.'

Her boss, Richard, hem-hawed the sort of agreement you gave someone who you had to agree with, for money.

Edie thanked him and hoped everyone else in the office knew she did nothing to invite his whisky-breathed attentions.

As Richard guided him away from her desk, her G-chat popped up on her screen. Jack.

'Young lady, may I tell you, in a completely platonic way, how much I'd like to have sex with you?'

Edie boggled and then noticed the inverted commas. She almost guffawed out loud. Then, gratified, typed back:

Ahem, Olly's a valued client. He's family . . .*like the Wests were family* *seasick face*

Without knowing it, she was sunk. She had picked up the baton from Jack. The journey to ruin starts with a single step.

Jack
The only thing worse than his pick-up patter is his wine. Have you tried the Pinot Grigio? BLETCH

Edie
I think you'll find my copy describes it as having

a tingle of green plum acidity and a long melony finish, perfect for long afternoons in gardens that turn into evenings

Jack
Translation: a park-bench session wine, aromas of Listerine mixed with asparagus wee

Edie
The bouquet could be described as 'insistent'.

Jack
I've actually looked it up for the lols. 'A fruit forward blend of ripe, zesty flavours. Will transport you to Italian vineyards.' Will transport you to A&E, more like.

If this sort of instant familiarity had come from a single male colleague, Edie would have treated it as clear flirting. *Obviously.* But Jack was Charlotte's boyfriend and she was sat right there, though, so this couldn't be flirting. It was G-chat, but not a G-chat-up.

They became messaging mates. Most mornings, Jack found some witticism to kick things off. He was catnip to someone with Edie's quick wit, and he seemed entranced by her. He had an easy self-confidence, and ran on dryly humorous remarks and giant Americanos.

In the boredom of office life, the ping of a new message from Jack on her screen became inextricably associated with pleasure and reward. Edie was like a lab rat in a scientific experiment, pressing a lever that gave her a nut. To follow the analogy, sooner or later it'd give her an electric shock, and she'd prove the mechanics of addiction by keeping on pressing for another nut.

It was all a bit of fun.

Even when the conversation naturally strayed into slightly more serious, personal topics. Amid the anecdotes, the casual intimacy and larks, she found herself telling him things she hadn't told anyone in London.

Edie found her spirits dip at home time on a Friday – a funny reversal – realising there'd be no more 'special chemistry' chatter until Monday.

Eventually, there were text-jokes from Jack at the weekend – *saw this, thought of you* – and favouriting of her tweets, and explosively she'd even occasionally get the notification he'd Liked an old photo of hers, buried in the archives on Facebook. Truly, the footprint on the windowsill of social media courting.

Jack would sometimes say in front of Charlotte, during the Friday night drinks, that he'd shamelessly distracted Edie at work. Charlotte tutted and chided Jack and apologised to Edie – and then Edie definitely felt a whisper of guilt.

But, why? For conversation that Jack was openly acknowledging in front of his girlfriend that he instigated? If it was anything untoward, it'd be secret, right?

There was enough plausible deniability to park a bus.

7

What Charlotte didn't know, and Edie didn't admit to herself, was that the devil was in the detail.

It was unlikely Charlotte would be blasé if she knew Jack got *joke-or-is-it?* jealous whenever Edie had been out on a date. 'Oh my word, just imagining the stress of you as a girlfriend though . . . ' Jack would say. 'Getting you to tone down the potty mouth when you meet the parents. You bringing them a gift of black pudding sausage.'

They both imagined this intangible ideal and happy-sighed and laughed, Edie pretending to be outraged by his ongoing teasing about her supposed northernness, when in fact it was thrilling he was contemplating her as his other half. There was such a *tenderness* to it.

Jack played the role of a best friend, confidante and, well, sort-of boyfriend. And she wanted him to.

Eventually, Edie realised she'd crossed an invisible line, without ever intending to. This mistake wasn't one big decision, it was a series of smaller, unwitting choices.

She was never going to act as long as he was with Charlotte, though, so what did it matter? A crush added a sparkle to your day, it was a calorie-free, non-carcinogenic, cost-free joy.

Only, she found out it did have a cost, some four months after Jack first G-chatted her.

Jack hadn't wanted a mortgage, and definitely not in commutersville. One lunch time, Charlotte popped a bottle of Moët and handed round fizzing plastic cups. 'We've completed on our house!'

What? Jack never said? And he and Edie shared, well, pretty much everything, she thought.

It felt like a betrayal. She'd had, as her friend Hannah liked to say, her world view bitch-slapped by reality.

She messaged, as soon as Jack was back in his seat: *'Didn't see this coming?'*

Ack, I know right! She wore me down & got her way in the end. Hold me and tell me it's going to be OK, E.T. x

That was it? That was all she was going to get?

Edie's strength of feeling over this development knocked her for six. She could have it out with Jack, push him on why he'd not mentioned it, but then, it wasn't her business. It was prying into his life with Charlotte and implying she was owed personal information. It was distinctly not cool. She'd argue with herself: *Well, you go on dates? Can he not buy property with girlfriends?*

But it forced Edie to take a hard look at how her hopes had been building, quietly and unobtrusively, even to her.

She resolved to avoid banter, and for a while, he kept his distance too. But after a short time had passed, and he reappeared on G-chat as sparky as ever, it was difficult to change gears, without it being a giveaway. She *had* to play it off as business as usual, or the jig was up.

Something that began so lightly was now the cause of much fretting for Edie. She spent evenings scrolling through Jack's emails and texts, looking for proof of his reciprocal feelings for her. '*X' marks the spot.*

Jack was also once again saying that Charlotte wanted things he didn't: weddings, babies. Wood-burning stoves and 4x4s.

Edie now avoided talking about all this, and yet equally avoided what it told her about him. Refusing to look at the great big health and safety warning sign, saying: DO NOT PROCEED BEYOND THIS POINT. HAZARDOUS MATERIALS. MANAGEMENT ACCEPT NO LIABILITY.

It dawned on Edie that he didn't tell Charlotte about their chatting because he thought it was innocent. He told Charlotte because he was an accomplished liar, and those liars hid in plain sight.

There was only one person to take this to. Her best mate, Hannah, who inconsiderately lived in Edinburgh.

Edie bucketed it all out by last orders in a nice old man's type boozer on the Royal Mile on a bank holiday trip to the far north.

'You know,' Edie said, trying desperately to wear it lightly, 'I might be better with it if I understood him and Charlotte. They're so *different.*'

Hannah shook her head, dismissively.

'Selfish jokers always like a woman who runs the show. They have a basic respect for finances and efficiency. If not fidelity.'

This had the CLANG of ugly truth.

'Take it as a sign you don't know him as well as you think you do, not that she's wrong for him,' Hannah said, adjusting her poker-straight brown hair in its top knot.

This sort of common sense wasn't what Edie wanted to hear. She wanted to be told Jack was fatally in love with her and hadn't found the courage to tell her.

'This wasn't your idea, you know,' Hannah said, picking at peanuts in the ripped-open packet between them. 'You didn't want to end up here. He's been messing with you and he doesn't care if you get hurt, as long as he gets his entertainment. The butterflies and rollercoasters that you don't get when you're settled. And you're friendly and obliging; some blokes take advantage of that openness.'

Edie knew the word she wasn't using that also applied. *Needy*. He exploited a neediness she'd not admitted to herself she had. Needy Edie.

Hannah had been with lovely dependable Pete since university, though, Edie thought. Perhaps she doesn't understand what a complicated jungle it is out here.

'Does he even know I've been hurt by it, though? Maybe he doesn't know I care,' Edie said.

Hannah shook her head.

'He knows. If he didn't know, why keep things that didn't help, from you? Why not say, by the way what's your views on this place on RightMove we're seeing on Saturday?'

Edie nodded, morose. 'Don't laugh at me. But could he be confused about his feelings?'

'He's not so confused he can't co-sign mortgage papers. Bottom line. If he wanted to be with you, he'd be with you. However infatuated he is, he doesn't want to be with you enough to do anything about it.'

Hannah had special dispensation to be brutal, because she was a surgeon (kidneys) and when she'd had a bad day, someone had died. 'I lost someone on the table,' was a phrase that kicked Edie's complaints into touch.

Edie couldn't find any way out of this last logical point. Her lip went wobbly.

'Fuck, Hannah, he's broken me. I feel as if there's no one else in the world who will ever be right for me, if I can't have him. And I'm thirty-five. I'm probably right.'

Hannah put her hand on her shoulder.

'Edith,' – school friends didn't hold with her 'Edie' revisionism – 'he was not right for you. If he's treating his girlfriend like shit by doing this, if you ended up together, he'd treat you like shit too. That is an eternal truth, and you know it.'

Edie couldn't allow this to be true, even though she knew it couldn't be truer than Darwin being right about the ape thing.

She whimpered that *maybe* he didn't want to hurt Charlotte.

'Haha!' Hannah said. 'Oh wait, you're serious?'

'Also,' Edie said, knowing she was truly rummaging at the bottom of the Christmas stocking with this one, with the unshelled Brazil nuts you could never find a nutcracker to open, 'he once said that I'm unpindownable and intimidating, I've been independent for so long. Perhaps he thinks I'd be a risk . . .'

'Oh yeah, so hard to catch that you're sat in another country crying about him over your weekends! Exactly the sort of thing that manipulative bullshitters say,' Hannah said. 'Ugh. Sorry, I really don't like him, Edith.'

Edie sort-of agreed and yet thought if Hannah met Jack and was exposed to the full force of his charm, she'd understand. And that perhaps Edie shouldn't have said so much, because now if Hannah and Jack ever met she'd have to do some serious repair work on his image. This was such a triumph of hope over rationality, she wondered if he'd made her loopy.

So, all things considered, Edie should've seen the engagement coming.

Yet the Friday when Edie spied Charlotte pink-cheeked with excitement, fingers of her left hand clasped by a cooing secretary – it was like someone had put a fish hook in her stomach, attached it to a flatbed truck and accelerated away.

Edie pretended not to have seen, and slipped out to a client meeting, which she didn't return from. She got a text later that night.

Hey you. Where were you today? Didn't see you in Luigis's after work? And yeah so I'm getting married, what's up with that? Gulp. Are we growing up? Please tell me we aren't . . . I'm not ready for the La-Z-Boy recliner yet, E.T. Jx

She threw her phone across the room, drank three-quarters of a bottle of gin and danced around so loudly to Kelis's 'Caught Out There' that the couple downstairs complained.

It was in many ways worse than if she and Jack had a full-blown physical affair. That infidelity was incontrovertible; making fury and hurt legitimate. An emotional affair required two people to agree it had taken place, even while one person lay in tatters. Her dad once told her about 'quantum super-position' which seemed to boil down to something both existing and not existing at the same time. This, to Edie, summed up her and Jack.

She couldn't complain. She should never have got entangled with someone who was with someone else.

It was like trying to go to the police to report that you'd had a knife pulled on you during a drug deal.

8

The problem with waking up after a day like yesterday, Edie discovered, were those few seconds of freedom before you remembered what had happened. A psychological prison break where you didn't make it to the perimeter fence.

She had finally passed out in twitchy exhaustion around four a.m., roused by the alarm on her phone at five. For a split second, she couldn't remember where she was, why she was looking at a flowery bed canopy or why she was so tired and wrung out. When it all came rushing back, it was almost as bad as realising her fate the first time round.

Edie jumped up and ran to the bathroom, dragged a flannel across her puffy eyes, threw make-up in the general direction of her face. She pushed every possession into her trolley case, swallowed hard and squared her shoulders. None of this should be happening. She should be sleeping off the previous night's consumption, and later sharing a full English with other hungover refugees from the stop-when-you-drop service of a hotel bar. Instead, this.

In the pin-drop quiet deserted dawn on a Sunday, her heart was pulsing, ker-thunk ker-thunk.

Any traces of sleepiness from her grotty hour's rest were chased away by the gigantic adrenaline surge as she turned the lock to open her door. She half expected to find a crowd of snoring people with outstretched legs, weaponry like unplugged irons in their hands, a boobytrap tripwire at her feet.

The hotel was silent, and Edie winced as if the squeak of her trolley case was making the noise of a jumbo jet taking off. She pushed the handle down and picked it up. She reasoned with herself: what percentage of people will have stayed awake, patrolling the building? What percentage of people, bar Louis, would be able to visually ID her as the fallen woman anyway?

She breathed deeply and jabbed her finger on the button to call the lift, as her skin glowed and prickled with the combined heat of an intensely bright yellow summer morning and the slick of guilty, fearful sweat. As per last night's vomiting episode, she knew that once the practical problem of getting out of here was out of the way, the creeping psychic torture would be far, far worse.

The middle-aged man on reception looked startled as Edie rolled her case out of the lift and said, testing her croaky voice: 'I'd like to check out, please.'

He stared at Edie for a moment, putting two and two together, and Edie felt like a celebrity for all the wrong reasons. She had some dark glasses somewhere in her bag, but wasn't going to put them on until she hit exterior sunlight. Only Stevie Wonder was allowed to wear sunglasses indoors without being a tit, even Edie's predicament didn't change that. She wished Hannah was here. She wished she had just one person on her side, to vouch for her. Although she knew Hannah would have some vigorous words for her, too.

'Could I order a taxi to the station?' Edie said, 'I'll wait out there.'

The man nodded in embarrassed understanding. Given her state, Edie couldn't help but think that he was thinking *was this woman really worth it.*

Edie pushed through the revolving door, into the car park and came face to face with another human being. She tried not to startle at seeing the 40-something mother with curly hair, a very small baby in her arms and a toddler bumbling around at her feet. Thankfully, Edie didn't know who she was, and the woman smiled at her as a reflex response, suggesting she definitely didn't know who Edie was.

'Morning!' Edie said in a peppy, sergeant major-ish voice.

'Morning! Nice one, isn't it?'

'Gorgeous.' *Appalling.*

'You're up early!' Her eyes moved from Edie to her case, and back again. 'And you don't have this lot to contend with,' she jiggled the baby, who frowned at Edie with its suspicious crumpled face.

'Haha no, tons of work to do. Big project on. Thought I'd best get home.'

Oh God, taxi, please turn up, and soon.

'Do you have far to go?'

'London.' Edie swallowed, with a dry mouth. 'You?'

'Cheltenham. We won't be going til his nibs wakes up

though. *Far* too much red wine. Have you been at the wedding, too?'

Shit.

'Uh. Yes.' Edie gripped the handle on her trolley case more tightly.

'Awful business, wasn't it? Stanley! No digging up handfuls of earth, thank you. Clean play only or we go back inside.'

Edie couldn't be more grateful for Stanley's sort of muck raking.

'Seems Charlotte found Jack having some how's your father, or snogging or something, with another guest. Unbelievable,' the woman said. 'Can you believe it? On your wedding day? To be carrying on with another woman?'

'Huh,' Edie said, trying to make an incredulous-yet-also-disinterested face. 'Wow.' She shook her head.

The woman shifted the baby to her other Boden trouser-clad hip.

'. . . Did you not know?'

Shit.

'Uh, I knew . . . something had happened. I didn't know exactly what,' Edie said, quickly. *Think.* Think of something to say to keep her occupied. 'Where are they now?' Edie said, mindlessly.

'Charlotte left with her parents. You know her parents? They have the big white house over on the other side of the green.'

'Oh, right. Yes.'

'Poor, poor thing. I can't imagine what she's going through.'

'No, dreadful.'

The woman was contemplating Edie more carefully now. She was wondering why she was really stood outside the hotel before six in the morning, looking like a bedraggled Walk of Shamer, and feigning improbably little knowledge of the previous night's earthquake.

'How do you know Jack and Charlotte?' she said hesitantly, asking for confirmation of a hunch.

'I work with them.'

There followed an acutely uncomfortable few seconds where the woman's face became a taut mask of revelation. It was as if she'd seen a WANTED poster over Edie's shoulder.

A minicab finally swept up the drive and Edie could've thrown herself arms wide across the windscreen in exultant relief.

'Bye!' she said to the woman, who was staring dully at her, not noticing Stanley was now eating gobfuls of soil.

The driver helped Edie haul her case into the boot and she hopped into the back like a scalded flea, in case the woman started screeching that the man from Blueline Taxis was unwittingly aiding and abetting a dangerous felon.

9

As the car turned through near-empty roads, Edie couldn't resist looking at her phone. If it had been hard for her father to grasp why they pulled duck-face selfies, she imagined explaining to him why, at a time like this, she would investigate things that were guaranteed to violently upset her. Because the big online glass palace full of funhouse mirrors was where half your reputation lived, now.

Edie had a flurry of a dozen or so Facebook messages. She opened them, nauseous with foreboding. They were distant acquaintances, the social media version of phishing scams – feigned concern and closeness, to gather information. Bloody hell, how shameless.

Long time no speak! Heard something kicked off at the wedding yesterday. Are you OK? Laura x

It's been a while, hope all is good! And WOW: is what people are saying true? What happened, Edie? Hope everything is still going well at your company.

I've had a second child since we last spoke! Best wishes, Kate

Hi. Do you know what people at Ad Hoc are saying? I felt I had to tell you . . . don't know whether it's true. Terry PS we worked together from 2008-9

Edie gulped and hammered delete-delete-delete, only skimming the first few lines of each. *Long time no* – DELETE.

She had messages **(3)** in 'Other,' i.e., from people who weren't in her friends list. She guessed they'd be more savage. U R A RANSID FIRECROTCH TART was all that 'Spencer' had to say. She deleted and blocked.

She also deleted and blocked a total stranger called Rebecca who used lots of words that couldn't be published in a family newspaper. Edie wasn't upset by the language, the ferocity behind it was frightening. As if she actually would beat seven bells out of Edie if she could only get her hands on her.

Speaking of which . . .

Edie. This is Lucie, I am Charlotte's chief brides-maid and best friend since our university days. Since you are too gutless to face me and got your ridiculous friend Lewis involved in your devious games (that's right, I worked out you swapped rooms with him, and I hope you enjoyed the sign I left on your door 'Please Do Not Disturb I'M SHAGGING SOMEONE'S HUSBAND'), I am forced to tell you here what kind of person you are. It's no exaggeration to say you're the worst person I've ever met or heard about. It's one thing to try to steal someone else's man but to DO IT ON THEIR LITERAL WEDDING DAY beggars belief. I hope you realise you have ruined a woman's life and wasted countless thousands on venue hire, catering and transport. I can't imagine she will want to keep the photographs either. Will you pay her back? Methinks not.

I know Jack to be a good guy despite this mistake and don't doubt for a second you've been offering it to him on a plate, trying to break them up.

I hope you are happy now you've got your wish but you won't be because terrible people never are.

Lucie Maguire

She'd learned Edie's name, at least, and it sounded as though Louis got a nice memento.

The activity overall was an odd blend of frenzy of attention and rejection: Edie could see her friend numbers had dipped, yet a lot of people wanted to talk to her – another couple of notifications pinged as she browsed. She clicked through, stomach churning, to Charlotte's Facebook page and saw, 'This Link May Be Broken'. This link is very broken. She didn't blame Charlotte for coming off entirely. In fact, that was one small mark of respect she could offer, and do the same.

Edie deactivated her own page. Why provide a toxic waste dump site.

'You're off early,' said the taxi driver.

'Yes,' Edie said, blearily and blankly. 'Lots of work on.'

'The trains won't start for a while yet.'

'Oh. I best get a coffee then.'

'The café might not be open for a bit either.'

'Oh. Yeah.'

Edie spent the next few hours waiting for a connection to Leeds, hiding in the loos for fear of running into other wedding guests, then staring unseeing out of grimy windows, feeling a queasy mix of listless and terror-struck. This wasn't, she accepted, one of life's wrinkles. This was one of those jolt-crashes that nearly threw you out of the dodgem car. She felt so morally unclean, it was like she needed a whole-body blood transfusion.

She could call Hannah. But she couldn't face it, not yet. Hannah would be raging at Jack but might not see Edie's role in it as much better. Edie didn't yet have enough distance on this to work out how even those closest to her would see it. And if her best friend withdrew her support, Edie would collapse completely.

After rewording it three or four times, she risked a text to Jack.

Hardly know what to say, but, what happened & why? Call me if you can. E.

No reply. She didn't think there would be one. Ever, possibly. She needed to message Charlotte too, but that was going to take more time and thought.

Once she was through the door of her cupboard-sized flat, she flopped down on the sofa and burst into heavy, heavy sobbing. She wanted to scream those childhood complaints, that This Was So Unfair and It Wasn't Her Fault.

This was Jack's fault. He'd chosen to marry one woman and kiss another, and both were paying a horrendous price. Edie was furious with Jack, but most of all, she was mystified. If he'd wanted her, even so much as for an affair, why choose the first few hours of making an honest woman of Charlotte for his rankest act of dishonesty?

By lunchtime, she steeled herself to call their boss, Richard. Leaving her job, without one to go to, wasn't only a professional disaster, it felt personal. She hated letting Richard down, and she writhed at the thought of him being repulsed by her behaviour. It was one thing to be despised by the Lucie Maguires of this world, another to disgust people whose good opinion you really valued.

Richard was an incredibly handsome black man and so impeccably dressed, Edie imagined he'd walk away from a plane crash adjusting a cufflink, with one extra waistcoat button undone. ('He doesn't sweat,' Jack said. 'Literally or figuratively. Ever.') His wife was a high-flying prosecutor, and they had two eerily well-mannered kids. The secret nickname among their colleagues was 'the Obamas'.

Everyone said Richard had a soft spot for Edie and she was his 'little favourite'. Edie didn't know if that was true. If it was, she could only think it was down to the fact that she dealt with someone as smart as Richard by being absolutely straightforward. A lot of others responded to his fearsomely cool intellect by bullshitting him, which was, to use a Richard phrase, the wrong play.

He answered his mobile immediately.

'Edie.'

'Richard, I'm sorry to bother you on a Sunday.'

'OK. We can skip the explanation as to why.'

'. . . Can we?'

'Louis helpfully put me in the picture.'

Setting aside what this told Edie about Louis's loyalty, she said: 'I'm so, so sorry, Richard. I'm handing in my notice. I won't be coming into work tomorrow so you don't have to worry about a bad atmosphere or anything.'

'You're required by your contract to work four weeks' notice.'

'I know,' Edie said. 'Under the circumstances I thought you might . . . let me off it. I can take part of it as holiday owing?'

'I'm not clear which half of the unhappy couple will be reporting in yet. Am I supposed to have two staff on gardening leave, and a third functioning from behind a vale of tears?'

'Sorry,' Edie said, in a small voice.

Richard sighed.

'Why did I break the no couples rule? Mind you, even when your employees aren't a couple, it's no guarantee, *eh.*'

Edie said nothing.

'Look, your extra-curriculars are none of my business, except when it affects my business.'

'Richard, I'm sorry. If there was any way I could come back I would, but I can't.' Edie tried not to sob.

'I don't want decisions made about that, yet. It so happens I have a suggestion for a solution that might suit us both. A very short-notice job has come in, I was going to talk to you about it tomorrow. Have you heard of the actor, Elliot Owen?'

'Er. Yes. From that swords and sandals show?'

The conversation had taken a surreal turn.

'That's him. A friend at a publishing house has *on their knees* begged me to spare a copywriter as a replacement to ghost-write his autobiog, after the last guy walked at the last minute. Or the first minute, the one where they met each other.'

'OK . . .' Edie grimaced.

'He's back home in Nottingham to do some TV thing. "One for the cred not the bread," I'm told. There's a three-month window starting now to get all his hilarious stories out of him, before he's off to America. Then four to six weeks to type the thing up. You're from Nottingham too, am I right? So, go. See the folks. It's good money. Then afterwards, we'll look at how the land lies in the office.'

'I've never ghost-written a book before,' Edie said. 'I don't know how.'

'No, but how hard can it be? This will be one of those "separate kids from their pocket money" jobs where you pretend this vacuous pretty boy has amassed a lifetime of wisdom at twenty-five and everyone just looks at the pictures. You're plenty literate enough to make him sound halfway articulate.'

Edie fell silent.

'Seriously, it's stenography. He talks, you marshal his self-aggrandising drivel into something vaguely coherent.'

Edie swithered. On the one hand, this sounded fairly mad. On the other hand, her boss was offering her a way of paying her rent for the near future. And Richard was right: as an alternative, he could contractually insist she worked her notice in the office. Anything was better than that.

'OK,' Edie said. 'Thanks for the chance.'

'Great. I said Tuesday to start, his people will be in touch. They'll courier the cuttings over to you, so drop me a text with your folks' address. By the way - I pass this on with a wry eyebrow raise – they, and I quote, want you to "really get under his skin and get some real meat out of this". Try to ignore ground that's been covered already in his press.'

'Mmm-hmmm,' said Edie, with the firm assurance of someone agreeing to do something they had no idea how to do.

'Check in with me, every so often.'

'Will do.'

There was a pause where Richard heavy sighed again.

'And this part of the conversation is strictly off the record. I couldn't care less about the rights and wrongs and who-did-whats of your superannuated game of kiss chase with Jack Marshall. But I'm disappointed in your taste.'

Edie was surprised at this, and could only say:

'Oh?'

'You've always struck me as a bright woman, with a lot about herself. He's an irrelevant person. Learn to spot irrelevant people. Don't expect someone who doesn't know who they are to care who you are.'

Edie, surprised, nodded meekly and then remembered he couldn't see her.

'OK. Thank you.'

'Oh, and Edie. I'm sure it's not necessary to say this, but in the circumstances I'm going to go belt and braces.'

'Yes?'

'The advice was about getting under his skin, not his clothes, and let's set aside the "real meat" thing entirely. For fuck's sake, don't get off with Elliot Owen.'

10

Edie paid first class to get back to Nottingham, even though it was an extravagant amount extra, travelling on a Monday. The last luxury for the condemned woman, a Big Mac and large fries on Death Row.

It was tough, she knew, to equate her native city with the Electric Chair. Nevertheless.

In their twenties, everyone who'd escaped to The Smoke had shuddered at the thought of moving back to wherever they'd come from. Edie had fitted right in. They were the ones who'd got away, and they revelled in their success every weekend. On Fridays, when Edie drank in Soho pubs, everyone spilling out of the doorways, she felt she was at the centre of the universe.

Then slowly but surely, the tide turned. People married and planned babies, and wanted good schools and a garden. They didn't go out to explore the capital's cultural riches and superior shopping at the weekends anyway. Even those who didn't have families got sick of the commute, the cut-throat competitiveness, the gargantuan property prices, the way London geography made social spontaneity impossible.

Gradually, the very same people who'd proclaim loudly after a few pints that the rest of the country was a backward dump full of UKIPers, began to romanticise home. Being in striking distance of the grandparents, being able to have a dog, a friendly local where everyone knew your name. It taking ten minutes to get into town was a desirable convenience, not a sign you were in Shitsville, Nowhereshire.

As Charlotte said, when justifying St Albans, *Now you can get a decent coffee and a cocktail most places, you don't need to be in London.*

And Edie once again was the odd one out, because she didn't feel like that. London wasn't about drinks. It had always felt a huge achievement to her, and carried on feeling like one. London was anonymity, London was freedom. London was where Edie had reinvented herself. A London address, albeit a cramped one-bed rented flat in Stockwell, was almost everything she had to show for living, aged thirty-five. Yes, every friend she'd made at the agency prior to Ad Hoc had moved out. It became a social exodus, after thirty. But Edie stood firm.

As the countryside sped past the train window, she kept thinking: *STOP. You're heading in the wrong direction.*

She only went home at Christmas, if she could get away with it. It was bleak, for Edie. It was particularly hard as it felt as if everyone else she knew returned to some Cotswolds vision from a supermarket advert, in holly-wreathed timber-beamed farmhouses with spray-on frost edging the windows. There was excited discussion about traditions: smoked salmon and fresh pyjamas on Christmas Eve, Frank Sinatra while you opened your presents, champagne and blinis and Monopoly and snowflakes on smug kittens.

Standard procedure for Edie went like this: she would invent a reason why she had to work until Christmas Eve morning (cursing the years where it fell on a weekend, and elongated her agony).

She'd feel guilt at the disappointment in her dad's voice when he'd say: 'Oh, can you not get away any earlier? Oh, OK.'

Richard would have to shoo her out when he saw her in the office.

'I don't want to go,' she'd lament.

'You're condemned to a green and pleasant city with a university boating lake, not fucking Mordor. Now get lost – you're only reading the BBC News site, and the cleaners want to get in.'

Edie would catch the train at St Pancras, ending up on the service that was crammed with inebriated last-minuters. On arrival in Nottingham, she'd go straight to Marks & Spencer, buy as much food as she could carry and a large bunch of flowers. Then she'd clamber into a taxi to Forest Fields, about ten minutes' drive north of the city centre.

She'd get the cab to drop her at the end of the street, so her sister Meg didn't hear the rumble of a Hackney engine and give her a lecture on how it was ecologically much better to get a bus, here, LOOK. (Having the timetable thrust into her hands as soon as she was through the door made Edie want to go everywhere on a motorised golden throne powered by unicorn tears.)

Trying not to let spirits sag as she entered the poky, ramshackle semi, wreathed in fag smoke, books stacked against the walls and on the stairs, wallpaper peeling. Edie would hug her father, Gerry, hello. He was always in a moth-eaten jumper, his craggy face like an Easter Island statue. You would never guess that Edie, her dad and Meg were related, they looked completely dissimilar. (Edie couldn't help think that was telling.)

Meg had a very round face to Edie's pointed chin, small cornflower blue eyes to Edie's vast and doll-like dark ones, and patchily bleached mousy hair, which she wore in matted dreadlocks, gathered into a pineapple-style ponytail.

Edie would unpack the food into the fridge, while Meg loitered and complained at the Oakham chicken touching her tofu wieners, generally acting as if Saudi royalty had come to stay.

Meg was a militant vegan and if Edie wanted anything resembling a Christmas roast, she had to bring it herself and fight for its right to party. (She'd offered to take them to a pub for lunch in the past, but Meg thought it was outrageous exploitation of the proletariat who had to work on a public holiday.)

With relief, Edie would chuck her flowers in a jug which, in the chaotic tip of a kitchen, was akin to pencilling a beauty spot on a corpse. Then she'd faux-cheerily open a bottle of wine. Glugging it took the edge off, and helped abort the annual argument about whether her father and sister smoking stood in the back doorway, freezing faggy air rushing in to the kitchen, did in fact constitute 'not smoking in the house'.

They'd long ago cancelled the gift giving on Christmas

morning. Edie's father was on an academic pension and Meg was mostly unemployed, and no one had a clue what to get for each other anyway. So they got half-drunk while Edie tried to make seven dishes in a small kitchen without anything meat or dairy so much as *looking the wrong way* at Meg's spartan ingredients.

Meg would slowly build up a head of steam at the fact that Edie dared trample on their 'cruelty-free lifestyle' in this insensitive way, and cava-pissed Edie would stop herself from saying it felt pretty cruel to appetites.

With her sister and father parked in front of a rerun of *The Snowman*, Edie had to clear the piles of mouldering *New Scientist* magazines from the only-used-once-a-year dining room table and cobble together clean crockery that sort of matched.

They'd eat a botched-together lunch with a Gaza Strip in the middle made of candles, separating Edie's Henry VIII food from a glowering Meg's bean banquet. If Edie's dad recklessly praised anything on Edie's side of the table, Meg would say: 'The succulent flavour of murder. The lovely taste of unethical slaughter. I'm having to eat with death filling my nostrils.'

Edie would likely snap: 'Well we're having to eat with hippy grief filling our ears,' and Meg would rejoin: 'Yes, anything other than your choices is *hippy*. Why don't you just join the Bullingdon Club, Bernard Matthews.' And so on.

And that was it; that was magical Christmas Day. If they could find something on television to agree on, it provided a few hours of respite, but if tempers frayed, or Meg got on to politics, all bets were off.

There'd been a particularly bad row two years ago when Meg had a long soliloquy about scandalous under-funding in the NHS. Edie snapped and said: 'You know how they pay for the NHS? Taxes, from people who work, and PAY TAXES.'

In the ensuing fight, Meg called her a 'consumerist chimpanzee' and a 'Nazi in a dress' and Edie said *Some Nazis did wear dresses so that doesn't make sense, which you'd know if you didn't skive off sixth-form college to smoke weed and call the tutors "head wreck fascists"*. An observation that really calmed things down.

Their dad went to the dining room to play his old piano. He treated trying to defuse arguments between his daughters as bomb disposal; he might cut the wrong wire . . . better to stay back entirely.

Edie got a mid-afternoon text from Jack, last year, that said: '*Do we need to talk about how this is in fact, the worst day invented?*' and she could've kissed her phone; whirled around the room hugging it, while humming. The happy few hours of text tennis with Jack that ensued was the only pleasure to be had that day. He got it, he hated Christmas too! Soulmates! And his jokes about his in-laws – 'the outlaws' as he called them – were so funny.

The only other respite in the entire experience was if Edie could get out for a Boxing Day pint with her school friends Hannah and Nick, yet this was increasingly difficult. Hannah had a gorgeous place in Edinburgh and had taken to inviting her parents to come to her, and Nick had a wife – a real Nazi in a dress, from what Edie could tell – and a small child, and recently said he couldn't get a pass out.

On the 27th, the day she went back to London, Edie felt near-euphoric. She tried to hide it from her dad, but the haste with which she packed and the fizziness of her mood was hard to completely conceal.

The two key emotions of Edie's visits home were guilt and disappointment, one feeding off the other. The more disappointed she felt, the guiltier she got. Despite best intentions, she could never effectively hide her hating being there, always playing her part in the three-hander Mike Leigh film they were trapped inside.

She got through this nightmare by having her London life to flee back to. It relied on there being a cast of people down south who thought of her as funny, sparky Edie, who coped, who enjoyed life. Who wasn't a failure of an absent daughter. Who wasn't a deeply disliked sister.

Now she'd been reinvented again, and not by her own design. She was reviled Edie, the home-wrecking whore. London hated her now. Nottingham didn't want her or understand her, either.

As the train pulled into the destination, Edie's eyes brimmed with hot tears. Three months here. The phrase 'all my Christmases' usually meant a massive treat, didn't it?

11

Edie's dad was delighted to see her, making her feel the usual remorse she wasn't glad to be home. She'd wrestled with whether she could get away with staying in a hotel and concluded: no, not without badly hurting his feelings, and anyway, hotel plus her London rent = exorbitant. Home it was. Sorry, Meg.

'Three months?' her dad said. 'I don't think you've been here this long since before university!'

Edie grit-grinned and said he must be right. They hugged in the narrow hallway, with the dappled Artex walls that had reminded younger Edie of rice pudding. She rolled her trolley case to the foot of the stairs and hung her coat on the banister. They'd lived in this cramped but homely house since her dad retired early, on ill health grounds, when they were still kids. He'd had a nervous breakdown, but they never referred to it as a nervous breakdown.

'We've become a fully vegan household,' Meg said, by way of greeting, appearing from the kitchen in a T-shirt saying BITCH PLEASE with a picture of Jane Fonda doing the Hanoi Jane fist, and geometric-print leggings that pouched at the crotch. 'So don't bring anything of meat or dairy nature onto the premises or it's going straight in the bin.'

'Don't be daft, Megan,' their father said, all jocular, 'She can have the odd bacon cob if she wants one.'

'Bacon cob?' bellowed Meg. 'No she CAN'T! Have you ever heard a pig's death rattle?'

'No, but you hum it and I'll try to keep up.'

Once again, she and Meg weren't really talking about what they were talking about. This wasn't about bacon cobs, it was about Meg repelling Edie as a rebel force invading her territory.

It hadn't always been this way. Edie had been a hero to Meg when they were younger, and Meg trotted behind her like a duckling. Edie had been excessively protective of Meg, almost as much proto mother as older sister. Things started to change when Edie went to university and after she moved to London, Edie returned to find she'd become a fully fledged villain. Her popularity, once so simple, so powerful, had completely curdled. Once lost, it wasn't possible to get it back. Meg was perpetually resentful, as if Edie was a giant fake, and every word out of her mouth only confirmed it. Edie had probably shouted: 'What IS your problem?' many times at Meg, yet non-rhetorically, it was a good question. Edie gathered that it was because Meg deemed Edie's life choices the choices of a sell-out; a false, superficial light-weight.

'It's fine, I can eat meat out of the house,' Edie said, trying to keep to her resolve of no fighting on the first day.

Meg 'hmphed' at this, with an air of irritation at a typical Edie ploy.

An assertive rap of knuckles against the flimsy wooden front door made them all jump.

'Did you bring back-up with you?' her dad said.

Edie dodged past him and answered, suddenly nervous that it'd be a gift-ribboned turd in a box or something with 'Love From The Office' and she'd be forced to explain it.

A motorcycle courier said 'Thompson?' – and handed over an A4 envelope, while Edie used the plastic wand to scribble on the electronic receipt-of-delivery device. The adrenaline subsided as she inspected the publishing house watermark and realised it was the Elliot Owen Files.

When Edie closed the door she saw her father and sister watching, once again, as if Joan Collins had wafted in.

'Cuttings. To help me interview this actor for his auto-biography,' she said.

'What an interesting project,' her dad said, kindly. 'Has he been in anything I've seen?'

'The fantasy show *Blood & Gold*. If you've seen that.'

'Ah. No. Didn't look like my bag. Tolkien is enough questing dwarves for one lifetime.'

'The one with the sexist attitudes to women where it's all "Oh, look, my bubbies have fallen out of my lizardskin jerkin, *again*,"' Meg said, and Edie laughed.

'Exactly.'

Once again, Meg looked irked that Edie hadn't disagreed with her.

'Why are you writing a book about him, then?' she said.

'For the money,' Edie said.

'You don't have to say yes to everything that pays money, you know,' said Meg.

'No, just some things, so you don't have to live off gruel. Can I put my things in my room, Dad?' Edie said hastily, before Meg took off from the runway.

'Yes, of course. I've moved the washing out of it and most of the wardrobes are free.'

Edie made noises of thanks and, envelope clamped under one arm, began huffing her giant case up the stairway, made narrower by the books lining each step. The books were on their way to or from a bookcase, stuck in mid-flight.

She felt Meg watch her progress, suspiciously and sullenly. Edie could explain she wasn't back at home to mess up her life, or to show off, and that her own life had gone spectacularly to shit.

But what would be the point? Even if Meg believed her, she'd no doubt think Edie brought it all on herself by being a sex puppet of the patriarchy, or whatever.

It wasn't that Edie violently disagreed with most of Meg's principles, even if she didn't want to be vegan herself. The fact was there was no point agreeing with Meg about anything – because Meg's views existed to establish the difference between herself and most of the rest of the world, specifically her older sister. When Edie concurred, it was viewed by her sister as some sort of spoiling and tarnishing gambit.

Edie flubbed down on the bed – she was touched to notice her dad had put clean sheets on it, and old blue faded ones from her childhood, too – and considered unpacking. But it was too much like accepting the length of her visit.

She had hoped that, if nothing else, Nottingham would make her feel better about what had happened to her life in London. Sat staring at the old built-in wardrobes, from the days her dad still did carpentry, and the bare emptiness of this box room without her things in it – bar a few old musty dresses on plastic hangers inside the wardrobes – she felt worse.

In a vacuum, there was nothing to stop her howling, no routine to cling to. She put her toilet bags in front of the mirror, the one she'd gazed into a thousand times while applying copious amounts of kohl before a teenage night out drinking an illicit concoction she and Hannah had devised, 'Poke', a blend of port and Coke.

She dug her phone out of her coat pocket and saw she had a text from Louis.

Hey babe, how you doing? Xx

Not great, but thanks for asking. You spoke to Richard? X

Yeah, I wanted to save you the hassle. He was cool about everything, as always. How long are you off for? Everyone misses you, you know <3

Hah! Yeah, Edie betted that was what everyone was saying. Louis was such a snake on wheels. This was his dream: a catastrophe that overlapped on the personal and professional Venn diagram. He could be excited onlooker and major political fixer, whispering in everyone's ears, with the sole hotline to the villain of the piece. This was Edie's

Vietnam and his *House of Cards.* He'd deleted the Instagram picture to distance himself from Edie, and called Richard purely to stir and get a measure of her fate. Now he wanted Edie to tell him whether she'd been sacked, so he could be bearer of that news, too.

That's nice. Three months.

OMFG, three months! Paid leave?

Did Louis think she was stupid? Did he not realise she knew he'd look up from his phone and say 'My God, listen to this, she only got a three-month holiday out of ruining Jack and Charlotte's wedding'? Louis knew what Edie knew, that a false friend was the only kind of friend she had left in that office.

Not leave, on a project in Nottingham. How's Charlotte?

No reply. Of course not. Edie asking after Charlotte didn't fit the story and there was nothing in answering it for Louis.

Edie got up off the bed, and thundered down the stairs. Her dad was fishing a tea bag out of a mug in the kitchen.

'I meant to say, dinner's on me tonight, as thanks for having me! We could go out. Or get fish and chips. Or, chips for Meg. Whatever you like.'

'I'm cooking,' Meg called, from the front room. 'The kidney beans are already soaking. Also that chip shop doesn't use separate preparation areas. I asked them and everything's contaminated. And I don't want to give them more profit anyway.'

You wouldn't be, would you, Edie thought.

'Uh, OK. Maybe tomorrow?' Edie said, heart plummeting, as her dad nodded. Meg was an awful cook. That wasn't anti-veganism, just a fact. Meg had never met a seasoning she liked to use. The one consistency all her curries, stews, hotpots and casseroles achieved was 'non-toothsome sludge'. She eschewed recipes as creative constraint, and generally just mashed some stuff into other stuff.

Most terrible cooks were aware they were terrible, and limited people's exposure to it, thus they weren't a danger to the public. Meg was either blissfully unaware or strangely sadistic – the more Edie pushed it round her plate or her dad declared himself 'pleasantly full', the more she'd heap spoonfuls of it out and say, 'This is full of iron,' or similar.

There was an aggressive piety to forcing it on them: it wasn't for the food to get nicer, it was for their minds to get wider.

She trudged back up the stairs thinking she'd eat Meg's Sewage Slurry tonight to make nice, then tomorrow, go to Sainsbury's and try to fill a cupboard with edible items. She might even hide a packet of Polish sausages inside a large bag of rice.

Back in her room, she was at a loss about what to do in the middle of a Monday afternoon, when not at work. She physically ached for the life she couldn't go back to. She wasn't only separated by geography from it now. She couldn't even indulge herself with a crying jag, and come down for dinner pink-eyed and puffy, and have to explain what was up. The envelope with her name scrawled on it sat in the middle of the bed.

Sod it. There was no avoiding Elliot Owen. She was probably one of the few women in the country that this opportunity was wasted on.

12

It was strange to get to know someone through their press before meeting them, but Edie guessed it had been a while since Elliot had met anyone who hadn't met him in print first.

What was that quote about Paul Newman, something about, 'He was as nice as you could expect for a man who hadn't heard the word "no" for twenty-five years'?

The photogenically brooding Elliot Owen couldn't have heard the word no for at least five now. From women, possibly ever.

His bio details weren't very colourful. He was thirty-one, not twenty-five, as Richard had said. Same age as Meg, though he'd been busier. Born to a comfortably middle-class family in the leafy Nottingham suburb of West Bridgford, went to a state school with a better OFSTED score than Edie's, joined a local TV drama workshop, got spotted by a scout. He moved to London and ended up in a boring medical drama, did a bit of time in a soap, and a very quickly canned sitcom.

He was the love interest in a video by a terrible American

emo-rock band for a song called 'Crumple Zone', which was a huge hit in the States and got his face known. It landed his breakout role in *Blood & Gold*.

As Prince Wulfroarer in the epic and boisterous fantasy series known for its stabbing, shouting, tits, scheming and tits, he was suddenly 'sex in a wolf pelt'. A swaggering, high-born Northern warlord – rallying cry; 'For the Blades of My Brothers!' – he fell in love with a servant girl called Malleflead. Sadly that had proved his undoing, as Count Bragstard had also set his Machiavellian sights on her.

Prince Wulfy had therefore died on the end of a pointy weapon at the end of last series, uttering the heartbreaking words to his distraught shag-piece, before he bit on the fake blood capsule: 'I am my Kingdom' (his catchphrase), 'but I would sacrifice it all for you.' His demise prompted much speculation about whether female viewers would desert in droves.

Edie was resigned to Elliot being at best, boring, and at worst, an obnoxious brat. The fact the last ghost-writer had exited immediately was a very bad sign.

She didn't think this expectation was prejudice on her part, it was straightforward logic. Take one male ego, rain down this much attention, employ someone whose sole job it was to blast his armpits with a hairdryer, and so on. Pay him millions, spooge a luge of adoration all over him. To come through that and *not* be an arsehole would take someone of spectacular character. Which meant you were gambling on a man not only being given his physical gifts, but also bestowed with Gandhi-esque substance.

You might as well pop down to the shop on the corner and expect your lotto ticket to pay off your mortgage.

Edie leafed through the photos of him on set in whichever raggedy-beautiful Eastern European country doubled for 'Easterport' or 'Goldendale'. (Edie hadn't seen much of *Blood & Gold* and could never keep the fictional geography straight.)

Elliot's dark brown, slightly curly hair was dyed boot-polish black for *Blood & Gold*, and he wore dragon-green contact lenses. He had one of those squared-off jaws that a draughtsman could draw with three swipes of the pencil, and full lips that Edie envied, they were the sort she'd always wanted.

It was obvious why he'd been such a hit. It wasn't sensible or interesting good looks, in Edie's humble opinion. It was silly-to-the-point-of-ridiculous, pin-up handsomeness, to appeal to teenagers who hadn't developed a more complex palate yet. The sexiness equivalent of strawberry milkshake.

She remembered Charlotte and others in her office all swooning and sighing over Elliot Owen, and Edie saying, 'Meh, looks like the one in the TRAINEE BARISTA T-shirt who makes your cappuccino sour and gritty', and Jack laughing in approval. Then Jack repeated the rumours he 'played for Man City, not Man U' and all the women chorused *noooooooooo*.

Edie had best buckle down to this homework – she also had a stack of celeb auto biogs, and they made drear reading – so she didn't give him an excuse to kick off when she fumbled a question to which there was a well-known answer.

She'd start with a recent Sunday supplement profile. She flipped past moodily blue photos of Elliot resting his forehead on his forearm, with an expression as if he'd just been given terrible news. Headline: FANTASY CHAMPION.

It's considered good manners to dip your headlights, at night, so as not to dazzle the oncoming traffic. When Elliot Owen strides casually into the dramatically under lit environs of the hip East Village restaurant he chose for our meeting, you can't help wonder if he wishes he could flip his full beam off, at will. As he asks the wait- resses for his table, they virtually crash and burn in the blazing glare.

Jesus wept, seriously?!

Raymond Chandler once described a 'blonde to make a bishop kick a hole in a stained glass window'. In the 21st century, Owen's a brunette who could leave a nunnery in smoking ruins.

Yes, that's how religion works, Edie thought, nuns simply haven't met sufficiently fit men and so married the Son of God as a fallback. *These people.*

With effortless good manners, Elliot inquires what I'm drinking. 'Diet Coke, right?' He summons the waitress, who is caught still staring at us. If Elliot's noticed, he doesn't let on: an old-fashioned gentleman, under the modern-casual shirt and jeans. 'Can we have a Diet Coke, and which beers do you have?' The waitress almost trembles as she offers Budweiser. 'Ah, not a big fan of Budweiser. Clearly not spent enough time here yet,' he says, with that sleepily devastating smile, as the waitress almost ovulates. 'But that will be fine.' And where is 'here'? America, or the spotlight he's now occupying? He's seemingly come from nowhere . . . 'Or Nottingham, as we like to call it,' he corrects me, sharp as a tack. There's that impossibly disarming smile again.

Christ, this is some hardcore drivel, Edie thought. Man In Ordering Beverage Shocker. He's just a person who has to poo like the rest of us. Also, is that a dig at Nottingham? She flared with indignation, which was a bit hypocritical, she realised.

New York has its fair share of celebrities and its most fashionable inhabitants are well trained in ignoring the famous. But Elliot Owen is so white hot right now, even those who aren't looking over at us are still looking.

How exactly do you look and NOT look at the same time? Edie wanted the female journalist to show her working. She was also curious how you show someone to their table in the style of a crashing car. Or 'almost' ovulate.

The reason, of course, is Blood & Gold, *the fantasy series that sparked many a female fantasy about its heroic, flawed, tragic lead, Prince Wulfroarer. With*

Byronic looks that could unlace a bodice at thirty paces,
Owen bestrode the pitiless landscape of the 'Eight
Islands' like a warrior Heathcliff, spliced with Mr Darcy.
And like Mr Darcy, had his cold, proud heart melted
by a woman of inferior class. In the hands of a lesser
actor, the Prince might've been a . . .

Oh God, *enough*, Edie thought and started skimming. Right, here was a bit about the Nottingham series.

The world is Owen's oyster right now, yet he makes it clear
that he's not interested in the low-hanging fruit of decorative
roles. His first job, since hanging up Wulfroarer's armour,
is a relatively low-budget gritty thriller set in his native
Nottingham, called Gun City.

Written and directed by Archie Puce, the enfant terrible
of British drama who made a splash with his BAFTA-winning
science fiction film INTERREGNUM, *Puce is notorious for*
pushing actors to their limit, and giving studios, and the
media, hell.

Both Owen and his US co-star, Greta Alan, are taking a
huge pay cut to be part of Gun City, *as the two detectives*
unravelling the mystery behind a young woman's corpse,
found spread-eagled and naked in a fountain in the middle
of the town centre on Christmas Day.

'When Archie got in touch, I was thrilled,' Elliot says.
'Everyone wants to impress people who are hard to impress
and Archie is very much in that category. When he
explained the thinking behind Gun City, *examining the*

*real law-and-order problems facing the region, I knew I
wouldn't be able to live with someone else taking this role.
Not least because it's my stamping ground. It's great to
spend some time at home.'*

Edie shouldn't be rankled, but the whole thing irritated her.
As if the city was going to be grateful for rich ex-pat Elliot
Owen giving it lots of publicity as a crime-ridden grot hole.

The rest of the cuttings didn't live up to the swooning
hagiography of the Sunday magazine piece. The papers and
women's glossies were mainly interested in the fact Elliot was
dating a hot British actress called Heather Lily. (Two flowers?
Impossibly fragrant.) They featured together in recent paparazzi
pictures in New York; Elliot in that very self-conscious
'off-duty' outfit of no-doubt hideously expensive binman's
style donkey jacket and artfully battered brown boots, carrying
Starbucks cups. His blonde girlfriend only a perfect Dairylea
triangle nose peeking through a bundle of thick blonde hair,
with a tiny sphere-of-fluff dog on a lead bouncing behind
her. Why did starlets always have dogs? Maybe it was the pissy
cat lady stigma.

Hmm, Edie conceded the angle of Elliot's jaw was caught
nicely in photo number five, as he stepped out to hail a yellow
cab. She caught herself getting sucked into the whirlpool of
trivia and thought, you really had to wonder at a society that
was fascinated by *couple buy coffee*.

She put the cuttings back inside the envelope and laid back
on her bed. Her dad had yet to find the funds or the will to
fix the damp problem at the back of the house, so the off-white

walls in this back room sagged and bloated like a wedding cake that had been left out in the rain. The ghostly remnants of her teenage self filled it, from the greasy blots left by Blu-Tack on the walls, to shreds of ripped-off stickers (the New Kids on the Block phase.)

Edie was once obsessed with glow-in-the-dark stickers, peppering her navy-blue bedroom ceiling with a constellation of white-green paper stars, crescent moons and comets.

She lay in her bed and stared at the universe on her ceiling in the late afternoon murk. Edie used to lie there thinking what a big world it was and how, one day, she was going to strike out into it.

That had gone well.

13

'Whereabouts, love?' said the taxi driver, as they both peered at deserted acres of not much at all, some ugly squat container buildings and trailers dotted about.

It seemed making dramas – the fictional sort – was less thrilling than Edie expected. When she got details of her first on-set meeting with Elliot Owen via his flunkies, she expected to be told to meet at somewhere like the Council House, which they were re-dressing as a haunted library, or something.

Instead she got the coordinates to an industrial estate at the south of the city, near a race track. A pile of churned mud. Oh.

Edie could see some vans in the distance, and possibly the odd human.

'Just here, thanks,' she said, doubtfully, wondering at the wisdom of having worn a small heel and her beloved tartan coat with brown fur hood. (Jack always asked if it was 'real gerbil'. She HAD to stop thinking about Jack.)

She picked her way towards the vague signs of life in the distance, men in North Face jackets, holding walkie-talkies.

If she squinted, beyond them she could see some arc lights and maybe cameras.

As Edie drew nearer, she realised what she thought was 'someone telling a funny story, in a heightened excitable voice' was in fact, a person having a massive rant. A wiry, bespectacled man in a long narrow beanie hat was having a meltdown, hopping around, gesticulating at a deeply dismayed looking member of the North Face team.

They were gathered round in a circle, staring at something. As the people shifted, Edie glimpsed the focus – a figure of a garden gnome, in a hat with a bell, holding a watering can at a jaunty angle.

Edie suspected, due to the sense of cowed deference, that the shouter was *enfant terrible* Archie Puce – being terrible if not *enfant*. The words faded in.

'—back and get me what I FUCKING WELL ASKED FOR, THE *FUCK* IS THIS? Do you grasp the significance of Buddha, Clive? Do you realise why this scene where Garratt smashes up a statue of BUDDHA in ANGER is IRONIC? I mean should I even BOTHER MAKING ART, WITH THIS SORT OF CLOWN WORKSHOP OVERT COCK-ENDERY?'

Lots of shaking of heads and chewing of lips and shuffling of feet. Blimey, Edie didn't think even divas did shit fits on day one at 10 a.m.

Archie waved a sheaf of paper in his hands and read from the page.

'*Garratt sees the terracotta figurine, and gripped by an unreasoning fury at its ironic juxtaposition in these war-torn surroundings, destroys the smiling round-bellied icon of peace as he hurls it at the fence, again and again. As it shatters, so does Garratt's hope.'*

Archie looked up at Clive.

'Perhaps I should have been more explicit for the hard of thinking. He is committing an act of ICONOCLASM. What is iconoclasm, please?'

Clive looked pretty miserable and very pale. He scratched his cheek. 'Smashing up . . . religious stuff?'

'OH, A BREAKTHROUGH. Religious "stuff". So, on the one hand, Buddha, an enlightened sage of the sixth century and figurehead of a faith. What do we have here as substitute?'

Archie picked it up.

'A gnome. A small old cunt with a pointy beard found in suburban gardens. Do we see the difference? What does smashing a gnome up signify? GOOD TASTE?'

Edie was suddenly gripped by an urgent need to laugh and had to choke back a honk as it surfaced.

Archie read the lettering on the base. 'Ninbert. So we have two options, Clive. Either we found a new religion based on THE CULT OF FUCKING NINBERT OR WE BUY THE RIGHT ITEM WHAT STRIKES YOU AS MORE FEASIBLE WITHIN OUR SHOOTING SCHEDULE?'

Clive was in that deeply unpleasant situation during a bollocking where you were required to explain the unacceptable and dig yourself in deeper.

'Sorry it's just B&Q didn't have any garden statue Buddhas and then I . . . looking at comparative size . . .'

'Size?'

Clive nodded.

'My head is comparative in size to a large gourd. Should I replace my head with a large gourd, Clive?'

He shook his head.

Archie hurled Ninbert in the air, and booted him with the toe of his shoe, causing onlookers to duck.

'What's in there?' Archie said, spotting another B&Q bag, beyond Clive's legs.

'Uh. Another one.'

'Get it out!' screeched Archie.

Clive miserably produced the second gnome, which was lying on its side, insouciantly smoking a bubble pipe, which seemed in the circumstances likely to inflame Archie. 'Who's this, Dildo Baggins?' He inspected its name. '*Boddywinkle.*'

Archie kicked that gnome clear of the group too, with a menacing zeal.

'This production,' he pulled his hat from his head and threw it on the ground, 'is a PROPER SHITTERS' PICNIC.'

An obliging runner nervously ducked in and snatched the hat up.

'LEAVE MY HAT WHERE I PUT IT, YOU ARSE-FUCK!' screamed Archie.

The runner darted in and threw it back down again.

A silence where no one said anything, for fear of being an arsefuck. Edie couldn't back away without it being noticed. She stood very still, as if she was a small shivery mammal in an old wildlife programme and a tiger was prowling around nearby. Unfortunately, Archie's boggling eyes swept over the company for fresh meat, and Edie had rather made herself stand out by being dressed as a cute librarian in an indie movie, instead of the regulation fleece.

'Who the fuck are you?'

Edie cleared her throat as everyone turned and stared.

'Edie Thompson. I'm a copywriter . . . I'm here to interview Elliot Owen.'

Archie ignored this.

'Since you've decided to join us without invitation, let's hear your thoughts on Buddha being substituted by Ninbert and or Boddywinkle.'

'I haven't read the scene.'

'Well neither has Clive, clearly.'

'Erm,' Edie was sweating inside her coat. '. . . Why would there be a statue of Buddha lying around on an industrial estate in Colwick?'

There was a pause while Archie Puce went, well, even more puce. Then his features twisted in an unpleasant fashion, as if he'd thought of something cunning and done a sly fart at the same time.

'Why is there a fucking gnome out here?'

'. . . Because you sent Clive to B&Q?'

Edie couldn't be sure but it seemed as if there was a beat of shock followed by some suppressed laughter-snorts. A harassed-looking woman at Archie's elbow who'd previously stayed neutral stepped forward and said briskly:

'Can I see some sort of ID?'

Edie dropped her bag to fumble for her wallet and the crowd dispersed, amid mumbling. When Edie looked up,

Archie was stalking back towards the set and the air pressure had reduced considerably.

'When did he say he'd see you?' the woman said, handing Edie's driving licence back to her in disgust.

'Just to be here at ten.'

'Alright, wait here.'

The woman turned on her heel and left Edie feeling like turning up at the appointed place and time had been the most presumptuous thing she could've done.

After ten minutes, the irascible woman with a walkie-talkie trudged back to Edie.

'Elliot can't see you today, sorry.'

'Oh. Can I—'

'That's it. Sorry.'

'OK . . .' Edie tried to say more but the woman had already turned. She hit the taxi number on her mobile and tried not to feel stupid, as people milling nearby glanced at her.

Usually, Edie would be very pleased to find herself with what amounted to a paid day off. Time tooling around by herself felt a lot less appealing now she had huge anxieties and a guilty conscience, with no online rabbit hole to tumble into, either. She wanted to be busy-busy-busy to avoid all the bad thoughts.

Also, while she appreciated he was an important man, she suspected she'd had her first taste of the behaviour that caused the previous biographer to exit stage left from the Elliot Owen Story. Edie had a very nasty feeling she was going to fare no better, and be what Boddywinkle was to Ninbert.

14

Edie finally had a reply from Jack. Six days after he'd unpinned a grenade and lobbed it into the middle of several lives at once, then scattered before the smoke had cleared.

She was getting ready for what could be grandly called 'an evening out', applying her make-up, peering into the old milky mirror of her youth with the plastic red frame, rummaging around in a cosmetics basket that had a topsoil of shattered kohl pencils and lidless grey eye shadows.

The name that used to give her such a sting of excitement appeared on her phone screen. Now it just stung. Involuntarily, Edie recalled how his lips felt on hers before she pulled away. She hadn't allowed herself to think about that until now.

Hi you. So. Sorry about everything. Hear you're up north for now? Take care. Jx

That was it?!

Trembling slightly, Edie hammered out three different replies of varying sarcastic rage, and deleted each of them in turn.

This man had dabbled with her heart like it was a finger-painting kit and he never *ever* took responsibility for the consequences of his actions.

But if she got too emotional, he could simply drop the conversation. How did Jack always manage to shield himself from feedback? Actually, he couldn't, not without her help. She needed to breathe deeply and be smart, here.

Hi yourself. 'What were you thinking' might be a cliché but, what were you thinking?

Near-insta ping back.

I wasn't, clearly. I know you weren't either. Apologies for inviting you to a wedding that had an 'aftermath' in place of a 'reception'. Man alive. Jx

And this was how Jack's wiles had sent her slowly mad. Within seconds of receiving this ostensibly self-deprecating reply, Edie realised he'd apologised, but neatly stopped her screen-grabbing the conversation and using it as proof of his guilt. To her, it worked as Jack's usual easy charm: 'I assume nothing from your momentary reciprocation'. To anyone else, it read as if they were equally to blame.

She had to find a direct question to ask that he couldn't wriggle out of. She steeled herself and typed:

But why decide to kiss me?!

'Edie! Time to get going?' her dad called from downstairs. He'd volunteered to drive them to their dinner. Edie had thought the best way to get her dad and Meg out was to promise to pay but let them choose the restaurant. Which meant, Meg choosing.

As they crushed into the back of her dad's old Volvo, footwells lined with old newspapers, Edie wondered why her dad burning a fossil fuel was OK with Meg, but taxi drivers doing it was not.

Meg also gave them a long explanation about rewarding venues that offered solid vegan options, to justify picking Annie's Burger Shack. Edie suspected the ethical reasoning boiled down to Meg fancying a burger. She was just relieved that Meg hadn't found some café full of nubbly seed-filled discs of tempeh and hemp burgers that looked like something you'd leave on a bird feeder table.

It took a lot longer to get a response from Jack this time and given the starkness of her question, Edie wasn't surprised. *Evade THAT, motherfucker.* She tried not to twitch her phone out of her pocket every sixteen seconds as they rumbled towards the city centre, to see if Jack had replied.

By the time they were seated at Annie's, had the menus and ordered drinks, bingo, a reply finally limped in. Edie had started to grind her teeth that he'd simply ignore her.

I was drunk and all over the place & I thought we had a special connection. Events overtook me with the wedding, I didn't have my head straight. Honestly, E.T., I can't say sorry enough. You don't deserve any of this.

Nicely played. 'I thought we had a special connection.' The nickname. Once again, nothing that could be easily passed on, without people who'd already made up their minds taking it as tacit confirmation that Edie was pursuing Jack. But was she reading too much into it? Did Jack realise he was safety-proofing it? Edie wondered if she was paranoid. *Just because you're paranoid doesn't mean everyone isn't out to get you.*

She asked herself whether she should care what *those people* thought. She did, though. She couldn't help it. Could she ask ano—

'Ahem,' her dad coughed, and nodded towards her phone, as Edie listlessly fiddled, eyes straying to it for the umpteenth time. 'Something interesting?'

'Hah no!' Edie turned her phone over, with some effort, screen facing down. She wasn't going to discuss Boy Trouble with her baffled father and hostile sister, and especially not when the story hinged on her own awful transgression. And Edie badly needed a space where everything was business as usual, even if that meant, 'still not great'. 'It's nice in here,' she said, with polite-fake enthusiasm.

Annie's was in a grand, high-ceilinged old lace warehouse in the Lace Market, quite a glamorous room for fast food, filled with the clatter of shoes on stripped wood and the burble of background music vibrating on wrought-iron fittings. As Edie glanced round the table, her dad in a faded cable-knit jumper, Meg in her denim dungarees, she realised how long it was since the three of them had been anywhere together.

On her birthdays, she usually took them to the local pub

and vigorously batted away her dad's offers of meals, pretending she didn't want the fuss, knowing he wasn't well off enough and it would be too awkward for Edie to stand the bill on that occasion.

Three bottles of beer arrived and Edie felt the pressure, despite her low mood, to jolly it all along. She had suggested they go out, after all.

'Good choice, Meg,' she said, making them clink glasses, *cheers.*

Meg looked at her impassively, obviously figuring out what stripe of bullshit this was. Edie considered her enthusiasm might contaminate Annie's, so quickly added: 'Do you, er, come here often?' She laughed at herself.

'No, I can't afford it. I've been once, when the home did a day out.'

Meg worked for three days a week at a holiday care home for the elderly, ill and extremely infirm. It was a noble and decent thing to do, but Meg thought her three-day-a-week work for very little money conferred sainthood upon her, and her saintliness came at a price she didn't pay. She drew state benefits to which she wasn't – in Edie's view – strictly entitled, while her dad picked up the rest of the slack, financially. Edie had tried to nudge Meg to look for a full-time or better-paid job in the voluntary sector, but it was like trying to lion tame wearing Lady Gaga's meat dress.

Thus *I can't afford it* was imbued with her usual sanctimony and implied Edie had no idea, living high on the hog. It wasn't an act of God that meant Edie had more money. It wasn't a secret of the elite, the whole 'working five days a week' trick, was it?

'Did they have a nice time?' her dad asked Meg, pouring some more beer out of his bottle.

'It was a bit of a 'mare. Roy came, you know the one with the bone tumours? He got brain freeze from drinking his root-beer float too fast and ate too many onion rings and started puking everywhere. The next table were totally out of order about it.'

From Meg, 'totally out of order' translated as anything from calling for Roy's execution to 'preferred to move out of the range of the spray'.

'Maybe they didn't realise he was poorly,' their dad said.

'Oh my God, of course someone's poorly when they're yakking chunks everywhere.'

'I meant his cancer. Vomiting in public is quite a tearing up of the social contract.' Edie's dad gave her a wry look and she thought, *Oh no you don't, I'm not getting involved.*

'It was INVOLUNTARY, it's not like he wanted to huey,' Meg said, eyes blazing, and her dad clucked and soothed and said he was only kidding. Meg turned her gaze on Edie and Edie knew she was thinking, *He's only like this when you're here.*

Edie edgily checked her phone and saw she had a text message from Louis. Almost certainly something she should leave for later, but she didn't have the restraint. She'd only fidget and fret about its contents otherwise.

Hola E. How's home? OK BIG news . . . Jack & Charlotte are BACK TOGETHER. Can you believe it? X

Edie stared, put her phone back down with a bump, and gulped her beer. Yes, she could believe it. She realised now she'd half expected it. What did Louis say about Jack, he was a kind of smooth-talking Houdini? You could tie his hands and drop him in a tank and he'd be out by the end of the show.

Her reaction was stronger than she expected. Not because she still wanted Jack herself. Or, she didn't think she did. This development made her inwardly howl with frustrated anger. They'd made it up. Jack had been forgiven. Once again, his misdemeanours had cost him nothing. (Well, unless you counted the wedding, but it sounded as if the bride's family picked up that tab.) And kissing her had no more meaning than a moment's confusion.

Jack's timing in making peace with her wasn't accidental. He must've known she'd hear about this, and hate him for it.

Wow. So all is forgiven? Ex

Not sure ALL. But he's back in St Albans. Apparently he went up to Harrogate to see her parents and sisters to apologise. He's mounted the full-scale I'm Sorry I Don't Know What Came Over Me tour, we've not seen the like since Hugh Grant after the prostitute. (Not saying you're a prostitute lol)

LOL OF COURSE NOT. Thanks, Louis. Always one to give the knife a quick twist. Edie could've cried, screamed, thrown her phone across the room. Her life had been trashed by Jack's actions, but there would be no forgiveness or reconciliation for her.

'What're you having?' said the friendly, buxom young waitress with the nose ring and magenta hair tied up in one of those *Dig For Victory* poster headscarves, pen poised above pad.

Edie could barely focus.

'Uh. A cheeseburger, please,' she said.

A pause while the waitress looked perplexed and said: 'A plain burger, with cheese?'

'Yes?'

'Meat?'

'Where?'

'Do you want a meat burger rather than veggie or vegan?'

'Oh. Yes.'

'And for your sides?'

'Just . . . chips?'

'We do curly fries, Cajun wedges or just wedges?'

'That's fine,' Edie said. 'I mean, the fries are fine.'

'Any sauces?'

Dear God, stop demanding things of me.

'Just ketchup, thanks.'

'Ketchup's on the table.'

The waitress gestured with her pen.

'Oh yes. Thanks.'

Her dad looked baffled and Meg frowned suspiciously at Edie, as if she might be doing the space cadet thing as London aloofness. They went on to give more detailed orders – 'The Lemmy, vegan, plain wedges, American mustard side' – that made Edie realise she hadn't got into the spirit of the thing at all. She had ground to make up already.

'And a portion of onion rings,' she volunteered. 'For the table.'

'For the tapeworm,' her dad said.

Don't think about Jack, Edie instructed herself. He doesn't deserve to be thought about.

15

Edie was thinking about him. *Jack and Charlotte were back together.*
It wasn't only that Edie resented them sorting it out and sparing
Jack's arse. It was that she knew what this meant for her.

If Jack had been restored by Charlotte, it'd make Edie the
only real bad guy. Friends might mutter about Jack in private,
but in public, it was disloyal to Charlotte. They'd have to
redistribute the weight of their disapprobation and put it all
on her. So now the official story would go: reunited against
all odds, once the scourge of that hussy was eradicated.
Charlotte could forgive Jack, but not Edie?

Ping, another Louis text.

*PS Listen, I don't know when the best time tell you this is but in
wake of J & C sorting it out, Lucie put an email round everyone
at work asking them to print out and sign a petition for you to be
sacked. No one's signed it though. Xx*

. . . Yet. Edie sagged with the weight and shame of it. She

couldn't go back, no matter what Richard said. Even if Jack and/or Charlotte left of their own accord, she'd be hissed at. Why should she lose her job and not Jack, though? So he walked away with the job and the wife?

'Do your work really need to get hold of you this often?' Edie's dad said, as she turned the phone face down on the table again.

'It's not work, Dad, at half seven at night,' Meg said, faux-sweetly.

'Oh.' Her dad's eyes widened. 'Are you courting?'

'No,' Edie said, forcefully.

Then, with not inconsiderable effort:

'Sorry. Being hassled about something work-related, by a friend. How was everyone's day?'

'Not bad, thank you,' her dad said. 'Radio Four and pottering. Have you clapped eyes on the elusive star yet?'

'He's saying he'll see me at his parents' house in West Bridgford on Sunday. Well, his PA says he's seeing me. Believe it when I see it. Or him.'

'Sunday? Funny hours you have to work.'

'I have to be available whenever he's available. I spent today reading more cuttings about him. God knows how you get a book's worth of words out of a thirty-one-year-old's life story. I'm going to have to do a lot of padding.'

'It's so stupid that we write books about people who've been in films rather than aid workers, and people who've actually contributed to society,' Meg said.

'Hmm yeah,' Edie said, nodding. 'It is. Or anyone who's thirty-one, really.'

She said this before she realised it sounded like a dig at Meg.

'Alright, *Yoda*.'

It was tiring, being around someone who not-so-secretly despised her.

The food arrived and Edie was glad of something that could unite them, the simple pleasure of stuffing your face. They carried trivial conversation through food and a second round of beers, with Edie asking a string of questions about things and people she'd missed in Nottingham. There was no foothold for Meg to complain about her being lordly.

'Oof. I feel as if my innards are trying to knit me a beef vest,' her dad said, exhaling and patting his stomach.

'Your colon will be sluggish with decomposing animal protein,' Meg said.

'Not my colon,' her dad said. 'Business is brisk, let me promise you. Nice frock, Edith,' he added, as the plates were cleared away. Edie was in a dark blue, long-sleeved cheap-buy dress that she'd pulled, crumpled, from her case. She'd not worn it much as it had a wide strip of lacy material across the bosom that acted as a cleavage viewing window. She reasoned no one here would be interested in taking the opportunity.

In a misguided attempt at paternal even-handedness, her dad added: 'You'd look nice in that too, Meg.'

Meg wrinkled her nose. 'No thanks, that's a very *Edie* dress.'

'Oh, an EDIE dress,' Edie said, doing shock-horror palms. 'What could be worse?'

'You know. It's a bit "Have you met my breasts?"'

'Megan!' her dad said. 'Settle down.'

Of all the things to mock Edie about at the moment, the idea she was a showy tart really was going to hurt the most. In front of their dad, too: cringe. She took a deep breath.

'Why do you have to be so horrible, Meg? Do I ever say anything critical about your clothes? No.'

'God, it was only a joke,' Meg muttered. 'Chill out, Cranky McCrankerson.'

'And I'd have thought it's not *totally* feminist ethics to comment on another woman's chest like that, is it? Didn't you just "slut shame" me?'

'Oh, here we go.'

'No, there *you* went.'

Meg squeezed the American diner style tomato-shaped tomato sauce holder and said, reflectively: 'As George Monbiot said, if hypocrisy is the shortfall between our principles and our behaviour, it's easy to never be a hypocrite, by having no principles.'

'I have no principles?'

'You called me a hypocrite.'

'Well. Cheers. Thanks for dinner, Edie!' Edie said, in sing-song voice.

'Oh, what a surprise, you had to throw that in my face. I didn't ask to come here.'

'Actually, you did.'

Meg scowled and Edie tried to regain self-control because she was angry enough to say *plenty* more.

This had escalated quickly.

'Sod this, I'm having a smoke,' Meg said, pushing her chair back with a loud scrape.

She disappeared off, digging the Rizlas out of her kangaroo-like dungarees front pocket for her roll-up. The waitress reappeared and Edie muttered: 'We'll have the bill please,' as her dad looked uncomfortable.

Edie felt bad for him. It surely wasn't nice, having children that couldn't stand each other. Edie wasn't able to face a sullen car journey and the four walls of her bedroom yet.

'Dad, you keep the peace and take Meg home. I've texted a friend and I'm going to meet them round the corner, so I'll be back home in an hour or two,' she lied smoothly, as smooth as when she was fourteen and sneaking off to meet boys.

Her dad nodded, as Edie tapped her pin number into the card reader and handed it back.

'Tonight was a nice idea, you know,' he said, and leaned over and gave her shoulder a squeeze, with the unspoken addendum, *just terrible execution.*

16

A friend called a big-ass glass of wine.

At the arts cinema café bar up the road, Edie got herself a thumping beaker of red and found a relatively quiet corner. She sat alone, back half-turned to the room, free to play with her phone unfettered and do some discreet weeping. She was overdue some self-pity. Edie indulged in leaking-eyes-and-holding-fingers-horizontally-underneath-to-catch-the-water crying. Everyone around her was far too lively-drunk to notice the dark-haired woman dissolving in the corner.

Everything was so fucked in so many ways. Her life wasn't great. She wasn't, by any stretch of the imagination, living her hashtag 'Best Life'. But it was hers and it worked, sort of. Now what?

She'd talk to her dad tomorrow and say she'd move out to a flat for the next few months. He'd object vehemently. She'd have to insist that she and Meg under the same roof was a recipe for disaster. Her sister hated her, she didn't know why, and that was that. It just wasn't tolerable when the world at large hated her too.

Edie had a sudden and overwhelming urge to speak to someone who loved her, and understood her, and confess all. Little chance of Hannah answering at this time on a Saturday night, mind you . . .

'Edith!'

'Hello! You're there?!'

'Of course I'm here, this is my phone.'

'I know, but it's a Saturday night.'

Edie put a finger in her spare ear to block out multiple other conversations and Tracy Chapman's 'Fast Car'.

'I was just thinking I should call you.'

'Noel Edmonds' cosmic ordering,' Edie said, feeling her chest swell and trying not to wail HELP ME, OBI WAN KENOBE, YOU'RE MY ONLY HOPE.

'You sound funny, where are you?'

'I am funny. I'm crying a bit and I'm in a bar. In Nottingham, actually.'

'Really?! That's a coincidence. Why are you crying?'

Edie steeled herself. She should've done this sooner.

'Ready for a dreadful story and a big pile of I Told You So? Hang on, why is it a coincidence?'

'I'm here too. At my parents'. Where are you?'

'Urrr . . . Broadwalk? No, wait, Broadway. The cinema.'

'Can you hang on ten minutes? I can cab it to you.'

Could she hang on ten minutes? Edie wanted to do a lap of the café-bar, face daubed with woad, whooping war cries of joy.

Quarter of an hour later, Hannah appeared in the doorway of the bar, fists bunched in the pockets of her jacket, ponytail whipping from side to side as she scanned for Edie. Hannah wore big eighties-ish secretary spectacles with coloured frames that somehow made her look even more attractive. Edie would've looked like a serial killer's wife.

She waved and did a two-finger point at the two glasses of red in front of her. Hannah was as tall, lithe and handsome of face as she'd ever been – she'd skipped the puppy fat and spots of adolescence entirely. She was born aged thirty-five, in more than one way. The only sign of the years passing was that her delicate Welsh skin had acquired a network of fine lines you could only see up close, like varnish crackling on pottery.

They hugged across the table and Edie said, not completely able to staunch the waterworks: 'Oh, it is so good to see you. Why are you here? Home, I mean?'

'Tell you in a minute. You alright? Is your dad OK? Your sister?'

'They're fine. It's me. I've been an idiot.'

Edie relayed the wedding carnage. Hannah was quiet, sipping her red wine, brow furrowed. 'I never liked the sound of this Jack. That's certainly not changed. To be honest, I thought you were going to tell me his girlfriend caught you showering together or something.'

Edie's jaw dropped.

'You don't think I'm the most despicable woman who ever lived?' Edie said.

'I think you fucked up in the heat of a moment but you'd hardly be the first person to do that. Also, he jumped you, right?'

'Yes but, I kissed him back though,' Edie said, morose. 'I kissed someone's *husband*, Hannah, on their *wedding day*. They'd only said vows about forsaking all others a few hours before.'

Hannah sipped her wine and put her head on one side.

'Hmm. What would *not* kissing him back have looked like in that situation? I mean, even if you'd stood there, it'd have looked bad. Sounds like he lunged and you were buggered, really. I can't judge you. My dad always says, only beat yourself up about the harm you did that you meant to do. That's on you. The harm you did by accident, feel bad but let it go, ultimately it's not on you. Only way I got through junior med school, was with that in mind.'

Calling Hannah tonight was the best idea Edie had had in a long time.

'Yes!' Edie said, feeling a rush, a *flood*, of gratitude and relief. 'Who would possibly expect it? If I'd had any time to think it'd have been a "no".'

'Toxic arsehole. Please tell me he's out of your system?'

'God, yes,' Edie said, nodding vigorously. 'I was already well on my way to over him by the wedding.'

She said this, not knowing if it was wholly true. Would she have replied to that first post-honeymoon G-chat? Probably, yes. In a guarded way. She was an addict. Addicts weren't to be trusted. Addicts lied to everyone, and themselves in particular.

'If you're looking for my reputation, however, it's in the toilet. I had to come off Facebook, I was getting a barrage of abuse,' Edie said.

'Well, you know my views on that merry shitshow.'

Hannah was an avowed loather of social media.

'I've got news, too, as it happens,' Hannah said.

'Yeah?'

'Pete and I have split up.'

Edie paused, glass of wine halfway to her mouth. 'What?' she said dumbly. 'That sounded like you said you and Pete . . .?'

'. . . have split up.'

'No?' Edie said. It was as much a statement as a question. Hannah and Pete couldn't simply 'split up' any more than the Queen and Prince Philip. Together since university, inseparable, finished each other's sentences, each other's equal and opposite reaction. This was unthinkable. This was like your parents divorcing.

'I don't know where to start,' Hannah said, and Edie heard the unusual tremor in her voice. 'We'd been not happy for so long we'd forgotten what happy felt like, so we were numb to it all. I couldn't bring myself to say the words, I kept losing my nerve. I lay in bed at night thinking, "I'll do it tomorrow" and then the next day was never the right day to do it. I went away on this training course and shagged someone else so that I'd done something definitive I couldn't take back.'

'*You* had an affair?' Edie said. This was un-possible.

'Not sure if it's an affair if it's a one-off? I fell off the fidelity wagon with a thud, yes. I knew Pete and I were over and had to push myself to make it real. I haven't told him. I'm not proud of it, but there it is. It was as if I had to prove to myself we were over, as well as him. I came home two weeks ago and finished it.' Hannah paused. 'I was

112

going to call you before now but I needed to get it straight in my head and we had to tell the parents and everything . . . With Mum having the MS flare up, I wanted to pick my moment . . .'

Edie nodded. She owed it to Hannah to be as supportively hard-to-shock as she'd been for her.

'I had no idea. You seemed so steady.'

'*We* had no idea. Or we had some idea, but it was like carrying a weight. Sooner or later you forget you're carrying it and think you always walked with a stoop. Fuck, Edith, I can hardly bring myself to admit this to you, but I found myself thinking: we can't split up because we've just had the floors sanded. We were seriously staying together because of sofas and tiles and stripped floors. Like the beautiful house had become this *tomb* we were *interred* in together.'

Edie had forgotten how smart Hannah was. It was intimidating she was so good with words when Edie did words for a living. You'd hardly let Edie tinker with your urine-filtration system.

'We didn't want a wedding or kids and so it was possible to drift, you know? And the whole constant mantra about how *long-term relationships are hard work* and *everything has its ups and downs* and *you're going to be annoyed by their toenails* and *stick with it* and *the grass only looks greener* and so on. It's actually very hard to tell when you should split up with someone. All I knew was I was waking up every morning thinking this can't be it, until death. When your relationship is making you feel life's too long, something's gone awry.'

Hannah's voice had become thick, and she sipped her wine.

Edie felt bad that Hannah had obviously churned on this a lot, with her friend so many hundreds of miles away, not able to help.

'You should've said . . .'

'I didn't want to say it out loud until I was sure. You know that's me.'

Edie nodded. She'd done the same over HarrogateGate, after all. Waited until she could face saying it.

'. . . I'm moving back to Nottingham,' Hannah continued. 'I was here for a job interview at the Queen's Med yesterday and they've offered it to me. I don't want to hang around in Edinburgh and bump into Pete all the time. I can't stand the whole access arrangements to mutual friends thing, I want a clean break. My mum's not getting any better. I start in two weeks.'

'Oh my God! Both of us back at the same time, what are the chances?'

'You're not staying, though?'

'No,' Edie said, with a small shudder, although why she thought London was the safe haven was unclear. 'I technically have my job to go back to.' As if that made it more appealing.

'How lucky are we, to at least end up here at the same time in our hour of need,' Edie said, as Hannah returned from the bar with more massive glasses of red that were going to wreak flamboyant revenge in the morning.

'Well, qualified lucky,' Hannah said, into her glass, and smiled.

'OK, *we* know our lives are a shitty mess. To the outside

world, I am a celebrity biographer and you are a superb renal surgeon and we have most of a bottle of Shiraz to neck.'

They clinked glasses.

'To being together in our time of need,' Hannah said. 'Shall we look Nick up? Have you heard from him lately?'

Edie shook her head, guiltily. She'd not seen Nick for eighteen months, bar trading the odd 'did you see this' funny email. Nick was a friend they'd made in sixth form. You might say he was 'Eeyore-ish' although 'prone to mildly depressive episodes' might be more accurate. With bizarre juxtaposition, he had a very sunny local radio show where he chatted with old dears and played Fleetwood Mac.

Aged twenty-four, he'd made a catastrophically bad choice of sour, bossy wife in Alice. Hannah had once described marrying Alice as 'an act of self-loathing'.

It seemed as if it was so much strife for him to wriggle out from under the yoke of oppression, it was easier to turn down social occasions. They had a young son, Max, and Nick had pretty much been grounded by Alice, forever.

'Do you think A Town Called Malice is letting him roam around free range, yet?' Hannah said. They had called her this for some time.

'I doubt it,' Edie said.

'I want to talk to him, you know. Life is too short to put up with being unhappy.'

Edie nodded, though she suspected it was futile. 'We should definitely let him know we're back.'

Now she thought about it, Nick had been unusually quiet on email, even by his standards. Maybe Baby 2 was on the way and he didn't want to face their creaky-polite *erm great what wonderful news.*

'If he tries to avoid us, we can call in to his radio show,' Hannah said.

Edie agreed. 'We could even ask him out with Alice? Turn a new page?'

'We could. I bet that page will say Yep Still A Cow on it though.'

When she rolled in later, revived, Edie was surprised to find her dad waiting up for her, watching the television with a glass of Glenmorangie.

'Haven't waited up for you to come home for quite a few years,' he said, smiling.

Edie had to say it fast or she'd lose her nerve. 'Dad, I'm going to find somewhere else to stay, tomorrow. Me and Meg is too much stress for everyone.'

Her dad didn't look surprised.

'Look. Give it a week or two. The settling in was always going to have its rocky moments.'

'She hates me!' Edie said, in hysterical whisper-squeak. 'I don't do anything to provoke her and she gets at me, all the time.'

'I know you don't. She doesn't hate you. It's very difficult for Megan. She sees you as the success who gets all the glory and her feathers get ruffled. I'm not excusing her behaviour tonight and I've had a word. But she really does suffer with some sibling envy, I think. Let it settle down a bit. For me.'

Edie already knew she couldn't refuse her dad this. Her shoulders sloped.

'. . . OK.'

'It is good for us to see you, you know.' He gave her a hug and Edie surrendered to it with that waterlogged feeling in her heart. 'You never know, one day we might even be good for you.'

He said this with such forced-lightness and sadness that Edie had to squeak 'Night', before she teared up.

17

The Elliot Owen Story had started in the somewhat sleepy but 'sought after' suburb of West Bridgford. It was a place Edie had lived, long ago. Her brain had been too small to record many memories but she had a few. They flashed on and off like old jumpy sound-free sunny frames of a Super 8 Cinefilm and Edie turned her internal projector off.

Elliot's parents' home was large and comforting, the doorway partially hidden by clematis. He would have one of those mums who used to pack his ingredients for Home Economics into a wicker basket with a pristine gingham tea towel on top. Edie used to buy her supplies from the local inconvenience store, while missing the bus and factoring in a sneaky fag. She rang the solidly middle-class, stiff brass bell and waited, prickly with anticipation.

Elliot answered the door himself, which surprised Edie a little. His neon-green eyes met hers, and there he was, in the sculpted flesh. A fact that was both shocking and completely banal at the same time. It was ridiculous to be surprised he answered his own door, the man had to be by himself *sometimes*.

He wouldn't have an Alfred, as if he was Bruce Wayne. (Would he?)

She kept her expression steady and said: 'Hi, I'm Edie,' and as soon as she said it, felt irrationally foolish, as he had a mobile clamped to his ear and she was talking over him. Elliot made the 'point to phone and make twirling finger to indicate the call is running on' gesture.

He wedged the door open with a pristine white sneaker-clad foot as Edie brushed past him into the house, nerves jumping like fizzy beans. She'd sternly told herself not to wilt and thrill at being in his presence, yet it wasn't possible.

It didn't matter how indifferent you declared yourself to be to the particular celebrity, seeing someone famous in the flesh had a weird hysterical buzz of cognitive dissonance. Edie couldn't quite compute Elliot Owen's proximity, even though it was a simple thing to understand.

The clean-shaven, dark-haired man in the stripy jumper in this suburban hallway had the same face as the dishevelled hero she'd seen charging around in battle on her telly. Her brain roared IT'S HIM IT'S HIM OH MY GOD IT'S REALLY HIM.

OK, the sight of Elliot didn't knock Edie out or make her almost ovulate. He was just 'people', except a pumice-stoned, cleaner, clearer, more bone-structured, symmetrical version. He looked like he'd smell of cut apples and fresh linen. And like all famouses, was smaller than the towering, glowering hunk she was expecting. He was a fairly good height, if on the slim side.

Elliot opened the door to the sitting room with one hand and Edie took that as direction to go and sit in it.

She thought he'd follow her, instead he went into what must be the kitchen next door. He'd only half-closed the sitting room door so Edie could hear most of what he was saying.

' . . . that's not it, though, is it. Why would I do that? Tell Larry that I'll pay the deposit and if I can make it I can ma— oh bloody hell, Heather, *really*? Is this how we're going to do it? You know what my schedule is like . . . oh WELL when you put it like that . . .'

Edie had a jolt of realising she was overhearing a domestic between Elliot and his famous girlfriend. Something actually newsworthy – well, if you subscribed to our messed-up twenty-first-century news values – was happening on the other side of that white glossed door, with an audience of only Edie. Not that she could do anything with it, if she valued her employment.

She wriggled out of her coat and laid it neatly on the arm of the sofa, got her Dictaphone and notepad out. She felt the hum of her jittery anticipation: she'd once again steeled herself for the first meeting and once again, he'd hit pause. And how was he difficult last time, exactly? Was he going to toss his curly hair around and get shirty at her opening questions? She wished she could've spoken to the outgoing writer, though that might not've helped.

The row continued offstage.

'I don't understand why you're being so stroppy when you *knew* . . . what the fuck's the dog's quarantine got to do with me?! Oh, I invented rabies, my mistake.'

Edie scribbled 'Inventor of Rabies' at top of her notes,

giggled idiotically to herself and then heavily scored it out. More disorientation: in *Blood & Gold*, Elliot had a cut-glass English RP *madam I'm afraid I must ravish you at once* voice. In real life, it was a soft Midlands burr. Not Nottingham-*Nottingham*, a middle-class version, still with the flat vowels. Actors put voices on, who knew!

Edie considered that this humdinger with Heather Lily wasn't going to put him in the best mood for their chat. Or maybe it'd help, maybe he'd be fired up and unguarded? *Think positive.*

The room's décor was standard issue for a comfortable, 2.4 family in this postcode, if a little staid. There was a thick deep beige carpet, a floral sofa set with those napkin-like thingies over the back – antimacassars? A varnished oak cabinet, the type that definitely had gummy-capped bottles of Advocaat and Martini Rosso behind its doors. A clock in a glass dome with a metronomic swinging device gave a hypnotic tick-tock-tick-tock.

Elliot's parents were away on a cruise, his agent had told Edie, so he'd opted to stay here rather than a hotel. She added lots of strenuous caveats about not disclosing this address to anyone, which offended Edie, as if she was going to go on Reddit and post GUESS WHAT, GUYS.

The cabinet shelves displayed childhood portraits in chunky silver frames. Elliot had been, as expected, an angelic-looking little boy, marble skin and molasses-dark hair. Edie could see how he'd got a role as a Celt warrior.

His younger brother was completely dissimilar, as Meg was to Edie – blond, stouter, blunter of features, still handsome.

'. . . that a threat? Are you serious? Take him then, I honestly don't care what your fork-tongued friends say about it, do you? Huh, clearly. Wait, WAIT. So on one hand you're saying you'll have to take him if I don't show, as if that's going to cause me to kick off, but I'm an uncaring bastard for not kicking off? What kind of stupid trap is – oh really, Heather. Have a word with yourself.'

Yeah, maybe she has a word with herself and you have a word with me, how does that work for you?

Edie deduced the argument had something to do with Elliot not dropping everything and attending Heather's birthday in New York, and Heather's subsequent threats to arrive on someone else's arm. It sounded like it had turned into a full-scale 'you never put me first' which showed no signs of burning out any time soon. Edie checked her watch. She'd been here twenty minutes. *Tick-tock.*

She could check her phone. She did some listless scrolling, although with no Facebook and no friends, there wasn't much to distract her. She'd not looked at Twitter in an age. With a jolt, she saw some abuse on there: messages from Lucie and probably friends of Lucie asking her how she could sleep at night. Edie quickly shut it down: not now. She read news sites, she did flower doodles on her notepad, and tried not to think about how the number of people who reviled her was enough to fill a village hall, with garden overspill.

The beautiful people and their imaginary problems saga continued next door. She checked her watch. Forty-five minutes. This was turning Naomi Campbell – and not only

122

that, he was on the bloody premises. It was perfectly within his power to end the call.

At fifty-two minutes, when Edie's chest was tight in irritation with his manners, Elliot went quiet, banged about for a few seconds, then entered the room.

He flopped down on the sofa and barely looked at her. Edie waited for an apology about keeping her waiting, none was forthcoming. Anger was a useful cure for awe, anyway.

'Hi, I'm Edie,' Edie said, and ran into an instant roadblock. You usually introduced yourself to get a name in return. Given she patently didn't need one, it left the line dangling.

'Hi. Yeah. This project. I don't know whether Kirsty spoke to you. I really don't want to do it.'

Edie summoned courtesy with some effort and said: 'Oh. I thought we were meeting up because you wanted to do it?'

'Nah, my agent signed me up for it. I really don't see the point. The whole thing is just an exercise in ego.'

Hahahhahaha and you hate indulging your ego, I can tell, thought Edie.

'Soo . . . should I tell them it's off? Or . . . should you?'

'We've done all the paperwork, so it's going to be a pain in the arse. Can you just draft as much as you can without me for the time being, and I'll take a look?'

Oh right, so you want the money but you won't do the work. This is just BRILLIANT. Next time anyone told Edie they fancied Elliot Owen, she wouldn't make the Trainee Barista coffee joke, she'd throw one over them.

'I can draft something but it really needs your input. I was told the publisher wants, uhm, real meat.'

Elliot had been rubbing his eyes and they suddenly snapped open in a not-very-friendly way, like she'd poked a crocodile with a stick.

'"Real meat"? What the hell does *that* mean?'

'Er . . .? Things that haven't been anywhere else, I suppose.'

'Gossip and generally invading my private life? No fucking way. I knew this was a disaster.' He said this to an invisible third party, instead of Edie, although she felt entirely invisible.

'We could work on what we wanted to leave out and. . .'

'No no no. This is trashy.'

In another time, and another place, when she hadn't been shredded by humiliation, flattened by shame, involuntarily thrown back to her home city and forced into a bruising encounter with a truculent narcissist, Edie might've handled this more diplomatically. As it was, she was boiling with fury.

'I don't understand your attitude. You've signed off on this and presumably accepted the money. The idea is you collaborate with me and we both get a good book out of it.'

Elliot's eyes widened and she felt she finally had his attention, at least.

'Oh yeah, you're going to write a *good book*. C'mon. We both know this is one of those hack job cash-ins you see in the bargain bin at the supermarket. Like Danny Dyer's *A Cheeky Blighter* or whatever.'

Edie could think of a few titles for Elliot's right now.

'Well it's definitely going to be a hack job if you won't be interviewed properly.'

Elliot ran a hand through his hair and again appeared to look offstage to some imaginary PR handler.

'Sorry for your disappointment.'

Edie was humiliated, and spoke before she thought.

'This isn't disappointment, it's anger at having to work with someone being completely unprofessional. And spoiled.'

'Woah!' Elliot's eyes were round.

Edie had gone too far and they both knew it.

'This must be the rapport-building phase to win the subject's trust,' Elliot said. 'Tell you what . . .' a pause here while he realised he couldn't remember her name, 'I think we've established this isn't going to work.'

He got to his feet and pulled his stripy grey jumper over his flat stomach.

'Great meeting, thanks a lot.'

'Yeah, thanks a lot,' Edie said, with similar sarcastic intonation, and briskly showed herself out, to spare him the effort he wasn't going to make.

18

What a wanker! Would you believe it? What an utterly inter-galactic astrotwat.

Edie was already replaying lines from that brief encounter in her head, almost chuntering quotes out loud in the street, in the way of deeply indignant people.

Her phone buzzed in her pocket and she slipped it out. *Richard.* Her rage march to the nearest bus stop was stopped in its tracks. She let the call ring out and saw the words New Voicemail appear ominously on the screen.

It would be a check in, a 'how are you getting on'. *I had a row with him and the project is cancelled*, Edie imagined herself saying. *Oh, and his agent might hear I was . . . forthright.*

She swallowed hard. That would be an awful conversation. Even worse than the one about the wedding. Then, she hadn't owed Richard quite as much. He had since taken pity on her and extended her this lifeline. She knew he wanted to keep her, not Jack – it was Edie he liked, Jack, not so much, and Richard always said employing people you liked was good business sense. He'd maybe even choose Edie over Charlotte, if it came to a *her-or-me* stand-off from one of his best account managers.

Edie would now repay this faith by embarrassing him in front of the publisher contact and letting him down entirely. At least the last writer to walk out hadn't burned the bridge behind him. And she'd been warned that Elliot was difficult. Elliot Owen was a star, and being an arsehole was a clear perk. That was what was nagging at Edie throughout their confrontation. Not that she wasn't well within her rights to sound off, but that they weren't on an even footing when it came to losing your rag. He could be mardy, she was expected to keep her cool in the face of complete unreason. She was supposed to sweet-talk, wheedle and cajole, and in her ire at the Heather delay, she'd lost sight of the mission.

She didn't see a way out of calling Richard back and copping to this mistake. Richard's disgust and disappointment with her, she couldn't handle. She couldn't lose another friend. One of the very few real ones.

There was a possible plan B. Could she bear to try it? It was a vile prospect but on balance, the marginally less vile of the two. She vacillated. She stared at the New Voicemail, as her heart thumped.

Even though it was unlikely to do any good, she'd have to at least try to see if there was a chance of rescue. Richard would surely demand she tried anyway.

With lead in her shoes and a stomach full of ball bearings, she walked back down the street to Elliot's house, and rang the bell again. Her nerves now had nothing to do with his fame, though it hardly helped.

One of the problems of meeting celebs was knowing that you'd comb over every stupid thing you said afterwards, even if they'd not remember you five seconds later. It was certain she was going to have the full Gollum body cringe whenever Elliot Owen's name came up. This might be an even worse cringe than 'Charlack'.

He opened the door, leaned on the door frame and peered at her, inscrutable apart from the sullen set of his mouth.

Edie cleared her throat.

'Hello again. Er, OK, that didn't go quite how I planned. How about this. I write some draft copy and you see if you like it. We do a few interviews but you keep the topics to things you're comfortable with. We'll see how we go.'

'I thought a moment ago I was a spoiled unprofessional twat?'

Edie bit down '*you were*' and said: 'Sorry, I shouldn't have snapped like that. Obviously I was thinking about what I'd been—'

Elliot interrupted.

'Have you been told to come back here and persuade me?'

'No.'

Elliot folded his arms. 'Liar.'

'I'm not lying!'

'It's still a no, I'm afraid.'

'Look. *Please*, can we – I'm in an impossible position . . .'

'Get down from your stool, there's no point doing the ballad.'

He had a sharper tongue on him than Edie expected. Elliot went to close the door and Edie near-shrieked.

'Stop, stop! No one's told me to apologise. But I have to do this book. I can't go back to my office, and face everyone I work with. Please.'

Elliot opened the door again. 'Why not? Did you insult them too?'

'I kissed someone's husband on their wedding day. Both he and his wife are my colleagues. My company is weaponised right now. I asked to be sacked and my boss gave me this to do instead, while it blows over.'

Arrrgh *shut up, Edie.*

That part might've been best left out, especially as Elliot had done a double take. This was a large gamble. Edie reasoned that throwing herself on his mercy was the only thing she had left; but on the other hand, it could be repeated to make her look like a completely incompetent fruit loop, and embarrass Richard further. Short of pulling a gun on him, however, she had nothing.

There was a pause. Elliot shifted his weight and frowned.

'You kissed someone's husband on their wedding day? Like on the cheek?'

'No. *Kissed*-kissed.'

He lifted his eyebrows. 'Christ.'

'Yeah.'

'In front of who?'

Asking questions had to be a cautiously good sign.

'No one, we thought . . . then the bride saw us.'

'Y'kidding?'

'No. They split up on the spot. I should say here that he kissed me. I didn't try to kiss him.'

'Not sure you're the person I should feel sorry for in this anecdote, but whatever you say.'

There was unexpected wry humour in his tone.

'I might not be. I'm begging you not to send me back to London yet. I'm from Nottingham too, so it's good to be home . . .'

That was an openly craven untruth, Edie thought.

'. . . I'm not as lucky as you though, my family are all at home. Hah.'

She was gabbling now. Elliot folded his arms. His expression closed again but Edie had an inkling she might just have won a second chance. If it was a no, surely the door would be shut by now.

'Please,' Edie soldiered on. 'Let's *try* to do this book. There's got to be a way of making this work, so that I—'

Elliot chewed the inside of his cheek and held up a palm.

'. . . No rubbish about who I'm seeing though, I can't stand all that.'

'Agreed,' Edie said, feeling giddy with shock that he'd relented. 'You sign off everything I write, so no surprises. I'm quite good at writing. You might even like what I do.'

Elliot made a sceptical face and scratched the back of his neck, exhaled.

'I'll give it a go, but no promises.'

Edie could fist pump, while doing a knee slide. 'Absolutely. Understood.'

'I don't have many scenes on Friday so I should be done by afternoon. How about we do it over a pint?'

'Sounds great.' Edie beamed.

'A-right. I'll get Kirsty to ping you the details.'

Elliot closed the door in her face.

Edie walked back down the street with a spring in her step, grinning like an idiot in relief. Elliot was . . . she wouldn't say she *liked* him. At least he wasn't a completely inhumane monster though. She might be able to break through to some sort of kernel of humanity, then grossly exaggerate it for the benefit of his fans.

She listened to the message and pressed dial on her phone.

'Richard! Hi . . .'

19

Her father had clearly said more to Meg than Edie realised. Meg was quieter, contrite, and even apologised.

'Sorry if I was rude about your dress,' she mumbled, when Edie was in the kitchen making a cup of tea on the following blazing hot Wednesday morning. Their dad was at the supermarket. 'Was only meant to be a joke.'

'Don't worry about it,' Edie said. She was going to exploit the moment to say something like, 'I do have principles you know' but then had the twin thoughts: *don't push it* and *why bother.* Also maybe the woman hiding in her home town in shame wasn't in the best position to make that case.

Edie was glad of the temporary ceasefire though.

'Want one?' Edie asked, gesturing to her tea-bag dunking.

'Ah, no. Winnie and Kez will be here in a minute.'

Meg had mentioned she was having some friends over for a barbecue this afternoon. Edie had perked up – 'ooh, barbecue!' and considered dropping Hannah a text to see if she could join them. Then she remembered it was a *Meg* barbecue. Disintegrating

Sosmix nut-turds would sit there smoking meatlessly on the coals, instead of burgers and chops. Also, Meg's friends often conducted themselves like Fun Prevention Officers. Although Edie had met Winnie and Kez a while back and they seemed more docile than the more fighty social justice warriors of Meg's acquaintance. Did none of them have work to go to on a Wednesday, though?

Meg didn't offer for Edie to join in and Edie didn't want to, so she thought it tactful to go up to her room and stay out of their way. She started drafting The Elliot Owen Story, according to the How to Write a Novel book she was consulting. Though it had to be said, her data was thin stuff. He could've had the basic consideration of an interesting origins tale. The prequel to 'grew up handsome and got famous' didn't have much storytelling value.

After half an hour of pecking at her laptop, Edie heard music and clanking around in the back garden. She glanced out of her bedroom window and did an involuntary gasp. '*What* the . . .'

There was brazen, unexpected nudity, right in front of her: neither Winnie or Kez were wearing any clothes on their upper half.

Winnie, a voluptuous twenty-something with curly hair, had unleashed stupendously huge mammaries. They were swinging gently like udders as she checked the foil-wrapped packages on the grill. Edie winced at her leaning too far and getting broiled breasts. Kez was her physical opposite: wiry and tiny to the point where you might mistake her for a teenage boy, at first glance. She had cornrows, a giant tattoo of the words 'CAN U NOT' across her very flat stomach, and nipple piercings like Frankenstein's bolts.

Mercifully, Meg was clothed. She was in what could be best described as dungashorts, with a striped vest underneath. They were all swigging from cans of Strongbow, smoking roll-ups and playing some music from a beat-up ghettoblaster that had a boom-digga-boom-digga bassy rumble. One of them had brought a thin, grey dog with mange, which sat on the concrete patio looking as embarrassed as Edie felt, head on paws.

I mean, *really* though, Edie thought. You could celebrate your natural form and the wind on your skin any place you liked, but Wednesday afternoon in your friend's dad's garden seemed not the natural order of things. Society has taboos for a reason. Also, the narrow garden was overlooked by about a dozen windows. They'd make this house a magnet for perverts. Edie imagined saying any of this to them and realised she'd sound like an eighty-three-year-old, writing a letter to the *Telegraph*.

She checked her watch. Her dad would be home soon. She didn't want to be here where he got in and tried to conduct a stuttering, startled conversation with them. Edie bounded down the stairs, picked her bag up in the kitchen and put her head round the back door. They were all clustered round the barbecue, gnawing on corncobs.

'Hi,' Edie said, shading her view from the sun, trying very hard not to make eye contact with any nipples, 'Just wondered if you wanted anything from the shops? I've a lust for a mint Magnum.'

They looked at her blankly and Meg said: 'Nah, we're good, ta.'

Good and NUDE. Whatever next, Meg.

'Oh, kay.'

'Excuse me!' A woman's head appeared, over the garden fence on the right-hand side, the other half of their semi. She was maybe late sixties, heavily made up, thin, dyed-brown hair in peaks, like a feminised Ken Dodd. She too was holding a fag aloft. The concept of 'getting some fresh air' around here was somewhat confused.

'Excuse *me*. Why should we all have to look at your bits and smell your jazz cigarettes? Have some respect for others.'

Edie's jaw dropped. She was fairly sure Meg's jaw dropped. The somewhat stoned-looking Winnie and Kez gawped.

'Put some clothes on, for heaven's sake. You're women, but you're not ladies.' The woman who *was* apparently a lady took a drag on her fag, puffed and surveyed them. 'Mind you, I'm not sure she's a woman.' She gestured at Kez.

'We don't care about your fascist ideas of propriety, you old ratbag,' Meg said. 'The Western sexualisation of breasts is not our concern.'

'I doubt anyone will be sexualising Laurel and Hardy any time soon. The state of them!'

'Oh, nice body shaming. This is private property, you can't make us do shit.'

'Are you asking men to put their tops on?' Winnie asked the neighbour, shielding her eyes from the sun with a palm.

'No, dear, because they don't have knockers.'

'Not all women have breasts and not all born men are men

anyway,' Meg said. 'Don't impose your preconceived gender normative assumptions on everyone.'

'I think that wacky baccy's gone to your head, love.'

'Free the nipple!' Meg said.

'Well yours aren't free. Not that I'm complaining.'

'I have impetigo!' Meg said.

This was the first Edie had heard of it. She remained glad her sister was clothed though.

The woman villain-laughed uproariously and her head disappeared again.

'Oh my God,' Meg shook her head, 'I didn't realise we lived next door to *Margaret Thatcher.*'

Kez was unperturbed by the sickening tirade, squirting lurid mustard into a hotdog bun.

Edie judged it safe to retreat. She was at the front door when she heard screaming from the garden, and not joyful high spirits screaming – bloodcurdling howls of shock.

She dashed back through to see the woman from next door had returned, cackling delightedly as she drenched the three of them with a hose, which she wielded like a gun in a western, fag in other hand. They danced in the spray, holding their faces, chests bouncing. If any deviant was watching from a window, it was a *wet dreams come true* moment.

'I'm calling the police, you mad old bitch!' shrieked Meg, pink in the face, pale dreadlocks plastered to her wet face, as the drenching ceased.

'You do that, my love. And I'm sure they'll be interested in your drug-taking. In fact, I'm going to call them myself. How about that, eh.' Her head popped away again.

Meg dried her face on a grease-stained tea towel.

'Mental cow,' she muttered.

'You don't think she's going to call the police, do you?' Edie said, nervously.

It wasn't just the weed. She had long had a suspicion that her dad was falling behind on all sorts of necessary admin, like TV licences and that shattered brake light on his car. It was a consequence of being short of money, and possibly also a remnant of his breakdown. Edie nudged him when she could, but she wasn't here to oversee it, most of the time.

The police turning up on the doorstep, confronted with a toked-up Meg, two more traveller-types with their baps out, and a mouthy, pushy neighbour? Edie couldn't see it ending well.

As she passed her next-door neighbour's front door, on her way to the shops, Edie paused. Maybe she could sweet-talk her sister out of this, pour oil on troubled water. On an impulse, she tapped on the flimsy wooden door with its whorl-like glass panels, somewhat apprehensive.

'Hello,' she said.

'Who are you?' said the woman. In full length, she was wearing a blue and pink housecoat of a sort that Edie didn't think had been manufactured since the 1950s.

'I'm Edie. I'm from next door.'

'Oh, are you sick of the boob show too?'

'Er, no. I'm from *that* next door. That was my sister you were talking to. She was the one who was dressed.'

The woman leaned on the door jamb and looked her up and down.

'Not seen you around.'

'No, I live in London.'

'Huh.'

'I just wanted to say – I know my sister can be a bit full on . . .' Edie lowered her voice; Meg would kill her if she overheard this. 'But please let's not all start calling the police. It's not necessary. There won't be many days warm enough for topless sunbathing anyway. I'd say this was a one-off.'

Edie sincerely hoped this wasn't Incident No.702 and nudism was Meg's new jam.

The woman gazed at her with crepey lidded eyes, her eyebrows above plucked into croquet hoops, which gave her a slightly Hammer Horror look.

'Are you back to London soon, then?'

Edie couldn't tell if this was conciliation or not, so played along.

'Uh, no, I'm not. I'm working up here.'

'What do you do?'

'I'm a writer. A copywriter. Right now I'm writing a book about an actor.'

'Which actor?'

Edie hesitated.

'Someone from *Blood & Gold*.'

The woman sucked on her cig and exhaled a train-like stream of puff from the corner of her mouth. Edie worked hard at keeping her face straight and not coughing.

'Ooh is it the dishy Prince? I like him!'

Edie couldn't resist a small moment of showing off.

'Er. Yes. The Prince.'

'He's from round here?'

'Yes. Well, Bridgford.'

'I won't shop your sister, if you show me some of this book.'

Edie was taken aback. 'I had to sign confidentiality clauses. I'm not allowed.'

The woman threw her head back and let go a cackle. 'Who am I going to tell, dear heart? My birds?'

Edie bit the inside of her cheek. It admittedly seemed unlikely this woman was a security leak. And the autobiog was anodyne. Still, Edie wasn't in a risk-taking frame of mind.

'I'm not allowed, sorry.'

'No deal then.'

The woman smirked evilly and delightedly. Ooh, you old rotter. Wait, Edie thought: she was loaded with Elliot press clippings. She could read any of those and she'd be none the wiser, right?

'There's not a lot of it and it's not very exciting. I've not even done the first interview with him yet. It's on Friday. So, go on then.'

'Next week?'

'OK. And you are . . . ?'

'Margot. See you next week.'

The door closed in her face and Edie thought: *This neighbourhood is nuts.*

20

Edie did a circuit of the pub without spotting Elliot, before realising he was tucked away in a corner, doing a Hollywood version of inconspicuous. *No cheekbones to see here, move on.* He was in a dark sweater and jeans and wearing a black woolly hat pulled low around his ears. It was completely unseasonal and made him look like a male model playing a criminal fisherman.

Lol, famous people.

'You're alright for a drink?' she said, smiling. Elliot was sat in front of three-quarters of a pint of beer.

'Yes, thanks. Sorry, I would get yours but I've found a safe corner, I'm best staying in it.'

'Sure,' Edie said, thinking, 'lying lazy arse.' The Stratford Haven was hardly hostile territory: a real ale sort of pub, it attracted a mixture of middle-aged men and sports clubs from the university. At early evening on a Friday, it was busy enough, but not madly so.

Once she'd obtained her civilian's G&T, Edie got her Dictaphone out and placed it between them.

'I'm going to take a paper note, too.' Edie had learned that people said more to you if you broke eye contact while you wrote.

Elliot nodded. He had an odd expression that Edie couldn't quite read, a mixture of attentiveness and apprehensiveness. He was obviously uneasy. Perhaps he spent all his time in The Ivy now.

'I thought we could start with your love of acting,' Edie said, sipping her drink, feeling a little foolish. 'When you first realised it was what you wanted to do.'

She'd congratulated herself on this being a suitably grown-up and flattering first subject for them to tackle.

Elliot sloshed his Harvest Pale around the glass.

'Hmm.'

'You don't like the question?' Edie said, very carefully, in the pause. She'd be handling him with kid gloves and sugar tongs.

'No. The question's fine. Do people honestly care about this? My "craft". Haha.'

He took a sip of his beer.

As Edie tried to work him out, Elliot glowered at her with his light eyes, framed by dark lashes, the look that had apparently unlaced bodices. Edie found him distinctly more chilly and forbidding than arousing and inviting.

'Yes, they're definitely interested.'

'But you're not?' Elliot said, with a small smile.

'What do you mean? I'm interested,' Edie protested, suddenly a little embarrassed. He had an odd way of throwing out attitudes she didn't expect.

'A-right. Sure you are.' The small smile spread into a laddish 'caught you out' grin.

'You're more northern-sounding than I was expecting.'

Weirdly, the portcullis went down, at what Edie thought an innocuous remark. Elliot looked hard again, although his voice was merely level.

'I'm from here. How was I going to sound? I didn't go to RADA. Or did you not read the Wiki notes?'

'No, I didn't mean . . . I'm from here, and I sound more southern than you.'

'You do,' he said.

Edie decided to say nothing. She kept getting it wrong, apparently.

'Hey, here's an idea . . .' Elliot said.

Edie smiled a polite tight smile. She'd like the general idea where she had a safe amount of intel in her recording devices, thanks very much.

'How about I ask you questions, too?'

'Uh . . . How do you mean?'

'I mean, to make this feel more like a conversation and less like an interrogation. You ask me stuff, I ask you stuff.'

This wasn't the snotty self-obsession she assumed was part of the thespian DNA.

Still, she also assumed he'd be capricious, so she'd see how long this whim lasted.

'. . . If you really want to.'

Elliot stretched and sat straighter in his seat.

'Acting . . . I didn't like school much and I wasn't very popular.'

Edie raised an eyebrow without realising she was doing so. Every celeb seemed to have this Cinderella story.

'Honestly, I wasn't,' Elliot said, reading her expression. 'I'm no good in clubs or gangs. I'm not a joiner. Growing up male is one long team-playing exercise. Ironically, I'm bad at pretending to be something I'm not when I'm playing myself, if you know what I mean?'

Actually, Edie did. In their first encounter, he didn't do much dissembling.

'Then a teacher I got on with suggested trying the drama club, and something clicked. It was amazing, I've never had that feeling, before or since. That sense of, "I didn't know I was looking for this until the very moment I found it."'

Edie scribbled this down. Elliot scratched his ear, under his hat.

'Aren't you hot in that hat?' Edie said, as courtesy-code for: *Why on earth are you wearing that indoors?*

'A bit. I can't take it off.'

Edie giggled.

'Why?'

'I'll get hassle.'

Edie had to tread carefully. They were on better terms, but only slightly.

'I know you're very well known, but we're not in the Chiltern Firehouse. There's only real ale fans in here. I think you'll be OK, as long as a hen party from Rhyl doesn't turn up.'

Elliot looked at Edie steadily, jaw clenched in concentration as if he was trying to figure out if she was joking.

'We'll do it your way then,' he said, and took the hat off. Edie felt a little smug. A bit of reality might be good for this man.

'You?' Elliot said. 'How did you end up writing an actor's ME-moir?'

Edie laughed and thought, He's sharper than I thought. Admittedly it had said he was smart in that Sunday supplement article, but given it had been such panting purple prose, no wonder she didn't believe it.

'I always had good language skills. I did an English degree in Sheffield and moved to London and fell into copywriting.' She paused. 'See, not very interesting.'

'*Everyone's* interesting,' Elliot said. 'Acting 101.'

'They're definitely not. Advertising 202.'

Elliot laughed, showing very white, straight film-star teeth, and Edie smiled and chided herself for the small tingle it gave her. He'd have forgotten her name again by tomorrow. In fact, she wasn't convinced he knew it now.

A man with grey hair in a cagoule approached them.

'Excuse me, me and my friend were wondering. Are you the man from the TV show? The one with the killer bats?'

'Yes,' Elliot said, with a practised smile, reaching over to shake his hand.

'I was wondering, could I have an autograph for my daughter? She's a big fan.'

'Of course. Do you have pen and paper?'

'Ah . . . No.'

Edie fumbled to tear off a sheet of her notebook and hand over a pen. Elliot inquired who he was making it out to and wrote the dedication, doing a well-practised one-loop-and-line scribble for his name. The man seemed as if he wanted to stay but couldn't think what else to say, and backed off.

'There you are. I've been made. Assume you know numbers of local taxi firms?' Elliot said. Edie nearly laughed in his face.

'I don't want to be, an, uh, Doubting Thomas but that was one man. We'll probably be alright.'

'You honestly don't get it, do you? It's like being out with my gran. *"Ooh, Elliot, they won't all have seen your Bloody Gold series, it's not even on the proper television channels.""*

He said this with enough warmth that Edie had to laugh. Elliot rubbed his eyes.

'It's mobiles. Nothing was as bad before mobiles, I'm sure. What's he doing right now?' Elliot said, inclining his head towards the autograph hunter.

Edie glanced over. 'I can't see . . . wait. He's talking to his friend and looking at his phone.'

'There you are. Pretty much everyone under seventy has a mobile now, right? He's texting where he's seen me.'

They stopped talking as the barmaid came over to clear Elliot's now empty pint glass. Oh. She wasn't taking his glass.

'Sorry to bother you, could I get a photo?'

'Sure. Do you want to take it?' Elliot said to Edie, smoothly, and Edie dumbly accepted the woman's iPhone, steadied the frame and snapped, the barmaid in her work shirt leaning in, Elliot smiling with one arm slung round her. Edie handed the phone back.

'I think you're amazing,' the woman said. She was trembling

slightly. 'And could you sign this?' she pushed a beermat towards Elliot.

Elliot picked up Edie's pen and scribbled across the beermat.

'There you go,' he said, and the barmaid backed off, hand over mouth, muttering *I can't believe it, thank you so much.*

'And the cameras on phones, of course. Magic,' Elliot muttered.

Edie suddenly sensed many pairs of eyes boring into her back at once. She glanced over her shoulder and saw everyone in the pub looking at them. A few phones had come out too, and Edie sensed they were being photographed.

'Found any love for the hat, yet?' Elliot said.

Edie felt as if she was in a zombie film and had given them a sniff of her live human flesh. The sense of everyone being silently hyper-aware of you, while pretending not to be, was creepy in the extreme.

'Uh,' Edie tried to concentrate on her notes and not fear that everyone was now craning to hear her every word. 'Acting. Your drama club . . .'

They made it through another five minutes or so of school years before the pub door flapped open, noisily. A group of girls spilled into the room. There was an instant craning of necks and whispering and scanning. The man in the cagoule was saying hello to them and doing the world's least discreet *'ee's-over-there* head jerk. Oh, bollocks. Elliot was right.

'How many?' Elliot said, unable to see what Edie was looking at, round the wall.

Edie counted: 'Five, no, six,' as if they were in the NYPD. (*Half a dozen perps at three o'clock, cover me.*) I mean, it was silly, not as if high school girls wearing lots of liquid eyeliner and glittery trainers were going to be wilding and monstering them. It was curiously intimidating though.

Elliot said: 'You can get out of the doors at the back there, can't you?'

'Yes?' Edie said, looking at the rear exit.

'Can you call a taxi and ask it to pull up in the car park? I'll hide in the men's. Text me when it's there.'

'Alright,' Edie said, bizarrely nervous at being on her own with this. Elliot moved towards the toilets, all heads turning in his wake. Edie called the taxi. She kept the phone pressed to her ear even after the call was over, to keep the girls at bay who looked poised to approach as soon as she'd finished talking.

Edie stuffed her things in her bag and minutes later, felt a wash of relief as a car with the taxi company livery could be glimpsed out of the back window. Wait. Bugger. She was supposed to text Elliot, but she didn't have his number. With the room watching, she legged it into the back corridor and tapped at the door of the men's loos. No answer. She pushed it open nervously and saw a man using the urinals, and a locked cubicle door.

'Elliot!' she called, making the weeing man startle and nearly piss on his shoes. 'Taxi's here.'

Elliot appeared, pulling his hat on.

They bolted out through the doors, Edie leading Elliot. It was unbelievably odd to be doing an Elvis Has Left The Building dash in a pleasant Tynemill pub that did sausages and mash and quizzes, and shared a car park with the Co-Op next door. Extreme famousness didn't seem as if it could happen here.

'Where to, love?' said the taxi driver, frowning at Elliot as he wriggled low on the back seat next to Edie, his hat yanked below his eyebrows.

'Just head towards the city centre,' Edie said, as the driver frowned some more. Elliot sank almost below the level of the rear windows as they drove past the gaggle of girls that had now gathered on the street, outside the front of the pub, as they saw their prey escaping. Some held phones aloft and took pictures of the departing taxi, as if they were press photographers besieging a prison van.

A few moments later, as they approached Trent Bridge, the driver pulled over, sharply.

'Is something wrong?' Edie asked.

'I'm not taking some toerag in trouble with the police anywhere. Go on, out you get. You can take your chances.'

Edie turned to Elliot, who was already holding out a twenty-pound note between finger and thumb to her. She passed it over, mumbling that it 'wasn't like that'. The taxi driver glanced at Elliot in annoyance, sighed, took the note, and they set off again.

'Which road?' said the driver.

'Roads? Where we're going, we don't need roads,' Elliot mumbled into his collar.

'You what?'

'Know any other quiet pubs?' Elliot said, to Edie.

'I think so . . .'

Edie had been arrogant, she realised. She no more knew

148

Elliot Owen or understood his life than any of his most ardent fans did.

The person sitting next to her was a stranger. She'd give him the basic respect of treating him like one, from now on.

21

'Can I let you into a secret? It's horrible. We're not taping yet, are we?'

Edie shook her head. She'd positioned the Dictaphone near her body, where it hopefully couldn't be seen by onlookers, but was yet to turn it on.

Edie nodded and felt guilt for the hat derision. The hat was back on. Elliot looked hunted.

She'd brought him to The Peacock pub, north of the city centre. With the mounted stag's head, flock wallpaper, wax-dribbling pillar candles and general air of cosy eccentricity, it was like the bric-a-brac-laden front room of an alcoholic uncle. Stevie Wonder's *Innervisions* played on vinyl on a turntable on the bar.

'The first day I realised how big *Blood & Gold* had got was when I got chased out of a newsagent by a fourteen-year-old-girl in Muswell Hill, like some reverse-sexism Benny Hill sketch. I went home, and this realisation bore down on me: *there is no off switch.* You can't get un-known in the same time you got known. The devil doesn't do refunds. You gave it away and you aren't getting it back.'

Edie was sorry the Dictaphone wasn't on now, this was much better quality stuff than she thought she'd get.

'Do you wish you'd never done *Blood & Gold*?' Edie said.

'No, I liked the show. I like the fact I currently have my pick of scripts. I wanted to do this for a living. I just wish . . .' He looked at Edie warily again. 'I wish I was a character actor. I don't want the fuss.'

Edie read that as 'female fuss' and nodded. She nearly made a joke about not enjoying the burden of sex symbolism herself, and then considered it was a bad idea for about five reasons. She was wearing her tartan coat, an old T-shirt and a plastic pineapple necklace. She was turning forty in five years' time, maybe a wardrobe rethink was in order.

'The fact that success gives you a new set of problems without solving all your old ones has come as a surprise. Do I sound a massive whiny twat? The money's nice, obviously.'

Edie smiled. 'You don't sound a twat. It's quite interesting actually. I always sort of assumed famous people secretly love the fuss.'

'Some do,' Elliot said. 'The truth is it was funny and weird and a buzz to me for about five minutes, and then the novelty wore off and stayed off. I can't go on the tube any more.'

'Can't you?'

'Nope. Getting spotted in an enclosed space, bad. Not worth the risk. One hairy experience on the Circle Line with some over-caffeinated American schoolgirls and I accepted it.'

Edie said 'huh' and watched as Elliot drew a small figure of eight with the bottom of his pint glass.

'My best mate from here, Al, sometimes gets a bit like: "Ah I don't like to tell you what I've been up to, I went on a camping holiday with the kids," and the thing is, he's having a better time than me. What about you?'

'What?' Edie said. 'Camping? I don't see how it can be a holiday if it's worse than real life.'

Elliot laughed. 'Whether or not you're having a good time. Are you happy?'

'Uh . . .' Edie stumbled into silence. She couldn't remember a time when anyone had asked her this. She'd not asked herself this.

'Probably not that happy. I mean, I told you what happened at work. The wedding.'

'You were seeing someone's husband?'

'No . . .' Edie shifted in her seat and thought how surprisingly exposing it was to describe yourself to a new person. This wasn't like a date, you couldn't do your best-foot-forward anecdotes. No wonder Elliot didn't enjoy it. 'He was my colleague's boyfriend. We messaged all the time, that's all. He started it. Somewhere during all the chatting, I really fell for him. We got on to, y'know, *deep* topics, all that. Then he kicked me in the guts by moving in with her, having said he didn't want the commitment. I didn't know what me and him had all been about. And on their wedding day, for reasons I will never understand, he finally decides to make a move on me.' Edie swallowed and said, 'Men,' with both palms up, as a nervous full stop.

'Oh-kaaay,' Elliot rolled his glass in his hands. 'Let's do the visualisation bit, like my therapist.'

'You have a therapist?'

'I'm an actor who spends half the year in the States, what do you think?' he deadpanned. 'Next you'll ask me if I have prescription sleeping meds.'

Edie laughed.

'What did you want to happen between you and . . .?'

'. . . Jack. Nothing if he was still with Charlotte. I wasn't trying for an affair. I wouldn't do that.'

'What did you want to turn out differently? He was always going to move on with his life, eventually?'

'I . . . suppose I wanted him to leave her.'

'The narrative in your head was that he falls for you, and leaves her, for you? I'm not judging here, I'm trying to understand.'

Edie was caught. Stevie Wonder was yodelling 'Don't You Worry 'Bout a Thing'. Easy for you to say, Stevie.

'Yes. I mean, I didn't understand why Jack wanted so much of my time, but not . . . me.'

Why was she telling Elliot Owen, of all people, this? Tragic.

'And all the way through this, he had to make the decisions, based on guesswork? You weren't going to tell him how you felt?'

'No.' Edie had never even considered that.

'You were waiting for him to give you things he never said he'd give you and you never asked for. You could have asked him what your "thing" meant to him. But you didn't. By default, you gave him all the power. Doesn't sound like he was trustworthy with it.'

153

Edie nodded, miserably.

'In my experience, hopeful silence is a tactic that is DFD.'

'"DFD"?'

'Destined for doom.'

'Is that a therapist phrase?'

Elliot laughed and Edie drank her drink and started to wish she'd said *No I ask the questions and you answer them, that's the deal*. He had just taken her apart in about three chess moves.

'Waiting for people to read your mind never works.' Elliot swigged his beer. 'One of my old acting coaches used to say the only thing that comes to those who wait is cancer. He was a jolly sod.'

Edie smiled, thinly.

'I'm not saying it's your fault. We all do it. You can only look what happened in the eyes and learn from it and try not to repeat it.'

'Thanks, Oprah.'

Edie made sure she said this with a grin, so he couldn't take the arse at it.

'Jump on my couch,' Elliot said, and they both laughed. 'I scoffed at therapy, you know, but you can get useful things from it, without disappearing up your own arsehole. It makes you pull the camera back and see how you're participating in your fate. Or not.'

Edie made polite noises, as while she had sympathy, she definitely didn't think the burden of being Elliot Owen was worthy of psychiatry. Also, she refrained from saying that it didn't sound as if his own relationship was going great guns.

At that very moment, as if God was a film director with

no fear of the absurd, the pub's music system started playing 'Crumple Zone', the emo rock ballad that was forever associated with Elliot's face. Elliot groaned and pulled his hat down over his eyes, slid down the seat.

'Do you realise, I thought I'd get well paid for wearing a Levi's jacket, squinting into the setting sun and driving a Mustang around the desert outside LA, in that video. And it was such a bad song that *no one would ever see it.*'

Edie giggled and had a *Hannah will never believe this* moment.

They turned the Dictaphone on and managed to gather another forty minutes or so of fairly anaemic material on Elliot's inception as an actor. Edie couldn't help wishing they could put the off-the-record material in. As himself, Elliot could be adroitly funny and surprisingly incisive. As Elliot Owen, Actor, he became tense, blander, more on message.

Their glasses were empty.

'Mind if I get going?' Elliot said, checking a no doubt horrifically expensive watch, concealed under his jacket sleeve.

'Oh God, absolutely, sure,' Edie, embarrassed that she'd relaxed and had opened her mouth to suggest another drink, as if the big screen's next hot property didn't have somewhere better to be on a Friday night.

'Will you be OK?' she said. Elliot grinned with those otherworldly white teeth.

'Yeah, taxi rank opposite. Ta, Mum.'

Edie blushed.

22

Edie knew her mobile − a smeary iPhone, plain black case, wallpaper picture of a carefree, sundress-clad Marilyn Monroe holding a flower − had multiple functions. She had never thought of it as a weapon. But it turned out she was carrying an incendiary device that could go off at any moment. What did Elliot say? *It wasn't as bad before mobiles, I'm sure.*

In the minutes after Elliot left, she'd started to think she might get used to being back in this city, and come to terms with her situation. The atmosphere in the pub was so welcoming, for a moment, she was almost content. Then the screen pinged with an email alert from Louis.

An email, on a Friday night? What could be important enough to merit that? Nothing good. She felt the usual adrenaline spike and stomach flop as she slid the unlock bar.

Hi doll. Hope things are good up north? So . . . Charlotte just put this on Facebook. Thought you should see it. I think she should let bygones be bygones really but I guess she's got a big

grudge. They're all drunk tonight I think. L Swag
Xx

Below his message was a screen grab of a Charlotte status, and the ensuing comments.

Hey I'm finally back on here. And yes Jack & I are
still together. Wedding day had a slight hitch (no
pun) but we're moving on. I guess you never know
who your real friends are until a time like this,
and it turns out some people weren't your friend
at all.

That could've been worse, Edie thought, though her skin burned with shame while she read it. Underneath she saw her old foe, Lucie Maguire, was the first to dive in.

Welcome back C! It wasn't your fault you let that
horrible girl into your special day. She will die
alone and her fat arse will be eaten by hungry
cats. There's plenty to go around lol. Love you &
the scrummy new hubster to the moon and back.
L xxxx

Over a hundred miles away, Edie gasped as if she'd been slapped. Someone she didn't know, hated her that much. Wait. *Dozens* of people she didn't know, hated her that much.

What Lucie said. What a total bitch. And errrr . . . aren't you supposed to be tempted by a BETTER looking woman? This is the whole Camilla/Diana thing again.

Who was she? I never even noticed her?

Sadie, nor did anyone else until she threw herself at him. Can you imagine having that little class?

Seriously, which one was she? Is this girl on here?

Chubby face, dark hair, big tits, red dress. Short. Waaaay too much make-up. No, she's disappeared! Stupid tart.

LMAO. I think I know who you mean. Completely throwing herself at every bloke and falling out of her dress. Ugh to infinity.

Edie would like to know where this evidence was coming from, but the roasting had a momentum of its own. It was powering forward and it didn't need facts as fuel, only feeling.

I hope if she ever gets married, someone completely trashes her big day ☹

Hahahahahha no one's marrying THAT. NO ONE. Pig in a ribbon.

Does she have a boyfriend? I thought she was there with someone?

A gay BFF. She's a forever single type girl.

OMFG I wonder why. And I wonder why she was JEALOUS.

Has anyone got a photo of this skank? I want to laugh at her loser-ness

The last comment was from Charlotte:

Ladies, thank you so much for having my back, I love you all. I will have to get rid of this now as I don't want her to be mentioned on my profile again. She's a nobody. C xxx

Edie stopped reading and looked up, lightheaded and nauseous. It was as if they were talking about someone else, but they weren't, it was her. Her name, her appearance, her behaviour. She was a virtual piñata. Her phone rang. Louis.

'Hello?'

'Edie, hi. Look, that email I sent you. Delete it, don't read.'

'I've read it.'

'Oh shit! Right after I hit send, I thought I shouldn't have sent it. Are you OK, babe?'

'Not really,' Edie said, in a small voice.

'Oh NO. Oh God, I feel so awful. I didn't like people

talking behind your back and I thought someone else might show you it.'

Louis truly was the worst sort of sadist. The utterly manipulative, cowardly sort. He wanted to have his cake and eat it. To get the savage thrill of passing all this on, and to soak up Edie's first reaction. And for her to thank him for doing it, to soothe him that it was *fine, no, don't worry, you meant well.*

As he was the sole person posing as her ally, falling out with Louis would leave her completely alone. Hah, who was Edie kidding: she was anyway. But no. She had no desire to make another enemy, however much he deserved it. You win, Louis.

'I don't get . . .' Edie had to gulp. The back of the roof of her mouth was frozen with a cold, hard pain, which had spread out through her nose and ears. 'I don't get why everyone is saying I'm a horrible person when it was Jack's decision.'

'I know,' Louis lavishly-sighed and tutted, 'Jack gets his fit arse out of any trouble, doesn't he? I guess they are saying things, but not to Charlotte's face.'

'Why did she take him back?'

Edie felt a tear roll a wet trail down her cheek. She brushed it away and disciplined herself to keep her voice steady. *Don't give Louis the satisfaction.*

'The same reasons you let him kiss you, I guess,' said Louis, with exquisitely judged nastiness.

'Thanks, Louis! Thanks a lot!' Edie said this loudly enough that a few people in the pub glanced over.

'Noooo, babe,' he said, in his serpent tones. 'I mean, he's *charming*, isn't he? And technically, they're married. There was a period where Charl could get it annulled. Jack obviously beat the clock, hah.'

Edie wanted to be out of this phone call.

'. . . How's it going with you and this actor? I cannot BELIEVE you're getting to meet Elliot Owen, I would die wanking.'

'Yeah, I'm meeting him in a minute actually, so got to go. Speak soon!'

Edie rang off. This was clearly going to be used as leverage for more Edie-bashing in the office – she knew exactly how Louis would operate, innocently dropping a chunk of meat into the cage and enjoying the ensuing feeding frenzy. Edie had considered asking Richard to keep it secret, then considered she might be pushing her luck.

She'd pay for this discourtesy to Louis, of course – she could picture the lip curl he was doing, right now – but all things considered, Louis operating as her enemy and Louis operating as a friend were pretty hard to tell apart.

Edie deleted the email, and deleted it again from her trash. She had meant to send Charlotte an email herself with some sort of explanation and a heartfelt apology, once the dust had settled. She saw now that all she'd do was stir things up, to absolutely no end whatsoever. Edie had fantasised that it'd be possible to repair some of the damage by grovelling and minimising what happened, but she knew it wasn't possible. She was the woman who ruined Charlotte's wedding day and nearly wrecked her marriage, and that was that.

No doubt Jack had dropped enough *Aw man, I suppose now when I look back, she was quite full on* . . . hints that Edie had led him astray, and it had got him back in the door. She finished the last of her wine.

The Peacock was at the bottom of Mansfield Road. She could walk home from here. Through the gathering dusk and noise of a Friday night that was only getting started for everyone else, Edie trudged the streets of her youth, past antique shops, a Caribbean food store, newsagents, real ale pubs, and some kind of strange empty-looking place apparently selling ballerina costumes and stick-on moustaches. Men cat-called her from a fried chicken shop doorway and she grimly ignored them.

Somewhere right now in London, everyone she worked with was massing in the Italian wine bar, gleefully ripping her to shreds, while she was up here, banished from the kingdom, despised. She felt bad Nottingham was associated with so much torment and exile, but honestly, who could blame her? The words from the rabble on that thread haunted her. Was she really a grotesque predator? Perhaps this was what it was like to have a mirror held up to you, and hear other people describe what they saw.

When she'd finished wrestling her key in the lock, Meg was waiting for her in the hallway. She wore an expression which almost made Edie laugh, even in this dark hour: chin tucked down, glowering from under her brow, cheeks puffed out with righteous indignation. It was so incredibly similar to stroppy child Meg, and gave Edie a pang of maternal love. Then, she twigged that this was no humorous simulation of childhood tantrums. Meg was blazing.

'You APOLOGISED FOR ME? How DARE YOU?'

'Wha—?'

'That old Nazi next door starts giving me shit again and says *oh and your sister says you'll stop getting your suck sacks out* blah blah and I was like WHAT and she says you WENT to TALK to HER and SAY I WAS SORRY? Could you BE a bigger traitor?'

'Megan, what's all this bloody squawking!' Edie's dad called from the front room.

'I didn't say that, I asked her not to call the police . . .'

'You didn't say we wouldn't go topless?'

'I said you probably wouldn't . . .'

'Oh my God, why are you such a cow?!' Meg shouted, clearly having worked herself into a state where no explanation from Edie would be good enough anyway. 'You had to go straight round and start making me sound the bad person, when she had a go at us for no reason. Just because you're so uptight you secretly agree with her!'

'Meg,' Edie said, feeling a volcanic bubble-up of rage she had no ability to quell, 'JUST FUCK OFF AND LEAVE ME ALONE. FOREVER.'

Her volume momentarily stalled Meg. Edie roughly pushed past her and bombed up the stairs, chest heaving, and slammed her bedroom door with enough vicious force she guessed her dad would leave it at least an hour before daring to approach her. Sod it, sod them all – she was going to have to move out, this was disastrous.

Edie looked around her shabby room, and her not-fully-unpacked case on the floor, a signifier of her feelings for sure.

She flopped on to her bed, face down, and discovered she didn't have the energy to cry. Instead she wondered, if she took too many aspirin and waited to slide away, how many people she'd hurt. Her dad. Meg, she supposed. Although she'd consider it as the all-time attention grab one-upmanship. Hannah. Nick. Richard. A pretty small number, for someone who'd reached thirty-five years of age.

The thing about her reputation, she finally accepted – it was like Elliot's anonymity. She'd given it away and she was never getting it back.

23

'You have to eat,' was one of those stupid admonishments, Edie thought. Like the way, whenever anyone said: 'There's nothing worse than . . .' they always named something there were tons of things worse than.

You don't have to eat, as long as you're not in the grip of dangerous disorder and food is available when you need it. You can get by on barely eating perfectly well.

And Edie had no appetite. Whenever she faced a plate of food, her stomach would knot in the misery of the memory of that online conversation. She even went back and forth over some of the lurid claims: she was throwing herself at every man? Could that be true, even if she thought it wasn't? Was she throwing without knowing?

Either way, there were undoubtedly many more people in the world who hated her than loved her; a startling thought. She was partly denying herself as punishment. As one of society's repulsive creatures, she was subsisting on a monstrous diet of forkfuls of Meg's 'Chickpea and Orange Gumbo' (beyond unpleasant, an aggressive act), 'Seitan and Date Curry' (a culinary date with Satan), and the odd packet of barbecue-flavour Hula Hoops.

The only person she didn't want to notice her 'nil by mouth' was her dad. He no doubt thought her wan appearance and palpable misery were to do with having to be at home, which upset her. Edie could explain, but what comfort was there in him hearing that story? The idea made her skin crawl.

When putting on a brave face for his sake, she tried to fix her sights on a horizon where she'd be happier. Back in London, at a different agency, maybe she'd meet someone. And the wedding story would be nothing more than an occasional flinch when someone she'd never met before said, 'That was YOU?' after it passed into urban legend.

She and Meg weren't speaking. The temperature inside the house had plummeted to new lows. She suspected Meg had a calendar in her room with the weeks crossed off until Edie left.

On a warm day in the garden, when Meg was mercifully at the care home and her dad was in the spare room marking exam papers (he still did work for the Open University), Edie was sat in the garden, waiting for her next call from Elliot's PA, reading a crime novel, trying to convince herself it could be worse. A murderer could be after her. She was failing: she'd take the Silent Skinner over Lucie Maguire, any day.

A head appeared over the fence. 'Where's my book, then?'

It was the Ken Dodd-like woman, Meg's nemesis. Edie had hoped she'd forget about this. Meg's wrath if she caught Edie sneaking across to the neighbours' didn't bear thinking about.

She had also sussed this woman was a hardcore eccentric, and from her recycling bottle collection, the sort of person who Richard codenamed a 'possibly volatile liquid'.

'Er. Do you definitely want to see it?'

'I said I did. Or are you backing out of our arrangement? I didn't call the Dibble on your sister.'

Edie, despite herself, smiled at 'Dibble'. The woman was holding on to the fence posts and staring at her beadily, expectantly. Edie had a stab of sensing the woman was lonely. Edie's visit was a bigger deal to her than she realised.

'I could come round now?' she said.

'Now is fine,' said the woman, and disappeared behind the fence.

Edie took her sunglasses from her head and walked through the house, collecting her laptop from the kitchen on the way. Hmm, should she tell her dad where she was going? It'd implicate him, if Meg asked. She checked her watch. Meg wouldn't be home for hours yet. Best to slip round and slide back, unobserved.

She knocked next door with her laptop under her arm and felt foolish. The woman answered.

'Hi! It's Margaret, isn't it?'

'Margot!'

'Margot, sorry. I'm Edie.'

'Yes. You said before. I thought I was meant to be the barmy forgetful old biddy.' Margot was dressed in a mohair top that made her look like a giant white rabbit, and black swishy silk palazzo trousers. She had a very full face of make-up, and the ever-present fag on.

Edie tightly smile-grimaced and thought bejeez, this is going to be hard work. The interior of the woman's house was infused with the warm scent of tobacco, a surprisingly anachronistic smell now. The décor couldn't have been more different to the threadbare middle-class retired academia look next door. The carpets were thick and pale powdery pink, the light fittings tear-drop chandeliers.

Edie was led into the front room, which had a giant flat-screen television and two rather beautiful grey and yellow budgies chirruping and hopping about in a domed cage. Some very flouncy cream-gold curtains with frilly pelmets were held back with tasselled tie-backs. There were funny sort of ornaments dotted about: a crystal ball with LED lights inside it, and a small plastic-looking tree with metal leaves. Edie had a feeling they all came from catalogues she wouldn't know existed. There was a vase of stargazer lilies, petals turning ochre-yellow and a shower of pollen dust collecting beneath.

Margot sat in a chair by the electric fireplace, a swan-shaped ashtray, a glass and a bottle of Martell cognac next to her. She didn't appear to have started consuming the daily dose, but Edie couldn't be sure.

She gingerly lowered herself on to an overstuffed peach sofa and said: 'If I open my laptop I can show you . . .'

Edie had selected a page of absolutely bog-standard back-ground detail on Elliot, material that had almost entirely been drawn from elsewhere, reworked to avoid any claim of passing off, and zero risk if Margot called the *Mail* with it.

'Oh,' Margot waved a claw-like hand, with a fan of bones

that stood out like piano strings. 'I can't see that tiny thing, dear. You'll have to read it.'

Edie adjusted herself on the sofa and thought teenage-resentful thoughts; *this is so weird* and *why do I have to do this.*

'It's quite scrappy and draft stage, so forgive me.'

Edie cleared her throat and started reading. Oh dear, it looked flat enough on the page. Read aloud, *Jackanory* style, it was truly thin stuff. *It was then that Elliot discovered a refuge in acting . . . parents had hoped he might prefer law and medicine but soon saw what it meant to him . . . blah blah Artful Dodger . . . blah blah the smell of the greasepaint.*

In mild embarrassment at the tedium, Edie didn't look up until she was interrupted by a funny wheezy noise. She glanced up to see Margot had nodded off.

No manners – but what a critic.

For a moment, Edie thought she was doing it for effect. Nope.

'Margot?' she said. 'Margot!'

The woman snapped awake and looked at her, then let go of an anarchic whoop of a cackle. 'Oh dear! Oh Sorry! I just drifted off . . . and I asked you to read it. Oh dear, hahaha.'

Edie smiled and tried not to be offended.

'It's a bit *banal*, though, darling, isn't it? Is he really that dull? What a shame. All trousers and no mouth. Where is the hell-raising? Where are the anecdotes?'

Edie felt a little stung on Elliot's behalf.

'He's not boring. I think he's just very guarded about what he can say because he's got so famous.'

'Why?'

'He could get into trouble.'

'With who?'

'Uh . . . The press could take things out of context.'

'So give them context. You're the writer, doll face.' Margot peered at her. 'You do have a doll face. Are you married? Stepping out?'

'No and no.'

'Good for you. Marriage is a terrible mistake.'

Margot leaned closer and Edie held her stomach in a bit, feeling self-conscious.

'You're young and beautiful, why not have a go at this boy while you're at it? Might liven him up. Or is he a homosexual? Sadly true of so many of the exquisite ones.'

Edie laughed at this.

'I'm not young, I'm thirty-five,' Edie said. 'Or beautiful, but thank you for saying so.'

Margot tapped her cigarette into the ashtray.

'What a shame. You won't believe it until it's too late. Don't waste the young and beautiful years being anxious, darling. There's plenty of old and ugly ones coming.'

Edie laughed politely again.

'I was an actress,' Margot said.

'Were you?' Edie said, politely and disbelievingly, wanting to leave again. What if the woman was full-tilt fantasist barmy?

'Not a good one,' Margot said, 'I was rather crummy. But I looked *bloody good doing it,* darling.'

Edie smiled.

'Were you in anything I'd have heard of?'

'I doubt it, you're too young. I've got a photo of a show,

here. . .*The Girl Upstairs,* it was called. It was a farce. You don't really have them now. Unless you count your sister's antics.'

Margot stood up, momentarily like a faun on new legs, steadied herself and picked up a framed black-and-white photo on top of a drinks cabinet.

'This was a promotional, you know, to publicise it. We toured all over the country.'

Edie took it from Margot's mottled hands. 'Is that you?' she said, knowing she sounded incredulous, and that disbelief was slightly rude.

'It was 1958, so I'd be twenty-seven.'

'What was your name? Did you have a stage name, I mean?'

'No, I used my own name, Margot Howell. My agent wanted me to change it, I think I probably should have.'

Woah. Margot looked *astonishing.*

Edie wanted to effuse, without being insulting. She mentally scored out her first two reactions: ~~you look so young!~~ and ~~you were so beautiful!~~ She settled on: 'What an incredible picture.'

Margot wasn't a bit pretty, back in the day. She was full on, sixties French chanteuse crossed with *Avengers*-era Diana Rigg's knock-out gorgeous.

The cheekbones, that remained fearsome in the present day, and the huge swivelling eyes had looked wonderfully sultry in her youth. Young Margot gazed out at the camera through whirlpools of dark eyeliner, her features set off to great effect by a thick black fringe, the rest of her hair worn up.

She was wearing a fitted black cocktail dress with a scoop neck, pulled tight under the bust into an eye-wateringly tiny waist. She had slender legs, pinched together daintily, and held a cigarette aloft. Fagging had been a lifelong love, clearly.

Men in tuxedos posed clustered around her, proffering lighters. It was such a well composed, glamorous scene it deserved to be one of those posters that end up in every halls of residence bedroom: like the Parisian kiss or Marilyn on the grate.

'I love this!' Edie said, half sighing.

'Those were the days,' Margot said.

She took the picture from Edie and replaced it on the cabinet, and Edie had a sense she was quietly gratified by her reaction. Edie couldn't help feel operatically sad for Margot that she'd once been so dazzling, and was now stuck here with two budgies for company.

Edie's phone rang and she was guiltily pleased to have an excuse to leave.

'It's my dad,' she said to Margot, 'I better take it.'

Margot nodded.

'Your actor. It seems to me it's his book and his name is on it and he could put what the blinking heck he pleases in it.'

Edie nodded back, and answered her phone.

24

Edie ran into her dad in their hallway, so he was saying: 'Whatever are you there for?' into his phone to her as she faced him.

They switched off simultaneously.

'Dad, don't tell Meg I went to see Margot, will you?'

'That old sociopath?' her dad said.

'Not a nice way to talk about my sister,' Edie said, doing a thumbs up.

'Why would you visit her?'

Edie decided to gloss over the bit with the tits, cannabis and threats to call the police.

'She wanted to read my book. Did you know she used to be an actress?'

'She must be going Method on the part of a histrionic old brandy-sodden harpy, then. The slanging matches we've had about the state of the front garden. I think she thinks she's living in the Versailles of north Nottingham. Either her eyesight or her mind's seriously going, if so.'

'Shhh,' Edie said, conscious the walls weren't that thick.

'Hah, really,' her dad said. 'The woman is not upsettable. Would that I could.'

'She's scandalous but she's quite . . . enlivening. And honest.'

'Hmm. Truthful and wise are not the same thing.'

Edie's phone rang again and she saw Richard's name.

'Ah, work,' she said, bounding up the stairs with her heart thudding.

'Hi, Edie? Some bad news, I'm afraid. The book project is cancelled.'

'What? Why?' Edie was shocked, and oddly bereft, as she closed her bedroom door behind her. She'd never wanted the job but now it was hers, and it had been snatched away.

'The "talent", as we're probably ironically calling him, has changed his mind again. Ac-turds, eh.'

Edie hard-swallowed and said: 'He seemed fine with it when I last saw him . . .'

'Oh no one's saying you did anything wrong. The good news is, they'll pay a hefty chunk of the fee for mucking you around. All's well that almost ends well. Now, we need to have a one-to-one meeting and decide how best to reintegrate you into civilised society down here. Jack Marshall and I came to a grown-up agreement that he should gift his singular talents to another agency.'

Edie sagged. '*And she lost Jack his job*' would be the view of the Lucie coven.

'So it's down to how you and Charlotte can make this work. I have no doubt you can.'

'Richard,' Edie said, tremulous, 'it's not going to be possible. She absolutely loathes me.'

'I'm sure you're not someone she'd choose as birthing partner or executor of her will right now, but everything is surmountable, especially when people want to keep being paid their salary. I will host a peace-making chat between the three of us that will be brief, to the point, and entirely tears-free. Unless they're my tears.'

Edie almost wailed 'No!' and bit it back. This was her boss. She'd brought him all this aggro. Still, there was no way she was standing in a room with Charlotte ever again, if she could help it. The thought of returning to that agency . . . It would be like a kindly headmaster making them shake hands in his study, but the playground would be an entirely different matter.

'I will suggest to Charlotte that if this is something she can resolve in a marriage then it's something she can resolve in the workplace.'

'Thank you,' Edie mumbled, because although Richard was offering her a deal she fancied as much as a rectal bleed, he was trying to fix things.

Edie made fake-positive noises of assent and put her mobile down. Why had Elliot changed his mind again? Was the cross-city dash really that bad? Had he found her prurient, unprofessional? It wasn't just her professional pride that hurt. It was plain old pride. She'd told him about her life, he'd acted interested. Hah, *acted* being the operative verb.

Her phone rang with an unknown mobile number and Edie very nearly didn't answer. She had a squirmy thought it might be some associate of Charlotte's, or Charlotte herself, Mafia-style, advising her that she wouldn't go back to Ad Hoc if she knew what was good for her.

Should she let it ring out? She hesitated, and then thought if it was something that had to be dealt with, now was probably better than a sweaty later.

'Hello?'

'Hi, Edie? It's Elliot.'

'Elliot!' Edie said, a little too loudly. 'Hello! This is a surprise . . .'

In the disarray of her bedroom, she saw last night's bra lying on the floor, and had to turn away so she didn't have to look at her floral M&S D cups while speaking to one of *People* magazine's *100 Most Beautiful People 2014*.

'Hi. I wanted to apologise for the project being canned.'

'Oh. Yeah. You went off the idea? Hope it wasn't my crap questions.'

'No, of course not . . . They didn't tell you why it was cancelled?'

'Only that you'd changed your mind.'

'Oh, man. You must've thought I was a right dickhead.'

Edie made vague noises of false denial. This really was a surprise. He'd gone to the effort of finding out her mobile number rather sending a message via his agent, too.

'It's this other writer. Jan someone. She's writing an unauthorised book on me. That's why my agent bullied me into doing this one, to spoiler her efforts. The idea is that we can't stop her doing it, but we flatten her book sales because people buy the proper one instead. You didn't know any of this?'

'No?'

It would've been nice to have been told.

'Yeah. She's going round my friends and family trying to

get some dirt on me. And yesterday, she managed to trick my gran into talking to her. My gran said, "Does Elliot know you're doing this?" and of course she says *Oh yes, he knows.* My gran told her things and then when we explained who this Jan was, my gran was in tears, saying she'd let me down. You know, I get they think I'm fair game and that I gave up the rights to any privacy when I said I'd be in a TV show. I don't agree with them, but I get the logic. But what the fuck did my gran do to her? How can you sleep at night, making an eighty-three-year-old woman cry?'

'That's vile!' Edie said, with feeling. 'Can't you tell her she can't use it?'

'The law around withdrawing consent . . . there's a longer version but basically, no. Once they've got it, they've got it.'

'Ouch. Really, Elliot. I didn't know.'

'She put something on my old school's Facebook page, fishing for "stories" about me. My mate pretended to have things to offer, and in private messages it was all, "I only want to know who he slept with." It's gruesome. I lost it a bit last night. Why are we dancing around, doing another book because she's doing a book, and letting her call the tune? Fuck that noise. So she makes a load of money. If she can still look at herself in the mirror, good for her. I prefer a dignified silence. I don't need the money.'

His reluctance made a lot more sense now. Edie wished she'd been put in the picture. She'd have approached the whole thing quite differently.

'I had no idea about any of this, Elliot. Did you tell the last writer about it? The other ghost-writer before me?'

'Hah, *that* guy. The one who said unless I could offer him things that were more lurid than her discoveries, we were going to "look ridiculous"? I told him to piss off.'

Oh. Edie had assumed Elliot Owen was an obnoxious and trivial person. It turned out Edie was a person with a third of the information. Judging without all the facts, wasn't that what her online critics were doing?

'I'm so sorry,' Edie said. She had nothing to lose in honesty any more. 'I got this really wrong, Elliot. I thought you were being flippant about the whole thing because you couldn't make up your mind, I didn't know there were . . . external pressures. I completely understand why you didn't much want to do the book now.'

'Spoiled, I think you said,' Elliot said, with a smile in his voice. 'Nah you were right. I wasn't my best self the first time you came round, what with the break-up with Heather.'

'You broke up?' Edie said. 'I'm sorry.'

'Don't be sorry, I'm not. Heather and I were business. She approached a relationship with a human like she was in the Build-a-Bear Workshop.'

'Hah.'

Edie had an intuition, for the second time today, that Elliot was lonely. Why say this to her otherwise?

'Anyway, I wanted to say sorry. Didn't you say that you didn't want to go back to London?'

'Ah thanks. I'll live,' Edie said. 'Thanks for thinking of me.'

A pause where they both perhaps wondered how to say 'enjoy the rest of your life' and exit gracefully. Given it was the last time they'd ever speak, and Elliot wouldn't remember her in a few days' time, Edie wanted to linger.

'You know, it's a genuine shame I don't get to write the book.'

'It can't have been that appealing to you. C'mon. You seem too smart for a load of halo polishing.'

Edie had worked out how to deal with Elliot, and it wasn't dissimilar to Richard. He could clearly handle honesty. Her mistake had been to think Elliot was going to be several degrees less intelligent than her. Wrong play.

She decided to voice something that had only properly crystallised at Margot's.

'I'd had this crazy idea. You know when we were chased out of Stratford Haven? When I got you to take the hat off? I wondered if we should ditch the whole sterile vanity thing and instead write it as a snapshot of what it's like to be you, at a time like this. "Life inside the bubble." We could use that anecdote as an introduction in the first chapter and do it as more "in conversation" than me pretending to be you.'

'Hmm, yeah. Interesting idea. As long as the publisher wouldn't find it too "out there".'

'They'd have to like what you liked, wouldn't they?'

'Guess so.'

'Anyway. I'm not trying to talk you into it. I don't think I'd do it, in your position.'

'Ah, true say.' Pause. 'Nice to meet you, Edie. Lovely name, by the way.'

'Thank you,' Edie said, feeling bashful. *A famous likes my name!*

'See you around.'

'Yep. Bye.'

Ending the call, Edie felt twitchy, unsatisfied, strangely bereft.

Yes, she was crapping herself about being forced back to London, but it was more than that. She'd adjusted to the idea of writing the book, and finally found a rapport with the subject. She disliked being in Nottingham, but now she was going to climb on a train and disappear again. Unfinished business. She was doomed to be constantly abandoning unfinished business.

She added 'Elliot Owen' to her mobile contacts, as a show-off memento. He no doubt changed his number weekly, like a drug-dealer, but it'd feel cool to have it. Her phone rang.

Elliot Owen.

Uh?

'Hello?'

'Edie. OK, call me an infuriatingly inconsistent typical fucking strop-throwing actor idiot. Your idea?'

'Yes?'

'It's good. Let's do it.'

25

You didn't need a photogenic horde of friends, whatever anyone said. Whatever lies the media and advertisers – and Edie should know – told you, you only needed a few properly good ones. And in Edie's case, perhaps fewer false ones.

Edie was walking through The Park at dusk, one bottle of wine and another of flat-warming champagne gently clanking in a bag against her legs, musing on this.

She saw now that her superficially popular London years hadn't been full of good friends, just people she knew. One unfortunate incident, and they all turned into enemies. Their regard for her blew away like a sandcastle in a gale, it wasn't built on anything solid.

She couldn't even confidently reach out to a non-Ad Hoc friend, Louisa. She'd left the agency years back for a rival firm, but stayed in touch for loud wine-fuelled gossipy catch-ups every six weeks or so. Louisa had recently got pregnant and moved out of London, meaning the nights with Edie had come to an abrupt halt. After the baby arrived, Edie visited with cuddly toys and clucked and tried to empathise with the difficulties of breastfeeding. But it was obvious while their raucous acquaintance had survived no longer sharing a workplace, once you took alcohol and geography out of the shared items list too, there wasn't enough left. Louisa kept asking when Edie was going to have a kid, and Edie kept gritted-teeth joking she hadn't yet found a sperm donor, and the relationship quietly drifted by mutual agreement.

Now this had happened, Edie felt pretty certain that being at home with a screaming newborn, husband working long hours in offices with other women about whom Louisa knew little, she would take a dim view of unwed groom-kissing colleagues, whatever the context. Edie could already see the pained expression and feel the loaded silence that would greet her admission in St Albans Pizza Express, Louisa turning to fuss with a griping infant rather than look her in the eye.

And this was pretending that Edie needed to tell her – it was much more likely Louisa *had* already heard, and was dearly hoping Edie didn't contaminate her by reaching out to her. Edie felt pretty sure she wouldn't hear from her again.

It was startling and humbling to realise how much time you could spend with people to whom you meant so little, and vice versa.

Hannah had once defined a true friend as 'someone you'd let see you in a vomit-stained dressing gown', and on this basis, Hannah qualified. (Their teenage 'Poke' cocktail was an evil drug.)

Edie hadn't felt good for so long. On the way to Hannah's new flat for dinner, the sun dappling through the trees in the quiet streets, she felt almost peaceful. The Charlotte conversation threatened to intrude, but she firmly pushed it away and locked a mental door on it. It'd pick the lock and come creeping out later. She was losing sleep to it, her eyes becoming shadowed with purple, which she diligently powdered over.

Edie pulled her phone from her pocket and checked she had the right house number. Oh, wow. Well played, Hannah. The Park was a private estate on the edge of the city centre, full of beautiful pink-bricked, ivy-clad Victorian houses, the whole area lit by gas lamps. Edie might've guessed Hannah wasn't going to give up the New Town in Edinburgh for any old place, but her flat was still a stunner. It occupied the bottom half of a huge, Gothicky-looking pile, sat at a bend in a tree-lined road.

'God, Hannah. This is incredible,' Edie said, handing over her Sainsbury's Bag for Life, after Hannah cranked a giant arched door open. Hannah was in her big specs and a 'didn't have time to change' outfit of sloppy jumper and spray-on jeans that looked better than Edie's dress.

Beyond her there was a large, light-filled hallway with Persian rug, that led into a sitting room with practically floor-to-ceiling windows, and a huge fireplace.

'Look at that ceiling rose!' Edie said, neck craned.

'Hah, it's full of original features. We're all old enough to get excited by ceiling roses now, aren't we? The ceiling rose age.'

'I doubt Nick is. He's definitely coming?' Edie said.

'Yeah. He was cagey though. A lot of "I'll tell you how I am when I see you." Ah.'

At that moment the doorbell rang and Hannah went to

answer. Edie looked around at Hannah's half-unpacked boxes, and stumpy palm tree in a wicker basket. She envied her having somewhere to call her own, like this. Edie realised her flat in Stockwell had only ever felt like a holding pen, on the way somewhere else. To someone else, she guessed.

Nick came into the room, holding a bottle of red. He had a small build with neat features and close-cropped, fair hair. People always took Nick for a decade younger than his years. He always dressed very nicely, in a discreet way, like today's small-checked shirt, Harrington jacket and desert boots. He had a quiet voice that belied an extremely sharp wit. He was perennially disappointed with the world, everything in it, and probably most of all, himself.

Edie and he hugged hello.

'How are you?' she said.

'Fucking awful. You?'

'Shite,' Edie laughed.

'Same here, but we have booze,' Hannah said. 'Shall we start with the fizzy?' She went to the kitchen to find cups.

And just like that, nothing could be quite as bad as it was before. Edie counted herself lucky, for the first time in an age. Yes she'd wound up on her arse, but with these two people it surely couldn't be all bad. She was aware it was by chance, and that made her feel guilty. She could've made more of an effort to see them in recent years.

'Alice and I broke up,' Nick said, accepting a half-pint tumbler of champagne from Hannah. 'Is my news. Old news, now. A year ago.'

'Oh God,' Hannah said, and both she and Edie made

awkward tutting and clucking noises that stopped short of having to express actual specific regret.

'A year! Why didn't you tell us?!' Hannah said.

'I was sparing you having to pretend it was a bad thing,' Nick said, with a small smile, which they returned, guiltily.

'Neither of you need to ask "what took you so long?" I don't know. But the bad part is that I'm not seeing Max.'

Nick swigged his drink.

'What do you mean?' Edie said.

'Alice said he didn't want to see me so I couldn't see him. I went to court to say it wasn't true and I wanted to see him, but the process took ages. By the time they were interviewing Max, asking if he wanted to see me, he didn't any more. He's only seven, he'd probably half-started to forget who I was. His mum had been telling him he hadn't wanted to see me on a loop. So there we are.'

There was a short pause, filled only with the low burble of Hannah's radio, tuned to a jazz station.

'That's horrific. She's stopping you, for what reason?'

'She said I was a crap dad, I never had any time for him when we were together. If I wouldn't be with her, I couldn't see him.'

'Can you appeal?' Edie asked.

'Nope. Nothing to be done, Max has to change his mind. All I can do is keep sending him Christmas and birthday presents. And paying. I *think* I should be paying, can we be clear.' He pointed at them each in turn, with gallows humour, and swigged his drink again. Edie felt the force and speed he was drinking at was slightly concerning. 'But you know, it's nice she still thinks my money's good enough, if nothing else.'

'You know what, Nick, I'll be honest. I thought your wife was a cow. But this has left me speechless,' Hannah said.

'I always thought she would do something like this. It's one of the reasons it took me so long to leave. That, and I'm a lazy twat. What's for dinner, by the way?'

Edie and Hannah had been gawping. Hannah recovered quicker.

'I had plans to make you this nettle pesto and homemade pappardelle dish, but I can't find half of my kitchen stuff so wondered if fish and chips was alright?'

Nick glanced in Edie's direction.

'Weed sauce? That sounds revolting.'

'It's a River Cottage recipe!'

'At Crapston Villas, nettles are things dogs piss on.'

'You've nominated yourself to get the fish and chips.'

'Suits me. I can have a fag on the way.'

It was agreed that Edie could keep Nick company on the short walk down the hill, and Hannah could spend the time unpacking the kitchen boxes that had plates and ketchup in them.

They set off with a scribbled scorecard of haddocks, mushy peas and gravy.

'You should've told us about what happened with Alice, you know. We'd never have abandoned you in a crisis. I feel so bad – I was emailing you videos of cats and I didn't know.'

Nick finished lighting up and pulled the cigarette from his mouth, as they walked on.

'Always time for cat videos. Ah, thanks. It wasn't a crisis, though. It was a slow dawning realisation that I'd jumped into a pit of shit and it came up to well above my knees.'

Edie nodded. 'Not seeing Max . . . it must be so awful.'

'It's pretty bad, yeah. I deal with it by not dealing with it. I don't think about it. If I did, I'd go mad. Confronting things is overrated, in my opinion. What's up with you, then? Hannah said you'd had some drama at a wedding and got ex-communicated down south?'

For the first time, Edie felt this story was not the biggest deal. She filled Nick in.

'It sounds as much him as you, to be honest, if not more. Why is it on you? You're single. He'd literally just got married.'

'Thanks for saying so. I don't know. It's easier to blame me, I suppose.'

'We've all had a bash at Thompson at one time or another, doesn't need to cause problems.'

Edie was caught off guard, remembering a cider-sodden attempt at a bag off in Rock City from Nick when they were nineteen, and his garbled attempt to declare sincere and lustful love. She'd turned him down, but with a surprising grace and maturity that belied her years. It was one of the few things she could look back on without guilt. She honestly often forgot, it seemed so long ago.

Edie blushed and Nick smiled.

She shrugged and gabbled: 'Wedding days . . . People get fussy about them being important somehow though, don't they.'

'Oh, they get completely het up. You're not supposed to

try to have sex with anyone else for the whole day, as far as I can work out.'

Edie laughed. And sighed.

'. . . I know I ruined someone's wedding. I have to live with that for the rest of my life. It seems hard to bear when it isn't something I chose to do, it happened to me. It sounds gutless, but it's true.'

'Of course it's true. You're alright, you are. Stop taking what other people say to heart so much. You're one of those people that people always want to be around. You light up a room, dear.'

'Aww thanks,' she said, self-consciously, glad they had to negotiate a road crossing. 'What about you? Have you moved on, are you seeing anyone?'

'Only the four walls of my Sneinton divorcé dad grief hole.'

Edie had forgotten how jaundiced-funny Nick was. She'd let their friendship drift because of the mad wife, yes. Also because she didn't think they had much in common any more, and he was miles away. A mixture of ignorance and laziness.

They queued for their order and while they were talking, Edie saw her face reflected in the stainless steel counter of the chippy. She saw a tired-faced person who nonetheless, looked fleetingly happy.

26

'Chippy dinners taste best outdoors, but they taste second best when you're in a new house that smells different and half your stuff's in storage,' Hannah said. 'Pete and I had one when we moved in, in Edinburgh too. It's the biz.'

They were eating out of unfurled paper and polystyrene pots, the room lit by tealights and a big Tiffany lamp, feeling fuzzy round the edges from champagne and wine drunk out of chunky glass beakers. Hannah always had the nicest grown-up things.

'We're all single for the first time since sixth form, then,' Hannah said.

'I was single before it was trendy,' Edie said, excavating the mushy pea tub. Fairground peas and candy floss: one of the few positive childhood memories.

'What happens now, do we all go on dating sites and start Veet-ing our privates?' Hannah said. 'If there's one thing to be said for long-term relationships, it's the freedom to have un-groomed genitals. Pubic fashions can come and go and you care not a jot.'

'Hairy's back in anyway. Hairy's the new bald,' Edie said.

'I'm not Veet-ing my balls for any woman,' Nick said. 'And I'm pretty sure demand for my bare ballsack is nil. When did people start liking this macabre stuff?'

'When we got the internet,' Hannah said. 'And everyone started panicking their lives weren't good enough.'

Edie said: 'Here we go,' to Nick, then considered that she was an extremely good case study for Hannah's *Social Media Is Evil* lecture.

'Society as we know it is fucked,' Hannah said, noisily squirting the plastic ketchup bottle on to her chips. 'Everyone pretends their life is great online. It's lies by omission. It's just one big lie by omission. It makes people feel constantly inadequate and anxious and envious. All our lives are a managed mess but look online and you get advertising.'

'At least I couldn't be accused of making anyone insecure,' Edie said. 'My life's a car crash. I had to shut all my accounts down. The only one I miss is Instagram. It's just cats and sunsets and eggs with avocado.'

Hannah brushed batter from her hands.

'I'm trying to work out what would've happened after the wedding, before Facebook,' Edie said. It felt so good to have people to share this with, at last. 'Everyone would've still been saying things about me, but I wouldn't have known what they were. We see things now we shouldn't see.'

'Exactly! And it's so dehumanising,' Hannah said. 'Here's the thing. We know more about each other than ever before, and yet we've never understood each other less.'

'Profound. I feel like we should be sipping water on a

panel show here,' Nick said, making light work of the last of his saveloy. Nick had the tastes of a filth hound and the waistline of a whippet, 'Called *The State of You* or something, one of those late-night ones. I'd put this on my show with you both as guests, but you'd only start bellowing about pubes.'

Edie guffawed. 'Don't you have a delay thing?'

'No, that's a myth, it's live radio. We have an apology-afterwards thing.'

'Is the show doing OK?' Hannah said.

'Not brilliantly,' Nick said, sipping his drink. 'Listener figures are down. I keep waiting for one of the older presenters to do an *Alpha Papa*-style siege, we could do with a bit of an enema in the staffing department. Not me, you understand. Other people.'

Edie guffawed again. 'JUST SACK PAT.' She paused. 'Ad Hoc let Jack go. He was the man, the husband,' she explained to Nick.

A small silence settled over them. Nick didn't know what to say and Hannah looked as if she was weighing whether not to say what she thought.

'You're not feeling bad for him, are you?' Hannah said.

Edie said: 'No. Not really,' in a small voice. 'I feel bad for being the cause of so much trouble.'

It might've been a tense moment. But it was shattered by a large white and tortoiseshell cat, with saucers for eyes, winding round their feet. It stared at them in a mutual: *Who the fuck are you?*

'I didn't know you got a cat!' Edie exclaimed.

'I didn't!' Hannah cried, and there was an outbreak of squawking.

'Why are we screaming, it's only a cat?!' Nick said.

The cat flattened its ears back and skittered out. Some investigations showed Hannah's flat had a cat flap left by the last inhabitants, still swinging in the breeze from the departing moggy.

Once they were settled back down and the cat had been thrown some haddock through the flap, Hannah said: 'While we're doing big talk not small talk. Do you know why this Jack didn't choose to be with you, Edith? I've been turning it over.'

'I guess I thought it was the reasons people always prefer one person to another,' Edie said, embarrassed, despite being in drink. 'Charlotte looks like Andy Murray's wife.'

'BEEP. Wrong. You would've seen through him, eventually. He was attracted to how sharp you are, but too lazy and self-serving to want someone who'd give him that much trouble as a partner. He kept you at arm's length, enjoyed the frisson, and stuck with the safer bet.'

Edie nodded. 'I suppose Charlotte's always been very starry-eyed about Jack. I liked him but I didn't really give him that sort of unquestioning adoration. I think that was part of it.'

It used to be difficult to analyse this beyond the bitterness-buzz of 'sour grapes' and now it was even more difficult with the guilt-buzz of 'wedding sin'.

'If he didn't have a major thing for you, why lunge at you during his wedding?' Nick said.

'Why not lunge at me before the wedding?'

'You might've lunged back harder! You might've treated it like it meant something! And he didn't want to risk *actually getting what he wanted*. Far too much trouble,' Hannah said.

She was too much trouble. That was it, throughout, wasn't it? It was an explanation that didn't pander to Edie's ego, either. Love for her didn't conquer all.

And it was the first time, the timing of that kiss made some sense. It wasn't about the moment she was the most dangerous temptation, it was when she was safest. Edie finished her champagne and held her glass out for more.

'Amazing. You two might've solved "Jack".'

Hannah lifted the bottle again.

'You built him up to be something he wasn't. We women are prone to it, I think. No matter how grown up and independent we think we are, I swear we have a brain illness from childhood where we think a man on a white horse is going to turn up at some point and fix everything. And when he doesn't turn up, and he can't fix anything even if he does, we think we did something wrong. But he never existed.'

'I wish there was a man on a horse to fix everything for me,' Nick said. 'He'd have Alice's head in a bag.'

There followed a short discussion where Hannah gave Nick her similarly unvarnished views on Alice and Nick more or less agreed and said he'd made a fatal in error in mistaking a bullying personality for a dynamic, charismatic one.

Post Jack, Edie was much less inclined to judge Nick. Yes, commitment to vinegar tits Alice was unfathomable from the outside. But look how Hannah could clearly see Jack was a glib time-wasting liar, who was going to sit on Edie's heart and squash it like a whoopee cushion. Edie was so addled by oxytocin, or whatever the love drug was, she couldn't allow it when she was in the grip of it. Maybe it was a simple matter of chemicals: it was hard to accept that someone who'd caused so much pleasure, was in turn causing you pain.

They put the detritus from dinner in a bin bag and stretched out on the sofas.

'I've had enough of this angst. What's Elliot Owen like, then?' Nick asked.

'If you'd asked me that before I'd have said a hissy-fit-chucking dickhead. But it turned out he was getting it from all sides. He's alright, I think.'

'Is he ridiculously handsome?' Hannah asked.

Edie made a 'hmm' face. 'Yes, I suppose. I mean, yes.'

'I never understand that question,' Nick said. 'No, there's a reality distortion field around him on screen and in real life he's got a face like a Halloween cake.'

They all gurgled.

'Wait, wait. I've got it. If you fall in love with him, and have an affair with a famous actor, it'll be – *Nottingham Hill*,' Nick said.

Edie grimaced.

'God, waxed scrotums though,' he added.

Hannah sat up and did a quizzical face. 'Eh?'

'I'm returning to the earlier conversation. Do you think actors do it?' Nick said.

'Shall I ask Elliot, and say it's for the book?' Edie said.

'Nick, you're disproportionately haunted by this bald ball-sack notion,' Hannah said.

'I saw someone, in the gym. I don't want to talk about it,' Nick said. 'Legal proceedings are still active.'

'If I sleep with anyone ever again I'm going to say "I apologise in advance" and hope that legally covers me,' Edie said, lying back and closing her eyes.

'I could get pants with "Warning: Graphic Content" on them,' Nick said.

Edie opened her eyes again.

'It's great the three of us being together again, isn't it?' she said.

'Let's make the most of it. Let's do things rather than saying *yeah great that sounds great* and then never getting round to it,' Hannah said.

'Agreed,' Edie said, and Nick nodded. 'Who can do dinner next? I can cook, but no real space at Dad's.'

'I have space but can't cook. You cook at mine, Edith?'

'You're on!'

The mood was broken by a wail from the intruder cat, who'd thought about it and decided he really quite liked battered haddock.

27

No male human had done a double take at the sight of Edie in a while. At least, not in a good way.

Was this the good way? She couldn't tell.

The man who answered the door at the well-appointed Owen residence the following week was late-twenties, and over six foot tall, built like a rugby player. He had blond hair, light stubble and a sort of brute, laddish handsomeness that some women went wobbly for.

He pushed his hands into the pocket on the front of his hooded top, and grinned, as if he and Edie already shared a secret.

'*Hello.* Can I help you? It feels like I could.'

Edie stuttered and smiled.

'Ah . . . I'm here to see Elliot?'

'Oh God, don't bother with him. We don't. He's a tonsured fop. A fruity ponce. A giant woofting ham.'

Edie laughed now.

He stuck his hand out. 'I'm Fraser. His brother.'

Of course. The other kid in the photo.

'And you are?' he said.

'Edie. Thompson. I'm ghost-writing Elliot's autobiography.'

'Why should you have to toil for him, the lazy fucker? He can write his own thoughts down, can't he? Such as they are.'

Edie giggled.

'Fraz, let Edie into the house, please,' called an unseen Elliot beyond.

Fraser stepped back, his fists still bunched in his top.

'I'm thrashing him at table tennis right now,' Fraser said. 'Don't give him an excuse to duck out before the thrashing is complete.'

Elliot was in the hallway, rubbing his forehead on the neck of his navy T-shirt. He was moist around the edges, curly dark brown hair slick and black with sweat, twiddling a ping-pong bat back and forth in one hand. His eyes and skin glowed with the exertion. Good grief.

Edie gulped and internally swooned a little and thought, *Cor, if I could get a stealth photo of you right now I could sell it for much MUCH coin.*

It must be odd to be around people who you must know had rapacious monetising vulture-thoughts about you, even if they didn't act on them.

'Do you mind if we finish our game?' Elliot said. 'I'll never hear the end of it otherwise.'

'She can play!' Fraser said.

'Maybe she doesn't want to play,' Elliot said.

'I'll have a go,' Edie said. 'I don't mind.' And it couldn't hurt in getting to know Elliot Owen better.

She hung her bag over the banister and followed them into the kitchen.

Elliot reached into a giant double-door fridge and handed Edie a bottle of beer.

She paused in surprise at the lack of accompanying words, and Elliot said: 'Oh sorry – do you drink?'

'You've been in America too long. That question in British is "Are you driving?"'

'I like this one!' Fraser said.

'Fraser! Behave yourself,' Elliot snapped, and Edie relaxed, realising she was in the middle of a slightly fractious sibling dynamic. She knew it well. And then some.

'Are you driving?' Elliot said, politely.

'I am not, a beer would be great, thank you.'

She accepted the cold bottle, and the opener, flipped the lid and copied Elliot in palming it into the nearby bin. She was so cool, she totally fitted in at a famous person's house! Oh wait. She'd also said she'd play sport. That might not be such a breeze.

'Don't worry, Fraser's only back from Guildford for a few days,' Elliot said.

'What do you do there?' Edie asked Fraser.

'Financial consultancy,' he said. It was hard to imagine Fraser consulting anyone's finances. He seemed more like a swimming pool attendant, or kids' TV presenter.

It was a beautiful garden, beyond the kitchen's French windows: an undulating expanse of well-tended grass with flower beds around the border and trees planted against high walls, making it entirely private. Imagine growing up in a place like this. A large ping-pong table had been set up in the middle of the lawn.

'Five minutes, I promise,' Elliot said, and Edie waved her hand to indicate no worries, plonking herself on a wrought-iron garden chair on the patio and watching them leaping around. Not the worst sight in the world.

What must be Elliot's phone, on top of what looked like a script, was at Edie's elbow. It pinged with a notification every three seconds or so, the screen lighting up again and again, like an activated burglar alarm. Sheesh. She made a note to self that if Elliot seemed peremptory and hassled, he might simply be at input overload.

'Edie, want a game?' Fraser said. She nodded and stood up. She had worn a black playsuit with a halter neck today, a slightly more fashionable choice than usual. She hoped it stayed put while she was jumping about.

Edie picked up her bat, the handle still hot from Elliot's grasp, and bounced the ball. A gentle knock over to Fraser's side, and he knocked it back.

'Start off slow, like your style,' he said.

'Fraser!' Elliot barked, taking Edie's seat. 'No smut.'

'Smut! That wasn't smut. Sign of a smutty mind.' Fraser angled a volley back at Edie. 'Also, *smut*? Is it 1931? Alright, P.B. Wodehouse.'

'P.G. Wodehouse!'

'. . . Pee Wee Herman.'

Edie giggled. She wasn't going to be any good at ping-pong but it didn't matter. Before long she was leaping around and cackling and pretend-bickering the rules with Fraser, pink in the face from the exertion and forgetting to care whether her arse looked like a bin bag full of yoghurt from Elliot's angle.

'You are so much better at this than my brother,' Fraser said. Elliot looked up from checking his phone and rolled his eyes.

'One last match, Edie?' Fraser asked.

'Can I have another match?' Edie said to Elliot.

'You're the boss,' Elliot said, pleasantly, getting up. 'Another beer?'

'Yes, thanks!' said Edie.

Hang on. Edie was having fun. She hadn't thought fun was going to be possible for a long time, and certainly not in Nottingham, and absolutely not around the diva thespian.

There was a light tap on her shoulder, and Edie, out of breath and laughing, tucking a damp strand of hair behind her ear, turned to see Elliot holding a beer out towards her.

He smiled at her, she smiled back, and something snapped into place.

28

If Edie had learned one thing from being around Elliot, it was that awe wasn't a limitless natural resource. Your body can't sustain awe. Sooner or later it gets tired of awe and wants a sandwich.

So while, 'I can't believe I'm drinking a beer given to me by ELLIOT OWEN', 'I can't believe I am sat on a chair recently sat on by ELLIOT OWEN', was the repetitive internal monologue for part of the ping-ponging, it simply wasn't possible to keep being amazed afresh by his famousness. Eventually it became 'Elliot? Yeah he's over there, making me lunch. NBD, as the kids say.'

They ate giant cheese ploughman baguettes at the breakfast bar. Fraser declined – 'Meeting the lads for some beers at Mudflaps. Oh, what's it called? Mudcrab' – and slammed out, noisily.

'Sorry about my brother. Please don't sue for sexual harassment.'

'Haha. He's nice.' Edie decorously picked a shard of a tombstone-sized slab of cheddar out of the bread. Elliot clearly wasn't one of those actors who didn't eat.

'He's a bloody liability. Any brothers or sisters yourself?'

'A younger sister, Meg. She's . . . yes, let's go with liability.'

'Eldest child mentality is definitely a thing, isn't it?' Elliot said, handing Edie a square of kitchen towel.

'Yes,' Edie said. 'It really is. They've got an extra parent and you've had a kid.'

'Haha, in one,' Elliot said, screwing up his square of paper, necking the last of his beer and looking at her over the bottle.

Edie noticed that his sly, laconic sense of humour made a return in Fraser's absence. Around his younger brother, he was wary and a little exasperated. It humanised him, this normal, fractious relationship. Edie felt she could slide in between the two of them in front of the telly and guffaw, snipe and referee away as if they'd known each other for years. Even if in reality, without this job, a pair of posh lads from the right side of town would have had nothing to do with her.

Edie turned on her Dictaphone, put it between them, staking a claim in 'this is business now'. She asked Elliot questions about what it was like, the first time he came home as a celebrity.

'Friends, I won't lie, it is weird sometimes. It makes you appreciate that thing about how you "can't make new old friends". Your best mates know you're still you and if you disappeared up your arse they'd let you know. You just have to still be able to hear it. New friends are trickier. The question of whether they'd still laugh at your jokes if you worked in Greggs is always there, hovering. You need to have good instincts. And you discover there's a strange subcategory – you're in this category, although it's mainly male . . .'

Edie sat up straighter: 'What? How?'

'People who pre-dislike you because they're so sure they're going to dislike you, they may as well get it over with. Frustratingly, they're often the smart people you'd quite like to like you.'

Hoo, boy. Edie had been seen through. 'That's not true,' she said, in a small voice that admitted it absolutely was.

'Paradox of fame: people refuse to treat you normally and then complain you're not normal. Put *that* in your so-called book.'

Elliot tapped her Dictaphone and gave a roguish smile and Edie thought: the one thing she hadn't thought Elliot would possibly be, was witty. Edie needed to steer the subject matter in an assured manner, reclaim some ground.

'Is this all true of romantic relationships too?'

Elliot leaned over and turned the tape recording off.

'Do you mean was Heather a catastrophic misjudgement and does her heart pump frozen blue Slush Puppy?'

Edie laughed. 'No I didn't, actually.'

'Say that we "wanted different things". She wanted to carry on being a petulant wazzock and I wanted to fire her into the heart of the sun. Also put "she's a free spirit, I don't think anyone will ever be able to tie her down" as euphemism for about as faithful as a bonobo monkey.'

Edie laughed and Elliot reminded her of Hannah now: *I do the words, stop being casually so good at 'words' when it's not your job.* Edie thought Elliot might be one of those actors that directors allowed to ad lib.

'Should I do the standard "What first attracted you to the gorgeous woman?" question?' Edie said and Elliot grinned.

'It was one of those things match-made by her people getting in touch with my people and saying she'd like to have dinner,' Elliot shrugged. 'I was flattered. You live, you learn. Or you don't.'

Edie smiled and didn't know what to say.

'Do you want a softer seat, by the way?'

'Er, yes. Sure.'

Edie followed Elliot to the sitting room; scene of their first, less auspicious encounter. A stereo was playing. Edie heard which song it was, with a twinge.

'Would you mind if we didn't have the music? Concentration breaker.'

'Oh. Sure.' Elliot turned the volume down to an audible whisper.

Edie squirmed.

'Off, if that's OK?'

Elliot gave a small look of surprise and clicked it off. Edie, a little disconcerted at having sounded a bit of a nag after all the carefree fun of the ping-pong, blurted: 'The album has bad associations for me.'

'Oh. OK,' Elliot said, looking perplexed.

Edie fussed with the Dictaphone and got Elliot to talk for another half hour about the mental realignment involved in becoming famous. She found it genuinely interesting, hearing about the journey few would ever take. Onto the front pages. Into a world where everyone thought they knew you.

The only moments where he became monosyllabic was when they got anywhere near the topic of fame's effect on opportunities with women.

'I dunno how to discuss any of that without coming off as a huge nause. Plus it's invading the privacy of other people.'

'You say that, but Heather is putting things about you two on Twitter.'

It was a slightly tabloid gambit, to set him against her. And Edie didn't know if Elliot knew this. She judged they were getting along well enough that she could chance it.

'You mean her picture of cats touching paws, hashtagged: "This Could Be Us But You Playin'"?'

Edie nodded.

'My feeling on seeing that is that it turns out I'd had a relationship with an adolescent and didn't realise. Operation Yewtree. Operation *Mew*tree. Don't put that in the book.'

Edie laughed. 'I'm hardly going to put things like that in!'

'Didn't we have a deal that I get to ask you questions too?'

'Didn't I bore you so much the first time we tried that, we gave up?'

'Hah, good attempt at deflection. OK, then. My turn.' Elliot sat back, one foot balanced on the opposite knee. 'What's the bad association with *Hounds of Love*?'

And just like that, the mood was ruined.

29

The lie or the truth? Edie didn't feel right, soliciting confidences from Elliot, then fobbing him off.

'It was my mum's favourite album. She was a Kate Bush fan. It reminds me of her. She used to listen to "Cloudbusting" over and over again. And it has that "Mother Stands for Comfort" song, brrrr,' Edie steadied her voice. 'Can't do it.'

Elliot's face fell.

'Oh . . . Edie. And your mum is . . .?'

'Dead, yep.'

The air hung heavy.

'Shit. I'm so sorry. I didn't think it'd be anything that bad or I wouldn't have asked.'

'I know,' Edie said. 'Usually there's a time this comes up one way or another. Really, don't stress.'

'How did . . . how old were you?'

'I was nine. She was thirty-six.'

Elliot paused and Edie decided to spare him having to decide whether to ask the next question.

'She committed suicide. Jumped off Trent Bridge. People

tried to talk her out of it for half an hour, then she did it.'

Elliot looked genuinely horrified now. How much by the information, and how much by having unintentionally provoked the sharing of the information, Edie couldn't tell.

'. . . She'd had depression for years. My dad had a break-down afterwards, couldn't do his job, he was a teacher, head of science. We moved from Bridgford to Forest Fields and he did supply work.'

Elliot rubbed his chin and frowned.

'I'm so sorry. Jesus, not sure *I* can ever listen to *Hounds of Love* now, so can't imagine how you feel.'

'It was a long time ago. I'm fine, honestly. It's not like it's a fresh wound.'

Nevertheless, Elliot was looking at her differently, and Edie started to wish she hadn't told him. She'd worked out years ago that victimhood could take over your identity. This was why most people she met in adulthood – bar Jack, the bastard – got the abrupt, no-frills 'cancer' version.

She didn't want to be That Girl. The girl with the sad story attached. She wanted to define herself, not be defined by an event over which she had no control, from a quarter of a century ago. That's what people with comfortable lives who were only playing the victim didn't understand, how they gave themselves away – if you'd actually been one, you were desperate to shed the label. You craved the normality that had been taken from you.

So Edie left out lots of colourful detail that made people's faces turn into tragedy masks. That they couldn't see the body because her mum didn't wash up whole. That she and Meg were bullied for it at school. That her mum's family blamed her dad for what happened and cut them all off afterwards, at a time when they were shell-shocked enough by having to work out how they functioned as a unit without the fourth member of the team. The helpful detail in the local paper coverage, that onlookers on the bridge had said to her mother: 'Think of your children.' That had burrowed deep into Edie. She thought about it every day of her life.

There was the rattle of a key in the lock and Fraser bounced into the room like a Labrador.

'I'm back! What did I miss?'

'We're working, Fraz,' Elliot said, rubbing the back of his neck, smiling at Edie. Actually, it had saved them both from an awkward silence.

'Working, hah. Hey, shouldn't I be interviewed by Edie too? I've got some memories of you I'd like to share.'

Before he could get a sense of the strained mood in the room, Edie said: 'Sure! That'd be good.'

'Not with him here though. I have to feel I can speak freely.'

'OK?' Edie said, with a look towards Elliot.

'Oh. Fine,' Elliot said, mock-offended.

He closed the door after him, making a small tacit look of apology in Edie's direction. She turned the Dictaphone back on.

'What do you want to know? Kid stories?'

'Actually we were talking about the craziness of fame.'

'Do you know, Elliot is now so famous that I'm slightly famous by being his brother? Honestly. I've had people meet me as prospective clients. The conversation's stilted and then they ask me about him and I realise it's actually about that.'

'No?' Edie was genuinely taken aback. She got her notepad out too.

'*Way*. One woman was flirting really hard. Imagine how tight his vetting procedures have to be. Creeps me out.'

Fraser leaned back on the sofa, his frame so much more hulking than the brother who'd just vacated the same seat. Edie searched his features for signs of Elliot, but they were completely dissimilar. She tried to think of a single physical attribute she and Meg had in common, beyond both being female. The small hands and feet, maybe.

'I remember when he'd been in that crap show about the doctors for a while, he came home and we went for pizza on Central Avenue. I didn't watch his show, because it was crap. I didn't know he was "known". I thought, why are people staring at my brother, has he left his flies undone? Then it dawned, oh, right. Yeah. I felt a bit scared, to be honest. Like he no longer belonged to us.'

Edie kept making notes, in the hope he'd feel comfortable to say more.

'. . . You feel a little bit ruffled by him hogging limelight for five minutes and then you see he can't go for a slash without hassle and you shudder your skin off. Now I think of it as there's two Elliots. There's my brother, who I know, and there's this other person who you see in the paper who looks like him and isn't him and I try to ignore completely.'

'Was it bothering you, reading about him?'

'Yeah, if I thought something wasn't true, which it usually wasn't.'

Fraser played with a lace on his shoe and hesitated.

'The thing about Elliot is, he doesn't trust many people. But he's stupidly loyal when he does. At school, if someone so much as looked at me the wrong way, he'd be right there, squaring up to them. You've seen my brother, he's not really that big a physical threat. He was lucky not to get thrashed. He was quiet and kept himself to himself and had got picked on a bit for it. So a lot of people who are saying they knew him well, they didn't. I know how much this "everyone wanting to be his friend" freaks him out, and it makes me protective.'

Fraser pulled his hooded top over his head and down over his eyes. 'Oh GOD why am I telling you this. I sound like I'm about to get my period.'

Edie laughed loudly. She'd thought being famous was largely great. Increasingly she felt the percentage of nightmare was greater than dream.

When Edie was leaving, she put her head round the kitchen door to say goodbye, but Elliot was on his mobile. Fraser was milling about in the hallway, waiting to open the door for her. The Owen boys had nice manners.

'Tell Elliot I said bye?' Edie said. 'Nice to meet you. Thanks for the interview.'

'Hey, come out for drinks next time I'm up? We're going to head into town with a group on the 20th.'

'Oh. Thanks! Uhm, I'm more of a colleague of Elliot's though? Wouldn't want to intrude.'

'Don't be a melv! You're totally welcome, Elliot likes you. And *I'm* inviting you. Come on! If you let me have your number . . .?'

'Er. OK,' said, Edie, smiling, thinking she could always find an excuse, and he'd no doubt forget. She listed the digits as Fraser tapped it into his BlackBerry.

She walked to the bus stop in the sunshine, turning the visit over in her head. It had been mostly good, she thought.

Her phone pinged with a text. Fraser.

And this is me! Good to meet you. Fraz x

Was he hitting on her in any serious way? Hard to tell. He seemed someone who flirted as naturally as breathed, and Elliot's eye-rolling around him seemed to confirm that.

Another text. Elliot.

Edie, I'm still squirming at having pushed you into talking about that stuff about your mum. Really sorry. Ex

She was touched. He'd done nothing wrong, apart from show an interest.

Please don't worry, it's fine. See you soon! Ex

As Edie's bus was trundling up the road past the cricket ground, and she was texting Hannah that she'd thrashed Prince Wulfroarer at ping-pong and he'd made her a Wookey Hole cheddar sanger, she had a jolting epiphany. Something that had been nagging at her, formed into a conscious thought.

Oh my God. Elliot's *gay*. *That's* what he particularly doesn't want unearthed in the unauthorised autobiography. As she went over the evidence, it started piling up. There'd been those murmurings online and Edie had set them aside on the basis every heartthrob actor was meant to be gay, with a beautiful beard (the female sort, as well as the Wulfroarer sort). The comments that Fraser had made, almost unthinkingly, about his brother being a fruity ponce.

Think about it: the way both Elliot and Fraser described his withdrawn, sensitive school years, and the arty refuge of the drama club. His disgust over the biographer wanting to talk to people he'd slept with. His lack of emotion over Heather, the peculiar 'we were business' comment. His ongoing reticence over discussing any laddish bed-post notching.

And also – Edie felt guilty about thinking this way, like a mini-Margot – his sheer *prettiness*. I mean, he'd make an incredible cover of *Attitude*. She'd sat there taking notes about everything he said, and not paying any attention to him.

'Ironically I'm bad at pretending to be something I'm not when I'm playing myself, if you know what I mean?'

CODE. Edie didn't know how it worked, if she should try to get him to talk about it? She thought about what Elliot said about the last biographer – that unless they could match the other unauthorised book in revelations, they'd look ridiculous. What if Edie's book was full of stuff about his blazing red-blooded Tom Jonesing heterosexuality, and when Elliot finally came out, it would be quoted as a notorious joke?

She'd have to find a clever, tactful way to float it. Hmm.

An email from Richard arrived, as mood-puncturing as an open-palmed slap round the face.

Edie. Congrats on persuading the flounce-off-er to flounce back in. What a precious gem he is, I want to wear him as a brooch. My condolences on your reward being having to do more work with the blithering penis. The publisher would like a meet up with you to discuss how it's going to pan out, but the good news is they really like your sample chapters. As luck would have it, I'd like to host that conference with you and Charlotte. When can you get to London next week? Cheers, Richard.

The muscles in her neck tightened and Edie had to fight back the rising panic. She'd have to call Richard and say she couldn't do it. She couldn't do it!

She had to do it.

Not only was refusing cowardly and ungrateful – Richard rightly judged this cold-water shock treatment was the only way of bringing her back – it could jeopardise the book. If she no longer worked for Ad Hoc, she might no longer be the biographer. Richard could quite reasonably and would very possibly say: 'If you won't do this, you can't do that.' He was far too smart not to spot the weak point to push.

Somehow, she minded terribly being off the book now. She had to see it through. A voice whispered: *Because you've got nothing else left.*

Edie's bus took a turn and they were on Trent Bridge. As usual, she stared at her hands in her lap, until they were on the other side.

30

Edie woke an hour before her alarm, in the way you did when you were anticipating a horrible day.

She stared at the blue ceiling, with its dampness tidemark of uric acid yellow, and wished herself into a thousand different realities that weren't this one.

She could hear the hum of activity below. Her dad and Meg thought Edie having a day-long jolly to the capital was another example of her fabulous life.

'Is the publisher paying for it?' her dad had asked, last night.

'Yes,' Edie said, emptily.

'How nice! You can do a bit of shopping or see a friend before you come back?'

'Mmm, maybe,' Edie had said.

'Nottingham's not proving too much of a punishment though? What with Hannah being around?'

'Not at all, I'm enjoying it,' Edie said, and Meg looked at her with her bullfrog expression – the one she wore when she was dying to say something sarcastic but didn't quite dare voice it.

After Edie had dragged her leaden limbs from bed and through a shower, she went downstairs. Every single action brought her closer to Oh Fuck O'Clock, today. One of the hardest things to explain to a child is why adulthood involved doing so many things you knew you definitely didn't want to do.

Edie's dad was at the breakfast bar, absorbed by a copy of the *Guardian*. It would be days old, her dad always said it took him that long to read it.

On the kitchen counter there were three bananas cut into coins, a jar of Nutella, a jar of crunchy peanut butter, and an eight-strong stack of thick spongy slices of white Warburtons. The greasy old Breville sandwich toaster had been dragged out, its shell-like indentations still scabbed with the last cheese toastie that had been crushed inside it.

'Meg's mise en place for her breakfast,' her dad said, looking up from his newspaper. 'Disturb it at your peril.'

Edie frowned at the huge jar of Nutella. 'Is that vegan?' She picked it up and inspected the label. 'Milk and whey?'

Her dad folded his paper: 'Dearest elder daughter. Before going down this road, consider you may well be right. But do you want to tangle with the Megosaurus at this hour of the morning?'

'The shit she gives me for making anything in here that isn't vegan, Dad!'

'I know, I know. Perhaps raise the . . . inconsistency at another time. Neither of my children could ever be accused of being morning people.'

Edie plonked the jar back on the counter and poured Alpen

into a bowl, resentfully, hoiking herself up at the Formica shelf breakfast bar next to her dad. She sploshed the Meg-sanctioned vanilla flavour oily soy milk on it, and glowered.

Meg came in, still in her New Model Army bed T-shirt and tartan pyjama trousers, head a dreadlocked bird's nest. Edie could remember her childhood sheet of perfect shiny Dairy Milk hair, she used to plait it for her. Meg grunted and set about making her choco-nutty-nana hypocrite's repast while Edie stared, resentfully.

Her dad made polite chat about the train times and Edie reminded herself, for the umpteenth time, not to come across as if she hated her home.

'Do you want me to bring you anything back from London?' Edie said, to the room.

Meg snorted. 'Penicillin? Culture?'

'Sorry?' Edie said, sharply, dropping her spoon back into her Alpen.

'You make it sound like you're journeying into civilisation or something. Like an opposite *Heart of Darkness*.'

'No, Meg, I was being thoughtful and considerate. An alien concept to you.'

Their dad was stirring his coffee very vigorously and clearing his throat.

'Well what could we want in London we can't get here? Uhm yes, a Big Ben keyring please.'

Edie opened her mouth and realised she didn't actually know. The point was, she was being generous and nice and once again, Meg was turning it into an attack on her supposed airs and graces.

'Why are you such a thunderous bitch to me, Meg? "Would you like a present" translates as me being some stuck-up Southern princess wannabe?'

'You always run Nottingham down, you know you do. I've heard you do it with your snob friends.'

This dated back to a flippant conversation that Meg had unfortunately overheard many years ago. With hindsight, Edie wasn't particularly proud of it and had been playing to the gallery with some posh colleagues who visited for the cricket. She'd said something about it only coming first in a competition with Derby. Edie should never have let them call for her at the house, or let them discuss their views on the city, stood in her hallway. Or played to their gallery. You live, you learn. Or you don't, as Elliot said.

Meg shrugged and went back to sandwich assembly. Edie couldn't let it go, her blood pumping. She was the only hypocrite around here, was she?

'Oh and by the way, I assume you're not vegan any more, what with having Nutella. So I'll be having my bacon and sausages now, thank you.'

Meg turned, doing her toddler puffed-cheeks fury face.

'I have ONE TREAT and you think you can use it against me!'

'As ever, it's one rule for Meg, another for ordinary hard-working families.'

'Oh my God what do you ever do for other people! Or the environment!'

'SAUSAGE!' Edie shouted, thinking this wasn't her finest hour as an adult.

'DAD, TELL HER!' Meg screamed. She threw down her fudged-up knife and ran out, breaking into noisy sobbing as she thundered up the stairs.

In the silence of the kitchen, her dad tapped his spoon against his cup.

'I did suggest that might go badly.'

Edie didn't often lose her temper with her dad and she knew, today of all days, she wasn't in a position to keep things in perspective. However. She couldn't take this.

'Dad! You heard what she said about London, she kicked off at me! She's in the wrong. And she's always getting at me. She can't complain when she gets some back.'

'No, she can't.'

'Don't make excuses for her constantly. That isn't going to help. Her, most of all.'

Her dad said, quietly: 'It's a shame. Meg had suggested we might want Nutella sandwiches too. She said it might set you up for your day trip. She was on the verge of being concil-iatory there and it went awry.'

'What?' Edie's face fell. 'Why didn't you say so?'

'I thought it'd be nice if it came from her. As a peace offering.'

Edie put her bowl in the sink, got her things and left the house quietly, Meg's blazing outrage radiating from behind her closed bedroom door.

She didn't want it to be this way. She wanted to find her way back to the times they'd put the old hairy blanket known as 'The Wolf' across their knees on a Sunday afternoon and watch *Ghostbusters*.

It was only once she was on the train, staring out of the window, morose, Edie realised what she had been doing. Having a barney with Meg wasn't just pressure-valve release on this tension. Edie was fouling the nest, so it would make it seem less awful to go to London.

It hadn't worked.

31

Edie could remember when St Pancras was a fairly dark and forbidding train shed, not the glittering temple to consumerism, continental mini breaks, flat whites and getting nicely spangled on champagne that it was now.

She tested her feelings, as she queued for the ticket barriers, on whether it still felt like coming home. She couldn't sense much beyond the numb hum of what awaited her in the distance.

A bleep on her phone:

Edie baby are you in today? Heard you were? Good luck. I'm at a client meeting so will miss you. Hugs. L X

Edie wondered if Louis had deliberately arranged to be out, to avoid having to pick a side, in public. She didn't know, that could be paranoia talking. She texted back her thanks.

The publishers of Elliot's book were in bright offices in Bloomsbury. Usually a meeting this size would be cause for apprehension; she'd never pitched a rejigged celebrity autobiography before, after all. Or written one for that matter, although it seemed pretty straightforward. She felt some nerves, but they struggled in comparison to the much worse nerves about the following meeting.

Once she was in the room, Edie smiled and lot and nodded a lot and said plausible things about *making it distinctive in the market* and *staying true to Elliot's voice* and they nodded back and said, in not so many words, OK do it, but don't scare the tween horses with too much miserablism. It helped she was riding in on the wave of acclaim of having persuaded Elliot back on board.

She couldn't be sure, but she got the feeling Elliot had given her full credit for talking him round.

After the publishing meeting, the terrible hour of three p.m. approached. Edie nursed a lonely glass of Pinot Grigio after lunch, to give her Dutch courage. It was pointless really; the amount of alcohol required to make what she faced tolerable would also make her legless.

Ad Hoc was located in Smithfield, between Soho and the City. The office was on the top floor of a high-windowed 1920s workshop block, sandwiched between a Victorian pub straight out of a Dickens novel, and what used to be a family-run Italian coffee shop, which was now yet another Itsu.

At ten to three, Edie left the nearby bar – she'd avoided the after-work favourite haunt – and trudged to the office like it was the gallows.

She headed up the stairs, feeling her heart punching against her ribs, considering the hundreds of times she'd walked up these stairs and into that room and not been thinking about anything more troubling than what she'd have for dinner.

Edie felt a rush of blood in her ears, and pushed through the door to see a small sea of staring faces. They'd obviously been clock-watching with bated breath for the appointed hour.

'Hi,' Edie said to the room, in embarrassment, feeling her face flare.

There was a murmured response, so faint she might have imagined it. It was agonising.

She glanced around. Edie didn't want to risk asking anyone anything, for fear of silence in reply, and headed instead to Richard's office.

Edie knocked, with a rapid pulse in her neck and her palms slippery with sweat.

'Enter!'

Richard was at his desk. Charlotte was seated in front of him, to the left. Her narrow shoulders, draped in a red cardigan, were rigid. She stared determinedly ahead, barely moving her head an inch to acknowledge Edie's presence. Edie remembered the sight of her bare shoulders in the wedding dress, and winced.

'Thank you for coming, Edie, take a seat. And thank you for being here, Charlotte.'

Edie lowered herself into the chair on the right.

Richard sat back in his seat and surveyed them both. He was wearing an immaculate dark tweed suit, perfectly cut, with an Oxford blue shirt. He looked, as per, as if he'd tumbled out of the pages of a Turnbull & Asser catalogue through the credit sequence of *Mad Men*.

'Now, I won't belabour this. We all have private lives. Sometimes our private lives intersect with our professional lives. Whatever our personal feelings towards each other, we still need our livelihoods. We can't change what has happened. We can stop it affecting more than it already has, if we are pragmatic.'

Edie breathed in and out, heavily, and hoped her voice worked.

Richard twiddled a solid silver ballpoint, clicked the nib in and out.

'Charlotte, can you see a way to work effectively alongside Edie, putting aside any rancour and keeping things strictly business?'

'Yes,' Charlotte said, slightly hoarse. She was nervous too. Edie felt for her. Neither of them wanted to be in this position. Was it possible, remotely possible, they could both sob in the loos after this, Charlotte tearfully ranting, Edie tearfully apologising, and eventually agree to let this lie?

Richard turned to Edie.

'And Edie. Do you think it's possible to park the politics at the door, and continue to work here, conducting yourself in a way that is respectful of Charlotte as a colleague?'

'Yes. Definitely,' Edie said, listening to how small and tight her voice sounded. She sounded like she hated herself, which she did.

Richard looked from one to the other.

'I'm not being Pollyanna here, and asking you to kiss and be friends—'

Richard paused for a fraction of a second as he realised

the poor choice of words, but recovered as seamlessly as if it was a difficult client meeting.

'—and book spa breaks together. I will not put you on any joint project if I can help it. But let's proceed on the basis that we're all adults, you've assured me that I will not have either or both of you back in this office at any point, due to controversy stemming from that unfortunate incident. We are drawing a line, right here, right now.'

At the word *incident*, from the corner of her eye, Edie saw Charlotte flinch.

They both nodded and murmured agreement.

'OK, Charlotte, thanks for your time and understanding. I'll have a word with Edie now, if you'll shut the door after you.'

Charlotte got up, making no eye contact with Edie, though Edie was desperate to exchange a glance. The hairs on Edie's skin prickled.

A tense pause after the door closed and Richard said:

'Thank you for coming today. I wasn't entirely sure if you would.'

'Ah . . . thanks,' Edie said, half-wishing she'd made good on that doubt. The tidal wave of adrenaline had subsided a little, to be replaced by a dull ache of humiliation and regret at her reality.

'Despite what the BMW driver who shunted my car earlier this week said, I'm not an idiot. I know the nature of what happened means any trouble is unlikely to come from you. If you have any difficulty, I ask you to keep a cool head, bring it to me. And perhaps avoid team nights out when the hooch is flowing, for the time being.'

Edie nodded, miserably. As if she was going to be first at the bar on a Friday. She'd be slow-clapped and hissed. Richard tapped his pen on his mouse mat.

'All good otherwise? How was the book summit?'

Edie croaked out a few assurances and Richard told her she was doing well.

'See you back here very soon, then,' Richard said, and Edie wanted to cry. She nodded, gathered her things and stood up.

'Edie,' Richard said, abruptly. 'As a friend, not a boss: ride out the storm here. Decency will prevail. Treat those two imposters of popularity and infamy just the same.'

Edie nodded vigorously because if she'd tried to speak, she'd weep. *Infamy.*

She opened the door, set her sights on nothing but the exit and bolted for it, once again feeling every pair of eyes in the room lock onto her as she scuttled out.

'Edie,' Charlotte said, catching up with her at the door.

Edie turned in surprise.

'Yes?' she spoke the word in a nervous gush.

This was it, this was where Charlotte buried the hatchet? If everyone saw Charlotte didn't hate her any more, they'd have to forgive her too. Wouldn't they? Edie's blood pumped fiery-chilli hot in her veins.

'This came for you,' Charlotte said, and passed her a plain brown A4 envelope with her name scrawled on it. Charlotte did the smallest smile. In truth, it couldn't truly be called a smile, more a twitch of the lips, but it broke the poker face she'd worn in Richard's office.

'Thank you,' Edie said, trying to inject as much sincerity

into those syllables as possible, in a pin-drop silence. 'Thank you for coming in today.'

'I was here anyway,' Charlotte said, evenly.

'I mean, the meeting.'

'Have a safe trip home,' Charlotte said, impassive.

'Thank you,' Edie faltered over whether to say more.

She couldn't judge the hostility of the interaction at all. It felt, cautiously, like they were on speaking terms, that they'd taken the first and most difficult step.

Charlotte returned briskly to her seat. She'd always been slim but Edie noticed her clothes were hanging from her; she'd clearly lost at least a stone in weight. Edie knew she didn't look her best either.

Outside, with shaky hands, Edie tore into the envelope and pulled out two stapled sheets of paper. At the top were the words.

Petition To Get Edie Thompson To Go.

We're asking you to have the basic decency to LEAVE. No one wants you here. If you tell Richard about this, we will get IT to pull your emails and go through them for anything and everything we can use to show him you're a treacherous bitch. Which, let's face it, you are ☺

Below were signatures. Edie scanned the list. Every single colleague had signed it, except for Louis. Edie read and re-read, then pulled open the drawer in a nearby bin and shoved it all in, letting it slam with a bang.

That was that, then. She looked up at the building and knew without question that had been the last time she'd ever step inside. She just had to work out what the hell to tell Richard. He'd said to bring him any problems, but as Edie knew all too well, some were simply beyond fixing.

32

Edie lay in bed and couldn't think of a single reason to get up. Was depression still depression when it was a natural consequence, given the state of your life? Who'd be happy in her current circumstances?

Her phone, plugged into the charger in the wall, went *zzzz-zzzz* like an angry bee in a glass. She rolled over and checked her messages.

Don't keep me in suspenders! HOW DID IT GO? L Dog X

Edie hauled herself upright and texted back:

OK I thought, and then Charlotte handed me the petition as I left. Thanks for not signing it. Ex

Beep.

<3 She stood over everyone and made them do it, E. Seriously. Ignore it.

Easier said than done. If it happened to Louis, the result would be a meltdown and a massacre.

Thanks ☹ you know what though, I've had enough of this nasty vindictive crap over something JACK DID. Someone Charlotte's still happy to spend her life with. Fuck all this bullying, Louis. They might not like what happened – neither do I – but bullying is still bullying. And I don't see Jack getting any of it. x

Beep.

You tell 'em, gal.

No, YOU tell them, Louis, Edie thought. Pass it along: I've had enough. She couldn't go back, so what did she have to lose?

There was a question here about how exactly Louis had dodged the draft in this war, but Edie was not yet minded to ask it. She hugged her knees and looked around her room.

The problem with having a nervous breakdown was, it was giving her bullies what they craved. She got up, getting her dressing gown from the back of the door and tying the cord, slowly but firmly. Simple deliberate actions, one step at a time. She wanted to talk to Hannah, but Hannah did a proper job, she might be in theatre.

N, can you dedicate Nirvana's 'I Hate Myself and Want to Die' from me, to me later? E xx

. . . Not on the playlist. I can do you 'Love Will Keep Us Together' by Captain & Tennille which is a very similar sentiment. Are you alright? X

Not as such, but I'll get there. X

Downstairs, there were flowers in the kitchen. She'd had time to kill at St Pancras and gone to Marks & Spencer, cursing Meg for making it so difficult to work out what would look generous and what would look pointed, after their row. She'd put some unseasonal Parma Violet lilac tulips in a jug. In another vase, there was a bunch of tiger lilies, still in their cellophane. She'd remembered the sad bronze-edged bouquet at Margot's, and hit on a nice thing to do.

Meg was at the hospice and her dad was out, the house was quiet. There was a window of opportunity to pop round, unseen and unchallenged.

Once a wan Edie was washed and dressed, she knocked at Margot's door.

She felt very 'best Brownie' holding her surprise gift.

Margot didn't look overjoyed to see her.

'Yes?'

'I got you some flowers!' Edie said, and pushed the package forward. 'To say thank you.'

Margot accepted them, squinting in confusion.

'For what?'

Not quite the reaction that Edie had envisaged.

'You set me off on a line of thinking that saved the whole project. About the actor saying what he thought? He nearly walked away from it but I persuaded him to do the book, the way you said.'

Edie was making an *eager beaver please be eager too* face. Margot looked bleary and indifferent, even irascible.

'He should've had more spine from the start. Kids these days.'

She walked back down the hallway but didn't close the door, and Edie awkwardly followed her inside, taking it for a tacit, if not very warm, invitation.

She could see down the narrow corridor to a galley kitchen where Margot, fag dangling from corner of her mouth, blasted a tap into the sink and dropped the flowers into the water.

'Want a drink?' Margot called.

'Oh. Er. Yes, thanks.'

There was the clink of glass on glass as Margot sploshed out something Edie feared couldn't be a cup of Tetley, given the lack of reassuring hiss of kettle. Margot came back down the hallway and handed it to her. She was wearing a lurid tangerine wrap dress that was drawn into a large ornamental clasp at one bony hip. 'That'll put hairs on your chest.'

Edie vacillated over whether to say 'No thanks, I don't drink what looks – and smells, urgh – like brandy at 11 a.m.' versus the potential wrangle involved in demanding a soft drink, and then having to stay to drink it in the resulting atmosphere. Edie decided to take the course of least resistance and accepted.

She sipped it gingerly, returning to the seat in the front room where she'd read to a snoring Margot last time.

'What's the story with you, then?' Margot said, picking up and tapping her resting cigarette into a swan ashtray.

'What do you mean?'

231

'You're a pretty girl, moping around. You obviously don't want to live there –' Margot jerked her head at next door '– Who would? Something's brought you here. Or someone.'

She blew out the smoke and fixed wintery eyes on Edie.

Edie was stung by the 'moping.' She'd been faultlessly polite and upbeat with Margot, she thought. She'd come off as a misery guts?

'I told you why I'm here. The book.'

'Hmm. Yes. That's what you said.'

Edie took a swig of the noxious brown fluid and felt self-conscious. She noted her default position, under attack, was to feel guilty, defensive and apologetic. With Margot there was an added Old Lonely Person pity factor.

'Who is he?'

'What?'

'The man who sent you back from London like a scalded flea.'

'No one. Why should there be a man?'

'Hah,' said Margot, unperturbed. 'Have it your way, darling. No man. None at all. Definitely not the man you're thinking of right now.'

Edie flared with rankled embarrassment. And yet: Margot was right, wasn't she? Edie jutted out her chin and told herself: you don't need to be ashamed. Well, you do a bit, but you can be honest in your shame.

'He was my colleague's fiancé,' she said. 'He and I used to chat at work all the time. There's this G-chat thing, where you can message each other. Like email but faster. He broke my heart and married his girlfriend. He kissed me on their wedding day and I kissed him back and his bride saw and they split up on the spot. They're back together now but everyone still hates me for it.'

Margot raised an already artificially raised eyebrow.

Hah, *stitch that*, Edie thought. There's some of that anecdotal hellraising you've been missing.

Margot tapped her fag.

'Are you in love with him?'

'Er . . .' Edie faltered. 'I thought I was, but not now. Not after what he's done.'

'You can't think your way out of being in love. You are or you aren't.'

'I don't know. He's not completely out of my system, I suppose, no. I want answers from him I've never had.'

He definitely wasn't. Edie had braced herself a few days ago, in a 'devil makes work for idle hands' moment, and looked up some of their old exchanges. She told herself it was to reassure her that she hadn't imagined it all. Actually, it was allowing herself to revisit their rapport. She was struck, however, by how much Jack had been playing a part. As had she. A two-player game where they never shared a rulebook.

Edie swallowed in the small silence that followed her admission, and hoped Margot would say something pithy and take no prisoners about getting rid of Jack that Edie could adopt as her mantra.

Instead she took a swig of her brandy and said: 'It was your fault as much as his. You won't get over him until you realise that.'

'*What?*' Edie said, disbelieving. 'How? He kissed me?'

'I mean the whole affair. Kenneth Tynan said *We seek the teeth to match our wounds*,' Margot said. 'In some way, this man was who you were looking for.'

'He wasn't!' Edie said. 'That's very victim blaming. So anyone who's had a really terrible time . . . been hit, even. They were looking for it?'

She was starting to have a lot more sympathy with Meg's 'fascist' verdict on Margot.

'I'm not talking about other people, I'm talking about you. You're no victim. How old did you say you were? Thirties?'

Edie nodded with a jerk of the head. She was getting more furiously upset by the second.

'Well forgive me, darling, but he can't be the first mistake.'

'Oh yeah, any single woman of my age, there must be something *really* wrong with her. God!'

'What have all these mistakes got in common? Ask yourself that.' Margot leaned forward.

Edie glared at Margot and knocked her brandy back in one, almost making her cough, and sullenly didn't answer.

'They didn't treat you well. They didn't take you seriously. Am I correct? You're choosing men who behave like you do. They treat you how you treat yourself. Badly.'

Edie took a jagged breath and stood up. Being confrontational with old people wasn't the way she was brought up, it wasn't in her DNA. But needs must.

'I came round with flowers to say thank you, because I thought it might be nice. Thanks for being so gratuitously horrible about me, when you don't know me.'

Margot gave a joyless hiccup of a laugh. 'I know you, alright.'

Edie marched out of the room and hoped Margot's door was a simple Yale latch because she couldn't stand to ask for help in getting out.

As she wrestled briefly with the door, Margot called from offstage:

'You need people to like you. Stop caring so much. It doesn't matter.'

'Great. Cheers,' Edie called back, and burst out into the street.

Why did she try? Everything she did went so hopelessly to shit. Better to do the bare minimum, always, and protect herself from further hurt.

She let herself back into the house, went upstairs and lay down on the bed. *We seek the teeth to match our wounds.*

Was that true? Hannah had said Jack was to blame, but Hannah was her best friend. Elliot had pointed out that her hopes with Jack were almost certainly going to be dashed. But Margot had flat out said it: Edie had consorted with a taken man, and got her dues. On reflection, she realised how passive she'd been with Jack. She took no interest in him until he took an interest in her, and then he'd set the pace the whole way. She'd vaguely assumed she didn't have the *right* to ask him what was going on. She certainly didn't have the guts. She had sat back and waited to be told what – and who – she was worth.

Edie didn't know how much time had passed by the time she heard the scrape of the key in the door and her father's tread on the stairs.

235

She'd received an email from Elliot's agent. Would she visit him on set to do the interview, tomorrow? He should have some time free in the filming schedule.

Yeah sure, not like she had anything better to do.

She rolled off the bed and went to ask her dad what he fancied for the dinner that she would cook, and barely eat.

33

Edie was unlikely to forget how she spent the last day of her thirty-fifth year: staring at an apparently unconscious naked woman on a pyramid of rubble, in a cemetery.

She'd picked her way to it along the graveyard's quiet path, under a beautiful green canopy of leaves. Edie used to come to Arboretum Park when she was a moody Goth teenager. She'd look at the names and ages on the headstones and think about how short and brutal life was, then ponder whether purple suited her and what she fancied for tea and potter home again.

Today she had to get past one of the walkie-talkie army to gain admission to the set. The site, set on a slope, was a swarm of activity, with the TV crew centred around a lissom twenty-something blonde model, dusted post-mortem grey by make-up artists. Her body, as pale and still as marble, naked but for a strange Elastoplast thing over her crotch, was draped atop the heap of Styrofoam stone. Onlookers with headsets and clipboards shouted the occasional instruction, sometimes prompting the corpse to magically stir and adjust the angle of her arms or legs.

It looked bloody uncomfortable, as well as exposing. Edie was shocked by the public nudity for about seven to ten minutes and found shock was like awe, not sustainable. Especially when the attitude of those around her to a spread-eagled unclothed woman was complete indifference.

The mini mountain the not-dead body was lying on was surrounded by zigzags of a strange white substance, which a runner told Edie was the serial killer's trademark pentagram of salt.

There was also blue and white police tape, flickering in the light breeze, and a cluster of police cars. Actors in high-vis tabards milled around, drinking coffee from cardboard cups.

It was a bright day, but a persistent mizzle was cast on the area by a rain machine, a rig of pipes spewing a watery mist overhead. Wasn't the promotional bumpf she read about how this show was going to expose the gritty truth of crime in the regions? Maybe Edie had missed it, living in her London ivory tower, but she didn't recall many serial murderers in these parts staging elaborate crime scenes with piles of rocks, supermodels and bags of Saxa.

There was a slight hush in the chatter and a sense of heightened tension as Elliot and Greta Alan appeared on set, emerging from giant sleek trailers parked a hundred yards away. Archie went in serious conference with them, headphones round his neck, arms gesticulating.

Elliot had his hands thrust in his pockets and was listening intently. Edie felt the strange sensation of wanting to call to Elliot – *yoo hoo, it's me!* – when seeing him in work mode, the way parents waved at children in school plays.

He looked different, in character. His hair was short but tousled, he had a five o'clock shadow and a black leather jacket with hooded top underneath.

His co-star Greta was a tiny porcelain doll with flame hair, in Coke-can-sized curls. Her improbably narrow waist was accentuated in a nipped-in jacket, charcoal pencil skirt stretched tight across slender hips. She was wearing a large pair of beige Ugg boots, stovepipes on her stalk-like legs. She leant on a lackey and swapped them for violently spiky black-and-scarlet Louboutins when about to walk into shot. They were just the thing for tottering after murderers: chasing a toddler would've been difficult.

After the clapperboard went down – *action!* – Elliot and Greta picked their way up the slope, towards the body. An actor dressed as a chief constable spoke to them.

Edie was too far away to hear much of the dialogue, though she felt she could guess what was being said. Elliot was clearly the sort of maverick to try to roll a naked body off a tower of rubble before forensics were ready, and tangle with the uniforms. And then have a heated argument with the Scully to his Mulder, and stride away in an alpha male strop.

Edie might be pre-judging, but from this one encounter with it, Edie thought *Gun City* looked like clichéd toss.

The only real point of interest was Elliot. Edie watched the way his posture altered when he was in character. The set of his jaw seemed different, he moved in an un-Elliot-like way, somehow. Edie didn't have an opinion on whether he was a particularly good actor but it was interesting to see the change take place.

However, even Elliot's tarry-haired beauty couldn't enliven the experience of seeing the same process repeated twenty-four times. My God, but the hanging around was mind-numbing. The circulation slowed in Edie's legs.

There was nothing for it but running down the battery on her phone, yet with her social media accounts still disabled, there wasn't much to see. A text pinged from Nick and she opened it eagerly. Nick was a good correspondent, he had a great way with a one-liner.

When she read his text, her face fell.

E. I don't know whether you know about this but I felt I had to tell you. I looked for you on Facebook because I wasn't sure if you'd come back on. I found this group. What an utter shower. I've reported it as abusive, you should too. Nx

It was a Facebook 'fan' page with 71 Likes. '**The Edie Thompson Appreciation Society.**' There was a photo of her used as the profile – the one from the wedding, in the red dress. It was billed as: 'For people who love the work of Edie Thompson, the world's best wedding guest.'

Was she really still such a point of fascination for these people, for a moment's stupidity, however ill-timed? Did they think the kiss was part of a full-blown affair? She struggled to put faces to most of the names here, and felt how tawdry and mean-spirited it was. There were various sarcastic and spectacularly unfunny, vicious conversations on it: '12 reasons

Edie should become a wedding planner!' with gifs. And – surprise – there was the atrocious Lucie Maguire, giving it some welly. It was jolting, it was also repulsive, wearying. She'd done a bad thing but these weren't good people. Or if they were, they were hiding it well.

And then she saw it. Eight words, glowing black on white, buried in an otherwise same-same conversation about her crime of husband theft. Edie had to re-read it five times to be sure this comment existed, and her eyes weren't deceiving her. She didn't know the man who'd posted it, only that 'Ian Connor' knew something about her he couldn't possibly know.

Edie knew, however long she lived, she would never understand how someone could have thought and typed those words, and hit 'post'.

She stared into the middle distance, seeing nothing. She stared and breathed and stared and shifted from foot to foot and texted Nick brief acknowledgement, put her phone back in her pocket and looked at the birds in the sky above and breathed some more. There were people around, but thankfully no one near enough to start side eyeing her in curiosity. Suddenly, Elliot was in front of her, filling her field of vision.

She tried to focus on him. She thought he might be aloof at work, but the opposite was true: he looked excitable and boyish.

'Hey there! You're not too bored, are you? Did it look OK?'

'Sure,' Edie said, absently. 'Very OK.'

'That's a relief.'

Edie got her phone back out of her pocket and stared at

it, dully, and re-pocketed it again. What was Elliot saying? She should try to concentrate. *Concentrate.* Forget that thing you just read . . .

'You alright? You look like you've seen a ghost,' Elliot said.

Without consciously deciding it would be a good idea to tell Elliot Owen, Edie started speaking.

'There's a group about me on Facebook. People who hate me, because of the wedding, saying harsh things, taking the piss,' she paused. 'And someone's said . . . they've said . . .'

Edie breathed in, and out. She felt tears brim and course down her face, though she hadn't known she was that close to crying. There was no warning. In an instant, her eyes welled and over-spilled. A facial flash-flood.

She wiped her eyes with the heels of her hands. Elliot was frowning at her.

'Come on, come with me.'

Edie noticed dispassionately that her legs didn't work. It was as if she'd finally reached systems overload with psychological torment, and her body had temporarily closed down operations.

She shook her head: 'I can't move.'

'Edie?' Elliot said, with a hand on her shoulder.

Edie tried to diagnose what she was feeling. Was she going to be sick? Possibly. Faint? Also possible. It was oddly similar to the sensation when she'd over-eaten a rich bow-tie pasta carbonara as a little girl. She couldn't work out what was happening to her or what she needed to do to alleviate it, only that she wanted to crawl out of her own skin. A kind of crucifying, overwhelming wrongness.

'*Edie?*'

'I can't move,' she said again, hoarse.

'Are you going to faint? You're very pale.'

'I'm always pale,' she said, weakly. 'I don't know.'

She felt her knees rattle perilously, and thought, please don't collapse here, now. Yes, Edie was going to faint. She remembered the warning signs from a couple of times in her youth: the feeling everything was coming closer and pulling away at the same time, like the *Jaws* special effect.

She held on to Elliot to stay upright, bunching his leather coat in her hands. She momentarily wondered if wardrobe personnel were going to flay her for messing up a two-grand jacket. Were people looking at them? She guessed so but she couldn't see and didn't want to.

'Do you want me to call a doctor? We have them,' he said.

Edie shook her head.

'You need to sit down, and have some water.'

Edie nodded.

With surprising decisiveness and ease, Elliot moved his hands to her ribcage and picked her up. Edie was thrown against him with a jolt, instinctively putting her arms round his neck. He linked his arms under her backside, as if he was carrying a child across a supermarket car park, and set off towards the trailers.

Edie hung on and stared over his shoulder at everyone staring back at them, and finally found out what it looked like when female onlookers almost ovulated.

After a brief, bumpy stride, Elliot put her down by one of the coaches.

'OK? Sorry if that was a bit Tarzan but you looked like you were going to keel over.'

'S'fine, thanks,' Edie said, rubbing at her face with her sleeve, at that moment more interested in making sure her gastric contents stayed in place than worrying if she'd felt like lifting a pissed-up sack of spuds. At least she didn't feel as if she was going to faint now. The adrenaline rush surprise of being Mills & Boon-ed by a famous actor had obviously helped.

'I got plenty of practice hoisting women aloft in *Blood & Gold*. Just be grateful I wasn't rescuing you from your rapist royal husband's funeral pyre, eh.' Elliot cranked the handle open on the trailer door and ushered her inside.

Edie could only manage a thin smile at this joke, but in the circumstances, that was incredibly high praise.

34

Actors' trailers were like little luxury holiday homes, on wheels. A rock'n'roll caravan.

'Here, sit down,' Elliot said, gesturing to a banquette that curved round a lacquered veneer table. He opened a cabinet next to a large flat-screen television and said: 'Water? Whisky? Whisky with water?'

'Whisky, thanks,' Edie said, with no idea whether this was a smart idea or an incredibly awful one.

Elliot sloshed two fingers out and set the glass down in front of her, pushing his way behind the table from the other side.

Edie said: 'God, Elliot. I'm so sorry . . .'

'Stop that. You have nothing to be sorry for. Do you want to talk about it?'

Edie remembered what had been said, and her guts spasmed again.

'Some man, someone I don't know—' she drew breath, 'He said maybe my mum killed herself out of the shame of having had me.'

Elliot's eyes widened. 'What a . . . Jesus. Wow.'

'It's just . . .' Edie gulped back more tears and put her hand on her forehead, 'I don't tell anyone about what happened with my mum. I say she died but I don't explain how. The only person I told was Jack.'

'Who's Jack?'

'The man I kissed at the wedding.'

'He told people?'

'He must've done.'

'Well, you already knew he was a dick.'

Edie's tears restarted and she wiped at her face hurriedly.

'Hey, y'alright . . .'

It still surprised her whenever Elliot sounded more Nottingham lad than fantasy fighting prince. This was such a surreal scenario, sat in his trailer, weeping. He put an arm round her.

'Everyone *despises* me. I already can't remember what it was like when I wasn't hated, now,' Edie said. 'It's torture.'

'Stop for a second. *They* hate *you*? Someone made a savage remark about the way you lost your mother, and *you're* feeling bad about yourself? They've revealed themselves as someone who's going to need a LOT of therapy to resemble a human being.'

Edie nodded.

'Look. That –' Elliot picked up his phone, lying on the table in front of them, and put it down again '–isn't real life. That person they're talking about isn't you. There's another version of you, multiple versions, other people's versions, walking around out there. You have to let it go, or you'll go mad. Trust me on this. Keep these words in your head: *Those who know me better, know better.*'

Edie nodded again.

'How could anyone be that cruel, to bring my mum into it? I know I did a shit thing, but I've not killed anyone . . .'

'Because you're not real to them, online. You're abstract. They don't think you'll ever see what they wrote, or care if you do. You're a game. A story. And the more of them there are, the easier it becomes for them. The snowflake doesn't feel responsible for the avalanche. Honestly, I can relate to more of this than you might think.'

'At least everyone likes you.'

'Not true. Angus McKinlay at *Variety* said I had the gift of making acting look difficult.'

Edie smiled and saw Elliot was trying hard to make her laugh and in that moment she adored him for it.

'OK. You're well paid though,' Edie said.

'True,' Elliot said. 'And those strippers don't buy their own brunches, let me tell you.'

Edie finally laughed, a weak, wet gurgly noise because of all the snot and sob.

Elliot squeezed her shoulders before withdrawing his arm and Edie sipped her whisky. Oof, that was strong. It did steady her a little, though.

'Thank you.'

'You're welcome.'

There was a knock at the trailer door.

'Yeah?' Elliot called.

A stout blonde woman with a headset put her head round the door. 'Elliot, we need you.'

'Fifteen minutes, max.'

The woman gave Edie a hard look, jerked her head in acknowledgement and withdrew.

'Elliot, go. Honestly. I feel awful I'm holding everything up . . .'

'Don't be silly. I needed a breather anyway.'

Edie still felt discomfited and her discomfort increased when, minutes later, the blonde woman reappeared, looking flushed and anxious.

'Elliot. Archie is asking for you, sorry.'

'Tell him I'm on my way,' Elliot said, calmly.

The woman was clearly itching to say more, but couldn't quite decide who to risk pissing off in the pecking order.

'Thank you,' Elliot finished, with a pointed intonation, as code for, 'so go away'. Edie had forgotten he could be steely.

'I like the George Michael beard,' Edie said, once they were on their own again.

'Haha. It's meant to be the tortured detective, "I sleep in my car" look. Not the "I drive my car into Snappy Snaps when stoned" one.'

Edie burst out laughing again and Elliot looked gratified.

'Feel any better?' he said.

'Much, thank you.'

In truth, it would crowd her mind as soon as she left, but this kindness still mattered. Edie drank more of her whisky, finding when she tried to breathe normally, the air still hitched in her throat.

Outside the trailer, they could hear a male voice, presumably shouting into his mobile. It got louder as he got closer.

'. . . Exactly how simple do I need to make it for you? Do we need to start with how a baby is made? When a man's feeling especially loving, his penis becomes large, that sort of thing? WELL FUCK THE WHOLE FUCKING THING THEN, YOU BUM FUCK. CONSIDER YOUR BUM FUCKED.'

Elliot put a palm over his eyes and sighed.

A brief silence, then a hammering at the trailer door and the wiry frame of Archie Puce was in front of them. He looked very like Dobby the House Elf, and favoured a hat that did look as if he'd put a sock on his head. He planted his hands on his hips. Edie quailed. Only Archie Puce would have a row on the way to a row.

'Elliot. We're stood around holding our dicks here. Put the girl down and join us.'

'Archie, I won't be much longer. This is important.' Elliot squeezed Edie's arm firmly as he said this, to stop her protesting. Edie now felt sodden with guilt but saying 'no it isn't', seemed too ungrateful.

Archie's gimlet gaze moved to the tearstained Edie.

'Without sounding a heartless wankrag, can she not have someone here to cuddle her who isn't on your hourly rate? Like her fucking mum, for example?'

'Archie,' Elliot said, standing up.

'. . . Let me check the cast list, is her mum in my show? OH NO WAIT SHE'S NOT. NO MUM. LET'S CALL MUM.'

'Archie! Shut up and get out of here this second unless you want to get someone else to play my fucking role in your fucking show!'

Archie looked startled to have got a Puce-ing himself. He glared at Elliot, who glared steadily back.

'Alright. No need to become exhilarating.' Pause. 'You kids enjoy yourselves, put your feet up.'

The trailer door slammed after him.

'I'm so sorry, go, please go,' Edie said, aghast, as Elliot sat back down, shaking his head.

'Oh, don't worry. A row with Archie is a rite of passage. I'd been worrying ours was overdue and I was going to get a reputation as a walkover. Greta and him have been daggers drawn over the standard of catering since day one,' Elliot said. 'Also he really won't be getting anyone else. He wanted Jamie Dornan first and then when he told his agent the fee, they thought it was a prank call.'

Edie was still desperate for Elliot to go back on set.

'You've been so generous. I've come to your workplace and caused you massive amounts of trouble . . .'

'Hush. No trouble.'

'And I haven't even done any interviewing.'

'Tell you what, I'll email you. I saw "relationships" looming in the list of topics. I'd rather just hammer out a few thoughts on that and be done.'

Edie thanked him profusely, although her treacherous wicked brain did whisper: *And that's convenient, so I don't get to ask the gay question.*

'Please, go back to work.'

Elliot checked his watch: 'Yeah, Archie's sweated enough now, I suppose.'

He paused at the trailer door. 'You're a good person, Edie. Goodness will get you through this.'

Edie said a heartfelt: 'Thank you. That means a lot, Elliot.'

She was alone. Or as alone as she could ever be, with her phone. As gratifying as it was to hear Elliot say she was nice, Edie couldn't help feeling that it was as much use as an ashtray on a motorbike.

A famous person she'd never see again, in a few weeks' time, liked her. While the world at large loathed her. She knew one thing. She wouldn't rest until she found out who 'Ian Connor' was.

35

Edie was having strange dreams about being rescued naked from burning pyres by men in ritual sacrifice masks who turned out to be Lucie Maguire, when she was woken by a noise. Because she was woken by it, she didn't know what it was.

After a few seconds of bleary blinking it occurred to her to check her mobile.

Nice birthday wishes from Hannah and Nick, the occasion delaying discussion of her latest online shaming.

And a text, from Jack.

Hey you. HBD. Doing anything fun for it? Hope all's well. Jx

How on earth did he of all people remember this date? He didn't even have the Facebook prompt any more. Smoother than Smooth FM. She remembered the latest betrayal, with a lurch. Pale, puffy-faced and newly thirty-six years old, Edie tapped her fury into her phone.

*You told people about how my mum died? How could you? I can't
believe the person you turned out to be.*

Seconds after she'd pressed send, Edie's phone lit up with
a call from Jack. She didn't expect that, and licked dry lips.
She couldn't let it ring out, she couldn't be the coward
here.

'Yes?'

'Edie. What do you mean? Told who?'

She paused and gathered herself at the sound of his voice.
It was light and gentle, and still had some power over her.

'I saw a vile Facebook group, ripping the stuffing out of
me. Some bloke I'd never heard of made a "joke" about how
my mum killed herself because of me.'

Pause.

'Oh my God, that's horrific. But why would that have
come from me?'

'I never told anyone else.' This was a difficult admission to
make.

'No one?'

Edie said a terse: 'Nope.'

'I didn't tell anyone . . .'

Edie let out a sour noise of disbelief as Jack said: '. . . Except
Charlotte.'

'Oh, *right*. Who hates my guts. Thanks for breaking my
confidence.'

'Only because after what happened, she was in full flow
and I said she didn't know you and didn't know what you'd
been through.'

'So it wasn't "don't blame her for what *I* did"? It's "cut her some slack, her mum died!" Jesus Christ! Some defence lawyer.'

Edie hated the subtext. *She's an unmothered hot mess, don't expect normal social mores from her.* 'What's it got to do with anything?'

'Edie, Edie – it wasn't a considered thing, it was . . . you're so much a mystery to people and keep yourself to yourself and I felt if she understood you better she wouldn't be so critical.'

'Could've accomplished a lot more by telling her that *you* kissed *me*, couldn't you?'

'Believe me, I tried. This was in Hour Twelve of the crisis talks.'

Believe me. Easier said than done.

'If you really care about the treatment I'm getting, you'll find out who this "Ian Connor" is, who made that comment. I'm going to find out one way or another.'

This was showboating. Edie had steeled herself, gone back and clicked his name. She was taken to a completely locked down profile, not even a friends list available, with a profile photo of Daffy Duck. A Google name search didn't bear any fruit either, unsurprising with a needle-in-haystack of a name. She was at a dead end.

'Ian, Connor. OK. I will if I can.'

'Right then. I've got a birthday to have, so if you'll excuse me.'

Edie hung up, the way people only did in films.

Coughing and shuffling outside her door, a timid knock, and she realised with a stab of horror that her dad had overheard that exchange. Oh God, please don't let him have caught the part about her mum . . .

'Come in!'

'Happy birthday, darling daughter!'

Her dad appeared round the door with shaky Game Face on. He must've heard a lot. He looked for a moment like he was considering asking about it, while Edie non-verbally tried to vigorously convey: DON'T. When she was eleven, they'd managed to have a conversation about where he'd put spare change to pay for sanitary wear without ever using the words 'period' or 'tampon', like a game of charades. Edie saw no reason to become sharers now.

He was holding a bunch of pink peonies, the blooms still in tight acorn buds, a box of Green & Black's chocolates clamped under one arm and in the other hand, a bottle of pink champagne. Edie realised this occasion merited even more acting happy from her than usual, and broke into a huge beaming smile.

'Dad, you didn't have to! They're gorgeous.'

'I know how much you like flowers,' he said, standing awkwardly as Edie took them. 'I didn't know what else to get you. Do you want vouchers?'

'Vouchers would be perfect,' Edie said, putting her champagne and chocolates in front of the mirror.

'Meg's at the care home but she's left you a stack of her contraband Nutella sandwiches.'

'That's nice of her.'

Edie thought: *Though I do know you ordered her to do it and she sulked the whole way through making them, Dad.*

'What do you want to do tonight? Shall we get togged up and go out for dinner?'

'I was hoping for takeaway pizza and a few pints in The Lion, if that's OK?'

'It's fine, if that's really all you want?'

'Definitely, definitely what I want.'

There was something to be said for 'performative' cheerfulness. It didn't make Edie cheery, exactly, but it was much better than wallowing. After Edie had showered, dressed, put her flowers in water and had two types of chocolate for breakfast, the gloom had lifted a little.

'What are you going to do with your first day of thirty-sixness?' her dad asked, from behind his days-old newspaper.

'Hmm. I'm going to do some shopping and treat myself to lunch in a park and maybe find some ducks to look at.'

'Sounds marvellous,' her dad said, and they shared a genuine smile this time. 'See you later, once I've got some marking done?'

It was a warm day, and Edie decided to walk the twenty minutes or so into the city centre, up the hill and past the cemetery, which was now back to being a silent garden full of peaceful dead people, rather than the site of the baroque staging of a still-warm sexy cadaver.

She remembered, as she passed, how it felt to be picked up by Elliot. If she blocked out the massive embarrassment factor, it was worth a swoon, in memory. He was surprisingly strong, for a lean-looking boy.

A funny thing happened, as Edie strode up the hill and down again, into the mouth of the city centre, her blood pumping. She felt her spirits rise. Edie remembered a very useful thing about herself that she was prone to forget: she had resilience. When things were bad, sooner or later, she fought back.

Edie once came home from a history GCSE lesson and saying to her dad she'd read a phrase about Cardinal Wolsey, he was 'energetic in the moment of reverse'.

'That's me,' she said to her dad, 'I'm energetic in the moment of reverse.'

Her dad laughed and ruffled her hair and said, 'You might feel differently when you get to the end of his story,' but Edie adopted it as her motto nonetheless.

So, she recapped: everyone online was tomatoing her. Her whole office had voted to get rid of her. She was a scarlet woman and a marriage wrecker. Edie knew she wasn't the person they were saying she was. She could get past this.

Hannah once said to her: 'Pretty much the worst thing that could've happened to you has already happened to you and you're still here and you're OK. That makes you very strong. That is powerful.'

36

Edie wondered if her dad had noticed the significance of her age today. They never spoke about her mum, really. Occasionally her dad would say *'just like your mother'* or *'as your mother used to say'* but it made them all stiffen and he didn't do it often.

Some things, Edie thought as she wiggled the straw in her iced coffee, sitting outside Caffè Nero, were too big to be chipped away at in small talk.

There was one group family photo on display at home, half hidden in clutter on top of her dad's piano in the dining room. In it, Edie's darkly pretty mum looked incredibly like Edie, but with the eighties perm and frosted make-up of the time, in a blue strappy sundress with elasticated waist.

Each of her girls were caught in the right angles of her elbows, Meg a grumpy-faced confused toddler, Edie with a kitchen-scissors fringe. Her dad was beaming, his arm slung round his wife's waist. They were in Wollaton Park, having a picnic, a tablecloth spread in front of them. Edie didn't know if the picture was taken by a stranger, or a fifth picnicker. She didn't ask many questions about the past. It made her dad's face cloud over. It was as if she was trying to catch him out.

Edie couldn't look at the picture without thinking how little time they had left with her. She remembered her mum wore a perfume that made her skin smell like crushed rose petals when she hugged her. Edie could recollect her letting her stand on a chair to stir cake mixes with sultanas in them, and feeding their pet gerbils, Sam and Greg, together. Or her mum tying bibs on both girls, sitting them at the kitchen table with poster paints to make a creative mess.

There were also signs of impending doom: her mum sobbing quietly at the strangest, most innocuous times. Edie once thought it was her gerbils squeaking, and realised it was her mother, trying to stifle the sound with her hand over her mouth, as Edie and Meg played on the sitting-room floor. There were days she didn't get out of bed and told Edie it was because her legs didn't work.

Edie used to worry whether she or Meg had done something wrong. She still looked back now and wondered what she could have done differently. There was a cliché she knew to be true: kids always blame themselves. Though in adulthood, Edie discovered pretty much everyone blames themselves. Unless they're Jack Marshall.

And she very clearly remembered the day when her mum didn't collect her from school. Instead, Edie was called to the headmaster's office. There was lots of urgent whispering and looking at her worriedly and then a chain-of-command error whereby the teachers thought the family were telling her, yet her tearful aunt picking her up from school thought the teachers had broken the news.

Her Auntie Dawn was ashen, gulping for air and squeezing her hand as she briskly walked her the short distance home, Edie side-eyeing her, curiously.

There was a police car parked outside their house, and Edie wondered if they'd been burgled.

By the time Edie peered round the living room door and saw her dad weeping, head in hands, in a house that was peculiarly thronged with people, Edie knew something strange and terrible and aberrant had occurred. What had been taken, to make her dad so upset? She checked, and Sam and Greg were still there.

Her mum would know.

She tugged on a passing uncle's coat and said: 'Where's my mum?'

He started in shock, and said: 'She's dead! Has no one said?!' and Edie felt he was angry with her for not knowing. Everyone fell silent and stared, and Edie said, like it was a bad joke and its time was up: 'I want my mum.'

She and Meg were told their mum had been very poorly, and the poorliness was in her brain. It had made her think swimming was a good idea when it wasn't, their dad said, and she drowned. There was a lot to think about there. Edie had dreams about black water like oil and weeds tangled in her mum's hair, pulling her down as she struggled to kick her way back to the surface.

Edie was a natural question asker, though she could tell it wasn't welcome. *Where did she swim? Was it cold? Was the water very deep? Why didn't people help her, wasn't anyone else swimming too?*

The vague, evasive answers she got, designed to play down the horror, only deepened the mystery.

On the day of the funeral, Edie and Meg were left to watch cartoons with a twitchy neighbour – long before the days of Margot in Forest Fields – as babysitter. Funerals weren't for children, they were told, and they could see everyone at the wake afterwards, at the house. That involved lots of cups of tea and Stowells wine boxes and bustling around. Younger Edie thought there might've been an odd atmosphere, although she didn't know what atmosphere the occasion should have. As her aunt left, Edie heard her talking to their dad in the hallway.

'Those girls? What's going to happen to them?' she said, in a tone that was more challenge than regret. She didn't hear her dad answer, if he did.

Edie looked at Meg smacking her favourite Transformer against the coffee table and thought: what would happen? How did you do life, without a mum? Weren't they meant to be quite essential? Who was going to make the packed lunches?

Faced with a father who was barely able to function as one parent, let alone two, and a five-year-old sister, Edie decided she'd have to step up. In the months following the funeral, she learned how to make ham and cheddar sandwiches. She discovered where the mop was kept. She mucked out Sam and Greg on her own. She comforted Meg when she woke up after a nightmare. At first she was very proud. Then she felt exhausted.

It was never enough. She could never be enough. Edie felt

like a dog chasing a car. The persistence of the absence was debilitating.

Every time their dad made them beans on burned toast or pizza that was frozen in the middle, Edie would think, vaguely: it'll be OK when Mum's back. She'll be back for my birthday. She wouldn't miss that, would she?

Then a classmate called Siobhan told her that her mum hadn't died swimming, she'd jumped off a bridge on purpose because she was mad, and she knew it was true because her parents had told her. Edie felt very angry with her dad then that she knew less than Siobhan Courtney.

She came home and asked if it was true and howled at him and he cried and then she felt so guilty, she didn't know which part of it all was making her weep. It set a pattern with her dad that would continue until . . . well. It continued.

When she turned ten, during the creaky, sad simulacrum of a birthday party in McDonald's – her dad was in the middle of what Edie would later realise was a nervous breakdown – she finally realised this loss was not going to diminish as time passed.

It would grow and grow, it would hurt and matter in new ways, all the time. The older she got, the more questions Edie had for her mum, and silence was always the stern reply. It was different for Meg: their mother existed mostly pre-memory for her, she had a much blurrier sense of Before and After, whereas their father felt the difference so keenly he'd been shattered by it. He couldn't – or wouldn't – talk about it. In the individuality of grief, Edie was on her own. Looking back, she could clearly see that her early teenage years, shinning out of her bedroom window to drink in parks with boys, was an escape from the pressures of her home life. Between those walls, she worked hard to be the person both her father and her sister needed her to be. Outside, she ran wild to let it out.

Sometimes, she hated her mother. If your parent died through an 'act of God' you were free to simply miss them, without hesitation or resentment.

As much as Edie knew that depression was an illness and she'd lost her mum to something as implacable as any other illness, her heart couldn't rationalise away the fact that her mum made a choice.

Her mum lied to their GP. She decided not to take her medicine. She left Meg alone in the house, unsupervised, and walked out of the door. Her mum had looked at the water below, thought about her family, and chosen the water. Anyone lecturing Edie needed to understand that emotions weren't logical and never would be. Their mum wasn't just taken from them; their mum left.

37

Edie's brutally short annual flying visits had left her with no time to explore her home city, and she was enjoying rediscovering it more than she thought she would.

Once she'd got past her It's Not London Though stumbling block, she was finding plenty of things to like in Nottingham. And, whisper it: she appreciated being part of a place that was less hectic, impersonal and sprawling. If this was simply getting old, it felt quite nice. When she was small, Meg asked Edie what it felt like to die. Edie carefully told her it was like a long sleep when you were tired. So maybe ageing was like a nice sit down after being on your feet all day.

A wander up into a tiny shopping arcade led her to a creperie, with white subway tiles, wooden furniture and a nice woman in an apron tossing them expertly in special large circular pans.

Edie sat at a round table outside the shop and wolfed down a posh pancake full of salted caramel. Her appetite was definitely making a comeback.

Her phone rang, a call from Hannah, and she answered it with a mouthful of food.

'Happy birthday!' School friends never forgot your birthday. Life truth. 'What we doing tonight then?'

'Are you expecting to do something tonight?'

'Yes. Of course. It's your bloody birthday and I've had a long and bloody week. What are you doing?'

'Right now I'm eating a big pudding for lunch and then I was going to find a park with ducks. Not sure where that is, though.'

'You're an indoorsy person, Edith. Don't fight it. I remember you on our geography field trips. You sat on the coach with your Walkman. Miss Lister had to drag you out by the nipples. Why no birthday plans?'

'I've said I'll go to The Lion with Dad and Meg. I didn't see the point celebrating being old and reviled.'

'This is quitters' talk. I tell you what you're going to do. You're going to buy a new dress, go home, put yourself in a hot shower, drink a glass of Poke while you're getting ready and me and Nick will come meet the family Thompson. What time?'

Edie wilted in the face of Hannah's purpose. 'Eight.'

'See you then. I warn you, I feel in the mood for dancing.'

Edie groaned and laughed and noticed, grudgingly, she felt happier than she did before. A follow-up text from Nick confirmed that the dancing was a nail-on.

She didn't just want to sneak past this birthday because she was a social pariah. With her nearest and dearest, she also feared letting go. Becoming hopelessly morose-pissed and weepy and ending up that middle-aged woman in the corner, lamenting her lost youth. And lack of a family that she'd said she didn't necessarily want, or not since Matt, but now wondered if she did, maybe a little too late. Edie had never powerfully wanted kids, getting very annoyed with people who did sympathy faces and sometimes openly made the connection with what happened with her mum.

The truth was, Edie had no idea if her ambivalence was because of what happened with her mum. She couldn't live an alternative past where her mum did take her meds to find out, could she?

Edie wiped her mouth with a napkin, consciously parked the dark thoughts and drifted round fashionable clothes shops with pounding music, telling herself she had every right to be there, among the truanting teenagers. She found herself a simple strappy black maxi dress, something she didn't need to try on to know it'd fit. She had been avoiding mirrors. The remarks on Charlotte's profile came back into her mind, whenever she saw her reflection.

Too much make-up . . . falling out of her dress. No one's marrying that. NO ONE.

On her walk home, Edie's mobile rang again, rattling in her handbag. The sight of the name gave her a jolt: at once entirely plausible and yet ludicrous.

It was a struggle not to waggle her iPhone in the face of innocent passers-by on Mansfield Road and point: 'LOOK, ELLIOT OWEN. *THE* Elliot Owen! Not someone with the same name or someone I put into my phone under that name as a drunken jape.'

'I use the Force-ps, of course.'

Edie couldn't speak at first for guffawing.

'You have to do it! Then you can be on classic romcom posters where you're standing back to back with your co-star. You're doing the "I give up" hands and shrugging, while the woman is pointing back at you with a *This Guy* expression.'

Edie was rewarded with what sounded like a proper laugh.

'I'll call my agent straight after you. What could possibly go wrong? Other than the placenta detaching. Sorry, spoilers.'

They laughed and Edie felt she should wind the call up during the triumphant riffing and before the uhhming and aahing started.

'Anyway I'm genuinely feeling the better for your pep talk. I'm bearing in mind what you said about "those who know me better, know better". That was good advice. Thank you.'

'Ah, great, glad it helped.' Pause. 'I think that "those who know me better" was Marilyn Monroe talking about how people thought her breasts were fake. But whatever works, eh?'

Edie let go of a honking divvy laugh that she regretted a bit, after they said bye and rang off.

As she walked up the street to her dad's, Edie saw Margot standing outside the door. She had the fag glued to one hand as usual, and a cake on a plate in the other. She was wearing a blousy cream dress, with ruffles. Edie remembered that photo of Margot: she still dressed as the siren she once was. It was quite cool, really, if you forgot the viperous personality.

'Hello?' Edie called, and Margot turned.

'There you are! My hand's going to sleep.'

'How did you know it was my birthday?' Edie said, neutrally, as she didn't much want to renew an acquaintance with this woman, after the sting of the unwanted amateur psycho-analysis.

'Oh I didn't, is it your birthday? How marvellously timed, then. Which one is it?'

'Thirty-six,' Edie said, reluctantly.

'Don't tell me the truth. Don't tell anyone the truth. You can pass for twenty-eight on a cloudy day, I'd say. Stick there until you're forced to go to thirty-four.'

Edie wasn't going to be won by flattery.

'If you didn't know it was my birthday, why have you brought me a cake?'

It was an impressive creation: a dome of mink-coloured icing, grooved by a fork and studded with walnuts. Margot had clearly gone to quite a bit of trouble.

'To say sorry, of course,' Margot said, gesturing again with the plate. Edie took it from her.

'This is an apology?'

'It's a cake, darling. A Café Noisette. Or a Noisy Café cake, as I call it. My ex-husband used to love it. It was about all he loved.'

'Why did you say those things in the first place?' Edie asked. If Meg was in, she was going to get hassle for this, and Margot had to pay off her arrears in full.

'I was a bit tiddly. Some people are simply born two drinks below par. It's a cross I bear.'

'Hmm,' Edie said, at a loss for what else she should say.

'Doing anything nice to celebrate?' Margot asked.

'Only the pub.'

'Have one for me, darling,' said Margot, stepping over the small dividing fence between the properties, and letting herself back into her house, 'Or two.'

Despite having already consumed enough sugar to give her the jitters, once in the kitchen, Edie cut a small slice of the Noisy Café. It was the best cake she'd ever tasted. Perhaps she could forgive Margot.

38

What would tonight have looked like if HarrogateGate had never happened? Edie wondered, while absently rotating a giant blusher brush under her eyes. It left her with two pantomime splotches of dusky rouge that she then had to disperse with her fingertips.

Thirty-six; not so much mid as late thirties. She'd have worked even harder to show she wasn't a sad single. Edie would've organised something like the Arts Club in Soho, squeezed herself into a full-skirted and deceptively tiny-waisted dress that required living off Cup-a-Soup and Diet Coke for a week beforehand.

Instagram would've been littered with pictures of her in the red-lit basement, drinking cocktails from teapots, or draped round Louis, Vogueing to eighties Madonna with assorted Ad Hoc-ers. If Jack and Charlotte had put in an appearance, Edie would have spent the whole evening conscious of his eyes on her. She would've been performing non-stop: 'I'm so fun and carefree.' Hah, the whole event would've been a performance.

And there would've been no Nick or Hannah. Edinburgh was a bit far for one-night occasions full of strangers from the advertising industry, and Nick was a London loather, whose wife never let him out.

Edie was struck by the surprising notion: she was much happier with this completely no-bragging-rights night in The Lion. It was a pleasant real ale pub with exposed red-brick walls and garlands of hop bine, walking distance from her dad's house. It was the kind of place where people brought rain-wet shaggy dogs in, and you might happen on a group of paunchy men hunched over an intense game of Magic: The Gathering, muttering spells.

When Edie, her dad and a taciturn Meg arrived, Hannah and Nick were already there. They waved them over to a table with a bottle of Prosecco in a bucket. Hannah was in a drapey pale caramel jersey dress, hair pulled back tight displaying her great bone structure; Nick in a thin blue shirt, buttoned to the collar. They looked like a bright, happy young couple, possibly liberated from little kids for a night.

They pushed a pile of presents across the table to Edie: a framed photo of the three of them in sixth form – 'Look at the denim and Doc Martens!' – a bottle of perfume, more chocolate.

'I was going to ask you what you wanted,' Meg mumbled and Edie said, hastily, 'Please don't spend your money on me! A drink's fine,' and Meg looked like she didn't know what to say and Edie fretted that sounded too patronising and dismissive.

Nick insisted on getting her dad's beer and Meg's cider.

Once settled, Hannah chatted to Meg, while their dad held forth on his adventures in home-brewing to Nick.

'The rhubarb wine was lethal. It didn't get you here,' he tapped his head, 'it attacked the extremities. Like a nerve poison. Left men unable to walk.'

'Would you make some more?' Nick asked. 'If you had an order?'

'I wouldn't toy with those forces again. Necromancy,' her dad said, shaking his head. 'It'd raise Aleister Crowley himself.'

Nick laughed and her dad looked gratified and Edie thought she should make him socialise more often. He was vehemently against online dating, or the *"How much is that doggy in the window" self-promotion*, as he called it. 'I'd rather drink ink.'

Meanwhile, Hannah asked Meg about work at the care home. Meg simply couldn't keep up the strop in the face of Hannah's intelligent, interested questions, nor could she get unwound at someone who saved lives for a living. Soon the table was harmony and half-cut bonhomie.

Edie glowed a bit. Her friends were so nice. This was so nice. In London, she had to strive to feel good enough for her social circle – carefully tidying the messier, less cosmetic parts of her life away. She'd never questioned whether the fact she felt had to put on an act was telling her something.

When they were two drinks down, Hannah leaned in to Edie and said: 'Nick told me about the Facebook group.'

Meg was temporarily out of earshot, petting a scrotty-looking Alsatian over by the umbrella stand.

Edie felt embarrassed about her online disgrace, even if in

front of her oldest and most internet-averse friend. Edie nodded. 'Lovely, wasn't it.'

Hannah looked at her, taking in Edie's discomfited expression.

'Here's an inspiring thought,' Hannah continued, in an encouraging tone. 'I've been thinking about your situation to avoid thinking about mine, I hope you don't mind.'

'I've been trying not to think about it either, so it's good someone is.'

'What if you and Jack had kissed, and the bride *hadn't* caught you?'

Edie paused. She'd never considered that option, in life's great (You Don't) Choose Your Own Adventure. 'Uh . . .?'

'This is what I predict. He'd have kissed you and enigmatically disappeared back into his oh-so-romantic wedding before you could ask him why. You'd be in a bigger, more confused mess about him than ever. He'd have gone off on his honeymoon to St Lucia and you'd be in purgatory. He returns a happily married man with a tan, and now you really shouldn't be putting him on the spot and asking what it's all about. So you bide your time, carry on playing along, thinking the answer will turn up eventually. Only he's given you this massive new bit of hope.'

Edie gazed balefully at the knots in the wooden table. 'I'd have been crying in some bar in Edinburgh after he led me another merry dance, and then the ultrasound picture would go up online, wouldn't it?'

'In one,' Hannah said.

Edie held her breath. All the times she'd wished so badly

for things to have gone differently, without thinking that *things continuing as they were* would've been pretty terrible, too. Jack was going to hurt her one way or another. This way, at least everyone knew what a bastard he'd been. She'd never considered that her desire for privacy and secrecy had suited Jack down to the ground.

'The way I see it, you're still better off going through what you're going through, than that fucker having got away with it yet again. Change is often painful.'

Edie nodded.

'You are frighteningly incisive.'

'Ah, well,' Hannah said. 'If I was that incisive I'd have made my own change and left Pete five years ago, before I was mean to him all the time. It's mainly the benefit of having no feelings involved in this, other than concern for you.'

At last orders, after Meg and their dad had taken their leave, Hannah announced they were 'definitely going dancing' and Edie caved easily, as drunk people do.

They got a cab and ended up in the Rescue Rooms, a nightclub-live-venue-bar-and-fast-food outlet rolled into one, with low ceilings and full of the smell of hormones and sticky soft drinks and chips.

Edie looked around the room and accepted 'old enough to be their mother' was no longer a figure of speech but a stark mathematical reality. They got some necessary hard spirits and seats by the dance floor, where the first up to throw their moves were wheeling around under a disco ball.

'Do you realise they're dancing to The Cure and New Order and The Smiths the way we danced to The Beatles and the Rolling Stones? Proper vintage parents' music,' Nick said.

Edie and Hannah groaned.

'Time bastard,' said Nick, shaking his head.

'Time bastard.' They clinked plastic glasses, and drank.

They ended up dancing to 'Billie Jean', in a swirl of dry ice that smelled like bacon crisps. With a cough-syrup-sweet plastic cup of rum and Coke in hand, Edie felt a swell of wholesome happiness that wasn't simply inebriation.

Struck by a theory that felt very clever when sloshed, she ushered Hannah and Nick to lean in, with a flapping wave of the hand: 'Some friendships, they're like favourite mix tapes. You hit pause but when you un-pause and play it again, you pick up right where you left it. You know all the right words and what comes next.'

They clinked plastic cups. 'I hope what comes next isn't a little bit of sick,' Nick said.

Woozy, Edie got her phone out: when you were elated, there were certain people you wanted to share it with.

The thought of the petition kept coming back to her, yet each time the recollection was dulled: it was losing its sting, by degrees.

When she piled in the door from the two a.m. taxi, sweaty, bleary of eye, internally chanting *two-Nurofen-and-water* to herself, she tripped over a gigantic all-white bouquet. Uh? She snapped the hallway light on and peered at the card on the box. *Edie Thompson.*

It was a ridiculously ostentatious, expensive arrangement: the kind of flowers you normally only saw on screen. An obscene mega-bushel of vintage roses, hyacinths, snapdragons and lilies. Edie would have to split it between three vases, at least. She pulled the florist's miniature envelope from the box and tore it open.

Happy birthday, Edie. I'm a fan. Elliot x

Edie clutched the card to herself and giggled foolishly. He liked her! A 'fan'? Wow. This was quite a souvenir.

Wait . . . Had she messaged Elliot tonight? She had a horrible feeling that she had. Edie pulled her phone out. No replies. With mounting trepidation, she looked at her sent texts. Oh Jesus, she hadn't asked him if he extreme waxed, had she?

Elliot! I am SO DRUNBK. I just wanted to say thank you for being so nice feel like I'm finally getting myself together. FRIENDS. It's all about friends isn't it? The good ones I mean. I love them so much <3 PS: I'm Cardinal Woolly. PPS I have to ask you something personal next time I see you. It's about balls & grooming haha. Edie xxx

Oh. God. He *used* to be a fan.

39

Edie was sweating out the hangover in the garden with her pulpy crime novel and a toasted Quorn ham sandwich when Meg joined her, carrying a portable CD player and a CD.

Edie raised her sunglasses and watched as Meg put the disc in, hit 'play' and sat back, silver Birkenstocks aloft on the lounger, hands crossed on stomach, eyes closed. The volume was a provocative act and Edie chose not to be provoked. She picked up the CD case.

'Balearic Wellness Moods,' she read aloud, over the burble. 'Doesn't seem very *you*, somehow.'

'It was a quid in one of the chazzas in Sherwood,' Meg said, not opening her eyes. It carried on thumping out its chilled-out vibes at a not-very-chilled out level and Edie scowled and tried to concentrate on murders in East London. Eventually she became aware of noise layered on noise, masculine tones and a brass band that weren't coming from Ibiza.

Meg opened her eyes and said: 'What the . . .?'

She turned her CD down a notch and the unmistakable vocal stylings of Frank Sinatra could be made out, soaring across the fence. There was some lusty singing along. *My kind of town, Chicago is . . .*

'It's that woman!' Meg said, turning her CD off and jumping up to peer over the fence. 'Hello?' she said. 'Can you stop being so petty and pathetic and turn your antiquated crap down, please?'

'Meg . . .' Edie said, in a warning tone, and was ignored.

'I'm enjoying a nice old singalong,' she could hear Margot in the distance, 'Same as you.'

'I'm not singing along!'

'Well no, there's no tune to yours, is there? Shame.'

'You're only playing your music to ruin me playing mine!'

'You playing yours is spoiling mine, duck. We are at what they call, an impasse.'

'Turn it off!'

'Ooh I love this one. *IS MY IDEA OF, NUTHIN TO DOOOOO . . .*'

'Fuck's sake,' Meg said, grabbing her CD player and marching indoors, as 'I Get a Kick Out of You' echoed around the garden, somewhat appropriately.

Margot's face appeared over the fence.

'Fifteen–love to me! Thanks to Frank.'

Edie tried not to smile.

'Have you two ever considered a truce?'

'Where's the fun in that?' Margot said, arms dangling over the partition, displaying a flashy bracelet. 'Whatcha readin'?'

'It's about a serial killer who poisons people in 1950s East End London.'

'I like gore but I prefer romances. Absolute sucker for a bodice ripper. Hey, tell your actor to be in one of those.'

'I'll pass it on.' Edie got a vision of Elliot as a muddy, sweaty Heathcliff, or as Regency gentleman, buttoned up and storming on about his restrained passion, and her heart did a little patter, as she winced. *Why did she send that stupid text, why . . .*

Edie's dad wandered out, a book under his arm, disgruntled look on his face.

'Meg says she's been chased out of the garden?'

Edie sat up straighter. 'She got a taste of her own medicine, more like.'

'Edith,' her dad sighed slightly, 'this never-ending civil war is unnecessary, you know. We can all rub along, if we try.'

'Dad!' Edie said, losing her temper, with immediate effect. 'I didn't do anything to chase her out of the garden, quite the opposite. I put up with her noise pollution and Margot—' she indicated the beady-eyed septuagenarian and her Dad noticed her, for the first time, 'fought back with some Big Band and Meg huffed off. She started it.'

'Ah, Margot,' her dad said. 'Hello.'

'Morning, Gerald.'

'Dad,' Edie said, unable to contain this any longer, even with an audience, 'why do you pander to Meg, every time she has a whinge? It's obvious she's being stroppy and unreasonable. You make it worse by indulging her.'

'I don't indulge her, I merely try to understand, and not pick sides.'

'Sometimes sides have to be picked.' Edie loved her mild-mannered father, but felt this was a consistent failing of his, all the same. For example, she could've done with seeing

Auntie Dawn being comprehensively told to stow it in an overhead locker the day of the funeral, though she appreciated her dad was vulnerable at the time.

'Hear hear!' Margot said. 'A pandered-to child is a monstrous child.'

'This child is thirty-one and my family is my business, thank you,' her dad said. He addressed Edie: 'I give up. I renounce my role as this household's Ban Ki-moon. May you scrap freely among yourselves and have your weapons uninspected.'

He retreated back into the house and Margot said: 'You've done nothing wrong, my love. The girl needs telling.'

Edie made noises of thankfulness while wondering if Margot's approval was a good sign or not.

'Can I ask you a little favour?' Margot said. Aha, Edie might've known. 'Next time you go to the shops, could you pick me up some lottery tickets? Here, I've written my numbers down.' Her head ducked down and reappeared, a scrap of paper clutched between magenta nails. Edie took it. 'Mr Singh usually goes for me but he's in Hyderabad til Wednesday week.'

'No trouble,' Edie said. 'You play every week?'

'Without fail,' Margot said. 'Never know when your luck might turn. Mine's been bad so long I am due a little windfall.'

'Has it?'

Margot disappeared and Edie thought she might've gone, but she reappeared after a few seconds' delay with the necessary fag.

'I had a nest egg, back in the day. Money from my theatre show, and I got a nice sum when Gordon and I divorced. I fell in with this absolute rotter, who convinced me to invest it in some ridiculous boondoggle . . .'

Edie loved Margot's vocab.

'And that was that. First the money flew up the spout, then he did. I was a very silly girl.'

'Is that why you moved to Nottingham?'

Margot leaned back and tapped her fag.

'My parents lived here for a few years when I was a child, lovely place on The Ropewalk. It's some solicitor's offices now. London's very spendy, of course, and Nottingham was the only other city I felt I knew. And I had barely a bean to my name. So here I am.' I simply chose from an *A to Z*. I thought Forest Fields sounded marvellously bucolic.'

Edie laughed. 'Imagine if you'd picked The Meadows.' It was funny how tough areas tended to have these pretty names, like the smoke-stained tower block in Judge Dredd's Mega-City One dystopia being called Peach Trees.

Edie felt a mixture of sorrow and admiration for Margot: things had not gone her way, but there was admirable *sang froid* in her wicked sense of humour and determination to enjoy her vices.

'You've gone a little pink, darling,' Margot said. 'I'd head back in. That sort of pale skin wrinkles like tissue paper.'

Edie smiled, put her sunnies on and got up. As she walked back to the kitchen, Edie could hear Margot humming to herself.

'My kind of town, Nottingham is . . .'

40

There ought to be a modern word coined to describe the greasy, snaky, clammy anxiety of being flatly ignored after a misjudged message, Edie thought.

After spending Saturday morning relentlessly checking her phone for a reply, she'd braced herself and sent a follow-up text to Elliot thanking him for the bouquet, and wince-apologising for her previous. And, nothing. For the whole of the weekend.

At least with less than diligent correspondents, you could console yourself they simply hadn't got round to it. However, despite his vastly busy international superstar lifestyle, Edie had always found Elliot prompt with his replies. This was unlike him. It was now Monday. She had to assume the personal testicle-grooming query was to blame.

Argh, why had she sent such a thing, *why*? How was it possible Drunk Brain could seem like Sober Brain and yet be so different? It was the most sinister impersonation of your usual judgment imaginable, taking place in your own head.

When she'd typed that text, Edie was high on life and full

of fun, unstoppable: convinced that obliquely inquiring after the hairiness of someone's scrotum was top larks. Now, she wanted to dissolve with shame.

She wished she could see the flower-strewn house without it having negative associations.

Meg assumed Edie was deep in self-congratulation, of course, and observed: 'He'll have got some lackey to send those. Just pushing a button, for him.'

'Yes, probably, thanks, Meg,' said Edie, still nursing her hangover, both physical and psychological. Meg chuntered about the air miles involved in exotic flowers and lest the Sinatra incident had left any doubt, Meg was making it clear that the amnesty around Edie's friends was firmly over.

Edie couldn't stop herself looking at her phone every five minutes, even though the blank screen was an ongoing rebuke. Oh God, even if you call me a dreadful arse, say *something*, she thought. There was nothing worse than nothing.

Edie had plenty of time to write, at least, and the work-in-progress manuscript on her laptop was looking pretty good, if she did say so herself. Her choice of quotes from her entertaining conversations with Elliot had brought out his sardonic, Northern side, without making him sound sarcastic, conceited or chippy. The insights into what it was like to get very very famous, very very fast, were genuinely interesting. There was zero gushing over Elliot being the Olivier of his generation, in the body of a Greek god, and yet he was coming out of it really well, she thought.

They'd yet to tackle the tricky chapters on romance – Elliot was dodging them, and so was Edie, what with the giant GAY?

question hovering over it – but other than that, this was an elegant solution that pleased everybody. The response, following some regularly emailed chapter updates, from the subject himself, his agent and the publisher had been highly positive.

Although the response from Elliot might be about to change. Edie writhed: what if he'd formally complained about her? It seemed unlikely, but then so did days on end of silence.

When her mobile finally rang with an unrecognised number on Monday evening, Edie's nerves did somersaults. *Sing Hosannah!* Maybe Elliot had lost his phone or something? Perhaps he never even got the text?! LET JOY BE UNCONFINED.

'Hello?' she said, tentatively but eagerly.

A female voice.

'Is that Edie Thompson?'

'Yes?'

'This is Sally, I'm Archie Puce's assistant. He'd like a word with you.'

'Sure.' Edie paused, waiting for Archie to be handed the phone. Silence. 'Now?'

'I'll send you a car. Where are you?'

'Oh. OK.'

Edie dictated her address and sat fidgeting until an unmarked dark Audi drew up outside the front window. On the journey, she fretted about what could require an abrupt summons with the Puce-inator. Last time she'd been faced with his volcanic temper, Elliot had stood between them. She didn't fancy a repeat, presumably without the person of greater status there to protect her.

This couldn't be to do with the testes text, could it? Her nerves told her *Yes, you fool!* but she couldn't fathom why Archie would've got involved. Was Elliot outsourcing her dismissal? Was she to be sacked – over discussing someone's sack?

The car with the inscrutable driver was driving her south, out of the rapidly darkening city, and she started to feel very uncomfortable.

'Er, sorry. Where are we going?' Edie asked, slightly apologetically, as they left the ring road.

'To the set,' said the driver.

She'd missed a few pages here, without a doubt.

'Where's that?'

'Wollaton Hall,' the driver said, in a terse manner that didn't imply he wanted to shoot the shit with Edie on the way there.

Her phone buzzed with a message from Jack. How times had changed: his message couldn't have been more unwelcome.

E.T. I couldn't get to the bottom of the Ian Connor thing, I tried, I'm really sorry. Charlie doesn't know who he is either, but you can appreciate I had to be tactful about why/who I was asking for. She agreed the comment about your mum was beyond. That page is gone. I had a big go about it. I did find this Twitter account, don't know if you could contact him there? I might leave it though, he's clearly an arsehole. (Anyone who's confused social media with the Yellow Pages is worse than ISIS, in my book.) Hope you're doing OK. Jx

Edie followed the link to a Twitter account. Another cartoon character avatar, this time Roadrunner. It was bland stuff, mostly whinging about the London Underground, and as Jack said, trying to crowd source answers to boring questions about the best place to buy Hunter wellies.

When she scrolled far back enough she saw Ian Connor's initial posts —**@EdieThomson how does it feel knowing you ruined a woman's life you slutty cow?** Swiftly followed by **@EdieThomson sorry I thought you were someone else.**

A thought occurred: if these were the first tweets, then the account had been initially set up to abuse her? It gave Edie a spinal chill.

She clicked her phone off again. This was a fantastically unhelpful pastime on her journey into the unknown here.

As they swept up the long drive through rolling parkland to the illuminated stately home, the buzz of lights and trucks around it, Edie's heart was in her throat. This face-to-face was hardly likely to be good news. *Why was Elliot ignoring her?*

41

The car pulled up and announcements were muttered through rolled-down windows. It was a different mood, this time. Edie sensed she was no longer an irrelevance, milling at the edges. A fair-haired, middle-aged woman was stood waiting to briskly convey Edie to a trailer at the perimeter of the set, her expression grim.

'Nice to meet you!' Edie said, hoping to spark a conversation and possibly a hint of what this was about. The woman pretended not to have heard her.

Inside, Archie Puce was pacing the narrow space, hat on table. The woman shut the door behind them and retreated behind Archie. She stood with arms folded, staring accusingly at Edie.

'Hello again!' Archie said, faux-cheerily, without any warmth. 'It's the Yoko Ono of my little television production! How's the bed-in for peace going? Because I feel fairly un-fucking-peaceful.'

'What?' Edie said.

Archie prowled right up to her. He wasn't physically large,

just incredibly imposing given his malign, livewire energy.

'Let me make this very simple, "Edie Thompson". Either encourage lover boy to leave your side and come back to work, or I will tell powerful people in this industry, who aren't blessed with my gentle nature, that you're responsible for our current unscheduled and very fucking costly hiatus. And trust me, they will treat you as tenderly as a beer-can chicken at a tramps' barbecue.'

Edie struggled to work out what was being said, aside from the vivid poultry-vagrancy threat.

'How am I responsible? I don't know where Elliot is,' she said.

'In bed, where you left him?' Archie said, eyes boggling with *j'accuse*.

'I'm not sleeping with him!'

'Oh, we all must've imagined the very low-budget remake of *An Officer and a Gentleman* you staged on my set a few days ago. I mean, I'm always picking women up! I don't even know most of them. I see them, I put them over my shoulder like Captain fucking Caveman and off we pop.'

'That wasn't anything romantic, I'd had some bad news.'

'Yes, I'm sure. Some bad and yet strangely sexy news.'

Jesus. Where angels feared to tread, Archie Puce was quad biking.

'Look, no less authority than the women in make-up say you're the only female in his life. So stop fucking flirting with me and tell me WHERE YOUR BLOODY BORE-FRIEND IS BEFORE I BECOME JUST SLIGHTLY TETCHY.'

Aha. Edie spotted the tactic: bluster you know more than you do, shake the target up, and see how many marbles roll out in the panic. She refused to quail before him.

'I'm ghost-writing his autobiography. You can't go round accusing people of shagging with no evidence!' Edie said, thinking as she said it, *you absolutely could*. 'I'm only working with him – I'm what she is to you,' she gestured towards the glowering onlooker woman.

'Sally is my wife.'

'Oh.' Bloody hell. Imagine being Archie's assistant and his wife. Mind you, she was probably the only woman he wouldn't sack.

'OK,' Edie said. 'If I was in bed with Elliot when you rang, why would I come out here? Wouldn't I fob you off and go back to my X-rated activities?'

She had him there. Archie pursed his lips and said nothing.

'What happened, when did Elliot disappear?' Edie asked, because she really wanted to know, actually. What if some sick superfan with duct tape and a Stanley knife had him in a basement, and was right now dancing around to 'Stuck in the Middle'? The thought tied her gut in knots.

'The Scarlet Pimpernel fucker got a phone call on Friday afternoon, no one knows who from . . .' Archie paused to glare at Edie '. . . and did one. Left. Off he fucked. His parents are somewhere in the Caribbean and his brother's skiing, so he's not with them. He was seen once that evening going into his house, coming out with a bag. We've been filming around his absence using his body double in back-of-head shots, but we're out of time and over budget. Forgive me if this is very "movie biz" technical, but sometimes you need the actual fucker who's starring in the thing, actually here.'

'I texted him about something on Friday night and didn't get a reply, either. That's all I know,' Edie said.

There was a brief silence where Edie felt she might be finally being believed.

'Well this is fucking great, isn't it?' Archie said to his wife. 'If he's shagging the last one, he's balls deep in Bel Air. Why do I work with actors, Sally? Tell me that? I'd rather run a cattery on the fucking moon. It's like they give Equity cards out to people who need Velcro-fastening shoes.'

Wait, Elliot could be back with Heather? He'd possibly absconded across the pond? Without saying goodbye? Edie felt surprisingly churned up, and hurt. He'd sat there and said those slighting things about Heather, then she'd snapped her slender fingers and he'd gone racing over the Atlantic? Jesus, actors *were* giant fakes. Team Archie.

'Alright,' Archie pinched the bridge of his nose, 'do me a favour. Try to get hold of him again, would you? And put some emotion into it. Really remind him you have breasts.'

Edie grimaced.

'Call it an old man's hunch, but I think you're going to have more luck than we have,' Archie said. 'And when you do get hold of him, wherever he is, tell him unless he wants to spunk his career into a crusty sports sock, he'll get back on this fucking set, pronto. Alright. BYE.'

A sombre Sally guided Edie back to the Audi. Was Edie

imagining that everyone they passed paused in what they were doing, and stared at her?

In the car, she turned the situation over in her head.

Elliot's phone was probably out of charge, on another continent, lying on the floor in a heap of hastily discarded clothes at Heather's. Yuck. Edie's disappointed anger at this development was a useful antidote to her embarrassment. At a loss for what else to do, she texted him again.

Elliot, I don't know where you are or what's going on, but Archie thinks I have something to do with it & just hauled me in for the hairdryer treatment. If you're not dead, could you at least let him know that much isn't true? Cheers. Hope you're alright. Ex

She stuffed her phone back into her pocket. She felt it buzz within seconds and thought: It can't be him. Her heart leapt: oh my God, it was him!

Shit, I'm really sorry, Edie. Where are you?

In a car, leaving the set in Wollaton. Where are you?

In a hotel in the city. Do you have time to see me right now?

He wasn't in California! Or with Heather. Edie felt incredibly relieved, aglow even.

Yes! Sure.

Tell the driver to take you to the Park Plaza. Don't tell him who you're meeting. I'm checked in under the name Donald Twain, just come up to the room.x

OK! See you in a bit. x PS 'Donald Twain'? Haha.

You clearly don't know your classic films, Thompson. No wonder you want me to do the playboy gynae one. See you in a bit xx

42

Edie had a moment of thinking like a secret agent and asked the driver to drop her off in Market Square, then walked the short distance to Elliot's hotel. Archie might ask the driver where he took her, and it did sound as if he had Elliot's parents' house staked out.

As the lift took her to his room on the fourth floor, Edie's jubilation at her invitation to see him receded. What if he was having a full-scale nervo? What if his room was littered with evidence of a painkiller habit, or some other very American way that 'troubled young stars' killed themselves? And Elliot swore her to secrecy, and she had to choose between breaking his most desperate confidence and being partly responsible for his premature demise?

Elliot answered the door in a grey T-shirt and black jeans, looking embattled and tired and yet also like he was doing the 'behind the shoot' photos for an *Esquire* cover. Edie's stomach did a lazy forward roll. The room beyond was softly lit, the window open to the nighttime air, and Edie was struck by how many women would be delighted to be here. And men, for that matter. She was mainly apprehensive, however: to the point of being slightly scared.

'Ah, it's good to see a friendly face,' Elliot said, with a rueful smile.

'I'm not sure if it is friendly yet, Archie gave me a serious bollocking,' Edie said, talkative with nerves, smiling back.

'Oh God, did he? I'm really sorry. Why the fuck does he think you're responsible for my not turning up to work?'

Well, quite. Sadly Elliot had summed it up. She feared plenty of people might've put Archie straight on the likelihood of Elliot being with Edie, if only Archie didn't terrify others to the point of speechlessness. Edie definitely didn't want to see the shock-horror on Elliot's face when she explained what had been assumed, so she merely shrugged.

'I'm hitting the mini-bar miniatures, feel free to join me,' Elliot said.

'I'm OK, thanks.'

The room seemed mercifully free of drug paraphernalia, unless you counted a mini Jack Daniels and half-empty Coke bottle, next to a toothpaste mug.

He poured a dinky Smirnoff vodka into it and threw himself down on to a chair.

Edie lowered herself on to the edge of the double bed.

'What's going on? Who was the phone call from? Archie said you took a call and left?'

'It was my publicist.' Elliot drank.

He didn't expand on this statement and Edie didn't know what she was supposed to ask first.

'. . . Why aren't you at home?'

'Because there's some mope sat in a car across the street watching the house. Suspect it's something to do with Jan. Or maybe it's just press. Either way, it spooked me.'

'I think that might be Archie.'

'What?!'

'He said "you'd been seen" getting your things on Friday evening. So he must've sent someone to your house.'

Elliot rubbed his eyes. 'God. It's been a horrible weekend, Edie.'

At a loss for what to say, Edie waited.

'When I said I didn't want the woman writing the unauthorised biography prying into my life, there was a particular thing I didn't want her prying into.'

Yup. His sex life. She wanted so much to give him a hug and to say that many had probably guessed anyway.

'The call was to say the shit is about to hit the fan and it's going to come out. I shouldn't have freaked, but I did. This job. You know, sometimes I really regret having chosen this job, Edie. And you can't say so, because then you're ungrateful.'

'You *can* say so,' Edie said, forcefully. 'You can say it to me, and kick a pillow round the room or something.'

Elliot smiled. 'Thanks.'

'Elliot, you'll get past this. Keeping the secret is obviously not worth the toll it's taking on you. You might even feel better once it's out in the open.'

'Mmm, I'm not sure it's that simple,' Elliot said.

'I know. I get it,' Edie said, with a vigorous and encouraging nod.

'Wait. Do you know about this . . .? And if so, who from?'

Elliot spoke sharply, the idea simultaneously occurring to him and angering him, and Edie sensed danger.

'No!'

Once again, Edie was rueing her lack of preparation.

'. . . I just meant that life hasn't always been easy for you as it might look, and maybe keeping this secret is why.'

'"This secret"? It does *sound* like you know, Thompson.'

Elliot looked serious, yet as he'd never called her a nickname before – OK, it wasn't a nickname as such, but he had jocularly referred to her by her surname – Edie relaxed a little.

'I don't. But isn't it possible I could've intuited it?'

'Intuited it? Like an astrologer, or a clairvoyant? Or did you hack my phone?'

Wow, had he not heard of gaydar?

'I'm a writer, and we've talked a lot.'

'Yeeees?' Elliot said, with a *pray continue* tone.

'Sometimes you get a sixth sense.'

'Pretty powerful sixth sense. More like a third eye.'

Oh for goodness' sake. Because he was such a bleeding raw hunk of unreconstructed machismo?

Edie plunged on.

'. . . I'm also a woman.'

Elliot boggled. 'All the secrets are coming out tonight, eh. What the hell does that mean?'

'I mean, like I said: you get a feeling, don't you?'

Edie had been inching into this chilly water and now it was up to her waist. Soon it'd be up to her neck.

Elliot was half laughing, half spluttering in incredulity. 'No, sorry, I don't know what you mean. A feeling. Have you got cosmic ovaries or something? Or like in that film, the chest that can forecast the weather? I'll be honest with you, I thought weather boobs were fictional.'

Hah, see! Only a gay man would be so confident to refer to her mammaries in comedic fashion, and never once glance down at them during doing so.

Edie hoped he wasn't going to be devastated when she told him she knew, but it was unavoidable now.

'Elliot. I know you're gay.' *Boom. Drops mic,* Edie thought, as the kids say.

Elliot's jaw dropped instead.

'. . . What? How?!'

Edie opened her mouth and nothing came out. She didn't expect to be asked to raise her evidence, she thought it would be enough she knew.

'Because you don't want to talk about being with women?' she offered.

Elliot gasp-laughed. 'So straight men sit around saying, "Oh aye look at the bangers on that, let me tell you about some classic intercourse I've had"? Where did you conduct your studies prior to me, Walkabout bars?'

Edie flushed hard red, up to her hairline.

'You think that's the secret, I'm in the closet?' Elliot said.

Edie nodded and wanted to fly out of the window. She could tell Elliot wasn't feigning this response.

'Wow,' Elliot said, one hand on his head. 'But we *have* talked about relationships . . . why was I with Heather, for one?'

Edie cringed.

'. . . Publicity? You said it was very . . . business-based.'

Elliot's face fell further. The curtains blew in the night breeze as Elliot absorbed this insult and Edie wanted to kick herself. How hard would it have been to simply ask him what he was talking about? No, she had to call him a secret botter with a beard. To his face, in a time of torment. Five out of five, Edie.

'This really wasn't the understanding I thought it was, was it. You had the same views about me as people who post below the line on the internet.'

Elliot made a sad grimace face. Edie felt terrible.

'I'm sorry! I didn't think it was a bad thing.'

'You just thought I was a liar, sure.'

'I'm sorry,' Edie said. 'I added up two and two and got seventeen. You know, once you follow a line of thought . . . argh. *Sorry*.'

There was a heavy pause and Elliot sighed.

'No, Edie, look. I'm sorry. I shouldn't have got you to guess. I'm being a mardy selfish bastard and lashing out at the one person who's in front of me, who also happens to be the one person trying to be understanding. I don't mind being thought gay, obviously, though I'm disappointed you thought I was closeted. There's also a bit of wounded masculine pride involved here that I've obviously not been coming over the way I thought I was.'

He gave Edie an apologetic 'forgive me' smile and she squirmed, because he was absolutely impossible not to love, when he was being self-deprecating. And he wasn't safely playing for the other team. She felt her stomach cave in.

'I mean. Why wouldn't I be out and proud and shopping at Santa Monica's Farmers' Market with my NBA player boyfriend, in matching muscle vests?'

Edie laughed and really wanted to give him a hug now. Order and harmony had been restored. Apart from the other giant unsaid thing.

'If it isn't about sexuality, what has the other biographer found?' Edie asked.

'My father,' Elliot said.

43

Pause.

'Your dad? He's away on a trip, isn't he?'

'She found my real father. Ugh, I hate the word "real". My real dad is my dad on the cruise, yes. The other man, the one who contributed to my DNA. Him. You definitely don't want a drink?'

'Maybe a gin,' Edie said, feeling she damn well needed it now. Elliot poured out a Gordon's with a fizzy tonic, the froth almost spilling over. He stared at the carpet.

'I found out I was adopted when I was eleven. I'd had a fight with Fraz and used to stomp off and climb the ladder to the loft. I always had dramatic tendencies, even then.'

Edie said nothing, riveted.

'I was poking around and I turned up adoption papers, for someone called Carl, from St Helens. At first I thought my parents had taken in a son who we didn't know about. Maybe he died, I thought. Maybe I shouldn't ask them and drag it all up and upset them. But I think, deep down, I knew that wasn't it.'

He looked at Edie and she had an urge to lean over and squeeze his hand.

She resisted it.

'Not least because it was my date of birth on the form. Yeah, DERP, right?'

Edie still said nothing, as she feared anything she said would come out sounding glib, or small. Elliot ran his hands through his hair.

'I mean, there's me as an already highly strung, imaginative, self-styled outsider and then I stumble across this information. My mind starts whirring: what if Fraser was adopted too? Then I looked up the old family albums, my mum in the maternity unit holding him, still got the cannula in her hand. No, he was theirs. Then I recalled there were no photos like that of me, with them, at that age. The odd Polaroid of me in a crib that didn't look like the one they put Fraser in. When I asked why it was: "No one took as many photos in those days, oh there will be more, somewhere." I realised I'd been fobbed off.'

Elliot drew breath.

'I slept with the papers under my pillow for three weeks or so, and then me and my mum were having words and I just came out with it. I wasn't intending to. Part of me still hoped there was some other explanation, and she'd laugh and say oh is THAT what you thought, haha.'

'. . . What did your mum say?'

'She was really upset. Devastated, in fact. They'd made a decision it was better for me not to know and of course, me finding out, and like that? Worst of all worlds.'

Edie nodded.

'She and Dad sat me down and told me the full unexpurgated version. I was adopted after my alcoholic father crashed a car while blind-pissed and killed my mother.'

Elliot looked at her and Edie stared back, open-mouthed. All this time she'd been thinking Elliot's life was charmed, uncomplicated and, before fame, uneventful.

'She was in the front seat, no seat belt. He survived. And amazingly, I survived, given I was in the back without a child seat. They found me in the footwell with barely a scratch on me.'

Elliot lifted an arm and pointed to a tiny mark near his elbow. 'I think I might've done this, but I'm not sure.'

'Oh, Elliot . . . God,' Edie said, with huge feeling. She remembered that solemn, lamp-eyed little boy from the family photos. He did look darkly different to the rest of the fair, middle-class clan.

'I should say, I can't remember any of this,' Elliot said, with a hand on the back of his neck. 'It's as much a story to me as it is to you. I was two years old.'

'Why hadn't your parents told you?' Edie said. Adding, hastily: 'I'm not judging, just asking.'

'They adopted me thinking they couldn't have kids themselves and my mum almost immediately fell pregnant with Fraz. They told me they uhmmed and ahhed and the scan showed it was a boy, and they thought, why not bring us up simply as brothers – they weren't going to treat us any differently, after all. I think they were in turmoil, to be honest: overwhelmed. They had years of wanting a family they couldn't have. Then when the adoption finally came through, my mum was unexpectedly expecting. From nought to sixty. It wasn't the greatest choice in hindsight, but there it is. It was made with good intentions.'

Edie nodded.

'And I think they thought they would tell me, at the right time. But the right time never arrived. It went on too long and became too big a thing to be broken to me. They worried I'd be really angry they hadn't told me, that I'd spin out. Push them away.' Elliot paused. 'Something I now have a lot of sympathy with, given my own choices.'

'. . . How do you mean?'

Elliot raised heavy-lidded eyes to hers.

'Fraser still doesn't know. I asked them not to tell him.'

The curtains riffled in the breeze and Edie repeated: 'Fraser doesn't know you're adopted?'

'No,' Elliot said. 'I begged my parents to keep it secret. We were scrapping a lot back then. Just big brother, little brother trivial stuff, but you know. I wasn't having the greatest time at school, either, and if it got out, if Fraz talked to his friends or whatever, I didn't want to become known for being "different" because of the adoption as well. Sounds so silly now, but when you're eleven, it's huge. You just want to fit in, you know?'

Edie nodded; yes, she did.

'And I wanted some time to come to terms with it myself before Fraser found out. I was worried that he'd feel differently about me, that I'd be the odd one out in my own family. You know, every time you've questioned your differences – *why was*

I not sporty like Fraz, why was I not confident like him – I felt like every time he looked at me, he'd see that story. That every time we fought, he'd think, *Well, you shouldn't even be here.*'

Elliot's eyes looked shiny for a moment and Edie twitched with the urge to help in some way, though she couldn't.

'Aaaannnnd. Can you guess the rest? As time went on, it was never the right time. It had gone on so long that not having told him became just as big a scandal, and one I was responsible for. Imagine, Edie . . .'

Edie felt the force of the trust he was placing in her. Although maybe there was no one else?

'. . . The drama stuff took off and I was more different from Fraz than ever. Home was the one place I was just myself. Fraser used to look at me funny in those early days when I was on TV, as it was. There was no way I was going to make that harder. "*I'm not your brother.*" It's a big bloody chat, isn't it?'

'You *are* his brother, though! You're as much his brother as Meg is my sister.'

Elliot smiled at her in a fond, sad way. 'Yeah.'

Edie recalled what Fraser had said about 'It was like he didn't belong to us any more.' Edie might go back and remove that line. Would they have to cover the adoption in the book, if it was going to be in Jan's? She'd worry about that later.

'And your da— *father*, he never came looking for you?'

Elliot took a sip of his drink. 'Nope. Nor me for him. So until this lovely bin-diver of a writer, Jan Clarke, called him a few months back, my father didn't know I was his son. Good of her to take it upon herself to break the news.'

He rubbed his eyes and gave a pinched, murderous scowl into the middle distance. Edie remembered the expression from *Blood & Gold*.

'*What*?' said Edie, disbelieving, 'How could he not know?'

Elliot picked up his mug again.

'He's not seen me for three decades. I presume the adoption agency would've told him who I was placed with if he asked, but as far as I know, he never cared enough to ask. I've grown up, I look different, I have a different name. No reason he would recognise me.'

Edie tried to imagine having a magazine thrust under your nose and being told Prince Wulfroarer was your long-lost spawn. She didn't have much sympathy for Elliot's father but it must've been quite the mind-blower.

'And if you say that I must've known this'd come out sooner or later, I did. I've been a twat. I buried my head in the sand and hoped it'd all go away and that Jan wouldn't be thorough enough to get hold of my birth certificate. My publicist has been pretty forthright that I've made it much worse for myself. You're supposed to control this sort of thing. Not wait until your manslaughtering father's trying to call your people from prison.'

'What? That was the phone call? The one that made you leave the set?'

'Yeah. He's realised there's money to be made in going to the tabloids and selling his story. It's now a race between him and Jan to see who can get into print first. My father will likely win because he's up for parole in three weeks.'

'Oh my God.'

'I know. So I've got to tell Fraser. Time's up. I've been such an idiot, Edie. You must think I'm an absolute goon.'

Edie shook her head, vigorously.

'No, I don't. I think you had to make a big decision, as a child. Your parents made a bigger one as adults that they probably regret now. It's not your fault. It was a lot to bear.'

Elliot stared at her.

'You're so kind, you are.'

Edie almost flinched at the pleasure of him saying this, with such sincerity.

'It's honestly what I think. You're being too hard on yourself,' she said.

'Yeah I know. And you're kind, so it comes out that way.'

Edie glowed. She hadn't been made to feel like a good person for quite some time.

'. . . Fraz is skiing right now so I can't get hold of him. He's back next week. I guess I should go down to Surrey. I can't do anything else about this mess, until I've done that.'

'It'll be OK,' Edie said, though it sounded rather thin.

'It'll be OK, or it won't,' Elliot said, flatly. 'I won't blame him for being absolutely raging with me. It wasn't fair for him to not know something the other three of us did, for all those years. And when that dust's settled, we'll see if things can ever feel the same again.'

There was a pause.

Elliot set his cup back down. 'God, I'm absolutely shitting it about Jan realising Fraser doesn't know. Imagine the coup if she got to break the news to him.'

Elliot looked at Edie, morose.

'I've been jumping like a cat every time my phone goes. And it'd be my fault. A stranger being able to hurt my family like this – it's all my fault.'

'No, it isn't your fault. You did the best you could at the time. All of us are making it up as we go along.' Edie paused. 'Fraser didn't have to find out he was adopted, did he? He should have some sympathy with you, too.'

Elliot leaned over and clinked his toothpaste mug against Edie's. They shared a moment of complete understanding and Edie felt a feeling she chose not to name, for the time being.

44

'Room service!' a voice rang out, startling them out of the intimate mood.

'Oh yeah, I got a club sandwich. Do you want anything?'

Edie shook her head and there was a pause while the door was opened, plates were put on the side table, a tip handed over and the door closed again. Elliot sat back down.

'Of course, as well as my brother hating me, there's the chance the public will hate me after my dad's story, too. My publicist explained, if my dad positions himself as the victim, it's very hard to get into tit-for-tat denials without looking like the bully. I'm going to have to "rise above", which means staying silent while horrible untrue things are said about me.'

Edie, mindful of how recently she'd ineptly made the hidden homosexuality allegation, wanted to be careful how she handled this.

'But. Your father killed your mum, and almost killed you. Surely people won't think he has much place to criticise you?'

'Yeah, that's what I said,' Elliot said. 'Again, it was gently pointed out to me he'll play that as *his* tragedy. You know, first I lost my wife, then my son.' Elliot stood up, inspected his club sandwich, picked up a triangle of it, and sat back down. 'It's so nice to see a decent human being, you know. All I've been doing all weekend is talking to people in Los Angeles about disaster recovery, and brooding. Very moody, like,' Elliot did his 'Crumple Zone' face and then grinned.

He bit into the bread and Edie smiled, shyly. She so wanted to be the friend he needed. She guessed pretty much any woman would, right now.

'You're very well liked and I think people know the way the grubby exposé works,' Edie said. 'Like you said to me, goodness will get you through it.'

'Ah, yeah, but that's obviously not true, I was just saying it to cheer you up.'

Edie laughed.

'How's that all going?' Elliot asked.

For the umpteenth time, Edie cringed at him knowing. If only she hadn't checked her phone at that time, on that day.

'It's still going. I feel like I know something about having to stay quiet while people say awful untrue things about you,' Edie caught herself. 'On a much smaller scale, obviously.'

'The feelings are the same. They don't scale up whether it's twenty people hating you or two million. I'm more worried about Fraser than I am about the entire readership of a newspaper. Joking aside, Edie. You did nothing to deserve what's happening to you. You know that?'

Edie smiled, thinly. 'I did kiss someone's husband on their wedding day.'

'Yeah OK, that was ripe.' Elliot smiled. 'Wow, he must've really wanted to kiss you though, eh?'

Edie flushed hard red and mumbled *Maybe erm perhaps he was intoxicated*.

Elliot didn't reply, and Edie found the fact he was thinking about her, concentrating solely on her, made her incredibly self-conscious.

There was a pregnant pause, filled with the muted acoustics from the next-door room: a flushing toilet and low hum of a television.

Edie swallowed and cast around for something to say.

'So you've never met your dad?'

'Yeah I went to the prison, on Friday. It was a spooky experience. He looks like me, played by Catweazle. He did some crocodile tears and then we got down to business. What amount am I going to hand over for him not to do the story?'

Edie grimaced. Finally in touch your father after all those years, and he tries to extort money from you. You could rationalise he was a desperate wreck, but as Edie knew, there was that shortfall between emotions and logic.

'Did you consider it?'

'I did, yeah.' Elliot looked pained. 'Once again, you must think I'm a proper dick.'

Edie shook her head. 'No, why?'

Did he really care this much about what she thought about him? Or was it a Stanislavski-level acting trick, to make you feel like you were important?

'It's weak, isn't it? Throwing money at the problem.'

'Not at all. I'd pay for what's happening to me to go away, if I could.'

'So would I,' Elliot said, looking directly into her eyes.

Edie's heart surged, but she didn't know if he meant what was happening to her, or to him.

'Anyway, again it was pointed out to me that if I give him money, he'll only spend it and ask for more. Then when he eventually does the story, it'll be called hush money and give his case even more weight. What a twat's circus, eh?' Elliot shook his head.

Edie had never been more glad not to be famous. She felt awfully protective of Elliot all of a sudden, in the face of this hatchet job. He acted in things, he made people happy. And these were his just desserts, alongside his chicken BLT on granary? Elliot got another triangle of sandwich and offered one to Edie; she shook her head.

'I've never done anything unprofessional like running from a set before. I couldn't handle Archie screaming blue murder at me, I'd have either punched him or burst into tears, so I legged it . . . Got to get the *difficult arsehole* rep at some point, right?'

Edie swelled with indignation for him.

'Tell Archie about this. All of it. It's coming out anyway. I hate that he thinks you're being a self-indulgent ponce when anyone would've lost it if they'd had that phone call. You had good reason.'

Elliot looked at Edie with an intense expression. 'Thank you. I best call him sooner rather than later if he's kicking off at blameless freelance writers. Sorry you got any of it.'

Edie said it was no problem and had yet another wince at Elliot finding out what Archie had insinuated. Elliot's phone started buzzing, the vibration pushing it round the side table.

'Ah, speak of the devil and he FaceTimes you. Here's Archie . . . I'll call him back when I've finished my sandwich.'

Elliot chewed and watched as his phone lit up and rang through to a voicemail alert.

'I'll leave you to deal with the Puce, then,' Edie said, getting up, not wanting to outstay her welcome. 'I hope things don't get very grim. I mean, I hope he doesn't use a swear word or anything.'

Elliot laughed, brushed crumbs from his hands and got up to open the door. 'God willing there will be no cursing.' He beamed at her. 'You do cheer me up.'

'Ah . . .' Edie did an 'aw gee it's nothing' shrug and felt awkward in her sheepish delight.

'Thanks for coming. You're a really nice girl, you are. C'mere.'

Elliot leaned over and pulled her into a hug. Edie submitted to it stiffly but as soon as she was in his arms, she didn't want to let go. Elliot felt so solid. He smelled vaguely of coconut and warm male skin. Nngngngng.

As they disentangled, he said: 'Hey. Is Cardinal Woolly a cat?'

Edie paused, then flinched at recognising the phrase.

'Oh God . . . no . . .' She knew what was coming next. 'No. Wolsey. He was an advisor to Henry VIII.'

'Ah, right. And there was me thinking you weren't making

314

much sense that night. And you have a question concerning balls? I do hope that's about ping-pong.'

Edie's face was burning as she shook with laughter.

'Oh, God, SORRY. It was a stupid joke between me and Nick.'

Elliot frowned slightly.

'Oh, you're seeing someone?'

'What?' Edie said. 'Nick? No? Only a friend.'

'What was the joke?'

'Oh, Elliot . . . don't make me explain, please . . .' Edie put her palms to her forehead.

'Nup, I have to know now, sorry.'

Edie closed her eyes and said: 'Nick is preoccupied with the fashion for extreme male waxing. He wanted to know if actors do it.'

She opened her eyes. Elliot was squinting.

'You do know I do acting–acting, not porn, right?'

Edie shrieked. 'I wish I were dead!'

'Wait. In *Gun City*, you think it's "guns" as in my arms?' Edie squealed some more as Elliot flexed a bicep. 'Bom chicka wow wow, etc. *Manscaping*, Edie, seriously. Maybe I'll do a book with Jan instead, she'd be more respectful of my privacy.'

'I will never drink again,' Edie said.

'Apart from that gin you just washed down.' If possible, her cheeks blushed even brighter, from the intimate teasing as much as the shame of asking about the state of his scrotum.

'Edie,' Elliot said, as the door opened, 'Thanks for tonight. I mean it.'

'My pleasure,' Edie said. 'I wish I had an answer for you.'

'It's enough to listen.'

Edie nodded.

As she walked down the corridor, Edie remembered Elliot's arms around her, she wished the pleasure being hers wasn't quite so true. Why did he pick her up on the mention of Nick, so fast? Why did he once pick her up, literally? Was that as significant as Archie had said? Why did the 'women in make-up' know her name, and her name alone?

Don't ask yourself these silly, mad, wildly hopeful questions, Edie Thompson, she cautioned herself. Only a fool breaks their own heart.

Especially twice.

These thoughts were enough to make Edie miss the fifty-something, henna-red-haired woman who passed her, shrewd eyes flicking to Edie and away again.

'Excuse me,' the woman said, pausing, in a sandpaper-rough, Capstan-Full-Strength voice. 'I've heard a rumour that Elliot Owen's staying here. Have you seen him?'

Edie hesitated before she said: 'No.'

She instinctively knew this wasn't a common-or-garden autograph hunter. The woman continued down the corridor. Edie swivelled on her heel and before she'd assessed the wisdom of saying the word, blurted:

'Jan?'

45

The woman turned back, momentarily frowning, and then her heavily made-up face broke into an expression of caustic delight. She had drawn round the outer edge of her lips with dark liner, giving her the appearance of an evil clown.

'*Well now*. And you are?'

Edie hadn't thought like a poker player, not a bit. She'd simply thrown her whole hand down on the table. All in.

'That's none of your business.'

Jan smirked even more and Edie felt the blunt stupidity of what she'd done. Had she passed Jan without comment, and texted Elliot a warning, she might have saved this. As it was, of course, she'd simply confirmed beyond all doubt that Jan had the right place.

Edie had no next move. She couldn't walk off, Jan was very nearly level with Elliot's door. If she knocked, Elliot might think it was Edie, and open it. Did he know what Jan looked like? She guessed probably, but Edie had heard of this woman, and yet had no visual ID until now. It couldn't be assumed. Perhaps Jan was going to pose as someone else, blather her way into Elliot telling her something . . .

'What you're doing is wrong,' Edie said, tremulous.

'And what's that?' Jan said.

'Interfering with someone else's life in ways you have no right to.'

Jan snorted.

'I have every right. It's a free country. Are you going to complain to every journalist who's written about him? Get your Basildon Bond out and a fountain pen. *Why oh why oh why . . .*'

'That's different.'

'Why?'

'Because they're not . . . ' Edie could say this, right? Oh God, *fail to prepare, prepare to fail* '. . . Visiting prisons and pulling birth certificates and causing distress to make themselves a few quid.'

'What you're describing is thorough journalism. The information is there for anyone who wants to report it. Information is a natural resource. I find things out, I don't make anything up.'

'Don't you think people have the right to a private life?'

'I've not put cameras in his shower stall, sweetheart.'

'You left his gran in tears.'

'Uh, no.' Jan held up a forefinger. 'She was A-OK when I left her. Not my fault if other people upset her, after the fact.'

Edie almost gasped. 'That's an incredible mental contortion.'

'You're the girlfriend, I take it?'

'No,' Edie said, sharply. 'Definitely not.'

318

'Mmm. What about the rumour he's done a Lord Lucan, can you help me there?'

'*No.*'

Before it could become clear that Edie was not going to answer questions but curiously, not going to leave either, Elliot appeared in the corridor behind them.

'Lord Lucan. I've murdered a nanny?' he said, pushing his hands into his jean pockets. 'Ey up. Made a friend?' he addressed Edie.

She wanted to screech RUN! which was somewhat ridiculous.

'I was telling *Jan* to leave you alone,' Edie said.

'Lovely new girl you have here, very spirited. What's her name?' Jan said to Elliot, sweetly.

'She's my biographer, and she's of no interest to you,' Elliot said.

'But considerable interest to you. What's she biographing in your hotel room at this hour, exactly?'

'Oh, you are a rascal,' Elliot said. 'If you're not staying at this hotel, I think the manager can throw you out.'

'Ah, but I am,' Jan said. 'Checked in just now.'

'We'll see,' Elliot said.

'I haven't used my real name, my love. And neither did you. "Donald Twain", you famous people can't resist showing off, can you? It always finds you out.'

Elliot looked startled for the first time and Jan visibly gloated.

'Your ex – ' Jan glanced at Edie 'I assume ex? – told *InStyle* magazine you were always Donald Twain and Dolly Grip in hotels. Research is everything.' Jan looked to Edie. 'You'll find that out, I'm sure.'

'Good on Heather,' Elliot said, with an expansive feigned smile.

'Shouldn't you call in at work? They're searching high and low for you, I heard.'

'You heard wrong.'

'I heard you were hiding at this hotel, and that wasn't wrong, was it? Don't you have a place to stay in the city?'

Elliot sighed, and turned his head to look up at the ceiling lights. 'What a life.'

'I make a living,' Jan said.

'I meant mine.'

'Oh sure. Crying into your piles of banknotes every night.'

Elliot looked at Edie and wore a look that was half disbelief, half laughing, and she returned it, shaking her head.

'Edie, forgive my manners. I should've offered to call you a taxi,' Elliot said. 'Want to wait in there?'

He opened the door and gestured at his room and Edie gratefully stepped past him and under his arm.

'Edie!' Jan cackled. 'She has a name.'

Elliot sagged at his mistake.

'May the best book win!' Jan sing-songed at Edie. 'I know which I'd rather read. The one with all the colour, or the boring whitewash by a fawning schoolgirl with a crush.'

Edie whipped round, face hot with embarrassment, ready to fire back. But Elliot slipped his arm round her and bundled her backwards into the room. He let go of Edie and slammed the door.

He picked up a remote control from the bed, turned the television on, and spoke in a low voice.

'She's doing that deliberately, to make you react like that. They get more from you in hot blood. Standard paparazzi thing too, they goad you for better pictures.'

'But, none of it's true,' Edie said.

Elliot shot her a look. 'I know.'

However, as Elliot rang the cab in a now-strained atmosphere, Edie thought maybe Jan was right. She found things out, but she didn't make things up.

46

'I smell bacon.'

Meg sniffed the air in the scrubby oblong of their back garden. She was wearing a muddy-coloured pinafore dress over jeans, and double-strap silver glitter Birkenstocks. Her hair was even more vertical than usual, bundled into a cantaloupe-sized bundle of whitened dreadlocks that sat directly atop her head.

'The filth?' Edie said, from her vantage point on her dad's old sun lounger, biting into slices of soft brown Hovis. 'Margot next door calls them the Dibble.'

Alright, she was being gratuitously provocative by referring to Margot as well, but Edie was officially sick and tired of Meg's reign of terror. The latest encounter with Elliot reminded her not to sweat the sibling small stuff.

And the thing was, Meg had blown her cover. She'd been sweet and biddable with Hannah and Nick in the pub on Edie's birthday. It was a reminder of the relationship she and Edie could have. Her friends hadn't weighed and measured every word out of their mouths around Meg, they'd strode fearlessly into the lion's enclosure and been themselves. In return, Meg had chatted away amiably, laughed at their jokes, offered things about herself. That night in the pub, Edie had got to see the Meg that other people were given, even people who were tainted by liking Edie.

And Edie losing her rag with her dad for enabling Meg had focused her: time to stop treading on eggshells from the eggs they weren't allowed to eat, and see how far that got her.

'*IS* that bacon?' Meg demanded.

'Yuh-huh,' Edie nodded, through a delicious illicit mouthful. She'd got the fat to crisp up in a curly brown frill, and smeared the bread with HP sauce. If she was going to pay for this, she was going to get it right.

'You know that's not allowed. I find bacon in particular very triggering.'

'Triggering how? You fancy some yourself? There's a few rashers left.'

'Triggering because I made my decision to go vegan when I heard the pigs being murdered at the abattoir in Spalding on that school trip.'

Veggie at that time, not vegan, but Edie didn't pick her up on the slight historical amendment. She had bigger pigs to fry.

'Yeah I've been thinking about this. Thing is, why do *you* get to say what goes? Why is your choice more valid than mine? Maybe I find chickpeas triggering, after the bad shits one time.'

Meg's face became stormy.

'That's bullshit. Chickpeas didn't die so you could have elevenses, for one thing. There's no moral equivalence, so don't start.'

Edie finished her half of sandwich and brushed her hands on her legs.

'Well, here's the bottom line. I asked Dad if I could have bacon, and he said yes. It's his house. His house, his rules.'

'He agreed with the no-meat policy, before you came back.'

'I wouldn't confuse "not being arsed to have the argument with you" for agreeing.'

'You are SO up yourself, aren't you,' Meg spat. 'You are so much better than everyone else, so special, you're "I'm so smart with my smart comebacks" Edie.'

'That's right, descend to the reasonless abuse section of the conversation, because you don't have a comeback,' Edie said, temper rising sharply.

'I was here before you!' Meg near-shouted.

'Yes, here, not paying rent and bumming fags off Dad,' Edie said. She'd unplugged the grenade and was preparing to lob it. This particular row had been on the way, ever since she returned. 'I give Dad money. That, right there, is why this bacon sandwich,' she picked up the offending remaining oblong of bread, 'has more right to be here than you do.'

'I don't have any money!'

'Because you don't have a job. It's not rocket surgery.'

'I was made redundant!'

'When, in 1981?'

'You are a horrible bitch! I can't wait until you sod off

back to London and leave us in peace, we're much happier without you!' Meg screamed.

Edie responded by taking a large bite out of her sandwich and doing a thumbs up. Meg stormed off back into the house. It wasn't ideal, but Edie had to test the theory that only by standing up to Meg would she vanquish her in this never-ending battle.

Edie's laptop was open on the sun lounger. As the back door banged shut loudly, the G-chat pop-up appeared on her screen. Mercifully, it wasn't Jack. Less mercifully, it was Louis.

EDIE EDIE EDIE! I S@@ YOU!

Hi Louis

When are you baaaaaack? It's SO boring without you IsweartoGod *nail painting emoji*

Hah. Louis had sussed she might be gone for good and wanted the exclusive. Not so fast.

Few weeks! All good at Ad H? x

Yeah. How's the actor boy? Have you rumped him?

Not yet but reckon I'm in there ☺

Boom. Pass that joke on as sincere if you will, Edie thought. Let it confirm all their prejudices about me. She wouldn't say she didn't care but she certainly cared a lot less than she used to.

REALLY hoping it turns out he likes cock instead.

If wishes were (hung like) horses

Hahahhaa! Ah funny Edie. MISS YOU BABE <3

Yeah yeah. There was something concerning Louis that was tickling the edge of Edie's consciousness, an important detail she'd absorbed but was yet to process. Was it the petition? Was it a key piece of information he'd let slip? It'd come to her, eventually. Telling Richard she wasn't coming back was the bigger issue, for now. She hated the thought of that conversation. He didn't respect quitters.

47

'Was that the dulcet tones of your sister I heard?'

Edie jumped out of her skin. She typed 'BRB' at Louis and turned to face Margot. Her auburn hair was looking even more Ken Dodd-ish than usual as she twinkled roguishly over the fence.

'Cherish her!' Margot said, gaily.

'Trying to.'

'I'm an only child. Brothers and sisters are the only ones who'll stick by you when you're old. Along with your children. Except in my case, of course.'

This seemed a change of (big band) tune. Margot put her cigarette to the side of her mouth and Edie felt too uncomfortable to ask what she meant. She thought of Elliot, and wondered if he'd told Fraser yet.

'I meant to say thanks again for the cake,' Edie said. 'It was absolutely amazing. Oh and I've got your lottery tickets!' she rustled in her handbag at her feet, and produced them.

The cake had been so amazing, that despite Meg knowing the provenance of the cake, and there clearly being eggs and cream cheese involved, Edie didn't think it was her non-sweet-tooth-having dad who'd snaffled a quarter of it overnight.

'I've made you another. Chocolate ganache. I'd got all my baking kit out so I thought I'd carry on.'

'Wow, that's incredibly nice of you,' Edie said. 'I'll have to share it out so I don't get tubby.'

Margot peered at her. 'You can take a few pounds more to my eyes. Mind you, they're old eyes. Want to pop in and get it now?'

'Uh . . .' Edie looked at her laptop. 'Yes!'

'Front door's not locked.'

Edie could hear Meg's angry music upstairs as she stuffed her laptop under a jumper on the stairs, closed the door quietly behind her and hopped the fence to Margot's.

She let herself in, through the door with the sticky seal, and once again marvelled at an environment so very different to the one on the other side of the bricks and mortar: a mini-verse of fluff, oyster satin and chintz.

In the kitchen, Margot was in a cerise batwing top, pouring champagne into flutes. An absolutely magnificent chocolate gateau was out ready in a biscuit tin, a crown of piped swirls of icing.

'Not for me thanks. Too early,' Edie said, waving off the flute. Kerrrrist. It wasn't even midday. 'Cake looks incredible.'

'It's my birthday!' Margot said, forcing the glass into Edie's hand.

'Ah! Happy birthday!' Edie accepted it and felt sorry for Margot's celebration being one she had to strong-arm a neighbour into. At a loss for anything else to say: 'Am I allowed to ask which one, in return?'

'Oh, I forget. On purpose.'

Margot saluted her with her glass, and sipped.

'Seems much better than the alternative,' Edie said, feeling the champagne go straight to her eyes. Daytime drinking made her brow feel heavy.

'What no one tells you, darling, is that some people are good at being young, and terrible at being old. I am one of those people. Don't get old, if you can help it. Go out on a high with a lovely big aneurysm at your sixtieth at the Dorchester, holding a Dirty Martini. Leave behind a beautiful corpse and wonderful memories. Do what they call a French Exit from the party, and don't bother with goodbyes.'

Margot was still very much the actress, Edie thought.

'I'll pencil one in.'

'Shall we have a seat?'

They took their glasses to the sitting room, with the frilly pelmets and the budgies. Looking again, they might be some sort of parakeet, they were too big for a budgie. Hannah had a point that Edie wasn't hugely at one with nature.

'Where's your mama, if you don't mind me asking?'

Margot pronounced 'mama' like an aristocrat rather than an American.

'She died,' Edie said, flatly. 'Killed herself when we were children. Depression.'

She was done with euphemisms and obfuscations. Elliot's experience had made her realise: often the secret weighed heavier than the truth.

'Dear oh dear. With two little kiddies? How selfish.'

'It wasn't selfish,' Edie said, with the calmness that came from having given this speech to herself many times. 'She was mentally ill and she'd probably stopped herself hundreds of times before she did it. Suicide's a desperate act, it's not selfish.'

'Beg to differ, darling, it can be. My ex-husband blew his brains out with a shotgun after an argument with his second wife's family at their holiday home in Gdansk. That wasn't unselfish, let me assure you. They had to hire a pressure washer to clean the loft and completely repaint it.'

Edie had no reply to this other than: 'Oh, God.'

'He always was a "See Me" person, Gordon,' Margot said, stubbing out the last of her fag. 'No pills and hot bath for him, had to make a mess.'

'Why did he do it?' Edie said.

Margot sparked up her next cigarette. 'He was a moody so-and-so, temper like an Irishman in a heatwave. Apparently it was something of a stormy marriage and he had a lot of debts. He wasn't good at marriage; God knows why he tried it again. Mind you, neither was I, for that matter.'

'Is he who you have the children with?' Edie said, carefully.

'Singular, one son. Yes. I don't see Eric. We don't get along.' For the first time, Edie could see tension in Margot's face. 'What happened?'

Margot hesitated. 'He blamed me for not being around much when he was younger. I wanted adventures, you see. I was "with child" too young, I was still a child myself. We had the money for a nanny and so I would leave him with her, and gad about, go out on the tiles. If I could go back and do it differently, I would. He sided with his father when we separated, went to live with him . . . I wasn't the best of mothers, admittedly . . .' she trailed off. 'And his wife and I can't bear each other. She's *quite* the sourpuss. So. That's that.'

She snapped her lighter shut. Edie imagined the force of Margot's personality and beauty in her youth, and could imagine it was like trying to keep a snow leopard as a house cat.

'Why did he side with Gordon?'

'His father told him I was a philandering drinker. His father was also a philandering drinker, of course, but somehow that was less of a crime. His wasn't the hand that rocked the cradle. Neither was mine, of course.' Margot gave a brittle, false laugh and Edie felt intensely sorry for her. So much bravado hiding so much sadness.

'You don't see Eric at all?'

'No,' Margot dragged on her fag and blew the smoke out in a haze, 'not for years. He blamed me for his father's grisly end. Gordon's canonised now, you can't touch him, in Eric's eyes.'

Edie gulped. 'Wow.'

'This is why I say to make it up with your sister, before it goes too far. You're bound to have your problems, without a mother around. But family is everything, darling. You don't get another.'

'You're the one who thinks Meg's mad!' Edie snorted.

'She cares, though. She's got passion. Nothing worse than someone who doesn't care about anything except themselves.'

This made Edie think about Jack. She felt in a different

mood to the last time she was with Margot, a more adventurous one. The Moët was helping.

'Margot, you know when you said I'd brought bad men upon myself? Do you really believe that?'

Margot smiled as she picked up her drink again. Edie noticed that, like all committed drinkers, Margot had a way of somehow drawing down half a glass of liquid in one sip.

'Have you ever heard the saying "critics are always reviewing themselves"? You remind me of myself. That's why I was hard on you.'

That, and the brandy, Edie thought. Oh God, would Edie gad about on the tiles, instead of care for a child? Was that what she was doing, in a way, when she ran wild in her teens?

'You knew me that well from one visit?'

'The walls are terribly thin, darling, and your brood spends quite a time in the garden, too.'

Edie smiled. Nosy swine.

'. . . You won't find someone who treats you as you should be treated until you start to believe you are worth the ones you want, the ones who aren't asking you to do any work. Find the man who appreciates you at your best, not one who confirms your worst suspicions about yourself. I saw a film a few moons ago, it said, pay attention to those who don't clap when you win. Gordon *despised* my career. He resented any success I had. He didn't want me to be happy, he wanted to keep me in a box. In my place.'

Edie thought about Jack. He had kept her in a box, like a pet. She was like the school stick insects, with a tea towel thrown over her cage at home time, her use as entertainment value over.

Margot sussed her train of thought.

'What was the last one doing? Carrying on like a cad behind his lady friend's back, trifling with you? *Refuse to be trifled with.* That would be a start.'

Margot tapped her cigarette into the swan ashtray.

'Don't wait for men's permission. Don't wait for anyone's permission, in fact.'

Margot, a feminist! Sort of. She wished Meg could hear this.

'This all sounds wise. The ones I want are very likely married by now, though,' Edie said, sadly.

'Nonsense. Opportunity knocks when you least expect it.'

Edie and Margot discussed Margot's ex-husband's terrible investments in stocks and shares and numerous infidelities. When Margot offered Edie the inevitable second glass, Edie declined on the basis of having work to do, but reminded Margot she'd very happily take her cake home.

'Would you like to go out for a drink sometime? Just local?' she asked, as she stood in the hallway, clasping the cake tin.

'The ale houses around here are complete fleapits, darling,' Margot leaned on the door jamb, striking a sultry pose like Lauren Bacall.

'In town, then. My treat. We could even get dinner too.'

A whole evening of Margot, hmm. Could be full on. Edie fancied the tales of the Swinging Sixties though.

'I shall certainly consider it,' Margot said, primly. If she was gratified by the invitation, she didn't show it.

'Enjoy the rest of your birthday,' Edie said.

'Oh, it isn't my birthday.' Margot waved a bony hand, decorated with a gobstopper-sized crystal cocktail ring.

Edie's jaw dropped.

'Then why did you say it was?!'

'It was the only way to get you to have a little champers. Loosen you up.'

Edie tested whether she was outraged, and laughed.

48

'Edie, there's a big wheel in Market Square,' Elliot said, delivering this non sequitur of an opening line from somewhere that sounded noisy.

'Yes. I've seen it . . .?' Edie said, phone clamped between raised shoulder and ear as she picked up her popped toast from the toaster and threw it on to the plate, between finger and thumb. She still got that spurt of nervy alert celebrity-presence adrenaline when Elliot called, yet she was also wearing the involuntary grin of someone speaking to a beloved friend. The lines were blurring around Elliot, and her feelings were getting smudged, too.

'Can we go on it? I've got the afternoon off. We've had all the lighting cables nicked. "By thieving rob dog gypsies," according to Archie, who's never met a PC term he liked to use.'

'Am I meant to interview you on Ferris wheels now?'

There was a pause where Edie fancied Elliot might be looking awkward, though obviously, she couldn't be sure.

'Er, I was thinking we could do it for larks, to be honest.

Who knows what secrets I might part with when I'm squeaking with fear, though.'

Edie laughed. It was nice to hear Elliot sounding happier. She wanted to ask about Fraser, but it needed to be face to face. Perhaps that was what this was about.

'Will it be alright, with the crowds? You won't get mobbed?'

'I reckon if we get on the wheel without me being recognised, yes. Call me when you get there and I'll appear, like the shopkeeper in *Mr Benn?*'

Edie agreed joyfully and rang off. She hammered out a text to Hannah and noticed her hand was trembling slightly.

Now the actor wants me to go on the 'Nottingham Eye' with him! My life gets ever weirder. x

Is this a sex euphemism I'm yet to learn? Hx

I wish! X

Edie sent that without thinking, then as the speech bubble appeared in lurid green, regretted it somewhat. What did she wish? What was going on . . .

DO you now? X

Ah. No, probably not. X

EDITH THOMPSON. STAY AWAY FROM MEN YOU SHOULD

STAY AWAY FROM. X PS got to tackle a radical nephrectomy now, your life beats my life.

'Does he summon you like some feudal overlord with a serf wench then? Like in his shitey television show?'

Edie started, she hadn't realised Meg was behind her.

'Big flappy Dumbo ears! Yeah pretty much. Only it's not work today, he's got a day off.'

Meg raised her eyebrows.

After touching up her make-up with extra care and telling herself it wasn't for any particular reason, Edie caught the bus into town and walked the short way down into the centre. She hit dial on her phone and sure enough, as she spoke to Elliot, he emerged from the crowds, woolly hat in place, ridiculous bone structure and glowing skin still a giveaway that he was an exalted personage. It was dismally grey, the fag end of the summer, and yet Edie felt wreathed in rainbows as he broke into a smile. She'd have to make sure she didn't become too used to this sensation. Elliot, too, was going to be gone as fast as a spell of good weather.

'Why do you want to go on a big wheel?' Edie said.

'What does a man do when he has it all?' Elliot said. 'It was this or LaserQuest. Or you know,' he gave a sly smile, 'twerking in NG1s in my disco tits T-shirt.'

Edie went red and rolled her eyes. 'Yeah yeah.'

They joined the queue and Edie heard murmuring and shifting of feet as, she guessed, a few people started discussing why that guy in the hat rang a bell.

Elliot sensed it too and made a small *hmmm?* quirk of the

mouth at Edie. He gently put his hands on her waist, moving her so she was standing directly in front of him, their bodies close. He positioned himself so he was gazing down on her as if they were a couple, sharing confidences, and incidentally, blocking their view of his face.

'Sorry, needs must,' Elliot said, in a low voice, in her ear, in a way that would make onlookers think they might be about to kiss.

'Pretty sure I'm not getting paid for this,' Edie said, mock-indignant, while her heart thudded and her skin tingled. Play-acting Elliot's girlfriend was too much for her nerves to cope with. It gave her disturbance of her blood sugar levels. She looked up at him and tried not to wear any expression that could be construed as adoring.

'I'd ask them to give you a bonus for special services rendered,' Elliot said, still joke-husky, 'but I'm thinking of your reputation, here.'

'Hah,' said Edie, cynical. 'That horse has bolted.'

'It looks fine from where I'm standing. Seriously,' Elliot said. 'It's how many people? Screw them.'

Speaking in low voices somehow gave Edie the confidence to say more than she would have, normally.

'What if they're right about me? What if I am a terrible person and a home-wrecking slut and they're the ones to say it? It's not as if anyone awful goes around thinking they're awful.'

Edie didn't know where that blurt had come from. She couldn't help herself from being herself around Elliot. No, it wasn't that. She *wanted* to be herself with him.

'Don't be soft. Did you want to cop off with a groom? Did you plot it on the back of a napkin?'

'No!'

'Well then. Did you . . . were you . . .' Elliot jerked his head.

'What?'

Elliot sucked in breath.

'Y'know. Sleeping with him?'

'No!' Edie was sure they'd covered this. 'I said I wasn't, didn't I?'

'Just confirming. Updating my spreadsheet.' Elliot surveyed her. 'It's quite an accolade that he'd risk so much for a kiss. Romantic, really. In a twisted way.'

Edie said, 'Oh God, believe me, it's not romantic,' and Elliot grinned. She had a funny sense he was impressed by her, though God knows why, on the current topic.

'Anyway want me to call him up as the Prince and tell him his head is going to be thrown in Tinkers' Pit?'

Edie guffawed.

'Haha! Ah . . . I don't know. Yes?'

'Think of it this way. You auditioned for a job you didn't get. Now the film's out and it's absolutely abysmal. Terrible reviews, you dodged a bullet. Someone else is his co-star in a total turkey.'

Edie knew Elliot was a smart wit but this couldn't all be off the cuff. He'd been thinking about it. Her stomach fluttered.

A light rain started to spatter and Edie pulled up the hood on her coat. As she turned her head, she saw no more curious glances. No doubt they'd not unreasonably decided that Prince Wulfroarer wouldn't be queuing for a fairground ride in the pissing rain with a tattily dressed lady.

'You look like a Jawa in *Star Wars*,' Elliot said, tugging at the fur trim, as Edie tutted and protested and enjoyed the affectionate teasing immensely.

Were they flirting? They were at the front of the queue and ushered into one of the cars, the safety bar slammed down over their knees.

As they began their wobbly ascent, then stopped again, Edie said: 'Have you spoken to Fraser yet?'

'No,' Elliot said, jaw tightening. 'I haven't been able to pin him down for a date to come and see him. It's tricky, I'm having to pretend it's just a jaunt. I can't say Clear Your Diary I Have Big Things To Say because he'll lose his shit and make me tell him on the phone. He was the kid who used to get up at four a.m. to open his Christmas presents.' Elliot paused. 'Not that I'm likening this to opening a Christmas present.'

'It must be stressful,' she said.

'Every time I think that Jan might call him, I get the jangles. I haven't been sleeping, the women in make-up are noticing the dark circles. I had to ask the hotel if they could bar Jan, because the thought of her lurking outside my bedroom was giving me squeaky bum time.'

The women in make-up, who knew her name. Was Elliot mentioning them on purpose? He appeared unperturbed. Obviously merely small talk. Edie should shrug it off. She was quiet as the car swung upwards again gently, squeaking on its hinges.

'Do you ever miss your mum?' she said, eventually.

She hadn't known she was going to ask something so stark, and personal. They were suspended in mid-air above the crowds and it shook it out of her. She'd never had this kind of solitude with Elliot, she thought, that's why these things were coming out. For the next ten to fifteen minutes, right in the middle of the city centre, they were alone.

Elliot looked at her. 'Yes, sometimes. It's a strange sort of missing, though. I didn't know her. Missing someone you don't know. It's more like a sense there's a blank that will forever be blank and never be filled in . . . Do you? I mean, that's a ridiculous question. Sorry.'

Edie nodded. 'It isn't. Yes. In the same way, really. I didn't have the chance to get to know her properly. It's a part of me that will always be missing. A dull ache, rather than a sharp pain. Lots of questions that I will never, ever get answers to. Sometimes I think about what I would give for one hour with her. Just an hour. To ask everything I want to ask.'

'Yes!' Elliot said emphatically, looking at her intently. 'You learn to live with that incompleteness. That's what other people don't understand. You have to make peace with this . . . *forever unknownness*. That's what's different between me and Fraz. He's very rounded, and complete. I sometimes wonder if I do this job so I can try on other personalities who are a bit more sorted out. People who know who they are . . . people who don't exist. So. That's healthy.'

Edie nodded again. This was dynamite for the book, though very probably too personal.

Edie had never considered if there was a parallel with her

loss, and choosing advertising. She could perhaps find one in running to London and building herself a new persona that was like a lavishly gift-wrapped empty box. Beautiful, shiny, full of foam peanuts. If her life was a memoir, it would be called *Display Model Only*.

'Is your dad OK? Did he remarry?' Elliot asked.

'No,' Edie said. 'No. He had a breakdown, the year after my mum died, it knocked his confidence. He ended up running out of a classroom he was teaching, in tears . . .' Edie found this hard to say, to think about what had gone on. The loss of dignity. 'He was a year head, and he had to go off long-term sick. That's when we moved to Forest Fields, down-sized. His life has seemed much more like coping, ever since, than living.'

Elliot reached over and put his hand over Edie's, gripped it supportively, and let go. She was silently ecstatic at the gesture, and the unexpected skin-to-skin contact.

As they drew level with the clock in the Council House, she thought: this was why you should never succumb to despair. One moment, everything looked lost. The next, the big wheel had turned and you were feeling on top of the world, surveying the rooftops and trading witticisms with a famous beautiful actor who even felt moved to hold your hand. (Briefly.) How bizarre and improbable and downright funny.

To underline life's absurdity, the rain made up its mind and started pelting them, and they had nothing to shield themselves with except hats and hoods. They were both half-wailing, half-laughing. The descent started and Edie squealed: 'Owen, you BASTARD,' heads shielded by their arms, soaked to their skin.

'Oh, sorry, Thompson. The whims of eejit thespians.'

They peeled themselves, sodden, from the car as soon as it swung to a halt. Edie guessed half her carefully touched-up make-up was now in oily pools on her cheeks, and didn't care. She was about to suggest a restorative coffee when Elliot pulled his phone from his pocket, wiped the water from it with the cuff of his coat sleeve and said: 'Balls to it, they've sourced some cables. I'm wanted back on set.'

Edie felt her face and spirits fall.

'Thank you for being excellent company, Edie,' Elliot said, and leaned in to peck her on the cheek.

At that moment, a scream went up from the nearby Five Guys burger bar.

They looked over to see a group of middle-aged women in quilted coats, pointing at Elliot and whooping.

'See you soon,' Elliot said, quickly. He angled his chin into his collar and set off down the watery pavement, suddenly reminding Edie of the iconic black-and-white photo of James Dean in Times Square, hunched in an overcoat against the elements.

Although with a very twenty-first century difference: Elliot with iPhone clamped to his ear, in place of the cigarette clamped between the teeth.

49

When had Edie last been to Sneinton? It was south of the city, walking distance from the city centre. Cheap housing, one good pub, a lot of other pubs you weren't advised to go into unless you were a Krav Maga master.

She had a watery memory of a really scutty party around here in her teenage years, where the trippy décor involved wilting daffodils Sellotaped to the wall at dado-rail height, a sink overflowing with tins of Skol, and someone dubious putting on a white-paper-sleeve video of German nuns urinating.

Edie knocked on Nick's door and wiggled the hand and wrist that had gone to sleep with the weight of the shopping bag. She waited, and knocked and waited, and eventually called his mobile. Nick had said it was a sad bachelor flat but it was a house, a semi. A pretty one, with a window box of pansies, which indicated a decent land-lord, as Nick wasn't known for touches like this. The area could be a bit fruity but his street seemed peaceful, and heavy with cats.

'I was having a fag in the garden, sorry love.' Nick leaned in to give her a kiss, a smoky whoosh of Marlboro Red accompanying his embrace.

'I like your shoes,' Edie said, glancing at the chestnut-brown boots beneath his turned-up jeans, which looked a little 'Madness nutty boy' to her untrained eye. 'Clarks?'

'They're Grenson's, you dozy mare!'

Nick seemed drawn and edgy, and his mood even stayed flat when Hannah piled in the door, sporting thick swingy new hairstyle in a treacly colour, with fringe. She looked about five years younger and Edie immediately began coveting it and thinking she should do similar.

'What do you think? My hairdresser says it's "bronde".'

'I think it looks incredible,' Edie said, circling her for the full effect. Nick muttered approval and went to get drinks as they sat themselves down on the front room sofa, which had been cheered up/disguised with a striped bedspread doubling as a throw.

'I thought, if Pete's parents say I'm having a midlife crisis, I should do it properly and have the new image too.'

'Does it feel like you're having a crisis?' Edie said.

'No. It feels to me like the crisis was the last five years and this is the part where I'm starting to sort it.'

Nick returned and handed them both beakers of red wine. Once again, Edie got that expansive feeling that she was exactly where she should be. It was so novel, she took a moment to recognise it.

Nick came back again, pushing the door to with the toe of his boot while balancing a mug of tea.

'Taking a break?' Hannah said, with a clear note of surprise in her voice.

'Yeah, I'm hanging from last night. Just boshed down Dioralyte though, puts you right back in the room, have you tried it? It's for diarrhoea. I'm giving you a total insider's tip here. Neck it down, and even if you're filthy, you can be back in the bar by seven.'

'Hmm,' Hannah said. 'Remember the part where I'm a doctor? Me condoning this doesn't sound consistent with taking the Hippocratic oath.'

'Look the other way. With me it can be the Hypocrite oath.'

'Where did you go last night?' Edie said, and as soon as the words left her mouth, knew the answer.

'Just in.'

'Nick,' Hannah said, 'you're drinking too much. It's worrying.'

'I know,' Nick said, playing with the turn-up on his jeans. 'I know.'

There was an uncomfortable silence, yet both Hannah and Edie let it be uncomfortable, to see where it went.

'. . . Alice is making me do counselling.' At their horrified expressions he added: 'Not "get back together" counselling, "sorting out a working relationship as divorcees" counselling.'

'That's good, isn't it?' Edie said, cautiously. 'If it means you'll get to see Max?'

'Mmm. I don't think that's where it's going though. So far, she wangs on about what a bastard I am at great length. I am "holding space" for her, apparently.'

'*Holding space*?' Hannah said. She wasn't one for pseudo-therapy speak.

'The counsellor says most people don't listen during conversations with their other halves, they just wait for their turn to speak. So in the sessions, the other person talks and you don't say anything or plan your response or play Angry Birds, you only listen. While imagining Alice being thrown into a medical incinerator. I added that last part myself.'

'Why do it if she doesn't want a better relationship?' Edie said.

'She thrives on conflict and when I had to accept I couldn't see Max, she'd won. I reckon this is a way of stirring it up again.'

'You need to see the counsellor separately and tell her your ex-wife is a toxin,' Hannah said.

'She seems to be loving Alice's righteous furies. She's being fed more shit than a fecalphiliac on a farm.' Nick shrugged.

'When you get your turn for Alice to "hold your space", talk about how it feels not seeing Max,' Edie said.

'That's all I'm hanging in for.' Nick twiddled the lace on his boot. 'I know I drink to blot it out. It's not even mysterious; the sadness cloud descends and I feel better after a pint. But there it is.'

'I'm not going to lecture you now, but we're going to keep talking about this,' Hannah said. 'There are other things you can do to feel better that aren't propping up the bar in 'Spoons.'

'Also, food!' Edie said. 'I'll start dinner.'

In Nick's red-tiled kitchen – Edie really liked this house – she made a huge pile of chilli con carne and they sat forking it from bowls while listening to Nick's latest mix tape and laughing at his terrible Single Man choice of décor, a bizarre painting above the mantelpiece.

'What *is* that?' Hannah said.

'It's Elton John singing "Candle in the Wind" to Princess Diana. A listener sent it in. Look, that's the candle, you see, hovering. It's very haunting.'

'Looks like Rose West and David Van Day from Dollar about to be hit by a flaming tampon,' Edie said.

'It's quite impressionistic,' Nick agreed.

Full of mince and goodwill, laced with alcohol, Edie had a powerful urge to declare something she'd only just decided upon. She held back, because as Hannah had said, she wanted to be sure before she said it out loud.

Instead she said: 'I think sometimes, shit things in life can't be learned from, they just "are". You have to live around them and with them. No one admits it, because it doesn't sound inspiring if you put it over a picture of a sunset. I was discussing this with Elliot yesterday.'

'*I was discussing it with Elliot yesterday!*' Nick said. 'Get you. Oh, as I was saying to little Kenny Branagh in The Groucho.'

'Classic mentionitis,' Hannah said. 'I see you, Thompson.'

'Oi! Hold some space for me. Elliot's a case in point, is all I'm saying,' Edie said. 'Anyone you think has it all worked out, chances are, they don't.'

'This is a long way round to telling us you've uncovered his whoring habit,' Nick said. 'What's his private pain then?'

'Yeah, what do you mean?' Hannah said.

'Nothing specific,' Edie said, and was drowned out by booing and catcalls from them both.

'You utter prick-tease!' Nick said. 'You've even got a coy gloaty little I Can Haz A Sekret face on!'

'No!' Edie said, laughing hard in that way that felt so therapeutic. 'OK, there is something. I can't tell you now because it'd make me a snitch. But I will eventually. When it comes out.'

'When it's in the papers anyway and not a secret. Thanks a bunch,' Nick said. Edie thought how much she'd like them to meet Elliot and then felt the force of its impossibility, and was a little sad.

'Phew,' Nick said. 'What a rollercoaster of a night. Acting man maybe is interesting but we can't know why. Can I have a wine now to soothe myself down?'

'Nope,' Hannah said.

'Tetleys it is then.' Nick got to his feet. 'I'll bring the bottle through for you two soaks.'

'Thank you for coming round,' he said, putting his head back round the door, 'You both cheer me up loads.'

'Me too,' Hannah said.

'Me three.' Edie leaned back on the sofa. 'Spend your time on the right people,' Edie said. 'It's one of life's big secrets, isn't it? I wish someone had told me when I was twenty. Don't make "friends". Make two friends. Find people you love to bits and don't want to confuse things by sleeping with, and keep them close.'

Nick held up a palm.

'Woah. There might've been a misunderstanding here.'

50

The serial killer in *Gun City* certainly didn't make life easy for himself.

This corpse – Edie had a bet with herself it was another lingerie model – had been placed atop a pile of books inside the Nottingham Contemporary art gallery, as a gruesome installation. It was a fair guess there was a pithy aside about qualifying for the Turner Prize, by a hardboiled DI.

The city-centre location for this part of the shoot had brought onlookers out in droves, and Edie had to squeeze past the fuss to get to Elliot's trailer, parked in front of the Galleries of Justice building, a little way along the road in the Lace Market.

Edie feared she might be in for a long wait, as Elliot was going to run the gamut of autograph hunters when he'd finished filming.

But within a half hour of Edie getting her things out and settling down to read her Kindle with a builder's tea, Elliot bounced in, Tigger-ish, eyes shining.

'Hi, honey, I'm home!'

Edie rolled her eyes and smiled and chewed her pen. He pulled his leather jacket off and opened the fridge, swigging from a bottle of water.

'Think that scene went quite well,' he said. 'You've got a drink, I see. Cool.'

Edie sat swinging her feet, feeling strangely like when her dad used to take her into school and leave her in the staffroom, colouring in. Elliot sat down opposite her and smiled. His short hair was tousled – did many detectives meddle with their hair using Wella Shockwaves? – and his teeth looked especially white against his detective's five o'clock shadow. Edie felt a swoon coming on and needed to quickly re-establish their irreverent rapport. She felt she knew her way around him now, they could recreationally squabble and easily make it up: the litmus test of familiarity.

'Elliot,' she said, 'can you explain something, about the show? Why would a serial killer go to all that trouble of breaking into an art gallery, instead of just ditching the body in a layby off the A453?'

Pause, while Elliot wiped his mouth and looked contemplative.

'He's the flamboyant sort of serial killer, isn't he?'

'But how many murderers take risks like that? I thought Archie was on about *Gun City* shining a light on crime in the regions. It's like something from a Thomas Harris novel.'

'Well, not everything has to be naturalistic . . .'

He boggled at her indignantly and she thought she might've genuinely annoyed him. 'It's ART, Edie Thompson! It's not meant to be anything like life!'

They both burst out laughing and Edie had a stab, a pre-pang, of missing Elliot before the moment arrived when they said their final goodbye, forever.

A rapping of knuckles disturbed them. Archie Puce popped his face round the door.

'Well done, Owen, that was a fucking triumph. Not just a pretty face. I'd need a doll to show you where that touched me.'

'Thanks, mate!'

He spotted Edie and visibly blanched. 'Oh. Hello again, Linda. You and your tambourine are just what our band needs, once again.'

Edie got the reference to The Beatles, with a spasm of embarrassment, and nodded curtly. 'Hello, Archie.'

'You completely disproved everything I accused you of when we last spoke, well done. I think the turnaround for a result was under two hours, wasn't it?'

Edie hadn't considered until now how it looked: she *had* found Elliot, she *had* persuaded him to speak to Archie. Just not using the methods Archie imagined.

Edie said nothing, and Archie stared some more, then withdrew.

'Linda?' Elliot said. 'What's he on about, disproved what?'

'He thinks it's funny to get my name wrong, or something,' Edie said, quickly. 'I said I didn't know where you were, and he's gloating that I must've done.'

'Oh.' Elliot frowned. 'What does he mean about your tambour—'

'We should crack on, on a bit of a clock,' Edie said, pushing

352

the Dictaphone towards Elliot. 'So, we're doing romance today.'

'Hell's bells. Buy me a drink first.'

'Hah. Er,' Edie shuffled her papers, pretended to look at her notes. 'Does fame make it easier to meet women? Or not?' Edie said. She didn't really want to know.

'Before we start, can we agree you'll find a way to say all this that doesn't make me sound grotesque? You're good at doing that.'

Edie nodded and smiled. Elliot smiled back and had some more water, keeping his eyes on her. He had spare energy to burn off, after that scene, Edie sensed, that was where the idle flirting was coming from. Wasn't it?

She'd have dealt with it so much better without Jan's 'schoolgirl crush' accusation. Edie felt she had to counter that, with every word and action.

'The thing about having been on a screen is that suddenly people start throwing themselves at you. I remember that from before *Blood & Gold,* you know, you can be in any old thing. And it's not really real attraction. It's not even that flattering. You know they're thinking, even if he's a crap shag, it's an anecdote. It's probably a rare chance for men to find out how it is for women: you're a trophy. I don't know about you but it does a lot more for my ego when someone likes me, you know, for my,' he sucked in breath, '*personality*. Not: Oh, you're that guy off that thing, OK you have my interest. That stops being flattering and starts being depressing veeeery quickly.'

Edie put her chin on her hand.

'I mean, if a man' – he gestured to the empty seat next to

him – 'had a fetish for talented copywriters and asked you out because he wants to have a copywriter on his arm, would you feel chuffed? Or would you rather date this man over here who's noticed all the particular reasons it'd be incredible to go out with you, Edie, the person?'

Which man? What? Edie felt her neck grow warm. 'Ah, yeah. See your point.'

'It puts me off, compared to when I had to work for it. You know, the greedy kid in the sweet shop becomes Augustus Gloop. I didn't want to start Augustus Glooping and sicken myself with my own behaviour.'

'Hah! Glooping. I like that verb.'

'Yeah, but don't make it sound like I'm saying women are Snickers bars.'

'You miss the thrill of the chase?'

'Argh, no, you see: that sounds creepy. It's just harder to find that natural slow burn of attraction where someone intrigues you and you intrigue them back and one day you wake up and they're all you can think about.'

Elliot looked at her steadily and Edie nodded and pretended she needed to write it down in her notepad as opposed to needing to break eye contact.

'It's hard to meet women who like you, for you?' she said.

'Well, what is "liking me for me"? I've been doing this job for a while now. It's a bit disingenuous to say I want them to love the kid from Nottingham.'

Edie once again thought, *Damn: you are sharp.*

'What about falling for your co-stars?'

Elliot clicked the record button off and said in a stage

354

whisper: 'Jeez, do you mean Greta? You might as well try to cosy up to a pair of secateurs.'

'She's so beautiful though.'

Elliot did a mock shiver. 'Yes, like the Arctic Tundra is beautiful. I wouldn't recommend trying to spend a night there.'

'Alright, Greta aside,' Edie said, and felt uncomfortably like a possessive girlfriend pushing to hear things about the past that she couldn't actually handle.

Elliot clicked the record button back on.

'When you're acting being into someone, surely that can slide into *actually* feeling it?' Edie continued.

'Nah not really, or not so far. What's exciting when you're kissing someone for real is that you chose to kiss each other. Take that out of the equation; they could hate your guts, but the kissing's in the script. It's not so hot. And you've got someone dangling a boom and a hairy-arsed crew watching and a director about to shout cut. The thoughts on your mind are not amorous ones.'

'And you've never . . .' Edie cleared her throat, it was next on the list and she wasn't clear enough of head right now to improvise an alternative, 'never done, an, er, nude scene.'

'Hahahaha.' Elliot was enjoying her discomfort hugely. 'No.'

'Would you do one if the role demanded it?'

Elliot started laughing in earnest, a blushing Edie squealing: 'What! It's a fair question isn't it?'

'It is, it's just such a funny cliché . . .' Elliot said. 'I mean, unless you're playing the lead in *The Naked Rambler Story*, you can stay zipped up for pretty much everything. It's rare a role *demands* it.'

'Is that a yes? Or a no?'

'Depends what's demanding it, I guess.' Elliot paused. He looked her in the eye. 'Or who.'

Edie hoped she wasn't looking like she felt. There was a terrible, embarrassing, loaded silence but Edie couldn't think of the words to break it.

'I mean, Scorsese. That's a yes,' Elliot said.

'Hah, of course!' Edie said, in a strangled voice.

If Hannah and Nick could see this, they'd be absolutely pissing themselves.

Edie usually had more poise than this.

'Can I ask you a favour?' Elliot said. 'I'm actually having trouble with a scene in *Gun City* and,' he lowered his voice, 'I don't want to rehearse any more with Greta than I have to. Would you read with me?'

'I can't act,' Edie said, warily.

'You don't have to be able to act, you have to be able to read.'

'What's the problem with the scene?' Edie said. She didn't like the sound of this, somehow.

'Edie, you look as if I asked you to skinny dip with me!'

Edie blushed hard again. She had never seen Elliot like this before: hyped up, mischievous and determined to get a rise out of her. Elliot saw her discomfort and relented, speaking in a more conciliatory tone.

'My character is an over-confident chauvinist type and I think he's meant to be very appealing to women in this scene, but I'm worried he's coming off as overbearing. I value your opinion and if you read with me, you can tell me what you think.'

Edie prevaricated. What if this was a love scene, of some sort? She didn't want the mind games of trying to work out whether to tell Elliot his fictional alter ego was 'appealing to women'.

'Do I have to . . .?'

'You don't have to. I'd be so grateful if you did, though.'

'Then, I suppose so . . .'

'Great! Thank you,' Elliot sprung out of his seat and returned with a thick, slightly dog-eared script, black Courier type on white A4 paper. He sat down next to Edie and she felt like volts had gone through her.

'Page 124,' he said, flipping through the pages. 'Take it from INT: NIGHT. *A rain-streaked window in a near-empty hotel piano bar, a pianist plays. Headlamps from passing cars cast an intermittent searchlight through the gloom. A slow pan to its only customers, GARRATT and ORLA, who are at a table alone. It's the first drink after work in a very long day. The mood is tense and they're both pointedly avoiding discussing what happened between them at the mortuary earlier.* You're "Orla".'

Edie swallowed hard. 'What "happened between them in the mortuary"?'

'They had a fight,' Elliot said.

'Ah.'

'Garratt, that's me, didn't agree about what the ligature marks on the neck proved.'

'Right.'

'We're always bickering.'

'OK.'

'Because you fancy me rotten.'

Edie stared as Elliot grinned.

'I did warn you, I can't act,' Edie said, finally finding one of the comebacks she knew she had in her.

51

ORLA
(pointedly keeping things business)
If the Jane Doe we have in Retford can be matched
with prints and DNA to the—

GARRATT
(interrupting)
Why are you being distant with me? Ever since the
Colwick case.

ORLA
I'm not being distant with you.
(pause)
I'm ground down by this job. The things we see. Why
do we do it to ourselves, Garratt?

GARRATT
We can't not do it. That's why. We see these things and

we want to run from them. And yet something pushes
us towards the darkness.

ORLA
We do run. We run deeper inside ourselves.

'Wow,' Edie said.
'What?'
'Bit purple, isn't it? Who's ever said something like that?'
'You did, just now. Stay in character!' Elliot remonstrated.

GARRATT
You see, I wanted to talk about you and me, and you
just turn it back to the job.

ORLA
There is no you and me.

GARRATT
Isn't there?

ORLA
(fighting hard to keep her usual composure)
I don't want to make things complicated with someone
I work with, Garratt.

She sips her drink, eyes still on Garratt. We sense her
nerves but also the tumult of her constrained desire.

Oh arsing hell. Neutral, keep face neutral and stare at script, Edie told herself.

> GARRATT
> There's nothing complicated about the way we feel about each other.

> ORLA
> Oh, it's always complicated. And you don't know how I feel about you.

> GARRATT
> The thought is in your eyes, every time you look at me.

Edie's heart raced. She couldn't scan ahead or she'd lose her place, start stuttering and the jig would be up.

> ORLA
> (defensive)
> What?

> GARRATT
> You're wondering if it would live up to expectations. You're thinking about how it would feel. Look me in the eyes and tell me you've never thought about it.

Elliot looked at her, and flipped the page. Edie almost coughed on her tea. Jesus *Christ*.

ORLA
I've never thought about it.
(But she breaks eye contact at the last moment, sipping her drink)

GARRATT
Once again, with feeling.
(pause)
I've thought about it. I'm thinking about it now.

ORLA
Good night, Garratt.

ORLA gets up, briskly crosses the short distance to the lift and hammers the call button. She knows she has only seconds to fight this, fight herself.

GARRATT
Orla.

He grabs her arm and pulls her into an embrace. They kiss, grinding against each other: it's urgent, passionate, with clear intent. The lift doors open and they stumble inside, together.

Edie glanced up and Elliot said 'And, cut. I'll let you off that part.'

He must've chosen this scene to rattle her. Surely?

'What do you think to Garratt? I don't like that line

about "I'm thinking about it now" at all. He sounds like an 0898 line. You mess with Archie's dialogue at your peril, though.'

'Uhm, yeah . . . It's quite full-on.'

'If a man you worked with said, "I'm thinking about it right now", you'd be a bit freaked out, right?'

'Yep. To the point of going to HR.'

'It's a short hop to "I'm mentally undressing you" and no one wants that.'

'Nope.'

Edie couldn't think of a single thing to say. She was going to ask about Fraser today, but it wasn't the time. Was Elliot messing with her?

'Edie,' Elliot said, leaning in, speaking in a low, confidential voice. 'I'm going to ask you something and I want you to be *totally* honest with me.'

'Yes?' she squeaked, pulsing with anticipation and apprehension.

'Is *Gun City* completely fucking dreadful?'

'Oh.' Edie gulped air, wondered what other question she was hoping for, and tried to think what the appropriately sycophantic response was to a celebrity fishing for a compliment. 'Elliot, I'm sure nothing with you in it could be completely dreadful,' she said, in a suitably prim "on message" tone.

Elliot laughed and the tension broke.

'Hah. I like you. You can stay.'

And there it was: Edie had a resentful stab at him saying those words, in that flippant tone. Not meaning it.

She was still palpitating over the things he'd said to her, in make believe. Pretending to feel things you didn't was no way to make a living.

52

Edie had known for a while she wouldn't be rebooting to her old social media accounts. However, as time had worn on, staying away felt less like self-preservation, and more like letting the bullies win. Also, she wanted to know what was going on out there, dammit.

She could go back, with new profiles, and a new outlook. She relaunched her Facebook. She used the photo of herself with Hannah and Nick from her birthday as her thumbnail: the three of them wound round each other in smoke-hazy Rock City.

She added Nick as a friend, and few others safety kite-marked as non-hostile and neutral, her dad's cousins. Within days, she got a request from Louis – no surprise he was constantly scanning the horizon – and left it pending. She didn't want a spy among the ranks. Nor did she want a fight, however. She'd use the 'oh I rarely check it' fib until she'd decided what to do.

Hannah organised an evening at hers, watching films. 'I've got *Zodiac* recorded, and I'm buggered if I'm watching that alone, so you and Nick can come round,' she said when she rang, a week previous. 'Also, it's not the pub. I've got Nick into coming running with me instead of booze. The language that's come out of him has been abysmal, but he admits he feels better for it. Do you think we should be discussing the Max situation more?' she added. 'I mean, not delve around in it. But draw it out of him.'

'Nick loves his bad-taste jokes. I think perhaps we should joke about it.'

'OK. That'll either go well, or extraordinarily badly. Let's balance on the knife edge.'

God, but Hannah's place was lovely. She'd unpacked since they were here last, and now there were candles in Moroccan-style holders casting handfuls of geometric patterned lights into chalk-white corners. The interloping cat was curled up on the linen-covered sofa.

'He's got his ginger feet under the table, I see,' Nick said, taking his shop-fresh autumn/winter coat off and hanging it up neatly. 'Shove up, Carrot Bollocks.'

Edie still hadn't taken her coat off, looking at the room. A certainty that had been forming was now fully formed.

'Something I've been thinking about,' Edie said. 'I might move back. To Nottingham.'

Hannah and Nick stared at her.

'*Really?*' Hannah said, in a tone of bare disbelief.

'Yes. Is it that surprising?'

'You've always been so London or bust, *he who is tired of London*. I honestly never thought you'd leave.'

'I didn't think you liked Nottingham much, either?' Nick said.

'I think it got tarnished with what it represented, some of the bad memories,' Edie said.

'Are you listening to these sick burns, Hannah? It's like she's pissing directly in our ears.'

'Appalling,' Hannah agreed.

'Not you two! You're the best of it. I meant family stuff.' They nodded.

'Well, I'd be over the bloody moon if you stay. That goes without saying,' Hannah said.

'This is ace, ace news, Tommo,' Nick said. 'It took us a while, but the Avengers have reassembled, haven't they?'

They all grinned at each other stupidly. Edie thought she might feel some loss at saying she was weary of London, but she didn't: only release.

Hannah arranged bowls of crisps, nuts, grapes and olives and they enjoyed some serial killing in foggy San Francisco in the 1970s. Hannah declared she was 'cacking herself' after they turned the lights back up.

'I don't know why you're so nervous, Hannah, they caught the guy,' Nick said. 'Oh no – wait, they didn't, did they, hahaha. At least he'll be very old now. He'd be buzzing after you in his mobility scooter like a homicidal bee.'

Hannah topped up their drinks and Nick said his colleagues were trying to set him up with a girl called Ros who was billed as 'lovely but a bit batty'.

'There are a lot of *lovely but batty* women out there,' Hannah said. 'You've done your time. You are not the council bat catcher. Steer clear.'

'It makes me wonder what my one-line summary would be though,' Edie said, slightly glumly.

'Foul mouth, great tits,' Nick said. 'Happy to help.'

As they flipped channels, they passed an old episode of *Blood & Gold*. Prince Wulfroarer, who looked exactly like this other guy Edie knew, moving in for a kiss with his servant wench beloved, Malleflead. Edie was suddenly rapt, watching their lips meet on the battlefield and swirling with conflicting feelings: jealousy, desire, and oddly, pride. There was someone she'd met, being someone else, on telly. Nice one, Elliot.

'He'll pay for that, in blood or gold,' Nick said.

'It was gold, then blood,' Edie said. 'Never trust a word out of Count Bragstard's mouth.'

'Oh ta, spoiler queen!' Hannah said. 'I was going to do a *Blood & Gold* marathon once I'd finished *Breaking Bad*.'

'Statute of limitations,' Nick said. 'Wulfroarer got killed off ages ago. Hang on, and if he hadn't been killed off, how would Elliot Owen be working here? Are you going to shout SPOILER KING at him if you see him in the street?'

Hannah rolled her eyes.

'You still getting on with him, Edith? It's nice to hear he's nice,' Hannah said. 'Oh, you know the secret you wouldn't tell us? He isn't gay, is he?'

'No! I asked him if he was. It went badly, and we established he wasn't.'

Nick gurgled with laughter.

'Loving imagining how you subtly teased it out of him. Did you ask if he was the kind of man who "finds Judy Garland fabulous"?'

'Shuttup!' Edie moaned. 'Last time I saw him, he got me to rehearse a sexy scene with him and I went full *Downton Abbey* dowager aunt. Mortifying.'

Hannah ate a grape and made a thoughtful face.

'Could those two things not be connected?'

'What?'

'You thinking he was gay, and him being very keen to prove his hetero-ness not long after.'

Oh. Actually, Edie had never considered that might've been the trigger. She remembered Elliot saying something about 'wounded masculine pride at not coming across the way he thought he was'. Perhaps that was it. She thought it was more likely than him suddenly discovering he had an Edie pecca-dillo.

'He was flirting with you?' Hannah said.

'Yeah, a bit. Purely to wind me up.'

'Why couldn't he flirt because he fancies you?'

'Because he's Elliot Owen! And I'm me.'

'You're very attractive.'

'I concur,' Nick said.

'That's very nice of you both, but he dates stratospherically gorgeous famous people.'

Hannah raised an eyebrow. 'And flirts with you.'

A pause, where Edie couldn't find an answer.

'In sort of related news, I've started seeing my fling from that training course. You know, the person I slept with, when I ended it with Pete?' Hannah said.

'Wow,' Edie said. 'That's great. Where does he live?'

'She lives in Yorkshire. Leeds.'

A pause where Edie and Nick looked at each other.

'Sorry, who . . .?'

'She is a she. I'm seeing a woman,' Hannah said.

A hush fell briefly, broken by Nick saying: 'This is the hottest thing to ever happen.'

Hannah threw a grape at him and started laughing while Edie said: 'Hannah, this is amazing news!'

'I'd been holding off telling you because I didn't know if the fling was a thing. I'd never been attracted to a woman before and I didn't know if it was a one-off. You know, too much pink wine girl gayness. And I suppose I still don't know if it's a one-off because it's only Chloe I like, in that way.'

Pause. 'Also Pete's parents have been real shits about the split and I didn't want to give them the satisfaction of saying "Our poor son ditched by the midlife lesbian".'

'My life sucks even more than I thought,' Nick said. 'Girl-on-girl action, flirting with famous actors. Hey, that's a thought –' he turned to Edie. 'Reckon you could get me an interview with Elliot, on the show?'

'Er. I'll ask. I get the impression his publicity schedule is locked down at very high levels.'

'Cheers. It would be like Viagra for the listening figures.'

Edie recalled Archie saying Edie could get Elliot to do things no one else could, that theirs was a special relationship. She had to shake this sort of thinking off, it was merely the ravings of a man-mental.

'Edith's moving back to Nottingham. I'm seeing a woman. We're having a truly surprising news day,' Hannah said. 'What next? Maybe you'll see the light and renew your vows with Alice, Nick?'

Nick stood up to go to the loo.

'I would rather lick the perineum of Piers Morgan.'

53

Edie wanted to ask Elliot what the deal was with Fraser, but every time she drafted an inquiry, she worried it looked prurient. If Elliot wanted to discuss it with her, he surely would. Then an aimless Saturday afternoon was unexpectedly punctuated by a text from the irrepressible younger Owen brother himself.

Edie! Still coming tonight, did Elliot remind you? We're going Boilermaker, I've put you on our guest list, it's in my name. PS I'm on 3% battery here so pardon my whoops if this conversation stops very suddenly. Fraz x

Thank you! What time? Sorry for using up some of the 3%. Ex

Silence. She could text Elliot, of course. Should she? She wasn't sure he knew she was going. Might be useful pretext to warn him, so she didn't have to see his look of surprise. After all, he hadn't mentioned it.

Hi Elliot. Just wondered if there was a start time tonight? Fraser was in the middle of giving me the plans when his phone battery died. Cheers. Ex PS presume you've not had The Talk yet

Her phone rang. Elliot. She had a ripple of discomfort that he'd reacted so fast. That was either a great sign, or not a great sign.

'Edie, hi! It's me. Er. You're coming tonight?'

His tone revealed: Not A Great Sign.

'Yes. Fraser invited me. Sorry, I thought you knew?'

Or at least I hoped you'd pretend you knew.

'No, Fraser didn't mention it.' Elliot hesitated. 'We've not had the chat yet, no. He's here with his wolf pack and I can't get a moment alone with him so far.'

'Oh.'

'He's got your number?' Elliot sounded edgy.

'We swapped numbers when we met, he said he wanted me to come to this.'

'Ah! OK. Sure.'

Ouch. Edie could tell Elliot didn't like this. She could hear his brain ticking over with the ticking off he was going to give Fraser. *It'd be nice if you'd checked with me . . . we have to work together, I'd rather not feel reminded of work when I'm out . . .*

'Unless I'm intruding . . .' Edie could hardly suddenly find she was busy, when she'd been midway through organising her attendance with Fraser.

'Not at all. You're completely welcome. It'd be great to see you.'

Arrrgh. Edie knew this was the polite awkwardness of Elliot now having to pretend he was fine with it and Edie trying to give him an out and Elliot not taking it because courtesy dictated he didn't, however much he wanted to.

'If you're sure?'

'Yes of course. Uhm, eight o'clock or so start?'

'Great.'

The trap shut and they were locked in it together. Edie had committed herself to going when she now wanted to pull out, and Elliot had committed himself to pretending he wanted her to go, when he was obviously going to call Fraser as soon as his phone was working again, and blast him about not sticking random copywriters on his guest lists.

Edie sat herself in front of her bedroom mirror and thought: *You have to try to look nice tonight.* No more avoiding looking at yourself, and dressing to disappear, ever since those people on the internet called you a tart. She couldn't go out on the tiles with the Owens and feel like she'd attract 'who invited Whistler's Mother' curiosity.

She had a shower, dried her hair and pushed it back from her face with a towelling headband, spending proper care and attention over her make-up. Edie told herself she wasn't larding it on, she was turning into a bewitching creature made of eyes and cheekbones.

Very attractive, that's what your best friends thought, said the angel on her shoulder. *Hah, yeah – your best friends! Strangers who owe you nothing say you're waaay too heavy on the blusher and top heavy,* said the devil.

Unfortunately, her hair had heard she needed it to play ball tonight, and decided to look lank, stringy and generally what her father called 'peely wally'.

In desperation, Edie ran some mousse through it, made two plaits and Kirby-gripped them to the crown of her head. She feared the look was slightly 'Princess Leia's let herself go' but there was no time left to get a proper blow-dry.

She chose a dress she'd been saving for a special day that had never arrived. A black patterned halter neck, it pulled tight under her bust and flowed over her hips, and made Edie feel neat of figure. It had that pleasing effect of putting skin on show without making her feel uncomfortably exposed.

God, she needed some Dutch courage though. Her pink champagne from her birthday was in the fridge downstairs. Edie popped it and sat at the breakfast bar, sipping it warily.

'Wowee, someone looks all dressed up with somewhere to go!' her dad came in. 'What a beautiful daughter I have.'

'*Dad*,' Edie said, in that obligatory embarrassed adolescent voice. 'But. Thanks.'

'What's the occasion?'

Edie flinched slightly that her extra effort was so obvious, then considered this was pathetic when she *had* gone to extra effort. As if her dad saying, 'Oh are you off to do some gardening?' was the desired image.

'I'm going for a drink with Elliot Owen and his brother.'

'Goodness, high society. Have fun. Tell them I am open to any calls asking for my daughter's hand in marriage.'

Edie winced and mumbled it was hardly likely. Was it the right time to tell her dad about moving back to the city? She thought not: she hadn't worked out the details and wanted to have a few more answers.

Meg loafed in and did a double take at Edie's appearance.

'What's going on?'

'I'm going out,' Edie said.

'On the game?'

54

It was easy to see how being famous could bend your ego out of shape and blow it up big, especially if your ego was of healthy size and made of very inflatable materials to start with.

This bar was usually one with a queue, but there was no queue if you were Elliot Owen. The simple practicalities of him not being able to inhabit confined spaces with members of the public meant first-class lounge treatment all the way.

The concept of this bar was a speakeasy, concealed behind a boiler showroom's utilitarian frontage. There were sample models nailed to the walls in the brightly lit, spartan reception, where people milled and kicked their heels until there was space free for a table in the hidden bar beyond.

Edie gave Fraser's name to the bored doorman behind the desk. He picked up a walkie-talkie and repeated her name into it. A crackle of static, a response and he nodded: 'Go on.'

Edie found herself in what appeared to be a store cupboard. What the . . . ? She worked out the door was a false wall, with a broom hung on it. Edie pushed on the dummy sink and she was into the dark and noisy main room, with a strong smell of incense. It was fair to say that Nottingham had changed a bit since Edie was drinking Snakey Bs in its more cobwebby historic pubs.

It was table service only, dotted with pot plants, and felt slightly like someone had hit the lights and installed a disco in a garden centre. She was pointed to Elliot's group. They had two large tables to the right of the bar that ran the length of the far wall, and what seemed to be an exclusion zone of two other empty tables in front that weren't in use but acted as a barrier from the civilians.

The crowd was intimidating. The boys were tall, well-dressed, active-looking types: private school Slytherins. The sort Edie would normally run a mile from. She took a moment to spot Elliot. He was seated in the darkest corner, a black sweater and his black hair rendering him a shadow, with people protectively and possessively clustered around him.

And naturally, they were thronged by beautiful women. They were punky, stylish and arty looking: shattered ombre bobs and backcombed side plaits, leather skirts and backless dresses. One Spanish-looking girl was in a crop top and jeans, exposing an incredible sculpted midriff. It reminded Edie that some figures were the rollover ball in the genetic lottery and no amount of hours in the gym were ever giving you a body moulded from rubber like that.

Yep. Thoroughly intimidating. Edie approached the table doing an apologetic-for-existing face and feeling about as sexy as a tortoise in a pitta bread. She deliberately avoided meeting

Elliot's eyes, and homed in on Fraser instead: the one who'd genuinely wanted her here.

As soon as Fraser spotted her, he broke from the group. He made a fuss of finding her a seat opposite him, pushing a menu into her hands and waving a waiter over. That was that: she was being looked after.

Edie went from, 'Oh God, why the hell am I here' to 'nicely buzzed, laughing and possibly flirting back' in fifteen minutes flat, with the help of a Negroni with a huge ball of ice in it, as recommended by her attentive companion. Yep, the Owen boys had nice manners.

Though she wasn't so naïve to not realise she might be getting special service, it was a surprise: Edie had assumed garrulous Fraser's previous flirting was simply because she was available to be flirted with. In the company of gorgeous women ten years her junior, she didn't expect to rate much more than a friendly hello.

Nevertheless, Fraser was taking Instagrams of the glow-in-the-dark cocktails and showering her with his undivided attention.

'Try mine!' He looked intently and somewhat lasciviously at Edie as she nipped the straw between her teeth and sucked. When Fraser didn't know she was looking, she saw his gaze sweep along her collarbones and down her bare arms. It had been a while since Edie had felt like someone fancied her, and it was welcome. Their senses of humour matched well enough to make them good chemistry for an evening out. She sensed Fraser wasn't exactly deep but that was OK, not everyone had to be.

After one particularly raucous bout of laughter, she glanced over at Elliot. He was staring at them with consternation that he quickly tried to conceal. Edie wanted to say to him: *Relax, I'm not going to drop you in it and say anything when inebriated.* Though his discomfort could also be because she'd ducked the red rope. She'd infiltrated a social occasion, without checking with him first. Not cool.

Elliot put a palm up in greeting, having been caught looking vaguely aghast, and Edie waved back. Elliot waved her over. There was a seat temporarily vacated in front of him. As she sat down he said:

'Is my brother being lewd?'

'Lewd,' she laughed. 'No. Or ribald. Despite the wenches and vittles.'

Elliot grinned.

'Got to have vittles. What do you think to the bar?'

'Fun,' Edie said.

'The city's changed a bit since our youth, eh?'

'Yes, I was just thinking that! Well, my youth more than yours. You youthful sod.'

Elliot said: 'I'm in no way being cheesy but aren't you around my age? I thought you were thirty, max.'

'Thirty-six,' Edie said, her vanity a little sorry to have to disabuse him. She wasn't going to go the Margot route though. Lying was a bad scene.

She thought he might do a poorly concealed 'over the hill' reel back but he said: 'Good genes.' Then she saw that look cross his face. *Oh God, I said good genes and her mum killed herself at that age.*

'Cheers, that's very good to hear!' she said, aiming for enough enthusiasm that he'd realise that it wasn't a faux pas.

Edie looked around and said, 'Whose chair have I stolen? Do they want it back?'

'Don't move,' Elliot stage-hissed, a hand on her arm, 'These are Fraser's friends. I like having some adult company.'

Edie beamed. That compliment landed.

They went on a Nottingham history tour, in conversation: the sweaty ceiling that dripped on the audience at gigs in Rock City, first illicit pints in the Old Angel, meeting friends at the Left Lion, buying Gothy teenage nonsense in Ice Nine.

Edie realised that she and the opinionated, articulate and sensitive Elliot would've been friends at school, if fate had thrown them together.

And a miraculous thing occurred, while they were friendly-arguing over the precise location of a long-gone bar in the Lace Market. She realised Elliot had become Elliot her friend, first, and Elliot the famous person, second. She saw what Fraser meant. The celebrity had become someone else, an assumed identity, not the man she knew.

'This music,' Elliot said, at one point, after INXS's 'Never Tear Us Apart' segued into the Simple Minds one from the John Hughes film, 'is exactly judged to make thirty-ish people feel nostalgic isn't it?'

'*Saudade*,' Edie said.

'What?' Elliot half-shouted over the din, not unreasonably.

'A Portuguese word that has no direct translation, it means "a profound longing for something or someone that is absent and might never return". Sort of turbo-charged, ultra-poignant nostalgia. "The love that remains after someone is gone."'

'Wow. And how do you say it?'

'*Saw-Dadi.*'

Elliot repeated it. 'I like that a lot.'

His eyes glittered in the darkness of the bar. Edie had an overwhelming urge to lean forward and kiss him on that incredible mouth. She couldn't hide from it or dodge it any longer; yes, she had the crush that everyone had. And not only that, she had it pretty bad. If feelings for Elliot helped switch her back on after the Jack debacle though, was it a problem? After all, nothing was going to come of it.

She succumbed to fantasy fiction for a moment and let herself imagine: *What if this moment was real? What if this was mutual? What if they went home together?*

As mad as that sounded, with alcohol in her bloodstream and Depeche Mode's 'I Feel You' pounding in her ears and his steady gaze holding hers too long – in a way that seemed to clearly *say something* – Edie wanted to let go briefly and dream it was possible.

Then she stopped herself, because it wasn't real, and at some point, the lights would come back on. When they did, no doubt some lissom creature would mysteriously appear at Elliot's side and disappear into the night with him. This girl would be someone he had a completely uncomplicated, physical-thing-only, sailor-on-shore-leave understanding with, brokered in whatever secret ways famous people organised their hook-ups. When that happened, Edie didn't want to feel sad. Knowing Elliot had made her happier, and she had no room for more sadness.

55

Nevertheless, if this girl was going to slink from the shadows, fair play, Edie had a difficult time guessing which one she might be. When Elliot had given Edie his yarn about not 'Augustus Glooping' his way round the sexual Wonka factory he found himself in, she'd taken it with a pinch of salt. Not least because she had no idea what counted as restraint in famous world. Perhaps one threesome a week was the monastic life.

Yet Edie had to admit that Elliot didn't appear to be looking at any of the gorgeous young things mothing around him. Not so much as a stray glance; although the lighting was low and the room was busy, maybe she'd missed it. His last girlfriend was Heather Lily, for God's sake. Edie hated to think what would be the minimum aesthetic criteria required to turn his head.

She shook off the mild embarrassment of thinking it was feasible there was attraction between them and excused herself to the loo, and then to the bar. Edie was encouraged to sit back down by the waitress and by this time, she saw her seat opposite Elliot had been taken by Fraser.

Something about the way their heads were angled, speaking closely, followed by a quick scan of the bar by Fraser, whose eyes fastened on her, suggested to Edie she might be being spoken of.

Fraser vacated her seat and indicated it was hers again.

'No, it's fine,' Edie said, gesticulating. 'I don't want to monopolise the Owens.'

Elliot pouted and cupped his hands round his mouth: 'Am I that boring?'

Edie sensed many girls watching this exchange, dearly hoping she'd stay where she was.

'No!' Edie said, pointing at herself, 'I am!'

'Come back at once,' Elliot said, pointing emphatically at the chair.

Edie made a mock-grimace and took her former seat again. This might be a one-night-only deal, her importance to him, but it was thrilling all the same. It was one night more than she thought she'd spend socialising with a celebrity.

'You know, I could get offended,' Elliot said.

'I thought you'd want to share yourself round!' Edie said.

'What am I, fucking hummus?!'

Edie shook with laughter and she could see Elliot was pleased to have amused her, looking at her over the rim of his glass with his funny-and-sly expression.

This was fun. He was fun.

Was he a real friend? Could this happen? Would they keep in touch when he was back in the States? The odd humorous email? Funny cat gifs? I mean, maybe not once the memory of this brief interlude in his life faded, but . . . She wanted to. Edie couldn't remember hitting it off like this with someone in a long time. Ugh, since Jack, she supposed.

'Real talk now. Do you like gifs of cats doing funny things?' Edie said.

'Of course, doesn't everyone? Have you seen the one with the cat in the helmet with the light sabre?' Edie shook her head. Elliot fiddled with his phone to find the link. Edie gazed at the top of his head and imagined running her fingers through his brown-black hair.

Elliot held the phone up for her and Edie watched, laughing, as a confused Persian jerked its head from side to side to the *whomp-whomp whoosh* of a light sabre being swung around a lounge.

A text appeared on Elliot's phone, over the screen, from 'Fraz'. Edie could read the words in the bright blue bubble of the preview window. Hah, why didn't he have previews turned . . . wait . . .

You say Edie's screwed up & more issues than the Beano? I say:
WOOF

56

Edie looked at it and blinked. She re-read it, as its meaning sunk in. It was like being hit around the head with a sandbag; the dull thud, the sudden pain.

Elliot was still looking at her expectantly, thinking she was enjoying cats playing *Star Wars*. She had seconds to decide what to do.

She whipped round, stood up and marched out, pushing through the exit, past the throng of people waiting to get into the bar where rumour had it, a famous actor was drinking tonight. That's a French Exit for you, Margot. She didn't care. She couldn't stay a moment longer with those people.

Edie scanned for taxis, heart pounding. There was one with its light on, parked a little way down the street ahead, outside Broadway cinema. She broke into a trot to get to it.

Elliot's voice rang out clearly, behind her.

'Edie! Edie?'

She marched onwards determinedly. Elliot ran ahead, cut her off and stood in her path.

'Let me past,' she said, looking up at him. Ugh, she couldn't bear to look at him and his stupid pretty fake face.

'What you read isn't what you think.'

'Huh. Leave me alone, Elliot,' Edie said. 'Really. I mean it.'

He looked stricken. Good. Edie knew she was making Meg's toddler huff gurn and didn't care. She was incandescent.

'Let me explain. I can explain.'

Edie folded her arms.

'Oh, OK, so you weren't running me down and saying to your brother, Don't bang a basket case?'

'Yes to the part about me not wanting my brother to sleep with you, no to the rest . . .'

'You said those things about me?'

'Yes, but if you'll let me give you the context . . .'

'What context could possibly make that OK?'

Elliot was going to try to minimise the damage and explain it away; of course he was. He didn't want to be the bad guy. If Edie let him persuade her there was any exculpation here, she was a rank fool.

And if it wasn't for that split-second fail with the technology, she'd still be giggling and confiding and thinking this man genuinely liked her. She'd been fantasising about going home with him, for God's sake. The blow to her pride, and most of all, the discovery of another false friend: it was more than Edie could withstand. She was going to let him have it.

'You know what, Elliot, I get that *you're kind of a big deal*, but you're irrelevant to me. I'm not a fan girl and you're just a bloke I'm working with for a very limited time. You didn't need to pretend to be my friend. I don't have some giant *need* in me to be befriended. Arm's length would've suited me absolutely fine. No loss.'

Elliot looked upset at this, and it only spurred Edie on.

'I don't give two shits about you, to be blunt, and I don't care if it's entirely mutual. So why do people like you—'

Elliot's face had been taut during her tirade, but at this, his eyes widened in shock.

'There's a "people like me" now?'

'—people like you act matey, then behind my back, say what a "nightmare" I am? Just avoid my company. Would that have been so hard?"

'I don't think you're a nightmare! Not in the least!'

Edie drew breath and went for the big finish. She didn't care what this cost her. She was so angry and distraught, she was practically seeing double.

'And when I told you about my mum, which I didn't want to tell you, by the way, but you put me on the spot. Instead of saying *Oh God Edie, how awful, poor you*, why not simply say: "Oh dear, you must be a really screwed-up mess." Oh no,' Edie put up both palms. 'That'd be a terrible thing to say, right? But you did. Behind my back. Which do you think hurts more? Which do you think makes you the better or worse person?'

'I don't think you're screwed up!' Elliot said, almost shouting. 'I think you're one of the sanest people I've ever met.'

'"Edie has more issues than the *Beano*,"' Edie quoted. 'It's a pretty big vote of no confidence, isn't it?'

Elliot winced.

'I was trying to deter Fraser, that's all. I was saying "high maintenance" – which isn't true – anything, to get him to flirt elsewhere. He was all over you tonight and it was a very hasty, ill-considered and ungentlemanly way to get him to back off. I'm dying here, honestly.' He ran his hands through his hair and Edie thought, Oh sod off if you think your *music video in a Mustang* expression is going to get you anywhere.

'Why is Fraser liking me such a crisis? Am I not good enough even for a casual thing? I don't think WOOF indicates a desire to wed, I think you're safe from me ruining the Owen name.'

'Of course not. Because,' Elliot paused. 'Because I didn't like the idea. At all.'

He stared at her, jaw set hard in a miserable yet defiant grimace. Edie knew what he meant: he feared if she and Fraser shared throes of passion, she might also share his secret. What a poor view he had of her character, when you stripped away the superficial.

'Oi! I am my Kingdom! Oi!'

They looked over to see a group of check-shirted lads outside the Rough Trade shop opposite.

'Are you the prince? Wolf Whorer!'

Elliot ignored them and turned back to Edie.

'Sorry you find the prospect of me and your relative so revolting,' Edie said. 'The one degree to Kevin Bacon and all that. Seems pretty snobby and vile, that I didn't pass your strict criteria for a worthy consort.'

'Oh . . . man. This isn't going right at all. It's not because I thought you weren't good enough for Fraz. Completely the opposite.' Elliot rubbed his chin. 'You were working with me and we were friends and I . . . felt like you . . . belonged to me, not him. I know how obnoxious that sounds, and I'm sorry.'

And the spoilt kid, dog in the manger thing where he didn't want his brother to put his lackey to another use. Edie understood a little more again but it didn't make her any warmer towards him.

'You could've said to Fraser, *Don't go there, she's my friend*, then? I still don't see the need for nastiness about me.'

'The reason I didn't simply say that to Fraz is − well, he hasn't won all those sporting medals for nothing. If he knew I didn't want him to do something, he'd take it as a challenge . . .'

'Oh my God, so what am I, PING-PONG?'

'No! Oh Christ. How do I say this now . . .' Elliot rubbed his forehead.

'Or you could've said to me: "Hey, Edie. Please don't boff my brother, it'll be weird, what with us working together?"'

'I didn't have the guts to do that.'

'Why not?'

'You might've said you wanted to. Can you really not see why I went to him and not you?'

'*Bros before hoes*, isn't that the line?'

'No! God.' Elliot put his hands on his head, in the style of a footballer who's missed a penalty. 'I completely get why you're raging after thinking I was talking about you in that way. But I'm telling you the truth.'

'No you're not. You didn't ask me not to sleep with Fraser because you thought: "Of course it's a done deal that Edie will take any chance she gets, don't you know what a desperate needy screw-up she is." Do you know, it's not a massive surprise, Elliot. I knew from our conversation earlier today you didn't want me to come. Not all your acting is so great.'

Phew, Edie was unstoppably savage. Elliot looked distraught. He was still only experiencing a small per cent of what he'd inflicted on her.

'That was *not* because I didn't want you to come! I was freaked out my brother had your number and might be sexting you dick pics, or something.'

'Hey. You're shorter in real life!' someone called, from across the street.

They looked back and saw the heckling group had got a few more members, some female.

'Fuck off mate,' Elliot said, and the group exploded into jeering, cackles, and 'oooooh, get you'.

'You need to go back to the bar before you get mobbed,' Edie said, 'And I want to go home.'

'Edie, I don't want to leave it like this.'

'Well this is how it is. I'm going to take my many issues home in that taxi. Good job it's a five-seater.'

'Get your tits out! Oi! Get your tits out for the prince!'

Edie turned and gave their latest male antagonist the V sign, producing more delighted screeching.

'Night,' she said to a stricken-looking Elliot, and wrenched the heavy door of a Hackney open. She didn't look back, but angered herself by worrying that Elliot was out there with no protection and hyenas around him. She shouldn't care. From now on, she wouldn't care.

57

When Edie was younger and she needed to escape the walls and ceiling of her home pressing down on her, she used to walk. And walk, and walk. Since she'd come back to Nottingham she liked having a compact city to traverse again, the distances she could cover made her feel like a Scott of the Antarctic explorer.

I am just going outside and may be some time.

Her father caught her slipping out of the quiet house before nine a.m. 'No hangover? My goodness. Where's my daughter and what have you done with her?'

Edie said something about how those cocktails were clearly a rip-off, couldn't even get drunk for your money any more, and disappeared swiftly before he could notice her downcast demeanour.

She walked down past the terraces of Forest Fields, up through the Forest Recreation Ground, once a year taken over by the organised chaos of Goose Fair, and through the Arboretum, following the tramlines into the city centre. August was nearly over and you could sense the cooler snap to the air coming, that smell of September.

Why bother to care about anyone? she thought, as she reached the city centre and bought herself a coffee in a cardboard cup, sipping it through the tracheotomy slit in the plastic lid. Most of them let you down. Most people were awful. The initial outrage with Elliot had given way to a deep, miserable disappointment in humankind. Her cynicism had said, 'too good to be true' about their friendship. Now, she was no longer sure it was cynicism, more like realism.

She expected mea culpas to limp in, and she got them by mid-morning.

First Fraser, trying to play Kofi Annan, with no success.

Edie, I'm an absolute arsehole for sending that text, blame me. Elliot just freaked because he thought I was going to try to take you home and I was totally paraphrasing. Please forgive him, I know he thinks the world of you. Fraz x

Edie texted back polite thanks to Fraser and absolved him of any criminal activity. She couldn't bring herself to reply to Elliot's near-simultaneous text for an hour.

I did a lot of apologising last night & I appreciate repeating those apologies is probably both useless and irritating, but anyway: I'm so sorry, Edie. I don't think those things about you, not at all, not even a bit. I said them in a panic. I hate the thought of hurting you more than I can say. Ex

The last line affected her. Then she remembered he was an actor, who read from scripts. In real life, he wasn't the person she thought he was. She couldn't find it in herself to say a false: 'It's OK.' Making him feel better meant making a doormat of herself. Why should she make him feel better?

What's done is done. Let's put it behind us and finish the book.

It wasn't just that he'd hurt her, it was how he'd hurt her.

She could've more easily forgiven overhearing standard laddish put-downs. '*Edie? Wow, nice enough girl, think you could do better though, mate, and you know she's thirty-six?*'

Being pragmatic, she would've been pained but not surprised to find Elliot had judged her and found her wanting in that respect.

It was the betrayal of knowledge of her past she couldn't stand, used to paint her as a clingy, flaky hysteric. Was that true, had she come across as someone with her shit very much not together? She wished so much she'd never told him about Jack, or the Facebook page. Or her mum. She'd made herself vulnerable and he'd thrown it back in her face.

And worst of all, Elliot should be able to empathise. He understood what it was like to get over something like that, the work it took to put it behind you. They'd bonded over exactly that. In fact, Edie could date her most tender feelings towards him back to that moment in the hotel.

Elliot was trying to cover it his betrayal with this bluster about not liking the thought of her and Fraser at it like knives – probably under his parents' roof – but there wasn't enough wallpaper to cover the gap, in Edie's view. It had stopped short of being a full explanation.

She walked home with her iPod blaring in her ears, New Order's 'Bizarre Love Triangle', which seemed to sum up the last year pretty well. Apart from the love.

When she got in, she checked her phone and found three missed calls from Elliot. Edie decided to ignore them, let him sweat overnight. She wasn't paid to speak to him on a Sunday and she didn't know what tone to take with him.

Polite but cold? Terse but businesslike? Raging harpy batcrackers, to play up to her stereotype?

Then, Nick was calling her. She had the 'grave walk', prescient shiver that this was more attention than she usually fielded of a Sunday, and something might be up.

'Edith?' Nick said. 'Are you alright?'

'. . . Yeah?'

'Have you seen it?'

'What?'

'You're in the *Mirror*.'

'I'm where?'

For a second Edie thought of fairytale mirrors, enchanted oval glasses that told Wicked Queens home truths. Then her brain aligned with the meaning: 'I'm *what*?'

'Go look online. Call me back.'

Edie pulled her laptop out and with shaking hands, brought up the *Mirror* website.

In the right-hand side bar, she saw, with a jolt that made her nauseous, a story with a nighttime paparazzi photo as illustration. She could recognise Elliot, and holy shitting hell, that was her with him. There were almost dots dancing in her vision, she was trying to take it in so fast. Caption. 'Elliot Owen fight with mystery woman.'

Her stomach rolled over and she thought she might actually be sick. Edie clicked the link.

58

He was beheaded in Blood & Gold, *after falling for the wrong girl – and heartthrob actor Elliot Owen may get it in the neck again when his actress girlfriend Heather Lily sees our snaps.*

The 31-year-old Brit was caught having a heated debate in the street with a mystery brunette – and it didn't look like they were discussing the show's controversial season finale.

The star, known to millions as Prince Wulfroarer, is back in his hometown, Nottingham, filming BBC crime series, Gun City. *And it seems he's wasted no time making himself at home.*

One onlooker said: 'It was obvious she was very upset about something and he was trying to calm her down. They were talking in an incredibly intense way and seemed to know each other very well. You don't expect to see Prince Wulfroarer having a slanging match outside your local!'

At one point, Owen appeared to hold his head in despair. When the emotional exchange was over, she jumped into a cab and went home without him – a move to baffle Owen's army of female fans.

The incident seems to confirm rumours that Elliot and his

*on-off love, Lily, 28, who's based in Manhattan, are 'on a break'.
Cryptic tweets posted by the Hampshire-born beauty last month
suggested she was upset by his failure to commit.*

*Our well-placed source said: 'Elliot and Heather have been
done for a while but he keeps begging her for one last chance.
She's been considering taking him back but this is likely to be
the last straw. Heather feels Elliot's played her enough. He
needs to decide what he wants.'*

*And it wasn't just Owen who got on the wrong side of his
new friend last night. His pretty brunette companion also made
her feelings known to a passer-by who tried to intervene in
the row, making a direct gesture with two fingers. She may
need this fighting spirit if Heather decides to pay a visit to
her man.*

**Do you know who the girl with Elliot Owen is? Call our
newsdesk now.*

Edie scanned down the photos. Her and Elliot's row, grue-
somely rendered in a series of poorly composed phone pictures.
There were Elliot's hands on his head, his expression hangdog
during Edie's tirade. Edie with arms folded, scowling, as Elliot
tried to placate her. And the pièce de résistance – Edie proffering the Vs to her antagonist. Oh, God. Oh no. Of course
that crowd had their phones aloft, of course they did.

She couldn't avoid ringing Elliot back now. The magnitude
of the situation suspended the rules of their current conflict.
You could no more scrap with someone who was helping
you escape a burning building.

'Edie,' Elliot said as soon as he picked up, 'you've seen the papers?'

'Yes,' she said. 'Elliot, I'm really sorry.'

A pause that she realised was stunned silence.

'Why are *you* sorry?'

'I should've realised we were being photographed and walked off faster. And not been flicking Vs at people.'

'Don't be daft. It was my stupidity, I followed you. And he was shouting about getting your tits out, I should've punched him.'

'That would be worse, right now, I think,' Edie said, palm on clammy forehead.

'I've spoken to my publicist. She says without more photos of us together, this is probably going to be a one-day wonder. I mean, other sites will crab the story, but in terms of *new* news . . .'

'OK,' Edie said, trying to get her breathing under control. She sensed a big fat hairy 'but' coming, in Elliot's tone.

'But, the appeal asking about who you are. They probably will do a follow-up story once they know. And it's not impossible Jan will stick her oar in, of course.'

'Right,' Edie said, dully. Oh God. She'd have to go downstairs and tell her dad . . .

'Don't worry about Heather turning up, by the way. She couldn't find Nottingham on a map.' Elliot hesitated. 'Not that you'd have anything to worry about even if she did.'

Edie grasped randomly at one of many, many questions.

'What was that about you begging Heather for one more chance?'

'Hah, classic wasn't it! Team Heather PR in full effect, there. Yeah, I wonder where they found this mystery source who makes me sound the wanker and her the embattled angel. "Elliot needs to decide what he wants." More embroidery than a crafting party.'

Edie wasn't about to be sucked back in by Elliot's knack for a pomposity-puncturing, witty turn of phrase. She accepted they had to work together on this, but full return to former friendship? Nope.

'What you have to do,' Elliot continued, 'Is warn friends and family that press might call and to not talk to them. Think of this as a fire and the more oxygen you starve from it, the quicker it goes out.'

'The problem is, because of what happened at the wedding, there's a large number of people who have it in for me. They'll grab the phone as soon as they see this and say they know who I am.' Edie hadn't thought of this, until she said it aloud. 'Meaning, the wedding stuff will probably come out?'

A heavy pause, one where she very much wanted Elliot to contradict her.

'Shit. I hadn't thought about that.'

Edie didn't know what to say. This was 360 degrees of terrible.

'Edie, anything I can do to protect you, I will. You don't deserve any of this.'

'I'm going to be notorious, all over again, aren't I?'

She took a deep shuddering breath and couldn't speak while she quelled the tears.

'Edie? Are you still there?'

'Mmm-hmm,' she said. A hoarse whisper: 'Just . . . *God*.'

She couldn't stop herself doing small sobs now.

'Shit, Edie, don't cry. Please. It's going to be alright. I'll look after you, I promise.'

Lovely words, that amounted to nothing. She'd been here before.

'S'OK,' she gasped. 'I'd best go tell my family.'

'I'm so sorry that knowing me has brought this down on you. Please let me know if there's anything more I can do. I can get my publicist to speak to you directly if it helps.'

Edie thanked him, but thought 'don't say anything' was pretty clear and simple.

'Also, Edie. About last night . . .'

'Let's park that,' Edie said, quickly. 'I can't handle that right now.'

Elliot acquiesced, sounding grim.

Edie went downstairs, and found her dad and Meg in the sitting room, watching *Antiques Roadshow*.

'Dad, Meg,' she said.

'That's a minging clock,' Meg said. 'I'd sell it. It looks like something you'd find in an old paedo's house.'

'Do paedophiles collect a particular sort of timepiece?' her dad said. 'Perhaps the police need to know about this.'

'*Dad*. There's something I have to tell you both.'

They both looked up. Edie opted for a blurt.

'I'm in the *Mirror*. The newspaper. Well, online. I had a . . . debate with Elliot in the street last night and someone took pictures. They're saying I'm his girlfriend, but I'm not.'

Moments later they were clustered round Edie's laptop

on the breakfast bar, her dad peering at it with his readers on.

'It's not the worst thing to happen, is it? Some silly gossip?' Her dad pointed at the third photo, where Edie, pursed lips, had her arms folded. 'Uh oh, I know that face. Poor lad.'

'Also. There might be another story,' Edie said, and Meg stared at her like she had jumped out of a fireplace in a shower of Floo Powder. 'Saying I kissed someone at their wedding. A colleague's husband.'

'*Did* you?' said Meg, with a look of disgust.

'Um. Yeah. He kissed me! It only lasted a moment.'

'Ugh. Marriage is such bullshit,' Meg said.

'It caused them to split up.'

'Oh dear, Edith,' her dad said, with an expression of consternation.

'Dad, I wasn't having an affair or anything like that!' Hmm. She was doing *something* like that. She was just eager to convey there was no sex involved, without saying it in so many words.

'They're back together now. But people at work think I'm at fault.'

Both her dad and Meg looked at her, at a loss for words, and Edie wished she'd copped to the whole saga as soon as she'd come home. As it was, the timing was doing her few favours.

'Wait, is that why you're here?' Meg said. 'In Nottingham? Were you sacked?'

'No, more sidelined. Until it blows over,' Edie said. Meg

looked at her and sniffed. 'Hah. I knew you'd only come here because you had to.'

'Let's hope it doesn't get an airing in the gutter press, then,' her dad said, stoutly. He glanced at the story. 'You do look very emotional. What was happening?'

Edie couldn't outright lie, not now. She looked at the pictures – she was quite clearly giving Elliot seven bells of hell. She'd have to go for a fudge.

'I saw a text I shouldn't have where Elliot said I was "hard work" sometimes. It dated back to when we were arguing in the early days. I'd had a few to drink and took offence. We've made up now.'

Quite a lot of mistruths there, but no way was Edie saying *He said I was mad because of Mum.*

'Who are you giving the Vs to?' Meg said, leaning over the laptop again.

'Oh. Some man who shouted at me to get them out for the lads.'

Meg grinned. 'Haha. Nice one.'

'You certainly look full of *personality*,' her dad said, with a smile. 'If not your usual infectious joie de vivre.'

'If journalists call the house, say nothing,' Edie said, 'Honestly, nothing. Just hang up.'

'The landline isn't in use any more,' her dad said. 'All we got were cold callers and a poor "Leonard" with Alzheimer's.'

'Mobiles then?'

'I'll be impressed if they catch me with mine switched on and Meg needs to have paid her bill.'

Edie had to admit the chances of either weren't high.

Well. This response was a surprise. Not good, but not that bad either. Edie still had a lurking sense this wasn't anything like the worst of it, especially if they got hold of the story about their mother. But she didn't say so.

59

It was hard to appreciate just how unpleasant it was to be in the press for a negative reason until you'd been in the press for a negative reason. It wasn't foul in the way Edie thought it would be, it was full on Is This Really Happening fever dream disorientating, and completely out of her control.

And even more unpleasant was having been in the press, and knowing you would be again soon.

There couldn't be any doubt on that point. Edie had a delirious half hour where she persuaded herself that by some miraculous chance, no one had recognised her. This ludicrous hope was quickly crushed when she had a flood of mysterious friend requests on her new Facebook profile. Text message tennis had clearly been pinging back and forth. Some were complete strangers to Edie, a few clearly journalists, but most astonishingly, half a dozen from Ad Hoc.

From signing a petition to get rid of her, to begging for a friending? Incredible. (Curiously though, Edie noticed, no contact from Louis. Gossip this big? He must've fallen down a manhole. Euphemistically or otherwise.)

Peering through the curtains on Monday, no follow-up story having yet appeared, Edie felt it was borderline safe to leave the house, albeit via taxi. She scurried from the front door to car door with head down, feeling both ridiculously paranoid and wildly reckless.

She should've known not to hang around with a very famous person and not expect some notoriety to rub off on her, like tacky wet paint in a narrow hallway.

'Hey, Christine Keeler, scandal girl. You know you're a bloody trending topic on Twitter?' Nick said – he'd appointed himself crisis manager – when she arrived for a huge sandwich lunch in tiny Brown Betty's cafe.

Edie abruptly lost an appetite for her Sloppy Joe.

'Oh God, what?!?'

'Here. Look. It's under the hashtag #whosthatgirl, trying to find out who you are. It seems Heather's unpopular among Elliot Owen's fans, after she said something in an interview about how they could never go back to dating "civilians". They've decided they like you, as one in the eye to her. I think it was the V flicking that clinched it. They're saying you're one of them.'

Edie hit the hashtag, the third down after #RuinARomanceInOneWord and #ifBloodandGoldwassetinBritain. She saw lots of bizarre captions on the photos of her and Elliot. 'LEGEND' and '<3 this skank' and the straightforward 'WHO DIS?'

A horrendous thought occurred; that this hiatus before the next story was merely extra digging time. She could imagine Lucie Maguire had run up a giant O2 bill calling every journalist in the country. Edie had warned everyone she could think of not to speak to the press, which wasn't many people. Her phone rang on and off with unrecognised mobile numbers, and when she listened to the voicemails before hastily deleting, it was anonymous voices, trying to sound ingratiating, offering her an incredible chance to tell her side of the story.

Nick protectively helped Edie into the Hackney to take her home, making sure they weren't being observed: although he was shaking with laughter throughout.

'Thanks loads!' Edie said, mock huffy. In fact, he was a tonic. Much better that than someone agreeing it was the end of the world.

Edie spent a restless afternoon until Meg got back from her care home shift and said: 'Uh. I think there's someone across the street taking photos.'

'*What?*' Edie said. She twitched the curtain and sure enough, there was a man cradling a long lens, leaning against a car. Edie was now under house arrest. It was a vile, cornered, hunted feeling. The only conversation available was Margot, over the garden fence. She didn't quite grasp the gravity of the situation.

'How fabulous,' Margot said, drawing on a gasper, free wrist dangling over the fence; her manicure, orange sienna. 'If everyone thinks you're having some *how's your father* with him, might as well have some. It's sure to have crossed his mind now, my love. Why be hung for a crime you didn't commit, I'm sure he'll agree.'

Edie didn't know whether to laugh or cry.

And then Tuesday arrived. As soon as she saw the title of the link, Edie knew this was the story she'd feared.

It was headlined: *'Who's That Girl? Colourful past of new woman in Elliot Owen's life.'* It was illustrated with photographs she worked out had been swiped from Facebook, as well as the phone images. They all seemed to design to portray a party girl – Edie saluting the camera with a cocktail, or posing with her arms slung round some of the Ad Hoc staff, big false eyelashed eyes cast to the sky, in playful mock-coyness.

Oh, God.

Speculation's been rife about the new woman in the life of Blood & Gold *star Elliot Owen, with fans anxious to uncover her identity.*

The pair were seen fighting in the street in an emotional encounter at the weekend, suggesting he and actress Heather Lily are over for good.

The Mail *can exclusively reveal that his mystery squeeze is Edie Thompson, 36, a writer working on his forthcoming auto-biography. Her visits to the set of his crime drama,* Gun City, *have left onlookers in no doubt that she's being very thorough in her research.*

'It's clear to everyone on set that they're madly into each other,' said our source. 'One day, Elliot had barely finished a scene before he was dragging her back to his trailer. He phys-ically picked her up and carried her. It was pure Prince Wulfroarer. We were told it was a case of "don't knock if it's rocking" and it ruined the filming schedule for that day. The production team was livid.'

His ex-girlfriend Heather has made no secret of her fury at the betrayal, recently tweeting 'When someone lets you down, rise above' and 'That which does not kill you makes you stronger.'

And it seems that dark-haired Thompson, who also hails from Elliot's home town of Nottingham, is no stranger to making waves when it comes to her love life.

Although thought to be single when she met Owen, she was embroiled in a love triangle earlier this year when she was allegedly caught in a clinch with a friend's husband – on their WEDDING day.

The marrying couple worked with Thompson at Clerkenwell-based ad agency Ad Hoc, and the controversy saw her put on leave – to write Owen's book. The newlywed husband, Jack Marshall, was sacked for the indiscretion.

'Edie's a homewrecker,' said one former friend of the ad girl. 'What she did to Jack and Charlotte was appalling, and she had no remorse. When Edie's around it's a strict case of lock up your men. I'm not surprised she's wasted no time in latching on to Elliot Owen. He has no idea who he's dealing with.'

TROUBLED PAST

While she's been writing the book on Owen, the sometime-advertising executive has been staying with her father and sister at their modest semi-detached house in a down-at-heel suburb of Nottingham. Her mother committed suicide in 1988 after suffering postnatal depression.

Jan Clarke, author of forthcoming unauthorised biography

about Owen, Elliot Owen: Prince Among Men *(out November 12th), says this turmoil may be what attracted the star. 'My book will include some explosive revelations about Owen's own past. It has been a lot more turbulent than people realise,' she said. 'No doubt these similarities drew them together.'*

A representative for Owen said the rumours of a relationship were completely untrue. 'It's purely professional, there's no romance,' said a representative for the actor.

Jan Clarke, what a surprise.

Edie's mouth was dry. She re-read the story half a dozen more times. *Troubled past.* It was deeply disconcerting, seeing your life served up to strangers in summary.

Edie's phone blipped with a 'WTAF EDIE?!' text and missed call from Jack and she ignored him. She owed him nothing. He'd thrown her to the wolves after the wedding, she'd throw him right back too.

With a very heavy tread, Edie walked downstairs and showed the story to Meg and her dad.

Her dad raised and dropped his shoulders, sighed. Meg read it, mouth hanging open, and audibly gasped at the opening of the last paragraph.

'Down at heel!' she said. 'Trust the *Mail* and its house prices obsession.'

Then she read on, and fell silent.

'Why did they bring Mum into it?' she said, raising resentful eyes to Edie. Her dad didn't look at her, which was worse than him losing his rag.

'I don't know,' Edie said, thickly. She thought Meg might

shout or cry but instead she was quiet. She apologised to them both but there wasn't much to say.

'And you're *not* courting this young man?' her father said, in disbelief.

'No,' Edie said, but rather than getting any vindication from the fact, it only underlined how pointless this all was.

Her dad glanced back at the story on her laptop and Edie felt hopeless – she could see both he and Meg weren't convinced, and they lived with her. Once it was in print, somehow, it stuck.

'Is there going to be more?' her dad said.

'I don't know. I hope not.'

Edie wanted to say more, but she had no comfort to offer and Meg made it clear she wanted to be elsewhere in the house. Edie went back to her bedroom and wept quietly. The only call – one of many her accursed phone buzzed with – she answered, was Elliot.

'Edie, are you OK? I'm in the thick of it here so sorry if the call is short,' he said, from somewhere blustery.

'Do you know what, I feel like puking,' Edie said. 'Yet completely flat at the same time.'

It was a different kind of shame from the wedding. That had an audience of everyone she knew. This was the world stage, complete strangers. A new dimension of humiliation. One that would live on in Googling eternity.

'Thanks for saying being publicly linked with me makes you want to puke,' Elliot said, and wrung his first laugh from Edie since the night of the fight. She laughed weakly, gratefully.

'Hey, and you have no idea who you're dealing with,' she said grimly. 'Who is this femme fatale I'm reading about? The worst of it is, it's hard to say "that's not true, or that's not true". Somehow it's built into a whole that's completely warped.'

'Yes! You see how it works now. Even when it's right, it's still wrong. I hope the denial shuts it down. We've got an advantage of not being in London here. They won't be sparing many photographers to hang around the Midlands. Also, my publicist is shit hot. She's working on a strategy. I will let you know what it is, when we know what it is.'

'Thank you.'

She noticed Elliot hadn't mentioned Jan's veiled threat about the adoption – had he told Fraser? She suspected in recovering from the fall-out from their fight, Elliot hadn't – and she thought it was decent of him not to make it about himself. But as much as she appreciated Elliot's support, it was different for him. He was used to being famous. He'd chosen it.

Hannah and Nick sent a group WhatsApp titled 'Tomorrow's Chip Paper', and promised Edie she'd laugh about this one day.

Her phone blipped with a waiting call. It was from Richard. Richard, who was still in Santorini until next week. Terrible omen that he'd call out of hours. Richard the workaholic fiercely protected the sanctity of his time out, as did his redoubtable wife.

'Only call me if a bomb has gone off,' he always said. 'And even then, if the field triage has been done and no one's bleeding out, ask yourself: as a non-medical man, what would I bring to the situation?'

'Hello, Edie!' he said, with robust and threatening cheeriness. 'My family are enjoying a late breakfast at a local taverna. And instead of being with them, enjoying Greek eggs, I'm on the phone to you. Can you imagine why that might be?'

'Richard,' Edie said, palm to forehead, 'I'm so sorry. Nothing that's being reported is true. I'm not seeing Elliot Owen.'

'I have your *Dear Deirdre* casebook photos here, and forgive me, you don't look like you're explaining your prose style to him. You know, I'm not filling those speech bubbles with debate over the possessive apostrophe.'

Richard was exasperated, but not shouting. Edie would have to take that as a good result.

'We went out for a drink and his brother flirted with me and there was a bit of a misunderstanding. It's all cleared up now.'

'It's his *brother* you're finicking around with? Jolly good. Owen looks delighted about it, I must say. You know, my employee engaged in verbals with a client in the street isn't exactly the Ad Hoc message I want to project.'

'Richard, I promise, it's not how it looks!'

'I fear what you're not grasping here is: how it looks, IS how it is. Unless you intend to embark on a nationwide door-to-door tour to explain your side of things, the papers have stolen a march on you.'

'. . . But as a client, Elliot is completely happy. I promise. The book's fine.'

'*He* may be. The publisher isn't.'

'What?'

'Yes. The bad news is, they've thrown a giant shit fit about the adverse attention. They want you to come down on Monday and explain why you should still write this book. The good news is, you can do a twofer, and meet me afterwards.'

Edie sagged. A double sacking. At least it saved her the trouble of telling Richard she was leaving.

'And, where the autobiography's concerned, make your case. I should warn you however, I think this is one of those occasions where the death warrant's been signed already.'

'But I've done so much work!' Edie said.

'Edie, call me a rule-obsessed stickler with an elephantine memory,' Richard said. 'You remember when I gave you this assignment? And I said, prime directive number one – *Don't, for fuck's sake, get off with the actor*? If ever there was an example of You Had One Job . . .'

He had a point.

60

Three publishing executives sat opposite Edie, across a board-room table in Bloomsbury, with A4 colour print-outs of the *Mirror* and *Mail* stories. Given they'd read them already, Edie assumed this was designed to intimidate and embarrass, and it worked. It had been a long, knotted-stomach train ride down, and the atmosphere was entirely justifying Edie's fright. There had been no more stories since last week, only canni-balised versions of the chief name-and-shame doing the rounds, yet Edie was far from certain that the worst was past.

'Before we start,' Edie said, 'I want to assure you that there's absolutely no improper relationship between myself and Elliot Owen. Those photographs were taken when I was invited to join a group night out, and everyone had had a little too much to drink.

'Everything's resolved now,' she concluded, into the silence where three pairs of eyes bored into her. The continuing silence said: *No. No, it isn't.*

'Let me explain our position,' said Becky, the Hobbs-clad and well-shod woman in charge, interlocking her fingers and speaking in a gently patronising and courteously hostile tone.

'We wanted a writer for this project who would remain invisible in the process. It's called "ghost" writing for a reason. We very much want a prestige slot in the market, to contrast with the downmarket rival releasing a book at a similar time.'

Edie tucked her hair behind her ear, nodded and felt she was in the headmistress's office, about to be expelled.

'Now we have *this* publicity' – she pushed the *Mirror* article towards Edie, as if Edie might want to refresh her memory – 'which doesn't spell quality product. And the autobiography has been mentioned in every single outlet that picked up the *Mail* story. You've made . . .' she looked down a list, 'the *Huffington Post*, the *Metro*, *Digital Spy*, the *Express*, *Just Jared*, the *Washington Post*. Need I go on?'

Edie *was* in the headmistress's office.

'We're in uncharted waters; we've never had a ghost-writer get this involved with a subject's life, and in such a public way. After much debate, we feel this episode is going to unnecessarily complicate matters for the reader. Unless you could offer special insights as a . . . partner—'

'I can't!' Edie said. Oh, to be believed for once. Imagine if she had as much sex as people thought she was having. She'd be walking like Yosemite Sam.

Becky paused long enough to make it clear Edie's interruption was crass and unwelcome.

'. . . No. Not least because you signed a confidentiality agreement.'

Trick questions, now.

'Unless you can do that, we see this as a lose-lose. It's

confusing to the consumer. It will be seen as his girlfriend's book now, whether we like it or not. And who knows what stories will come out next—'

'There won't be any!'

'You're sure of that?'

'Er. Well there's nothing new to say . . . Nothing true, anyway.'

Becky's eyes shot wide open. She picked up the print-outs and dropped them on to the desk again. 'But you're saying these things they printed weren't true?'

'No.'

'Then how can you be sure nothing more will come out? It doesn't have to be true.'

Checkmate.

Richard was right, this execution had been signed off at the highest royal level. This wasn't a debate about the decision, it was the delivery of it.

'We'll give you part-payment and pass on your material to another writer, and they'll finish the manuscript. We won't name you on the jacket but we'll give you a credit in the acknowledgements.'

'But . . .' Edie felt bereft, 'so much of it is based on conversations I had with Elliot. Are you going to pretend I'm not there?'

'The book is about him, not you,' said the younger woman to Becky's right, in a voice that made Becky seem an Edie fan, by comparison.

A knock on the door and a woman put her head round. 'Becky. Call for you? It's Kirsty McKeown. It's urgent.'

They sat in tense silence while she left the room. Becky came back in after five long minutes, pulled her chair up, cleared her throat and shot Edie a look that could, if not kill, significantly maim.

'Elliot Owen won't finish the book unless it's with this writer.'

Edie's heart swelled, despite everything.

The woman to the right looked irate. 'Can't we offer—'

'He's completely implacable on this point.' She glared at Edie, clearly communicating: OH 'NOT SLEEPING WITH HIM'? AND YET.

There was nothing left to say. Friends in high places.

'Please avoid any more situations that might be picked up by the press.'

'Yes, of course,' said Edie, in a small voice.

This warranted a direct thank you to Elliot. Edie stood in the street outside and dialled, checking she wasn't being snapped by anyone. In London, she was back to being anonymous, it seemed, thank goodness. People who wanted to be famous didn't know what they were asking for.

She got his answerphone. When Elliot called back minutes later, he sounded disquieted, his first words to her clipped and abrupt.

'They were going to throw you off the book?'

'Yes. Unless I wrote it from . . .' Edie hesitated, 'unless I wrote it from the perspective of being somehow involved with you, which I said I couldn't do, obviously.'

'Why didn't you tell me? If I hadn't happened to hear it from my agent, it might've gone too far for me to help. I could've stopped you even having to have that meeting.'

'I didn't know what you wanted . . .' Edie trailed off. Why hadn't she asked? It had seemed too helpless damsel. It felt too paradoxical to get Elliot to save the day as a mate, when the whole point was she was arguing theirs was a professional relationship. And yeah, she was avoiding him. 'And I thought maybe you'd find a different writer easier.'

There was a heavy pause.

'Edie, sod what I wanted, it would've been a massive waste of *your* work at this point. Unless you wanted to go?'

'No! Of course not! I really want to finish the book. I'm proud of what we've done.'

'Then why not ask me to intervene?'

'I didn't want to beg you for a favour. It wasn't your responsibility.' Edie hoped the fact she'd dismissed this option out of hand was a sign of impressive self-reliance, and not complete stupidity.

'Do you really dislike me that much, you couldn't bear to ask?'

It was clear Elliot was sure this was why.

'No!'

Edie didn't know how she felt towards Elliot. Not angry, any more, but not the same either. They'd moved past the text message in practical terms, but not emotionally, not for Edie. She was saved having to find the words to explain, because Richard appeared on Call Waiting, and she didn't dare leave him waiting for long.

61

Richard was the only man who Edie knew to do up a jacket button as he stood, like he was being announced as winner at an awards ceremony. Today he was in an incredible peacock-blue suit and dark wine-coloured shirt.

'Take a seat. What'll you have?'

'Thanks. A white wine?'

'Any?'

'You choose.'

Edie had expected a perfunctory coffee for this regrettable firing, but Richard had called to say, 'I'm still on Santorini time. Fancy a pint?' She met him in a refurbed Victorian pub, with overloaded hanging baskets and carriage lamps, beer-musky smell inside.

Richard returned with the drinks. Eyes were always drawn to him, because he dressed and carried himself like a person of note. Funny how crucial that was to garnering attention: meanwhile, Elliot in a woolly hat, hunched over, could largely go unrecognised.

When they were settled, Richard said: 'Well, now. Where to begin with the latest episode of The Edie Thompson Show. That was quite the mid-season-break cliffhanger. You're still on the book, you say?'

'Yes. Only as Elliot insisted.'

Richard raised an eyebrow and tried not to laugh.

'Did he now? Jack Marshall, and now that prancing tit. Not the hill I'd die on.'

'Elliot's decent!' Edie protested. 'Honestly. His early doors objections made a lot of sense, we just hadn't been copied in on his reasons.'

'If you say so,' Richard said. 'I agree he did you what my kids call "a solid" here.'

Richard swirled his pint around the table, as if he was drawing circles with the base of the glass.

'Now. In terms of your future at Ad Hoc—'

'Richard, I can save you having to break the news that you have to let me go. I can't come back to Ad Hoc anyway. There was a petition, asking me to go. Everyone signed it.'

'I know,' Richard said.

'And— Wait, you know?'

'Yes. They used the work printer and I found a copy in the overflow paper box.'

'Oh.'

'Master conspiracists, they are not.'

Richard sipped his lager and studied Edie.

'You know, my wife said after she met you at the last Christmas party, you have a high degree of emotional intelligence,' Richard said. 'And I agree. So, can you let me into the secret of how someone as intelligent as you, frequently behaves like a complete arse?'

Richard said this without edge.

'I don't know,' Edie said. 'If I knew, I'd stop.'

'I want good things for you, Edie. I've come to the conclusion you can't want good things for yourself. Perhaps you do consciously, but I think your subconscious is working against you. It's working for the other side.'

Edie nodded. 'You're not the first person to say this.'

'Speaking more as a friend than a boss here, you constantly let lesser people drag you down. Start dressing for the life you want. I mean that metaphorically. Although that chequered coat might've had its dog day afternoon.'

Edie laughed.

'However. You're talented, you're loyal, you're bright and witty, and very much the kind of person I want at Ad Hoc. I have a proposal for you. I want you to carry on working for me.'

'Thank you so much,' Edie said. 'I can't come back to the office that signed a petition for me to leave, though. Call me a wuss.'

'I sacked Charlotte. I also sacked Louis. I needed this holiday, I tell you.'

'What? Why?'

'Charlotte for designing the petition, and Louis for circulating it. I don't know what sort of madness gripped them, but if they want to re-enact *Mean Girls*, they can do it at someone else's agency.'

'Oh.'

This was why Louis hadn't been in touch for the last couple of weeks. It was too difficult to explain why he'd been let go. And that was how he kept his name off the petition: by doing everything but. Edie might've known. And – kerplunk – she finally remembered the stray detail that proved the extent of his betrayal. The smoking gun that had eluded her. She'd been too busy near-fainting at the time.

'The thing is, I'm incredibly grateful for the second chance,' Edie said. 'But I'm going to stay in Nottingham. I've liked being home. Well, not necessarily living on top of my dad and sister, but the city. I have my best friends there.'

Richard nodded.

'This doesn't change anything. My offer was going to be that you could work remotely. Copywriting can be done anywhere. When there's a client meeting, come down. We meet them off site, no need to be in the office.'

'. . . Are you serious?'

'Yes. I know you're diligent. Apart from when you're playing footsie with idiots like Jack Marshall. Or giving hell to preening actors in public. Plus you won't badger me for a pay rise for a while, you'll be so broken with gratitude and noticing how much further your money goes.'

Edie laughed, slightly incredulously.

'Wow. Thank you so much, Richard. This day's going dramatically better than expected.'

She not only stayed on the book, she could work for Ad Hoc from Nottingham? Guaranteed income. Work she enjoyed. Today, *love won*.

As Richard finished his pint, he pulled a folded piece of paper from his jacket pocket.

'I've waited until now to show you this as I don't want you to think it influenced my decision. I'd already let Charlotte and Louis go and decided to make you an offer when I got this. You can do whatever you like with it. As far as I'm concerned, I already thought he was an arch tosser. I'll be in touch when you've delivered the book to talk about how things work. OK?'

'Yes. Thanks, Richard.'

'Take care,' Richard said, and put a hand on her shoulder.

After he'd left, Edie unfolded the paper and read. It was a print out of an email.

From: Martha Hughes

This is a funny one, sorry for the unsolicited approach. I'm writing to you about Edie Thompson. I read the story in the Mail about how she was put on leave from your agency after being 'caught' with your employee Jack Marshall on his wedding day. I wasn't clear if she'd been sacked, as well as him? This is why I'm getting in touch, because if she is going to be sacked, I feel I have to say something. The story gave me déjà vu. I worked with Jack four years ago at another creative agency. He was in a long-distance relationship with someone else then, but I had no idea. He somehow managed to never mention it over the course of a lot of lunches on expenses and drinks after work. I was in an unhappy relation- ship. We got very close — not physical — and he was a shoulder to cry on for me during a diffi- cult time. Eventually he mentioned the girlfriend, Stephanie, in Leeds but by then I was in too deep to keep my distance. The girlfriend took a half-day one Friday, and turned up earlier to meet him than expected. She caught Jack & I out for a drink, just the two of us. A lot of screaming ensued, and I ended up feeling the villain of the piece. When it got round the office, everyone assumed we were having an affair. It contributed to my decision to leave about three months down the line. Even though I hadn't done anything, except perhaps not step back far enough when I should have. Reading about the wedding, I thought: he's done it again. The utter twat (pardon me) has led one woman on, while seeing another. It's his 'thing'. I don't know this Edie and for all I know she's been right round the office, and this testimony is neither here nor there. But I thought you should know.

When Edie finished reading, her eyes were shiny with emotion. She'd spent so long thinking she was to blame for what happened with Jack, and there were plenty of people willing to agree with her.

She'd been too weak, made too many mistakes and felt too

much self-loathing, to truly believe it was on him. In her darkest moments, she even thought *she'd* unwittingly seduced Jack, she'd messed with his equilibrium, and caused it all.

Now here was Martha, waving a wand like a Fairy Godmother. She had a power Edie didn't know anyone possessed. She could truly make her believe this wasn't her fault. *He pursued you. He pushed this. This is what he does. You're not a terrible person.*

Stupidly, it had never ever occurred to Edie that Jack had done it before. The whole trick was based on believing they had a unique special connection. But *of course* they didn't, *of course* this was his MO.

Thinking about it, Edie thought Jack might've mentioned a Martha. She was a dear friend who was lost to him as she stayed with a bad, insensitive guy and Jack had tried to help her but she wouldn't leave him and *why do great women settle for such useless guys, Edie? It's such a shame*, he'd said to her once, during a long rainy day's chatter. She'd thought *Cor, you're so caring*.

Edie felt as if a great weight was off her shoulders, she was elated, even giddy. And she felt strong enough for vengeance.

Not quite knowing why, Edie checked Ian Connor's profile again on Twitter. He'd shared the links to the *Mirror* and *Mail* stories with the caption: 'A slut never changes its spots.'

But, wait. The most recent tweet was moaning about the wait on his lunch. And it was tagged with the location. Ian Connor, if social media was to be believed, was sat in a pub about ten minutes' drive away, right now.

Seriously @TheShipTavern how hard can it be to heat through a lasagne? Have you gone to Italy for it lol. #wearewaiting

Her heart started thumping. A road forked in front of Edie. Put coat on, head back to train, avoid conflict, and almost certainly never find out who Ian Connor was. The infinitely easier option.

Or, go face to face with her harshest and most senseless critic of all. She thought of what Richard said about behaving like an arse. This wasn't arsery, though. This was the only way she'd ever have peace. It was her one chance of closure.

It was time to find out what a keyboard warrior did when you looked him in the eye and invited him to say that to your face.

62

Edie stepped out of the Hackney and wondered if this was quite mad. She breathed deeply once, twice, put her head down and pushed her way into The Ship. She glanced in terror at every anonymous male, momentarily taking any look in return as proof they were The One.

Then they went back to their conversations and she realised that most men met your gaze if you prowled around, goggling at them. Nevertheless, she had to keep searching for tell-tale reactions – Ian Connor knew what she looked like: he'd shared those newspaper stories.

As Edie rounded the bar, she almost yelped in surprise. At a table, sat Louis, Charlotte and Lucie Maguire, the fourth chair – Ian's chair, presumably? – empty.

Louis saw her first and, momentarily, it was a toss-up as to who was more shocked.

'Edie, what are you doing here?!' Louis said, in a strained impersonation of his usual sing-songy, sarcastic voice.

Edie forced herself to recover, even though she could hear her heartbeat in her eardrums.

'I'm looking for Ian Connor?'

Charlotte, Louis and Lucie stared dumbly at Edie, as if she was an apparition risen from a grave and pointing a bony finger.

'Shit *Terminator* impression,' said one of the suits from the next table. 'It's John Connor.'

They ignored the interruption.

'Who's that?' Louis said, eventually, trying to sling his arm over the back of his chair, casually. He looked as if he'd been caught with someone's husband. Edie knew how that felt.

'According to Twitter, "Ian Connor" is waiting here for food. You must know Ian Connor because he knows things about me that no one else does. Is he with you?'

'No? I've never heard of him!' Louis said, with feeling. There was a relief to it that made Edie think it was the truth.

Charlotte, in Breton top, hair in a neat bun, stared at Edie with revulsion.

'We don't know who you're talking about.'

Hmm, less confident. If Jack had indeed asked Charlotte about the identity of Ian Connor, she had some idea of what Edie was talking about.

Behind them, a barmaid juggling plates was angling to get past Edie.

'Sorry for your wait. I've got meatballs, the Thai curry and a lasagne?' she said.

Edie watched, saucer-eyed, as Louis put his hand up to claim the meatballs, Charlotte had a plate of slop the colour of an avocado bathroom suite put in front of her, and Lucie accepted the lasagne.

'Ian Connor ordered the lasagne too,' Edie said.

All eyes moved to the incriminating steaming china dish in front of Lucie, a boat of lava-bubbling browned cheese.

Edie looked at the seat next to Lucie. There was no coat, bag, glass or place setting. There was no one with them.

'*You're* Ian Connor?' she said to Lucie.

Lucie was rigid and pale. Edie didn't usually despise appearances, but she'd make an exception in Lucie's case. She was as unappealing physically as she was spiritually: beady ostrich eyes and thin lips under her blonded Toni & Guy salon hair.

'You have a sock-puppet Twitter account, that was set up to have a go at me? In the name of Ian Connor?'

Lucie cleared her throat. 'It's not *for you*. It's a private account. What's it to do with you?'

'When someone's giving me abuse online, it's my business. And it's not private; you haven't locked it, or I wouldn't be here.'

As her anger rose, Edie felt her fear disappear, evaporate like water on a brisk boil. These people only had the power you gave them. In person, they were small. They were scared.

'As Ian Connor, you posted the comment on that Facebook page, saying that my mother killed herself out of the shame of having given birth to me.'

Now Louis and Charlotte were staring at Lucie, who had turned as red as the setting sun.

'My mum committed suicide when I was nine. I don't talk about it, no one I worked with knew. It was a secret. You took that information from her' – she looked to Charlotte, who like hell hadn't known that Lucie was Ian – 'and you used it to make a joke online?'

The suits at the next table had downed their cutlery to watch the scene, slack-mouthed.

'I don't remember everything that was on there,' Lucie said. 'You've got a nerve, coming in here, after what you did to Char—'

'No,' Edie said, cutting across her. 'Don't hide behind what happened between us. You mocked someone for losing their mother, in the most horrendous way. Next time you *think* you're in the moral majority, Lucie, judging the rest of us, remember you're among the very worst. You're a coward and a bully. You have children, don't you? I was nine when I lost my mum, my sister was five. How would you feel if you died and someone took the piss out of your kids for it?'

She paused.

'She was called Isla, by the way. That was my mum's name. She was thirty-six, the same age as I am now. She was on Citalopram and Amitryptyline. She jumped off a bridge and drowned. When they dredged her body, it had got tangled up in a lock. My dad had to identify her by her wedding rings. Does it still seem as funny to you? Tell me when the punchline arrives.'

'You got off with her husband!' Lucie shrieked. 'Don't play the victim!'

'Yes, I kissed her husband,' Edie said, 'for about three seconds, when he all but forced himself on me. It doesn't make me non-human, does it? Quite the opposite.'

'You never said sorry,' Lucie said, but she was playing with her napkin now, lips pursed, face downcast. She'd lost and she knew it. What she'd done was abhorrent; her only protection had been her anonymity.

'Yes I did. I said sorry to Charlotte. She deserved my apology, I didn't owe you anything.'

There was a smattering of admiring applause from the next table.

Edie drew breath. She was on a roll. She was powerful, unassailable and had completely lain waste to their rapidly cooling lunch. She had a moment of divine inspiration. She removed the print-out from her pocket and tore away the top third, keeping Martha's name and email address for herself.

'Also, Charlotte. What happened on your wedding day was vile. It still didn't give you the right to do what you did to me, afterwards. You didn't treat Jack the same way – why not? Did you honestly think it was my idea, is that what he told you? You might be interested in this. It was emailed to Richard.'

She put the piece of paper down in front of her.

'Ta-ta, everyone. Enjoy your food.'

Edie turned and strode out of the pub.

'Edie! Edie?'

In the street outside, Louis chased her down. It was curious that he'd try, in front of Lucie and Charlotte. Maybe he had a very late-dawning attack of conscience. Maybe Lucie was not going to be able to throw her weight around for a while. Maybe he was sodded if he was going to lose the 'famous actor's girl' as a friend.

'Edie!'

He seemed surprised she'd stopped, and for a moment had no follow-up.

'I'm so sorry, darling. Honestly I am.'

'What for?'

'For not telling them to stop. It was like school, you know. If you didn't join in, you were going to get it too.'

'Yeah, terrifying,' Edie said. 'Forcing you to have lunch with them. Cramming meatballs down you. Monsters. Oh, and making you put that petition round. At gunpoint, I guess?'

'*Seriously*, babe! If I hadn't gone along with that stupid petition, my life would not have been worth living. Charlie knew we were friends and made me swear an oath. I didn't even know if you were coming back. It was the easy way out.'

'It was coercion? Pure survival techniques, and nothing else?'

'Yes!'

'In that case, how did they get the Facebook page's picture of me? It was the one of us together at the wedding, you took it? You'd been cropped out.'

'Uh . . .' Louis looked perplexed. 'The wedding . . .? That was on my Instagram. It was public. They must've scraped it.'

'No, it wasn't. You deleted that picture on the night of the wedding. I know, I checked. As soon as the Get Edie campaign started, you put distance between us. Yet you carried on acting like you were my friend, to get the gossip, to be on everyone's side and no one's side. In some ways you're worse than Lucie.'

Louis looked like he was regretting following her out now.

'. . . And when they set up a nasty page to take me down, you said *Oh hey yeah I've got a photo of her.*'

Louis didn't deny it.

Edie shouldered her bag. 'You know, I pity you, Louis. At least when I don't like myself, I still know who I am. You have a face for every occasion. When you're on your own, you must disappear. Who are you, when no one's looking?'

Edie left Louis stood there, trying to find an answer that'd get him off the hook, and walked away.

All these wasted years spent trying to get inconsequential people to like her. She never asked herself why she should like them.

63

Elliot had left Edie for another woman. According to the latest headlines, the love-cheat rat rotter had moved on to rumping his co-star, Greta Alan, and just like that, the press seemed to suffer collective and convenient memory loss about the woman he was supposedly sleeping with last week.

Pictures from *Gun City* had surfaced that appeared to prove the 'budding romance': they weren't filming (rehearsing, surely? Greta was in the Uggs, not the Louboutins) and had been 'snapped in a clinch'. Greta's arms were round Elliot, under his detective's leather jacket, and she was gazing up adoringly into his eyes.

Another anonymous on-set source was ready to confirm the relationship, in the same febrile tones they'd used to describe the fling with Edie. Apparently *everyone noticed their incredible chemistry from day one* and *Elliot has been showing the American beauty the sights in his home city* (nudge nudge) and they *didn't need much encouragement to dive into their love scenes together* (wink wink).

Edie was nowhere to be found in these stories about Greta,

bar one passing reference to 'rumoured involvement with his biographer, which reps for Owen denied'. She could see why – it was quite hard to explain how this stud had a tempestuous affair with Edie if he'd actually been wooing Greta. She sensed the media was much happier pairing Elliot with another famous person, especially when there was winsome imagery to go with the tale, and thus Edie was yesterday's chopped liver.

Edie knew she should feel relieved that her spell as Elliot's imaginary paramour was over, and she did. She also felt something else quite strongly too. But Elliot couldn't stand Greta, right? And if it had all been invention with Edie, this was more of the same?

She read and re-read the quotes and extrapolated the facts. 'Incredible chemistry' – actors. 'Showing her the sights' – actors acting in a show set in the city Elliot was from. 'Didn't need much encouragement' – actors. With the sum of the corroboration to this story, you could in fact only caption Elliot and Greta's 'clinch' as Two People Depicted Doing Job.

Nevertheless, Edie went back and forth over everything Elliot had said to her about Greta. He'd been privately scathing: but was he overcompensating? Why were they positioned like that, if not on camera? Edie had played Orla, too. Only she didn't get to act the part where they smushed faces and groins outside a lift. She twinged and ached, slightly, at the thought of it happening, even in make believe.

How did Edie feel about Elliot now? Friend, foe, 'other'? Unfortunately, she was staring mournfully at the tabloid fictions that did strange things to her stomach, when the man himself called her. Edie banged her laptop shut and took a second to compose herself, standing up from her desk to take the call, as if that was more businesslike.

'Hi, Edie. It's me.' Elliot's tone was resigned, no longer upbeat, none of the old bounce. 'How are you?'

'Fine, thanks. Glad to not be of interest to the media any more. Now you're with Greta.' She was aiming for playful here, it came out sounding stiff.

'Hah, right! Amazing, isn't it. Different day, same bullshit.' This sounded like a denial. It was a denial, wasn't it?

'I wanted to tell you I've spoken to Fraser. I'm doing a story with the *Guardian* about the adoption. It'll run in the next few days. It should help draw their fire from you.'

'You've spoken to Fraser?' Edie sat back down on her chair. 'How did it go?'

'At first, badly. You can imagine he was madly pissed off at me having shut him out, all those years ago. His point was: did you have so little faith in me that you didn't trust me not to reject you? When I asked did it change anything, he looked at me like I had two heads and said, 'What, after thirty years of growing up together?'

Elliot's voice had got more emotional and Edie wished they were having this conversation face to face. 'Then after a lot of shouting at me and slapping the table and shouting "Fuck!" and calling my parents on a satellite phone to shout at them too, he calmed down. I had to remember that I've had twenty years to come to terms with it, and I was expecting him to get his head around it in twenty minutes. But after a while, he started on how it should've been obvious we didn't share DNA when he saw me play football.'

Edie laughed, gently. Elliot was uncharacteristically quiet, and she sensed he was trying to sort her into friend or foe or other category, too.

'Anyway. He was also blazing about Jan and my dad, trying to make money out of it. He insisted I should spike their guns. I talked to my parents too and they agreed we should talk about it. The *Guardian* story won't discuss Fraser, but it'll explain my background. My real dad can do his version, but this way my version's out there to contradict it. I've said I won't be doing any other interviews about it.'

'This all sounds really positive,' Edie said.

'Edie, I'm sorry. If I'd not been such a coward then I could've potentially timed this better and stopped there being as much interest in you. I've said on the record that I'm single and Heather and I are no longer together, in this article. Not that the press ever takes my word for it, mind.'

Single.

'Oh,' Edie was touched. 'Thanks. It wasn't your fault.'

'It was, I should've been more careful than to let those photos get taken. I feel awful that you had your past raked over. It's one thing for me to choose a life where I get this attention, but I hate it when it affects my loved ones.'

What? Edie held her breath.

Elliot added: 'Or people I'm working with,' and Edie let the breath out. 'The *Guardian* piece will also effectively spoiler Jan,' Elliot continued. 'Hurray for that.'

'Why hasn't she gone to the press about the adoption already?' Her restraint in the *Mail* piece had surprised Edie.

'Apparently it's a fairly common thing, once a biographer's

dug some dirt – it's much harder to pulp a book once it's out there and you're less likely to launch legal action once the damage is done. They wait until it's safely on the shelves.'

'Oh,' Edie said, staring at the ceiling, 'I suppose that makes sense.'

'In light of this, we should cover the adoption briefly in our book, too.'

'Of course.'

She hesitated. Then, jocularly, with feigned lightness, pushing again: 'So you're seeing Greta now? Fast work.'

Please don't say 'Yes, funnily enough they've got this one right'! Please.

'Oh yeah, it seems I'm hooking up with her. No rest for the wicked, eh?'

Nope. Edie was going to need more than that.

'There was me thinking you didn't get on!'

Deny it, DENY IT.

'Ah well. I didn't read the signs, obviously. I'm never able to tell when women like me. Or don't.'

Ouch. It wasn't just the jibe: there was a deliberate Don't Come Any Closer reserve in his tone that had never been there before. There would be no return to the old joshing.

Embarrassed, Edie said sadly: 'Hah.'

'That said, I can't begin to imagine what dating Greta would be like. Those photos were just standard Greta touchy-feely moves. She's the same with everyone. Well, except for Archie. If you tried to touch Archie like that, he'd probably bite you.'

Edie wanted to say: *Thank God.* But she didn't.

'So. Can you make it to mine tomorrow for the interview? Is two OK?'

'Yes, sure.'

'This is the last one, by my schedule?'

'. . .Yes.' *Oh, no.*

Edie was sure there must be good, affectionate, friendship-mending words she could say at this point, but she was damned if she could find them.

64

When Edie arrived at the Owen family home the next day, Fraser answered the door. He was lounging around in sweats and Elliot was nowhere to be seen, a distant pulse of music signalling his whereabouts higher up in the house.

'*OK Computer*,' Fraser said, making a 'put gun barrel to temple and pull trigger' two fingers gesture. Edie smiled and hung her coat up and wondered if she was meant to know about his and Elliot's conversation. She should've thought to ask Elliot that.

'This blow-up between you and Lell. I feel awful about it,' Fraser said, at lowered volume.

Edie frowned.

'Lell?'

'Oh, Elliot. Sorry, kid nickname. Hah, that's weird, I never say that to anyone who's not family. Sure you're not an Owen?' He rocked back on his heels.

Edie guessed now that Elliot hadn't told Fraser what she knew. It was a very near-the-knuckle remark otherwise.

'Hah, pretty sure,' Edie said. That was a thought: Elliot

could have half-siblings he didn't know about. Press cuttings of the future.

'Just as well. This'd be some messed-up Luke and Princess Leia shit if you were.'

Edie laughed. Wait, who was Han Solo here? She didn't know, other than Fraser was good at flirting. He always managed to do the suggestive jokes without ever coming off as overbearing or greasy. He was like a big Golden Retriever: he might break things in his exuberance, but it was hard to be angry at him for it.

'Can you please make it up,? Because I hate Radiohead and he's not even playing their one half-decent album.'

'We have made it up,' Edie said.

'Errrrr, his complaint rock moods say you haven't.'

'We have. I've said I forgive him, and we've talked. It might be about something else altogether. Or someone.'

Argh. If there was a new girl on the scene, Edie was self-ishly glad she'd arrived too late to make the first edition print run.

Fraser pulled a face. 'Don't be soft. He's completely besotted with you.'

Edie's heart missed a beat and her stomach muscles contracted. *Besotted?*

'. . . He is?'

'Yes! He's gutted about upsetting you. Seriously, Edie. I wouldn't have come on to you if I'd known. You must've thought I was a right sleaze, hitting on you, in the circum-stances.'

The circumstances?

Fraser paused.

'He takes things hard, you know. He always has. I'm not asking you to do anything over and above, but at least tell him you don't hate him?'

'Of course I don't hate him!'

'Well right now, he hates himself and you're the only person who can help.'

'I'll speak to him,' Edie said, slightly stunned. Fraser wound himself round the banisters and bellowed up to Elliot that Edie was here. The music shut off.

'Ack, I am so sorry I messed up and made things difficult. You forgive me?' Fraser said.

'Course,' Edie said.

Fraser stepped forward and threw his arms around her in a bear hug. Edie patted him on the shoulder. When they separated, Elliot was on the stairs, watching them. He had one arm on the lintel above, which made his grey T-shirt ride up a little, exposing his stomach. Edie had to stop herself from wilting, a bit. Her heart rose up to block her throat.

'Hi,' he said, flatly.

'Hello,' Edie said. 'Fraz was—'

'. . . Fraz. Do you need a drink or shall we get on?'

'Let's start,' Edie said, feeling the chill of Elliot's disapproval.

As she fussed with her Dictaphone in the sitting room, she tried to make sense of what Fraser had said. *Besotted*?

She should try to clear the air, as she'd promised Fraser.

'Elliot, before we start. I want to say, about what happened. Outside the bar. Once and for all, apology accepted. Please accept mine in return, for screeching abuse at you?'

'Sure,' he said, neutrally. 'But you don't owe me an apology. I can't think about it without wanting to stab myself in my leg with a fork. If you want to see Fraser, it's cool by the way. I had absolutely no right to get involved.'

Eh? Hadn't they resolved that?

'I'm not . . .' Edie was going to say 'interested in your brother' but it sounded a little harsh. She settled for: 'Thanks. I don't.'

'That's cool too,' Elliot said, with a small shrug.

Oh. Edie had even less idea what to think, in front of this wall of indifference. Seeing Fraser was cool? It was obvious Elliot wasn't keen on her, in that way. She'd mistaken Fraser's meaning, and cringed slightly. 'Besotted' – you could be *besot* in a completely sexless way, right? She'd once been besotted with her gerbils.

They discussed the family background, the adoption, leaving out the Fraser-being-in-the-dark element. Elliot lowered his voice. 'He's taken it really astonishingly well, all considered, and I don't want to jeopardise that.' Edie nodded vigorously. 'I mean, he seems OK for now but it may hit him in stages.'

'And he doesn't know I know?' Edie whispered back.

Elliot shook his head. 'I wanted to keep the list of people who knew before him as short as possible.'

'Sure.'

They chatted the official biography, and by the time Edie had enough in her notepad, she hoped things between her and Elliot would've warmed up, but the thermostat remained resolutely low.

Filming on *Gun City* was days away from being finished.

'Um. Let me know if you fancy a drink before you leave,' Edie said, perkily, emptily, braced for rejection. She felt very sad. These weren't the terms she thought they'd part on.

'Sure thing,' Elliot said, in a tone that conveyed, *I won't*.

How did they get past it? How did they fix what had happened between them? Maybe her refusal to fully confront it was why. Edie had done some thinking, since she last saw Elliot.

As she stepped out of the front door for the last time, she turned abruptly.

'Elliot, I'm not dragging it up again for the millionth time to be annoying, but I have to ask something. What you said to Fraz. Why did you pick that to put him off, alluding to what happened to my mum? Why not have had a go at my looks or my personality or my writing ability' – Edie flapped her arms – 'or my stupid laugh and crap clothes, or something else. Why of all bad things, *that* bad thing?'

That was the crux of what upset her: that's what she'd been unable to forgive.

Elliot folded his arms and pushed at the door jamb with the toe of his Converse.

'There isn't anything bad to say about you. The only bad things about you are bad things that have happened to you. That was why.'

He looked up and met her gaze. If he thought that highly of her, why were things so perfunctory between them?

'Thank you,' Edie said.

'What for?'

'Letting me know.'

Edie extended her hand and said: 'It was great working with you, Elliot.'

He scratched his head as if she wasn't making much sense, paused and shook it.

'Likewise. Take care.'

Edie was yet again struck by the feeling there were a hundred more things they should talk about, and yet she couldn't think of anything to say.

65

It turned out Margot's 'maybe sometime' was a long form 'no', when it came to Edie's proposition to go for drink. It might not have helped that Edie's turbulent imaginary love life had delayed matters.

'Not fussed. I have all the grog I want at home, dear heart.'

'I know, but it's a change of scene! They have fizzy booze at The Lion, you know. I've checked.'

'It's my legs, darling. They're old legs.'

Eventually, through determined probing during the now-regular garden fence nattering, Edie wrung the truth out of Margot: a lifetime on the snouts had left her with virtually no lung capacity. She was housebound.

'My doctor said I couldn't run for the bus if my life depended on it,' she said, adjusting her 'Princess Margaret in Mustique' turban. It was a last burst of days of tolerable warmth before autumn set in proper.

'What about using a wheelchair?'

Margot's face contorted in disgust. 'A wheelchair, like a poor crippled sort? Or an old person?'

Edie laughed. 'Consider it role play. Acting a part.'

'The horror,' said Margot, rolling her extravagantly made-up eyes.

'What if I hired one, and we tried it, the once? If you hate it, we never need do it again.'

'Meryl and Beryl become very truculent when I abandon them.'

Edie hoped she hadn't named body parts.

'Who?'

'My lovely girls! The birds.'

'Ah. They can cope for a few hours.'

'Don't you have a boyfriend yet? What happened with the actor, has he moved on to pastures new?'

'No,' Edie said. She paused. 'I don't know.'

She'd re-read Elliot's *Guardian* interview many a time. He looked pensive and . . . well, devastating in the accompanying photo. His measured words about the difficulties of his real parents and generosity of his adoptive parents and the sympathetic tone of the piece made it hard to imagine anyone was going to be very hard on him, when his father made his effort to blacken his character. Edie had a brief look at the chatter online and it seemed the taint of tragedy made women more in love with him than ever. It made Edie feel possessive.

'I really did like that actor you know, and amazingly he maybe liked me at one point, but the trail went cold,' she blurted to Margot, carelessly.

'That's actors for you. They're itinerants, darling. Wherever they lay their hat is their home. If you want to settle down, you don't want someone laying his hat somewhere else by next week. I should know. Gordon's—' Margot made air quote marks, '"hat" was better travelled than Phileas Fogg.'

'Some sex would've been nice though,' Edie muttered, to much cackling from Margot.

She hadn't seen her dad walk into the garden, who overheard this and immediately remembered he'd forgotten something indoors. Both her father and Meg had softened slightly toward Margot since the awesome chocolate gateau. Meg hadn't officially tried it, of course. She merely conceded it looked tasty, based on zero first-hand information.

'I'll think about it,' Margot said.

That evening, Edie went to meet Hannah and Nick in the grounds of Wollaton Hall for the outdoor cinema.

Thoughts of Elliot infected her mind, hardly avoidable when she'd last been here when the place was a *Gun City* murder scene. Things were so different between them that night. She remembered Elliot drawing her into his arms. Hardly likely to happen now, she thought, glumly.

They unpacked their fold-out chairs and picnic food, and cracked open beers. 'Look, mine's got a cup holder in the arm!' Nick said, slotting his can of Stella into it. 'And I've got Marks & Spencer pork pies with hardboiled eggs in the middle. True contentment,' Nick said. 'Apart from the fact I will never know the touch of a woman again.'

Hannah prodded Nick's hand with a forefinger.

'There you go.'

'I am sated.'

'The temporary toilets are over there, for your clean-up.'

Edie always felt worlds better for being with her friends.

As the sun set, a safe distance from other cineastes, she told Hannah and Nick about the whole sorry saga with Elliot.

Hannah frowned at her and drew the blanket around her. She always felt the cold.

'Pass me another Mini Roll, please. Am I being very stupid or are you being very stupid?'

Edie frowned back. 'History would suggest it's much more likely to be me. So this is worrying.'

'He didn't want you to sleep with his brother because he wanted to sleep with you himself, didn't he? What am I missing?' Hannah picked the foil from her Mini Roll.

'Nah . . . I don't think it was that strong a wish, if it existed at all . . .'

Through a red-mist fug when they fought, had Edie missed this? Was that seriously possible? She'd thought he was just doubling down on bullshit.

'. . . Why not say so, if he did?' Edie said.

'Why does anyone not say so? It's intimidating, to come out with it, if you're not sure of the other person. Whoever you are.'

'OK, but now we've sorted it out and he's acting like I don't matter at all.'

Nick crumpled his first can and popped a second.

'Do you think sometimes you've treated this man a bit too much like he's from another planet? I mean, by the normal rules of interaction, I agree with Hannah, it sounds like he was into you.'

Hannah nodded.

'Look at his behaviour in the round. He sent you flowers,

flirted with you, confided in you. It's all pointing towards him liking you, not thinking you're a Steer Well Clear,' Hannah said.

They made a good case.

'Well if he did feel like that, the moment's completely gone. He doesn't feel like that any more. I'd go so far as to say he doesn't like me much.'

'He sounds more wary than anything. You know when you lost it at him, you said some harsh things?'

'Yes?'

'What, exactly?'

'Uh . . .' It pained Edie to remember. 'That I wasn't his fan girl. That we were only colleagues, not friends, and I didn't give two shits about him.' Edie winced. 'He knows I said that in anger, though. He knows I was lashing back.'

'He knows . . . how? You said so?'

'Not in so many words.'

Edie thought of her secrecy at Ad Hoc. Louis saying she was a mystery. Of her failure to ask Jack what the hell was going on. And about Fraser's reading of the situation between her and Elliot, which sounded like he was talking about strangers, Edie shrinking from saying: *Do you seriously mean you think Elliot's smitten with me?* Perhaps Edie's life badly lacked some plain speaking.

'You told him you had no time for him, and now he's behaving like he has no time for you.' Hannah smiled. 'Great mysteries of our age. Why not tell him you didn't mean it, and ask him outright how he feels about you?'

'It's too late,' Edie said.

'How do you know it's too late if you don't ask him?'

'We're not working together any more.'

'If he feels the way I'm pretty sure you hope he feels, you don't need to be.'

This was incontrovertibly true. How on earth could Edie ever ask *Elliot Owen* something like that though? What if he choked to death on his laughter?

The sky darkened, and the fog-wreathed Warner Brothers logo appeared on screen, to cheers. Edie sank into her seat.

It was preferable to think Elliot hadn't been into her. Because if by some astonishing, anomalous quirk of the fates, Elliot Owen had briefly fancied her, and tried to tell her, and she'd mucked it up, Edie would have to punch herself in the face for eternity.

66

Would Margot prefer a self-propelled or powered wheelchair? Edie accepted it wasn't the most glamorous decision for the wasp-waisted woman who used to have men in dickie bows and dinner suits fighting to light her cigarette. Still, those Sobranies had taken their toll, and wheelchair it was. Edie studied the Shopmobility leaflet and pondered how best to lure Margot to place her bony behind in one.

Please do this and take my mind off the actor?

She felt sure once Margot had enjoyed an outing, felt its benefits, she'd be up for more. She waited until G&T o'clock to pop round with it.

Edie knocked on the door, no answer. There were lights on, she was definitely there. Of course she was there, she was never anywhere else. She let herself in with the key from under the tub, calling: 'Margot! Hello? It's Edie!'

There was a low burble of noise from the front room, punctuated by birds cheeping. She peered gingerly round the living room door. Margot was in a patterned pink kimono, sprawled on the sofa asleep, head thrown back, a film she'd long stopped watching still playing on the television. Rosalind Russell leaned in to have her cigarette lit, in the 1940s.

Edie would leave the leaflet, and a note – was it alright to go poking about to find pen and paper? As she was nosying around the hallway table, a thought struck her. She walked back into the living room. Where was the snoring?

She gazed at Margot. And then she saw it. The candle-wax pallor. Her mouth open, slightly twisted. Her eerie stillness. The way her hands were clinging on to the sides of the sofa, claw-like. A grip that had frozen, possibly hours previous.

'Margot?' Edie said, frightened. It was a childlike fright. '*Margot?*'

She stepped towards and around her and examined her from another angle, feeling bizarrely intrusive. Edie had never seen a dead body before. When she read in news stories that it was 'obvious' someone was dead, she always wondered how they could be so sure. Maybe they were a few vigorous chest pumps away from spluttering back into life.

Looking at Margot now, she knew. Whatever had made Margot, Margot, was extinct, flown, gone. She was like a sculpture. Her pilot light had gone out.

Edie walked back to the hallway and picked up the telephone mounted on the wall, lilac plastic. She had the strangest sense that this was the wrong reality: that if she retraced her steps, she could walk back out the door, knock, walk in again and share a drink with Margot.

She spoke in a stranger's voice.

'Hello . . . Ambulance, please. It's my neighbour. No, I think she's dead. I'm not sure.'

Edie lowered herself on to Margot's chair, looking at the lipsticked fag butts in the swan ashtray, and stared at her body for what felt like an hour. Edie was numb. The birds hopped and squeaked and nibbled at their bird feeder. The knocking and commotion of the paramedics at the door made Edie jump out of her skin, even though she was expecting them.

Suddenly the house was filled with the bustle of strangers, people in green uniforms, speaking in confident voices. *What was her name, how long had Edie been here, did she know if she was on any medication.*

When someone with two fingers to Margot's neck, then wrist, shook their head, Edie had to fight back the first sob. It hadn't been fully real until someone qualified declared that it was. They thronged round Margot and Edie stared at her slippers, willing her legs to twitch.

'Looks like a massive heart attack, but we can't be sure,' said a stocky man with a kind face and Yorkshire accent, after fifteen minutes or so. 'She wouldn't have felt anything. It would've been quick.'

Edie nodded, blankly.

They loaded Margot's slight body on to a stretcher, her pink dressing gown cord dangling like ribbon. With the ambulance engine chugging in the background, they discussed next of kin with Edie. She told them about the son. She had to get out of Margot's house now – it was full of officialdom, pacing around. It gave Edie a jolting reminder of being nine years old again, in the house next door.

In a heartbeat, or more accurately, a missed heartbeat, everything that was Margot's was no longer private. It felt so wrong. *Stop. Come back. Bring her in. Wake her up.*

Edie stepped over the wall to her house, sweaty hand clutching her Shopmobility leaflet. In their front room, Meg was watching television. Edie had never been so grateful for her sister being alive.

'Meg,' she said, stood in the doorway, and felt her face collapse as she started speaking, 'Margot's dead. I just found her.'

'Oh, shit. From next door? The battleaxe?'

'She was my friend!' Edie said.

Edie fell on to Meg and put her arms around her, shaking with sobs, her tears soaking through Meg's saggy sweatshirt.

Meg put her arms around her as reflex.

'I'd got her this leaflet,' she howled, and showed a bewildered Meg. 'I was going to hire her a wheelchair. We were going to do things together. I wanted to take her to Goose Fair.'

Meg squinted. 'Won't you be back in London by Goose Fair?'

'No, I'm moving back to Nottingham,' Edie gasped. 'Don't worry, I'll move out of here.'

Meg looked confused and vaguely patted Edie's back. The floodgates had opened for Edie.

'Why bother to love anyone, Meg? They just leave. Everyone fucking leaves me,' Edie said, through another torrent of tears. 'I can't get anything right. Everything I try to do, it turns to shit.'

'Me and Dad didn't leave,' Meg said, but not resentfully. She was evidently startled, even disarmed, by the state Edie was in. She'd never seen her like this.

'No, true,' Edie said. 'You just don't want me to be here. That's a difference, at least.' She wiped at her face and smiled to show this wasn't said in anger.

'I do want you here,' Meg said, in a quiet voice. '*You* left. You left us. Whenever you come back, it's like you can't get away fast enough.'

'Only because I feel guilty all the time.'

'Why?'

Edie had never been asked this before. Probably because she'd never admitted it. She had to compose herself a bit more before she could reply.

'I tried to make up for Mum not being here, and I couldn't. You were disappointed in me, Dad still wasn't happy. I thought if I couldn't make it right, I was better off out of it. Rather than letting you down all the time.'

Edie saw tears slide down Meg's face now. She looked five years old again, to Edie. 'We didn't want you to go. It was like we were never good enough for you. We thought you were ashamed of us. That's what me and Dad thought. He said he understood, that he hadn't given you the start in life he wanted to.'

Edie stared at her younger sister. She hated the thought of them having had this conversation.

'I wasn't ashamed, why would I be ashamed?'

'We weren't London, or cool.'

'London isn't cool,' Edie said, half-hiccup laughing through her tears. 'It's lonely and quite shit for the most part. Is that what you thought, that I thought my family were a disgrace to me?'

'Yeah.'

'It wasn't that. It was because I wanted to make it better for you and I couldn't and I thought you hated me for it.'

'How could you make it better?'

'By doing Mum's job, I suppose. Looking after you and Dad the way she would have done.'

'We didn't want you to be Mum. We wanted you to be you.'

It was Meg's turn to stare at Edie in amazement. How had they never discussed this before?

Edie could only say: 'Oh.'

'Also, you did make things better, lots of the time. When I'm sad or I miss you or I miss Mum, I still make that hot chocolate you used to make me, remember?'

'Oh, God . . .? Yeah.'

Edie hadn't thought about that for years. When Meg was inconsolable for their mum when she was small, Edie decided on a combination of two great remedies: lying and sugar. She told Meg that if she stopped crying and drank her special hot chocolate (marshmallows, Flake, Carnation milk: approx 3,000 calories a pop, all ingredients available from the local inconvenience store), she'd feel better. Often, it worked.

'You took really good care of us,' Meg said. 'But you didn't have to. You could've stayed and been an arsehole, as long as you stayed.'

Fresh tears rolled down Meg's face and Edie wondered how she'd lost sight of her little sister. This was the same Meg who used to follow her around holding her pet rabbit Mungy, who used to hang on her every word, who nicked her clothes and copied her taste in music and idolised her friends. Somehow, through misunderstandings and distance and miscommunication, they'd drifted apart. They'd mistaken each other for enemies, rather than the closest ally they'd ever have.

'I'm sorry,' Edie said, putting her arms round her shoulders and holding her again, 'I'm so sorry for running away. It wasn't you I was running away from. I just miss Mum so much sometimes.'

'So do I,' Meg said, and they held each other as they both sobbed.

'Sometimes I'm so pissed off with her,' Meg said, when they'd steadied enough. 'I didn't even get to know her. How shit is that?'

'I get angry with her too,' Edie said. 'I think we're allowed. I think Mum would say we were allowed. Growing up without her hasn't been easy. It's been this giant unsaid thing hovering like a big Zeppelin. If we don't say it, we're denying how difficult it's been, and that's not fair.' Edie paused. 'How difficult it *still is*. It'll always be difficult. We have to miss Mum for our whole lives. That's it, isn't it?'

She paused. Somehow, naming the terrible thing took away some of its terror.

'I think I used to think there would be a time when it wouldn't hurt as much any more, or a place I could go where it wouldn't hurt as much. That's also what the running away was about. Home is the one place I had to face how much I miss her.'

Meg nodded and there was a fresh flood of tears from them both. They were crying out over twenty-five years of them, in the space of fifteen minutes.

'I read an analogy of depression,' Meg said, as they steadied, wiping under her eyes with a floppy cuff. 'About how killing yourself is like jumping out of a tall building when it's on fire. You don't want to jump out, but bit by bit, it becomes impossible not to because you're so scared and in so much pain. No one thinks anyone jumping out of a building on fire wants to do it.'

'Every time I think that Mum chose to go, I'm going to remember that,' Edie said. 'I know in my heart that she didn't choose it, but sometimes when it's hard to bear, being angry is easier.'

'You put things really well when you talk about your feelings,' Meg said.

'I thought I always have irritating smart comebacks?' Edie said, smiling.

'Yeah, those too,' Meg gasp-laughed.

They sat quietly, side by side, through the slowing of their sobs, Edie rubbing Meg's back.

'Margot said you had passion, by the way,' she added.

'She did?'

'Yes.'

The front door opened and closed. Their dad put his head round the door.

'I've got th— oh God, what's happened?! Are you alright?' their dad said.

'We're OK. It's Margot. She's dead,' Edie said.

'Oh.' Their dad looked from one blotchy tearstained face to another, and back again, his own face taut with incomprehension. 'Meg didn't kill her, did she?'

Their dad put his canvas shopping bags down at his feet and listened to the story of Edie's ghoulish discovery.

'Very sad. I'm sorry you had to be the one to find her.'

'She had to die. I had the easier bit,' Edie said.

He looked from Edie to Meg, perplexed, and could obviously sense the disturbance in the atmosphere. Edie knew she had to take this window while it was thrown open, before her dad stood up to make the tea and Meg loped back off to her bedroom.

'Dad,' Edie said, 'I've been talking to Meg. There's something I've never explained, about why I've stayed away so much. Meg says you thought it was you; that I was ashamed of you both, but that's not it. That was never it. I always wanted to make up for Mum not being here and I couldn't manage it. I couldn't be here and I couldn't stand letting you down. And I didn't want to face my own grief, especially not if it made you two sadder. I feel silly saying it, but it's true.'

She still had to force herself, against the ingrained habit of years, to say the 'm' word. She hadn't realised what a taboo it had become.

'. . . It wasn't because I didn't like being around the two of you. It was all about Mum. It was my way of dealing with it. I couldn't fix it, so I ran away. Fix or flee, that's what I do, I've come to realise,' Edie said. 'Mostly flee, I think.'

Her father frowned. 'Why would you need to do that?'

'I don't know. I made a decision really early on that losing Mum would be less bad if I did the things she used to do, around the house. If I looked after Meg. Then you had your problems . . .' she didn't want to make her dad feel worse about this. 'I thought it was my fault.'

Meg said quietly: 'I always wondered if she'd have been OK if she'd stopped at the one kid.'

Her dad shook his head.

'You have nothing to feel guilty about it, this is extraordinary to me. I had no idea. *I* should feel guilty, very guilty, I fear. Not you two.'

'Why should you?' Edie said.

'For not holding everything together better when she died, for losing my job. For not seeing how sick she was, and leaving her alone with both of you.'

Her dad's eyes were glassy and Edie realised how near the surface this was. Meg started snuffling gently and Edie put her arm round her.

'Mum's illness wasn't your fault!'

'No, but who's to say how differently things would've been if I'd acted differently. If I'd acted sooner.'

'Dad, that's mad,' Edie said. 'Neither of us have ever blamed you for what happened to Mum. She was seen by an emergency doctor the day before she died, wasn't she?'

Her dad jerked his head in agreement, not speaking.

'And she promised the doctor she wouldn't do anything silly. You couldn't watch her all day, every day. You couldn't have done more. Depression is an illness and no one would criticise someone who was widowed in any other situation.'

With these words, Edie realised this absolution was necessary for all of them. Her mum had an illness that killed her, and yet they were all still labouring under the guilt that it shouldn't have happened. That somewhere along the line, they each in their own way could've changed the course of history, and prevented or replaced that loss. You couldn't put a burden down if you didn't admit to yourself you were carrying it.

'Our job wasn't to stop Mum dying, because we couldn't have done that,' Edie said. These words were like a magic spell that could banish a curse. 'Our job has always been to just look after each other.'

Her dad nodded and tears rolled down his face. Edie got up to hug him.

'Meg, join in,' she mumbled into her dad's mothball-smelling old jumper and she felt her sister's arms around them.

'We're alright, the three of us,' Edie said.

'Let's have a cup of tea,' her dad said, when they broke apart and everything felt different. Except their dad's constant desire for tea.

'I wish I hadn't had fights with Margot now,' Meg said, wiping at her cheeks with the sleeve of her hooded top. 'She sounds like she could have been alright.'

'Nah, she loved it,' Edie said.

Before she could stop herself, Edie caught herself wondering if Margot could overhear from next door. Maybe Margot could hear from wherever she was now.

Would they have had this conversation without her? Edie didn't know, she suspected not. Guardian angels could come in very unexpected, and indeed inebriated forms.

67

The day after Margot's death, a thin, tall, dark-haired man, with familiar large eyes and bone structure, arrived outside her house with a removal van. He had an equally spectrally thin wife, her mousy hair pulled back from her face. Leaving the door hanging open, they filleted the house, Margot's chintzy bric-a-brac heaping up in the front garden.

'Human bastards,' Edie breathed, watching them from the living room window. Her dad stood next to her, sipping a cup of tea.

'Everyone has their story, and you don't know theirs,' he said.

'I bet if I did, I'd hate their dialogue and their character motivations and their . . . stupid faces,' Edie said.

'You sound like Megan,' her dad said. 'Is this a truce or a merging?'

He pretended to shudder and Edie leaned her head on his shoulder. He kissed her head and put an arm round her. The house had been spookily harmonious for the last twenty hours or so. Meg had wanted Edie to have her favourite bacon sandwiches to help with the trauma, and Edie had insisted Alpen was fine.

Edie watched as the parakeets in their cage, chirruping and hopping, were dumped unceremoniously alongside a bedside table.

'They're messing with Meryl and Beryl now, Dad! That's it, that's enough.'

Before he could stop her, Edie darted out to confront him. 'Eric?'

The man turned, looking taken aback to hear his name. 'Yes?'

'I'm Edie, from next door. I was Margot's friend.'

It felt nice, to say it.

'Take your word for it.'

'Well, that's how I know your name.'

Eric didn't respond.

'What's happening to the birds?'

Eric gave Meryl and Beryl a look that suggested he hadn't given it a whole lot of thought.

'RSPB? If we can get them to pick them up.'

'They'll probably want you to drop them off. There's a sanctuary at Radcliffe on Trent.'

Edie was being the archetypal irritating nosy neighbour and she didn't care in the slightest.

'I'm not a taxi service for budgies. If we open the door, they'll rehome themselves, no doubt. If they've got an appetite.'

'I'll take them,' Edie said, sharply.

'Be my guest, Bridie.'

Edie picked up the cage. 'Can I come to the funeral?' she

asked. Actually did you need permission, how did it work? Did funeral parlours have bouncers?

'It's only going to be small,' he paused. 'My mother made sure of that.'

His wife appeared in the doorway and said: 'Look at these slippers! How many Chihuahuas died so she could have warm feet?' Edie could've slapped her. And him.

'I'd like to be there,' Edie continued.

Eric sized her up, and shrugged.

'It's Thursday, three-thirty p.m., Wilford Hill. Flowers in lieu of charity donations. It's what Mum would've wanted.'

'Thank you,' Edie said.

She carried the bird cage back into the house.

'Holy guacamole, Edith, what's going on?!' her dad said, as Edie bumped and scraped the large cage down the hallway.

'I had to, Dad,' she hissed. 'They were going to dump them.'

Meg came down the stairs. 'Alright, animal activism! Yeah!'

'I don't want animals activated in here,' her dad said.

'It's like *Free Willy*,' Meg said. 'Edie has to free them from the yoke of oppression.'

'They don't look very free to me.'

'We'll build them a bigger enclosure, along the wall of the dining room. Or maybe just make the dining room their room,' Meg said.

'Oh yes let's turn my house into an aviary,' their dad said. 'As ever, the perfect solution is staring me in the face.'

'I said I'd take them to the RSPB,' Edie explained. 'This is a temporary rehoming, Dad, I promise. They're just passing through.'

Edie put the birds in the dining room, checked their seed and water bottles were full, and found her dad and sister in the kitchen.

'Will you come to the funeral with me? Thursday afternoon.'

'Oh, Edith. . .' her dad said, 'I don't know. I didn't know the lady all that well. And forgive me for saying so, but that's the way we both liked it.'

'Thursday's my day at the home,' Meg said.

'Could you swap it?' Edie said to her. 'It would mean so much to me to have you both there.' Edie hesitated. 'I want to be with my family.'

It was so simple to say, but she could see the effect her words had was profound.

Wilford Crematorium was south of the city, on a hill, with a winding road that often carried slow-moving funeral cortèges. Edie's dad drove them in the Volvo. They got out, her dad in an old work suit that was slightly too small for him, shiny from being ironed when it shouldn't have been. Edie was in an evening dress that didn't work with her tartan coat, while Meg wore a dark Pixies T-shirt with a black cardigan buttoned over it.

'Is this alright? I don't have anything plain and black,' she'd said.

'Margot would be fine with it, I reckon. She liked people dancing to their own drum. She might've liked "Monkey Gone to Heaven".'

In the bricked entranceway as they entered the crematorium,

Edie saw the flowers she'd sent. Lilies, roses and palm leaves, in a white, pink and green spray, the most ostentatious arrangement she could afford. 'Very princessy,' had been her instructions to the florist. 'She loved ritz and glitz.'

'That's magnificent,' her dad said. 'I'm very proud of you, you know. You're very caring. And generous.'

Meg leaned down and read the card aloud.

To marvellous Margot.

I hope paradise is an eternal cocktail hour at the Dorchester.

Thank you for your advice. You helped us more than you'll ever know. I was glad to meet you.

Love from Edie (and Gerry and Meg) xxx

Meg rubbed Edie's arm.

Inside the rather sterile modern room, there was Eric and his wife in the front row, and two other elderly women in a middle pew, who Edie suspected might be funeral-crasher day-trippers, although she couldn't tell for sure.

Margot's coffin was adorned with orange spray roses, a cheapy option, Edie guessed.

Frank Sinatra's 'My Funny Valentine' played. Eric had made one thoughtful choice, at least.

The vicar stepped up and read the passage from the Corinthians, which didn't strike Edie as very Margot-ish. He gave a short, tactful speech about Margot's vibrancy and beauty and her work as an actress. And how just because we didn't always see eye to eye with our family members doesn't mean we don't love them and let's carefully step round the lack of mourners here today and commend Margot to the care of the Lord, Amen.

He pressed a button, clasped his hands and bowed his head, and Margot disappeared through the curtains to a wash of nondescript classical music. Eric and his wife stood, chatted to the vicar briefly and left, without acknowledging the Thompsons.

I don't feel sorry for Margot, Edie thought as she watched Eric go. She's elsewhere. I feel sorry for you, because whatever she did, you lose out by caring so little for your fellow humans.

'Did she honestly have so few friends?' Meg said, as they walked through the car park.

'She was cantankerous . . . But I get the impression a lot of them were from her London days, and it's not as if Eric will have let them know.'

'Sad business,' her dad said. 'I'd have tried harder if I'd known.'

'She took real glee in the rucks. Shall we go for a drink, as a wake?' Edie said, as they climbed into the car. 'Quick one at the Larwood?'

They stepped from the hushed world of death and dying back into the noisy one of the living, and sat sipping a glass of champagne each – 'Trust me, Margot would be scandalised at us having anything else,' Edie said, buying a bottle – in a busy gastropub.

'To Margot,' Edie said.

'To Margot,' they chorused.

'Where do you think they'll scatter her ashes?' Meg said. 'If they do.'

'I hope the Dorchester, or the West End, or Cap Ferrat,'

Edie said. 'No windswept cliffs for Margot.' Edie weighed her next words carefully, though she judged if now wasn't the time, she couldn't see when it would be. 'Dad, do you still have Mum's ashes?'

'Yes,' he said. 'Of course.'

'I wasn't sure if you'd scattered them already.'

Her dad loosened the collar on his too-tight shirt. 'I'm sorry I've never spoken to you both about this. I've had to decide between telling you things and upsetting you, and keeping things from you, and I've not always judged it right. At the time, it got very fraught with your Auntie Dawn, she decided she had a claim on them. "Blood's thicker than water." I said well, in that case, surely the girls have a greater claim. You were too young to make a decision and then you were both growing up, getting on with your lives. I so wanted you both to be able to . . . emerge from the shadow of it, you know? And you have.'

He rubbed under his eyes, lifting his glasses, cleared his throat.

'Hence I waited. We can scatter them when you both decide you want to.'

'I would like to scatter them,' Meg said.

'We just need to pick a spot,' Edie agreed.

'Your Auntie Dawn had very fixed ideas about where they should be scattered.'

'Auntie Dawn can eat a bag of dicks,' said Meg.

'Megan!' their father exclaimed. Edie clinked her glass. Auntie Dawn and their Uncle Derek had often come across as more master villain and witless henchman than loving spouses and caring relatives.

'Mum's ashes belong to us,' Edie said. 'End of story. Dad, can you think where we'd scatter them?'

'Actually, I've had somewhere in mind for a while. It was a place your mum and I used to go when we were courting.'

'That's where we'll do it, then.'

'Unless it was the sex shop on Lower Parliament Street,' Meg said.

68

As they walked to the car, Edie said: 'I might go for a walk, actually. There's someone I want to see.'

While they had been toasting Margot, Edie had admitted to herself she missed Elliot, a longing that might even be yearning. It had been ten days since she'd seen him. Yes, she was counting. She missed the way they used to talk. She missed the way he'd instinctively get it, if she told him about Margot. She had an urge to share this with him. She had an urge to do a lot more with Elliot than that.

As Edie got quickly sucked into the vortex of second guessing 'what ifs' she had a simple clear impulse: *just ask him*. At least if he said it was never there, or it wasn't there any more, she'd know for sure. As Nick and Hannah had said.

And Margot had given her a speech about how 'no' wasn't the worst thing. It felt as if she'd been forecasting this moment. Edie felt like she owed it to Margot to take her advice. To take the risk. She pulled her phone out.

Elliot, if you're in Bridgford, can I come round & see you? There's something I really want to say. Edie x

Yes sure. Next half hour?

Edie was thrilled at the instant response but noted: no kiss.

Yes! If that's OK?

It's fine.x

Phew. A conciliatory 'x', if nothing else.

By the time Edie arrived at his door, it was obvious Elliot was a little apprehensive. He was polite in his greeting, but with a big question mark hovering over his head. They stood in the hallway, Edie hoping she didn't look too buzzed from the champagne, Elliot looking casually extraordinary in a black jumper.

'Er. You said you wanted to say something?'

'Yes.' Oh, God. The bit where you peered out of the plane and knew you had to jump was worse than the jump itself.

Edie cleared her throat.

'So . . .'

The inherent ridiculousness of what she was about to do struck Edie so hard she nearly laughed. The huge revelation of telling Elliot Owen she fancied him. Half the bloody world fancied him. You might as well nervously cough to Elton John he could probably make a go of the singing thing.

'I don't know exactly what happened between us, when we fell out that night.'

Elliot glanced at the floor. Edie took a breath.

'You once said that staying silent and waiting for your mind to be read is a tactic that is destined for doom, and I agree. And you're going back to America in a few weeks, so it's not as if I have forever to find out the answer. I thought maybe I should just ask the question.'

Elliot was impossible to read, his expression neutral.

'. . . And say, if that was all because you really liked me yourself, I want you to know, I like you too. A lot.'

'Thanks,' Elliot said, but with the smallest shrug of disappointment. Big drum roll, small firework.

She could see his point. It was a little too cutesome euphemism. Edie had come this far, she best make the carnal aspect clear.

'I've been to a funeral and had the sort of day where you're reminded life is very, very brief. I had this overwhelming urge to come and see you, and spend time with you. And if you want me to stay over, I want to stay over.'

'Stay over'! Oh God! Where did that come from? She was making it sound as if she wanted to do mani-pedis in front of *Pitch Perfect 2* with a tub of Cherry Garcia.

'"Stay over"?' Elliot repeated, pushing his hands in his pockets, 'What, as in sleep with me?'

Edie swallowed. 'Yes.' She breathed out, heart pounding.

You could do it. You could stand in front of someone and tell them what you wanted and it wasn't the worst thing. It was scary, but in a good way.

Elliot's expression was still impossible to read. He hadn't laughed or vommed, at least.

'What sort of sex?' he said, 'Hearts and flowers carry-me-up-to-bed-sex, or take-me-right-now-on-the-stairs-sex?'

Edie swallowed again and she broke into a light sweat. She hadn't tried to predict what Elliot might say; it's fair to say this was more of a challenge than she expected.

'Uhm . . .'

Perfect pin-drop quiet in the house. She could hear its bones creak.

She hit on an Edie-ish answer: 'Whichever's available?'

Elliot stared at her and eventually shook his head.

'I'll have to turn you down.'

Edie nodded. She made another useful discovery. It hurt, to be rejected directly. But not half as much as she thought it would. She wasn't embarrassed, and she didn't crumble. It was disappointing but crucially, it wasn't humiliating. There was something powerful in honesty.

'I hope you didn't mind that I asked, and that it won't make things too weird. OK, that's that done, then.'

She turned to leave.

'Edie,' Elliot said, 'don't you want to know why?'

She turned back. 'I'm assuming you don't find it an attractive enough prospect? I can probably live without the detail.'

'You've had a difficult day, and you're sad. If it was the hearts and flowers sort, I'd worry you only really wanted company and closeness. If it was the other, I'd worry you only wanted sex.'

Edie wasn't catching his meaning.

'. . . I said whichever, though?'

'That sounds like you mean this is casual.'

'Is that a problem?'

'Yes. I can't do casual. I was past casual . . .' he smiled, 'ages ago, I'm afraid.'

'I don't think I'm following you.'

'If we're going to do this, I want you to want me the way I want you.'

Her heart was racing. Oh God, if they *were* going to do it . . .? But the way that . . .? Edie hoped they weren't about to have a 'my desires are unconventional' moment.

'What sort of sex should I have said I wanted?'

'The sort where it doesn't matter, as long as it's with me. The sort where you mean it.'

Oof. Edie felt lightheaded.

'Sorry to be so direct, but y'know, we've come this far. If you don't know how I feel, it could be awkward in the aftermath.' Elliot paused. 'In summary, we can do it, just don't expect to have fun here, OK. I'm serious about you.'

Edie burst out laughing as her heart went *ka-dum ka-dum ka-dum*.

What did she say now? She composed herself, with some effort, given her legs no longer seemed to exist.

'You're asking if this is casual for me? I don't feel casual about you. I feel . . . everything about you.'

A long look and a silence stretched between them.

'Maybe, if you're staying, you could take your coat off?' Elliot said eventually, gesturing at Edie's favourite tartan number.

'Oh, hah, yeah!' Edie let out a goofy laugh and pulled it from her shoulders, turning to hang it on the banister. As she turned back to gabble something nervously, Elliot caught her, hands on her shoulders, and kissed her. He'd shaved since *Gun City* and Edie felt herself almost swoon at the soft brush of his jaw and sensation of his mouth on hers. It was confident – you'd expect that really, given the *Blood & Gold* practice – but gentle and warm and he tasted so *right,* and Edie had to control herself to concentrate on the moment and the man and not let her internal monologue shriek YOU'RE TOTALLY TOUCHING TONGUES WITH ELLIOT OWEN.

Why did things that were so simple, seem so complex beforehand? Of course they could kiss. Of course it would feel this right. Of course it would be this incredible. *Easy.*

From the sitting room, Radiohead's 'Creep' drifted out. Edie broke from his hold.

'. . . What album is this?'

'Er,' Elliot paused, pupils dark. '*Pablo Honey*, isn't it? Why?'

'I thought maybe you'd bought *The Best of Radiohead* and this encounter,' she gestured between them, '. . . would have to be cancelled.'

'Muso snob,' Elliot said, getting it, playing along. 'You wouldn't cancel it, you're well into it. Even if you found out my favourite song to have sex to was 'Two Princes' by the Spin Doctors, you'd still be saying *Give it to me, Elliot.*'

Edie laughed and didn't quite cope with the word 'sex' in proximity to the actual having of it and blushed scarlet.

Elliot laughed at her and kissed her harder and mumbled: 'I like you far too much. I like you so bloody much.'

They were on the stairs, Edie enjoying the weight of Elliot pressing down against her, while hoping they would make it to the bedroom, because she was far too mid-thirties for stair sex.

'Is this hugely disrespectful, on the day of a funeral?' Elliot said, in a very brief pause for breath.

'It's what Margot would've wanted,' Edie said.

In the moment where the music soared and Edie was looking up at the Owen residence hallway lampshade as Elliot kissed her neck, she thought she would live every last minute of her life – the good and the bad – for a second time, because it would bring her here again.

69

Edie's childhood bedroom had a plastic starlight canopy, Elliot's had a skylight through which you could see real stars.

They lay in each other's arms and misidentified the Plough, Sirius and Orion's Belt.

Edie liked the way that every time they pointed out a different part of the constellation above, they adjusted the position of their bodies against each other. The amateur astrology was something of an excuse.

'So now we've done it, I could do a kiss and tell?' Edie said.

'Yeah, knock yourself out,' Elliot said, rearranging the pillows behind their heads. 'You might want to wait to see if I properly break America, it'd be worth more after that. Are you thinking one of those *Sunday Sport*, "he went on as long as a docker's tea break", or *Sun* "incredible stud took me to O Town" things?'

'I dunno. Where do I stand legally if I'm making it up?'

Elliot burst out laughing. 'You weren't complaining, from what I could tell.'

Edie grinned and flushed.

'Could we have done this weeks ago?' she said, thinking about how little time she had left with Elliot. *Don't think about it . . .*'I was so hoping for something to happen, that night in the bar.'

'That night when you were flirting with my brother, kept trying to swap chairs to get away from me and then shouted you hated me? Why didn't I take those heavy hints?'

Edie laughed.

'You know, "I don't give two shits about you, Elliot." I heard a subtext there that wasn't *I'm falling like a ton of bricks for you too.*'

Edie winced and laughed and inhaled the warmth of him next to her and couldn't quite believe it. They were together.

'I thought you could see it in my eyes. Like Garratt and Orla.'

'Trust me, you're not easy to read.'

Edie remembered Louis saying something similar at the wedding, a lifetime ago.

'Also I've a suspicion Archie made all that shit up.'

'Haha. Point of order, I never flirted with Fraser, as such. Not my type,' Edie said.

'You never denied liking him, that whole fight. Afterwards, I thought you must be into him. I nearly said, when we were in the street, I'm absolutely crazy about you and the thought of you with my brother is the level end, but we had an audience. I draw the line at getting knocked back when someone's going to turn it into a Vine.'

'But you're *you*. Why didn't you say, long before that, "Bitch, I'm Elliot Owen, hop on it already"?'

'Oh yeah because that behaviour's really going to impress anyone worth impressing.'

'You must've known you were in with a good chance, though.'

Elliot turned to her. 'And some bloke ruined his wedding day for one kiss with you. I can see his point.'

Elliot kissed her again and Edie kissed him back and he had a palm on the curve of her bare hip, which made Edie feel like she had wasted too much of her life not feeling like this.

It was all quite quickly going to turn into a repeat performance, apart from the unmistakable bang of the front door downstairs.

Elliot sat bolt upright and listened to the drift of voices. 'My parents!' he hissed. 'Fuck!'

'They're not on a cruise?!' Edie hissed back, feeling every inch of her nakedness.

'Yes, they're meant to be back tomorrow lunch. Fuuuuccccck.'

He leapt out of bed and Edie was disappointed that instead of enjoying an Elliot Owen nude scene with an audience of one person, she was scrabbling desperately to find where Elliot had thrown her bra, and pull her dress over her head.

'Will they mind?' Edie said, in a hoarse whisper as she hopped around, dragging her pants and tights on underneath her dress, as Elliot's head disappeared into his T-shirt. 'They're not devout Christians, or anything?'

Elliot grinned. 'Nah. Not quite how I wanted to introduce you, that's all.'

They thundered down the stairs together, Edie behind Elliot, her heart banging like a gong, to see his parents stood looking up at them. Thank God, Edie thought, they hadn't done it on the stairs.

'Hello, Elliot!' His mum spied Edie. 'Oh! Now here's a surprise. You have company.'

She had silver hair in a sharp bob, Elliot's dad with the look of a retired barrister or cricket commentator.

'Hi, Mum, Dad.' He stepped forward gave each of them a hug, 'Uh, this is Edie.'

'Hello,' Edie said. 'Nice to meet you.'

She extended an arm to shake their hands.

'Well, now,' his mum said. They looked from Edie to Elliot, taking in their matching rumpled hair and flush, and smiled broadly.

'Edie's ghost-writing the autobiography,' Elliot said, for something to say.

This statement was the cause of some laughing from his dad that he turned into a small throaty cough.

'Elliot, we did call you to say we got an earlier connecting flight,' his mum said. 'But, most unlike you, you've not been answering your phone for the last few hours. How odd.'

'Oh yeah, it's in the kitchen somewhere,' he said, with a sheepish smile and a hand on the back of his head.

'We did want to warn you, so as not to disturb you at an awkward moment . . .'

'But as this nice young lady is merely ghost-writing your autobiography, that's put that suspicion firmly to bed,' his dad concluded.

Edie laughed out loud, before she could ponder if it was the right response. Fortunately it seemed it was and then everyone laughed.

'I'm going to get going, let you unpack and catch up with your son,' Edie said. She politely declined efforts to get her to stay, and the taxi beeped within minutes of discussing their foreign travels.

'I'll walk you out,' Elliot said.

As soon as Elliot had pulled the door on the latch he turned, grabbed Edie's shoulders, spun her round and kissed her deeply.

'Snogging in the garden, I feel like we're sixteen,' he said. 'Can I see you tomorrow? Can I see you constantly? Can I see you with no clothes on again?'

'Yes, yes, and no, I'm always clothed after the first time,' Edie said. She dawdled. Her heart felt so full. 'Elliot, thank you.'

'What for?'

'For everything. Today was a sad day, and the best night of my life.'

'Oh God, you ridiculous person. As if you owe me thanks.' He paused. 'Wait, I've just thought, it's the wrap party tomorrow. Would you come with me?'

'Er. Yes. Can non-*Gun City* people go?'

'Yes, we can bring dates.'

'OK, sure,' Edie said. Date. DATE.

He kissed her again and only a call from inside the house about whether Elliot wanted a cup of tea made them break apart.

'See you tomorrow,' Edie said, and walked to her taxi, completely unaware of her surroundings, lightheaded and love-drunk.

The driver had the radio on and as the lights of the darkening city flashed past, Edie was sure she'd never felt so electric and alive and sure that the John Grant song 'Outer Space' was written about the two of them.

On the journey, her phone buzzed with a text, and she pulled her phone out with a loopy grin on her face.

E.T.! Big stuff for a text, but I got your answerphone when I called you. So, me & Charlotte have split up. And you were one of the reasons. (Not that I blame you.) (My feelings for you are not, and have never been, your fault.) I need to see you and talk about things, all of it, once and for all. I'm in your neck of the woods tomorrow, at my uncle's in Leicestershire. Can I meet you? Maybe late afternoon/early evening? Let me know. Jack x

The grin slipped from her face. Sometimes you had to confront the complete crapness of someone you'd convinced yourself was wholly sensational, and accept your judgment had too been awful.

The tone of Jack's text nauseated her. HEY THERE. SO I'M ON THE MARKET. LET'S PENCIL IN FACE 2 FACE TIME SOONEST FOR ME TO OUTLINE THE EXCITING OPPORTUNITY THAT THIS REPRE-SENTS FOR YOU.

She'd had more subtle wooing on double-glazing flyers. He was one audacious bastard. She didn't answer. She didn't delete it, either.

70

The initial stages of seeing someone new were fraught with uncertainty and pitfalls as well as excitement, Edie had forgotten that: it was like wobbling down the street on a Christmas Day bicycle.

Tiny, daft things: would they hold hands? Yes, Elliot was a hand holder, and grasped for Edie's as they set off from the Park Plaza – which afforded more privacy than the parental home, now – to the *Gun City* wrap party, round the corner. There had been a brief interlude for reconnaissance when the hotel manager checked there were no photographers around outside, and then they set off together.

'There might still be some,' Elliot said. 'We can go in separately, if you want?'

'If you don't mind,' Edie said, slightly shamefacedly, hanging back. She really didn't want to be in the *Mail Online* again if she didn't have to be, however much she liked being Elliot's plus one.

'Is it in the upstairs bit?' Edie said, as they parted, her

stomach thrashing like a fish on dry land. It wasn't an ideal first date, being on show, like this.

Elliot side-eyed her, with an expression that suggested he couldn't tell if she was joking.

'The whole place, I think?'

Of course the whole place. Otherwise the downstairs would be overwhelmed with people craning their necks upwards to see the partygoers, and specifically, the fantasy prince. Edie was painfully conscious she should feel glee, and pride, and all sorts of ignoble triumph at being the woman on the arm of the man of the hour. She felt turbulent and conspicuous instead. First dates with someone you were mad about were plenty challenging enough, without being with a celebrity.

They dropped hands and Elliot walked on without her.

The party was in the Malt Cross, a Grade Two-listed Victorian music hall with wrought-iron balustrades, a vaulted glass ceiling and bunting criss-crossing the space above their heads. Her name was ticked off a list, and Edie wondered if she was going to have to introduce herself? As Elliot's what? She could get away with *the writer*, she guessed. Edie felt as if her real self was on a plane, a time zone behind her, yet to catch up with these events.

As she walked in, Elliot was waiting for her inside the doorway, eyes shining. 'Drink?' he said.

Someone with a tray of flutes was already zooming towards them and he handed Edie one. Within seconds, people had descended upon them, cooing with excitement at Elliot's arrival, their eyes combing over Edie with unconcealed fascination.

'Hi . . .' said Elliot, glancing back towards her. He tried to stay by her side and involve her in conversation, but the social currents were too strong, he was washed away, into some important-seeming group where Edie didn't want to follow. She wasn't going to do some awful clingy-sidekick thing. She adjusted a favourite black prom dress and thought maybe she should break out of black all the time. Edie could have gone shopping but she was far too busy with better pastimes than shopping, at the moment. ('Can I get away with wearing an old dress?' she'd texted Hannah and Nick. 'From all you say it sounds like you could wear kebab-wrap paper you'd found in the coach station toilets and he'd be into it,' Nick had replied.)

She sipped her drink and enjoyed the surroundings. She wasn't alone for long: someone called Gail who worked in props sidled up to her. She responded politely but increasingly sensed she wasn't just interesting, in of herself.

'You're here with Elliot?' Gail said eventually, after cursory small-talk preamble.

'Yes.'

'You're *with* him?'

Elliot and Edie had discussed this, if she was asked outright whether they were seeing each other. 'There's been so many lies told, I'm shagged if I'm going to add to them,' Elliot had said. 'I want people to know we're together.' Edie wasn't going to argue with that. She was his plus one tonight, with no ambiguity.

'Yes . . .?'

'As in, you're dating?'

'. . . Yes.'

'How did you meet?'

'I'm writing his autobiography.'

Gail scrutinised her face, and her clothes, and Edie sensed she was having conversations in two time frames: the present, and the one in the future, the reportage. *She seemed completely normal really . . . I asked her about how they met . . . about five foot four, no, not thin as such . . .*

Edie excused herself to the loo and felt herself trailing the gaze of various curious onlookers across the room. People didn't cherish the invisibility cloak of anonymity until it was forcibly ripped away from them.

And the thing was, no one wanted to ask her about *her* work. She was simply there to be judged as worthy, or not, of being Elliot's accessory. A single-issue campaign. *This is how it will be*, a voice whispered. *If you and he become a 'we.'*

There was a little kerfuffle near the doorway and Greta entered, shimmering copper-coloured hair piled on her head in a shape that Edie could only think of as 'Mr Whippy ice-cream cone'. She was in a diaphanous grey jersey dress that revealed glimmers of lacy underwear. She wafted straight over to Elliot's side, draped a pale reed of an arm around him, leaned up to whisper something in his ear. Elliot was right, she was tactile in a way that could look like seduction.

Edie had heard Elliot talk about Greta often enough to know there was no love lost: on his side, at least. Yet this otherworldly beauty, climbing him as if he was a tree, Edie seeing Elliot lean in and smile, say things in return that made Greta throw a swan-like throat back to laugh, while clutching her décolleté: it wasn't easy to be secure. Edie grabbed another drink from a passing tray.

'If it isn't the autobiographer!'

She turned to see Archie Puce, garden gnome circled with a gift wrapping bow tucked under one arm, staring evilly and delightedly at her.

'Your work ethic makes Stakhanovites look like stoned students! Will you never give yourself an evening off the close scrutiny of your literary subject?'

'Hello, Archie,' Edie said, surprised to find herself glad of the distraction. 'I'm not working. I'm here as Elliot's guest.'

'Indeed,' Archie said, giving Edie what she guessed he thought was a beaming smile, which made him look like a Skeksis from *The Dark Crystal*. 'If you ever decide to follow your amour into his profession, I see real potential. Your wounded innocence when I accused you two of copulating was an accomplished performance.'

'I wasn't lying, we weren't seeing each other then.'

'Of course not. Apologies for my confrontational style when my show was going over budget while he was getting his end away, but it's called showbusiness not show-friendship, sugar tits. Oh for fuck's sake, how hard can it be to make a decent margarita? People in this godforsaken backwater can't crush ice, apparently. No! No! Is that SPRITE, you depraved animal?'

Archie had been drawn by the activity at the bar and Edie was off the hook. She also fancied updating the latest version of the book with Archie's off-the-record verdict on Nottingham.

She decided to attack the buffet before the next hostile could approach her.

Unfortunately, the next person was the doorman, who tapped her on the shoulder right as she shoved a prawn canapéinto her mouth.

'Excuse me,' he said, 'there's a "Jack Marshall" outside, for you.'

Edie chewed and absorbed the shock.

'. . . He's not on the list. Do you want him let in?'

Did she want him let in? She had that power? This was the status of being with Elliot.

'No!' Edie said, swallowing. The bouncer nodded and pressed his earpiece, turned on his heel. Edie's heart pounded. What the hell? How had Jack found her here? The only people who knew she was here, present company apart, were her dad and Meg. Jack must've called the house. But he only had her mobile? Oh God, he'd called *at* the house, hadn't he? The wedding invite had been sent there, last Christmastime, so he had the address on file somewhere.

The bouncer found her again, face impassive. By now, Edie was in a light glossy sweat.

'He asked me to give you this.' He handed Edie a slip of paper and retreated. She unfolded it.

Edie. Sorry for turning up at your office party like a giant stalker, it was a last resort. I really want to see you to talk about everything that's happened and put it behind us. No pressure or offence taken if you're too busy right now, or ever, but I'll be at the deli-bar (Delilahs?) for the next hour if you can give me a minute to explain. J x

Before Edie could roll it up, hand it back and advise the doorman about where to forcibly insert it into Jack, she consulted her feelings.

This wasn't just about what he wanted. Not if she didn't let it be: it could be the rudest awakening Jack Marshall was ever likely to have. She'd emailed Martha to thank her for her vote with Richard, and Martha had concluded: 'Jack will get his comeuppance one day.' Was this the day?

It was very difficult to get a moment alone with Elliot as the man of the hour. The floor downstairs had been cleared into a dance floor and couples were waltzing around to something slow.

Pity about the tricky timing. How did she speak to Elliot without being overheard? Edie vacillated for some minutes, then made an impulsive decision, possibly partly powered by Prosecco. She wove her way over to Elliot, who immediately broke from the group he was with.

'I'm so sorry, are you OK? Let me get you another drink.' He leaned in. 'Another hour and then we'll go somewhere, just the two of us, OK?'

Edie took him by the hand. 'Can we dance?'

'Uh . . .?' Elliot let himself be swung into a close hold with Edie, her hand on his shoulder. She sensed many pairs of eyes on them. For a second, she almost abandoned her plan to stay like this with him, pressed together . . .

Edie leaned in close.

'Elliot, something's come up,' she whispered. 'I have to sort it out. Can you do without me for that hour? I'll be back before you notice.'

'What is it?'

'Jack's turned up and wants to have it out about the wedding.
I want to say my opinions into his face.'

Elliot pulled back, their faces inches apart.

'"Jack"?'

'The groom. From the wedding.'

Elliot's brow creased.

'*What*? What the hell are you seeing him for?'

Edie hushed him, though she couldn't really fault him for
this response.

'He says he wants to explain himself to me once and for
all.'

They resumed the dance hold and Elliot murmured in her
ear.

'Let me break it to you that's only half of his agenda, at
most. Isn't he married?'

'They've split up.'

'Oh my God, he's single! Better and better. You do realise,
he might, you know, have an interest in unburdening
himself with you in more than one way?' Elliot was hissing
now.

He glanced around to make sure they weren't being overheard and adjusted his grip on Edie.

'If he tries anything, I'll knee him in the goolies. Are you
really not OK with this?' she said.

'Er, not really, Edie, no.'

'You can't think there's anything between us? If I don't
see him, I'm letting him off the hook. Honestly, I really
need to be able to say my piece to his face. I promise you

that my only intention here is an interrogation and much swearing.'

'From where I'm standing, it's not quite that simple. You didn't go to his wedding planning to get off with him, I'm guessing.'

'That was then! This is my one chance to hold him to account for what he did to me.'

'If it's nothing romantic, can I come along?'

Edie laughed even though Elliot was clearly not joking. She'd not experienced Elliot quite this pugilistic since their very first meeting. Erk, when he'd split up with Heather, come to think of it.

'I'd bloody love to see his face if you did. Sadly, this is something I have to do on my own.'

Elliot pulled Edie closer as his voice in her ear became more menacing.

'So to recap: you're running off from our first date for this, and it has to be the two of you, no third wheels. It's lucky I'm not the jealous type. Oh wait, just checked. I am. As of now.'

Edie tried not to smile because having Elliot like this was also pretty great. A guilty pleasure, after the pain of seeing him with Greta.

'. . . Where are you going with him? Or is that a secret? I warn you there's a right answer and a wrong answer to this.'

'Delilah's? The deli with the bar, upstairs on Victoria Street. Elliot, it's not candlelight and violins. You honestly have no need to be worried.'

'Imagine right now that Heather's waltzed back into town

and I've dropped everything to see her, to clear up our unfinished business. And sorry, Edie, it's not romantic but it's terribly private, you can't come.'

Edie thought about that. 'I'd be well mad.'

'Yeah trust me, I'm not thrilled. I'd go so far as to call myself vexed.'

'Elliot,' Edie paused, got as close as she could to his ear and whispered: 'I'm in love with you.'

A nerve-wracking pause where Elliot said nothing, and when she looked, he was glowering at her. Edie's heart started thudding. Wrong thing to say? Too soon? Too not reciprocated? Oh, God . . .

The song finished and Elliot gave her a hug.

'Edie, don't casually tell me you bloody love me in a conversation where I'm getting angry about that tosspot, to win favour and put me on the back foot and make it difficult for me to object about something I have every right to question.'

'Sorry.'

'I'm in love with you too. See you in an hour or there will be hell to pay.' He swung in and kissed her hard on the mouth, in front of everyone, then stalked off back into the hordes, leaving Edie with cartoon birds circling round her head.

71

The café-bar Delilah was in an old banking hall, with high ceilings and decorative plasterwork. Edie guessed Jack chose it because it was hard to mistake for anywhere you'd have a date: raucous with ladies who lunched, or, at this time of night, cackled over rosé with their equally dolled-up friends. A place where well-to-do kids at the university took their well-to-do parents, and let them pay.

When Edie reached the top of the stairs, she saw Jack at a table at the far end.

He was in a pink shirt, very narrow grey flannel trousers and brown brogues. It wasn't a bad outfit, exactly, but showy in a way that wasn't Edie's taste, sort of upmarket man-at-Jack-Wills. With a small jolt, Edie realised she'd very rarely seen Jack in his civvies. A small thing, but a reminder of how little she actually knew him.

'I got you a Bellini,' he said, winningly. 'I hope that's OK.'

Edie nodded and thought to herself: I won't be drinking the Kool Aid.

'You look really well,' he said, with a glance at her dress.

'What was the event, something to do with the TV show the actor was in? Is he back in La La Land now?'

'I've only got half an hour,' Edie said, terse, ignoring him. 'Why did you go to my house?'

'You weren't answering my calls.' Jack pushed at the strawberry bobbing in his drink. 'Which I completely understand, by the way. I thought I had to make a gesture. Don't blame your marvellous father, I did press him quite hard,' Jack said, and Edie boiled. She suspected she was supposed to be awed at the effort.

'What happened to little E.T. then? Scrapping in the street with celebrities now? That photo of you giving someone the Vs was priceless.'

'That wasn't what it looked like,' Edie said, to shut it down fast. 'Nothing reported about it was true.'

'Hah, yes,' said Jack, joining in with a little too much enthusiasm. 'He's probably moved on to a *Doctor Who* assistant by now, or a member of The Saturdays. Sounds like it's a revolving door.'

She could see he thought he was being incredibly fleet-footed when actually Edie heard a lumpen insult. She didn't bother to pick him up on it: she didn't care enough to need his *no no no I just meant celebrities are fickle* denial.

There was something deeper in it than the simple bad manners of implying she wasn't enough for Elliot, however.

Jack didn't respect her. How had she never noticed that before? He was intrigued by her, entertained by her, attracted, sure. But no one who's playing you and duping you truly respects you, Edie thought, because it presupposes they're smarter than you. She would remember that, in future.

'What did you want to say?' Edie said.

'Ah. Straight in, OK,' Jack said, as if Edie was at fault for being too forthright. Clearly, she should've appeared to enjoy his jokes first.

'I wanted to give you a proper apology, in person, for the wedding. I unleashed the hounds of hell on both of us and it was a nightmare. I'm so sorry.'

'You didn't unleash them on yourself, did you?' Edie said. 'I missed the Facebook pages about you?'

'Hah, no, I didn't have that. But I had plenty. Trust me, you've never seen Charlie's dad in full flow. He has hunting rifles, E.T., he goes clay pigeon shooting. I thought I was in for a knee-capping.'

'Jack . . .' Edie paused, she had to judge this right. If she lost her rag too early, it was showing her hand. 'Are you asking me to feel sorry for you?'

'No! God, no.'

'Why did you do what you did?'

Jack sipped his drink. Edie studied his face and saw that there was nothing there. She felt nothing. She and Jack had simply fitted each other's needs. He wanted a woman to fall in love with him. She'd wanted to fall in love with someone.

'I've asked myself that a million times. The bottom line is . . . this is embarrassing to say . . .'

Here we go, Edie thought, here it comes.

'I'm utterly smitten with you, Edie. Always was. My

stupidity was ploughing on and marrying Charlie when I knew what my feelings were.'

He paused and Edie waited for it. The killer line he'd have worked out in advance.

'I turned round, you know, during the vows and saw you. You weren't looking at me, you were messing with Louis's buttonhole. And it hit me, right then. *That's the girl I should be marrying today.* When I followed you into the garden, I was drunk, I was all over the place. In a split second, I had to do what I'd wanted to do since the first moment I met you.'

Jack finished his speech, slightly flushed. She had no doubt he meant it, for as long as he was saying it. Edie left a short silence.

'You know how it looks though? You've split up with your wife a second time, and you turn up here, hoping to win me as a consolation prize?'

Jack shook his head emphatically.

'Look, I'm not proud of going back to Charlie, but she was a wreck, her parents practically had me at gunpoint, as I said. I'd ruined her special day, I felt I owed it to her. It quickly became obvious it was never going to work.'

'Well, that, and I gave your wife an email from another woman you'd mucked around.'

'What?' Jack raised his eyebrows. 'Who? When?'

Edie considered trying to get to the bottom of whether Jack was feigning ignorance, and decided she didn't care. Perhaps Charlotte hadn't wanted him to know Edie had helped her come to her decision. Because she didn't doubt it *was* Charlotte's decision to kick him out.

'There's a Maya Angelou quote that reminds me of you, Jack,' Edie said. Jack did a tiny 'oh really' polite expression with a nod, a look that settled as vanity. He was the kind of man that women had literary quotes for. Of course he was.

'It's: "When someone shows you who they are, believe them the first time." That was my problem with you. You were messaging me and flirting behind your girlfriend's back. What kind of man does that? I should've believed you were the man you showed me you were that first moment, but I didn't. I desperately wanted you to be someone else. The person I built up in my mind. I let you treat me badly, again and again. And because I refused to believe who you were, who you *showed* me you were, I ended up in that position at the wedding.'

'Edie,' Jack's face was a performance of innocent exasperation, 'it wasn't calculated. At all.'

'I believe that,' Edie nodded, 'You didn't rub your hands together and say, "I know what I'll do to that girl with the dark hair." You followed your instincts, without thinking about it much. And your instincts are bad and selfish. You deliberately didn't think, because it suited you not to look at what you were doing. From where I'm sitting, there's not much difference in you intending it, or not. Same effect on me.'

Edie could see Jack's mounting surprise at this chilly reception. She could also see him recalibrating, becoming sharper in the face of her anger. He thrived in adversity. Adapt to survive.

'You have every right to be pissed off at me, I'm not denying that,' Jack said. 'But if I'd been a proper bastard I'd have been trying to get off with you behind Charlie's back. I didn't want an affair. It wasn't fair, I wasn't going to cheat.'

'Noble,' Edie said, with a small smile. 'You're assuming I'd have gone along with that?'

'What?'

'You're assuming I'd have slept with you on those terms?'

'No! I was just thinking out loud, from my point of view . . . Oh God. I'm doing a *Strictly Come Dancing* routine across landmines here, aren't I?'

Jack gave her a small *Hey, I'm funny, we laugh at the same things though, right?* smile and Edie had a moment of authentic disgust at this man.

She'd been taken in by a mid-level-ability card sharp.

72

Jack might think he was whip smart, but he still hadn't sussed that Edie had *him* sussed.

'. . . That's what I meant at the wedding about cowardice. I got swept along, I didn't want to hurt Charlie . . .' he continued. He seemed to think if he chose the right lament, Edie would suddenly crumble, right into his arms.

'You didn't want to hurt Charlotte, so you flirted with me and kissed me, on your wedding day?'

'We were friends, there was no intention to flirt. We got on well. You know how it was, we sparked.'

'I know you constantly told me one thing, and did another.'

'How do you mean?'

'You didn't want to buy a house, you didn't want to move out of London, didn't believe in marriage . . .'

'Eh? I was letting off steam, I can't remember half the things we chatted about.'

'And yet it all meant so much that you're saying you're in love with me?'

Jack, greatly to Edie's pleasure, finally lost his temper a little. The mask slipped.

'I don't think I said *love*, did I?' he said, with a note of disdain. Hah, gotcha.

Not so charming now.

'Didn't you?' Edie said, with perfect indifference. 'Oh, *smitten*.'

Jack boggled at her. Giving no fucks was a superpower.

Edie's phone buzzed. A text from Elliot. She saw Jack see it arrive and try to read the name and she swiftly flipped her phone over. She could tell that he didn't like that, a spoonful of his own medicine.

'Look, I deserve this, I know I do. But you haven't given me a completely easy ride. You used to tell me about your dates, to make me jealous . . .'

Low blow. She did. In the context of everything he did.

'And I hadn't told my new firm exactly why I left Ad Hoc. That *Mail* story did me no favours, but I didn't complain.'

Edie frowned. 'Hang on, if you hadn't done what you did at the wedding, you wouldn't have got a mention in that story. Ass-backwards logic.'

'Edie. We could hash over who did what all evening.' Jack leaned forward and fixed his eyes on hers. He put a hand, palm down on the table, that Edie was being invited to hold. 'I've come here to say there's nothing in the world I want more than to see if, despite everything, there's as much here as I think there is. Look at this mess, what's it telling us? That we want to be together, no matter what chaos it causes. E.T., I think we're each other's happy ending.'

Edie wrinkled her nose and was about to say both vomit, and hahaha 'happy ending', when a voice behind her cut across them.

'Edie?'

Edie turned to see Elliot, hands thrust in coat pockets, glowering at Jack.

Jack placed Elliot's face, and went pale.

'I texted you,' Elliot addressed Edie, 'to see if you were done? I thought I could walk you back to the party.'

He transferred his gaze to Jack again, who was paler still.

Edie opened her mouth to say – *almost done* – and then realised they were done. Completely done. She'd heard enough of Jack's obfuscations and manipulations. And this was the ultimate farewell. Hollywood could not have scripted one better. There were practically fireworks spelling out Fuck You going off overhead, a marching band playing 'You're So Vain' as soundtrack.

'Yep, all done, thanks, Elliot,' Edie said, standing up, adrenaline coursing in a warm river, almost making her tremble.

Jack was open-mouthed at Edie, looking from her to Elliot and back again. Elliot held out his hand and she took it. He pulled her to his side, threw his arm around her shoulders and kissed the top of her head. It was petulant and territorial and Edie loved it.

In memory afterwards, Edie would imagine the café fell silent, although that might be due to how it felt right at that minute: the whole world was only the three of them, with Jack being served his arse on a plate with a sprig of parsley.

504

They turned and walked down the stairs. Goodbye, Jack Marshall, Edie thought. You're already designing the story about how your last love left you for that famous actor. Everything's material.

73

In the following weeks, Edie was asked by her friends and family 'what it was like' to be with Elliot, which was a strange question, really. As if she was knocking boots with an android, or a hologram, or someone who wasn't a thirty-something man from the Midlands who put on costumes to earn his salary.

She knew the subtext was: 'Don't you have moments of complete cognitive dissonance that you're only you, and you're bedding Prince Wulfroarer, commander of the dwarven army of Hellebore and most fancied man in the kingdom?' And the answer was she would have those moments, if she let herself. But she tried very hard not to, as if she did, she might ruin it. Edie didn't stand back and admire Elliot from a distance; she stayed close, literally and figuratively, and concentrated on the fact the attraction seemed very mutual. She might not have dated a famous before, but she'd been with men, and his machinery was just male like any other's. Edie could attest to that.

The prosaic truth was, going out with Elliot was like going

out with anyone else, with a few more practical cautions and restrictions. A week after they started seeing each other, a gossip column story appeared saying Elliot and Edie had 'rekindled' their love at the *Gun City* wrap party, but ironically, though it was now true, it somehow merited fewer column inches.

'It's because they only have photos of us at each others' throats,' Elliot explained. 'Pictures are everything nowadays. It might be best to be quite cautious and stay indoors a lot,' Elliot said on a lazy morning at the Park Plaza, picking at a room service tray at the end of the bed. 'If they get any more photos of us, it will definitely mean more stories.'

Edie said this was the slickest excuse for a boff-a-thon she'd ever heard.

'Do we honestly need one? You only have to look at me the wrong way,' Elliot said.

Edie wilted.

'Be honest,' he said, unwinding a croissant, 'is it massively off-putting, the attention?'

'I don't much like the attention, but no,' Edie said, leaning up to touch his face, 'it's not enough to put me off you. Not even near.'

'It's so great to go out with an adjusted person,' Elliot said. 'Heather lived for the attention.'

'Argh, don't bring her up *again* or I'll think you have an unresolved Taylor-Burton love-hate thing going on,' Edie said, succumbing to a sharp sting of green-eyed monster.

'Oh!' Elliot said, in mock indignation. 'The worm has turned! The worm who makes me well jealous all the bloody time. The worm is you, by the way.'

Edie laughed. 'I don't . . .?'

'I remember the lovely romantic ride on the big wheel I organised, and then I said all fake-casually "oh are you SURE you weren't sleeping with that married fella" and you were all "wait we've already discussed this" and I thought you'd seen through the fact I spent all my time brooding about you.'

Edie shook with laughter. 'I had no idea! I just assumed you had a crap memory!'

'Hmm,' Elliot chewed pastry, 'I felt a right tool.'

'Not as much of a tool as I felt in the *Gun City* read-through. What was that about?'

'Oh that,' Elliot grinned. 'That was, hand on my heart, fully professional in its aims. I was struggling with that scene and I thought if I played it with someone I *did* feel those things about, it might start working. As it turned out, you looked as if I'd walked in smelling of drink with my lad in my hand and were going to hit me with a rolling pin. I never did take the curse off that *I'm thinking about it right now* line.'

'You organised the big wheel to be romantic?'

'Yeah. Well, ish. Any excuse to spend time with you. That was what anything was about.'

'I best come up with some other things we can do together, then. Other than this. But still indoors.'

Elliot sighed: 'And you've got to meet my parents. They insist. The unfortunate post-coital encounter needs to be overwritten in the official version of events.'

'Ah OK. Oh no, that means by rights you have to meet my family too?'

Their eyes met and Edie sensed them both contemplate discussing why they were meeting the parents in week one of what was destined to be a fling, and decide not to tackle it. It *was* a fling, wasn't it?

'I want to meet your family. And your friends. I want a crash course in your life and times, please,' Elliot said.

'Hah, won't take long. The Tales of Robin Hood would've been tons better, they had an animatronic Friar Tuck.'

'You always do this, you always do the self-deprecating, put-yourself-down propaganda, Thompson,' Elliot said, propping himself up on the pillow, and pushing her hair behind her ear. 'It bears no relation to the reality of you, to the point where I spent some time early on figuring out if it was false modesty. You know, Archie's making his thudding jokes about you ruining my concentration and you looked like you wanted to die.'

'I did.'

'A lot of people wouldn't have minded the "you are very attractive" implication of all that.'

'I didn't think that was the implication, only that I was a bit . . . free with my favours.'

Elliot shook his head. 'I can see how you got yourself in a proper mess in the past.'

'I wasn't in a mess!' Edie huffed, but smiled.

'You know when you nearly fainted, that time?'

'Yes?'

'I walked back on set completely distracted and I kept thinking: Who *is* she? There's something completely compelling about you. Not just the beauty, or the being funny, or bright. You're someone who you meet, and can't get out of your head afterwards. It's an enchantment so powerful even my idiot brother felt it. Charisma, that's the word for it, but "charisma" always makes me think of smarmy gits. It's genuine. OK, maybe I'm overthinking all of this and it is your eyes. Edie . . . why are you crying, you spoon?'

74

Edie had forgotten Nick's request that she get Elliot to appear on his radio show, until they were lying horizontal at an undignified time that afternoon, listening to Nick host a phone-in on the new tram works, with a neat segue into the Lighthouse Family. She'd been explaining her enduring love for her two BFFs when the memory of her promise moved from back to front brain.

'I don't suppose you'd give him an interview?' she said, nervous that she might be overstepping some bounds that only famous people knew about.

'Sure,' Elliot said.

Edie sat up, screamed and hugged him. 'Really? Nick will be absolutely overjoyed.'

'Yeah. Whenever suits. I've done interviews before, you know.'

Elliot went for a shower and Edie texted Nick and said *ELLIOT IS ON FOR INTERVIEW!!* And Nick texted back with *I LOVE YOU/HIM/YOUR SELFLESSNESS IN UNDERTAKING THE DEBILITATING, DEGENERATE NAKED THINGS HE WILL MAKE YOU DO IN RETURN.*

They pre-recorded it the next day so they could use excerpts to trail it for a week and get the largest listener figures.

She and Hannah listened at Hannah's flat and Edie nearly combusted with pride at how warm, funny and insightful Elliot sounded. He even managed to make *Gun City* sound like it wasn't nonsense. Was any of it her effect? It was the first time Elliot sounded in public the way he did in private, to Edie. With some of his pithier observations and swearing edited out, obviously.

'Oh he is nice, Edith,' Hannah said, as she turned the volume down on her Roberts radio. 'You've actually chosen a nice one for a change.'

And Edie thought, he's nice because I chose, rather than letting someone choose me. *The girl that everyone wanted and nobody chose.*

Later, Nick and Elliot convened at Hannah's place, too. It was strange, seeing how awkward and guarded Hannah and Nick were around him at first, and realising that's how she'd been, too. However, a combination of witnessing how completely at ease Edie was with him, and alcohol, meant they soon loosened up. A bit too much, truth be told.

'I'm not usually into Puff the Magic Dragon bollocks,' Nick said, 'But *Blood & Gold* was alright. Better than that other one, anyway.'

'They should put that on the posters,' Elliot said. 'Word for word.'

And Nick drank enough to tell Elliot that Edie used to say she didn't fancy him and he looked like a trainee barista.

'NICK!' she and Hannah cried, in unison.

'The best relationships are based on honesty,' Nick said, unperturbed. 'I'm told.'

'It's OK,' Elliot said, mildly. 'I don't wish to embarrass Edie any further, but if this is how she treats a man she doesn't fancy, God help the one she takes quite a shine to. Probably swallow her prey whole and regurgitate him like an owl pellet.'

'In case it's not clear, I like him,' Nick said to Edie, pointing at Elliot.

On the walk from The Park to the hotel, Elliot said: 'Your friends are as sound as I knew they would be.'

Edie glowed and hung on to his arm.

'Nick doesn't get to see his son at all?'

'Nope.'

'I can't imagine that, not getting to see someone you love. Being separated by circumstance.'

It was funny that when there was only one off-limits, sensitive topic, all conversational roads seemed to lead back to it.

'Circumstance is the nicest word for Alice I've heard so far,' Edie said.

Another evening, they met Elliot's parents at Hart's for dinner.

Elliot wore a suit and looked so good in it, it made Edie shy. He walked out of the bathroom, doing up his cufflinks. 'Why the face? Do I look like a plum?'

When they were travelling down in the hotel lift, Edie said Hart's had reminded her she was seeing a boy from south of the river: 'Hart's is well posh for a first meeting.'

'Oh, they're just showboating as you're future daughter-in-law material.'

Elliot said this absently while checking his phone and his head jerked up as he realised what he'd said.

'A very roundabout way of asking me! *Edie Owen*. It works. Thus I accept. Tomorrow? West Bridgford registry office?'

Elliot shot over from his side of the lift and pinned her to the wall by the wrists.

'You're forgetting what a kind of big deal I am. I could call someone and this could actually be arranged. Turtle doves and Armani suits for the ushers and Maroon 5 for the reception. A finger buffet with cheddar and pineapple hedgehogs, everything.'

'You're on then,' Edie said, laughing against his chest. 'My answer is yes.'

They became the revolting people caught kissing when the lift doors slide open.

In the restaurant, Elliot reached for Edie's hand under the table, whenever there wasn't food in front of them. Edie imagined they were being discreet until Elliot's mother said: 'Elliot, dear, if you let go of her, she's not going to float away. She's not a balloon.'

Edie instinctively liked his parents, a lot. Like their son, they didn't feign interest, they were interested. They inquired about Edie's background and she gave them honest answers, and they asked sensitive questions. There was no snobbery whatsoever, a quality she could see they'd passed to Elliot.

She didn't pry about what had gone on with Fraser, but Elliot reassured that all was harmonious so far. There'd been no story by his biological father, so maybe Elliot getting in first and spoilering had worked wonders.

When he was in the loo, the whole restaurant surreptitiously watching him cross the room, his mum leaned over and said: 'I'm so pleased you're independent, and have such a good head on your shoulders. He doesn't need adulation, he needs a challenge. I can see you're that.'

'Congratulations, you were a huge hit,' Elliot said, back at the hotel.

Edie was a dimension drunk enough to chance saying: 'Still, daughter-in-law material is a high bar to clear . . .'

'Are you goading me?' Elliot said, gently pushing her further into the room, as Edie's stomach whirlpooled. *That suit.* 'Am I supposed to look terrified at the idea? Or are you suggesting that you think the idea is a joke?'

Edie could only laugh nervously.

'You haven't spooked me, I'm afraid,' Elliot said, pushing her down on the bed and looming over her. 'Not one bit. Try again.'

'. . . You have to meet my dad and my sister tomorrow. They both want to know if you can really talk to wolves in a special language and they'd like to hear you do some more of it.'

'Yes, now I'm spooked,' Elliot said, and they laughed as they kissed, conversations on the future parked again, for the moment.

When meeting her dad and Meg, Edie went for a down-to-earth venue.

'They're not going to be comfortable anywhere like Hart's,' Edie said.

'Good, we've just been there anyway.'

In the end, they opted for The Trip to Jerusalem pub, carved out of ancient sandstone caves.

'I know it's where tourists go, but now I'm in the States all the time, I get weirdly affectionate for the historic stuff,' Elliot said.

The States, all the time. Edie twinged and said nothing.

After a small warm-up where Edie found a stream of conversational topics, and Elliot joined in enthusiastically, her dad and Meg relaxed and treated Elliot like any friend of Edie's. Her father had never seen *Blood & Gold* and Meg didn't do reverence, in any great quantity. And they didn't get much time to chat, as they hadn't realised there was a pub quiz that night.

They joined in with gusto, Elliot and Meg debating the largest species of tiger, her dad adamant that the leader of military campaigns who had a boot named after him was Wellington, not Doctor Marten, as Meg had it. Elliot rubbed his eye and met Edie's, both trying not to laugh, and she'd never loved him more.

Edie sat there thinking: this is a typical Nottingham night out, with Scampi Fries, Nik Naks and a beer-dripped answer sheet. Elliot was one of them.

Only, except, he wasn't.

Edie had learned the rules of dating a famous person, whenever they ventured out to busy places with lots of people under the age of thirty. Walk briskly when in public thoroughfares, no eye contact. Show politeness when approached. Make swift departure once recognised.

516

And Edie was surprised: she got little to no thrill from Elliot's notoriety. He was special to her, she didn't like him being of interest to others, who didn't know him at all. She wanted him to herself.

Because Edie hadn't ever been in love like this. She hadn't known that losing yourself in someone could make you feel so *here*, so present, at the same time. When Elliot was with her and on her and in her and around her all the time, she'd never felt more like Edie.

They were the best days of Edie's life so far, but there were so few of them. She refused to think about it. It was the elephant in the corner of the palatial hotel room with the crumpled sheets.

75

On their last night, they went for dinner early. Elliot had a 'first light' call for the airport. He'd already said his goodbyes to his family and transferred his luggage to the hotel. Edie felt the size of the compliment that he wanted to spend the remaining time with her.

They went to a Persian restaurant in a quiet back street, with Formica tables and giant servings of kebabs on skewers and dill-flecked mounds of rice. Another discovery of famousness: if they went to places no one expected to see a famous, no one saw a famous. There were stylised paintings on the wall of Eastern women in veils, with huge almond-shaped eyes, mouths like tiny bows and centre-parted dark hair. 'Looks like you,' Elliot said, with an adoring smile, and Edie fluttered.

As they dawdled their way back, Edie thought perhaps they'd say goodbye without discussing it. Without ever saying: 'What was this?'

A light rain started and Elliot drew Edie to his side.

'I'm about to escape this weather for the land of the lotus

eaters. LA and its no seasons, how weird is that. Nothing to mark the passing of the year.'

'Hah, yeah. Make the most of the mizzle while you can.'

'It's not the weather I'm going to miss.'

'Ah you'll be back soon enough,' she said, avoiding his eyes.

'Not if I'm in some network show with a punishing schedule.'

'Mmm.'

They walked the remaining distance to the hotel in silence, Edie agonising over whether to say something.

Once inside the room, it was obvious the mood wasn't going to clear by itself.

Edie fussed nervously with her handbag while Elliot closed the door and leaned against it.

'Edie,' he said. 'Why are we avoiding this? Are we going to talk about it?'

'About you leaving?'

'Yes.'

'I know you have to go, I just don't want to think about it.'

Elliot studied her and Edie suddenly didn't know what to do with her hands. They hung heavily at the ends of her arms and she had to find something to do with them. She pushed them under her armpits.

'Do you not think I care, and I'm going to say, *See ya, thanks for the good times*? Or is this about you? I've been going mad trying to work out if you're hedging because you think I'm hedging or if you really are hedging.'

Edie didn't know what to say to this. *Both*.

'Unless I've got this badly wrong, you're my girlfriend, aren't you?'

Edie smiled.

'I'd like to think I am.'

'Then why aren't we talking about this? Look, Edie,' Elliot paused, 'you're too important to play games with. I love you. I don't want this to end tomorrow. I want to be together.'

'I love you too,' Edie said. She wanted to have said it again, before anything else.

Elliot stepped forward.

'Come with me, come to LA. You can stay in the apartment. And then depending on what happens with me and the jobs, we'll plot our next move. Together.'

Edie smiled. 'And become your green card-less sponger girlfriend?'

'No! What's mine is yours,' Elliot said. 'It's an adjustment, that's all, you'd need a little time to find things and until then it's a break, on me. Fuck's sake, why earn all this stupid money if I can't look after people I care about? What else is it good for? Or, if you're really bothered by working in the States, we could come back to London as soon as possible. I'm never in the place in New York as it is. You know, whatever. Whatever you want.'

Wow, his international jet-set life, where money and geography really wasn't a consideration. For a split second, Edie let herself feel what it would be like to be lady of that manor. And just as quickly, she let it go.

'Thank you.'

Her voice came out sounding lower than she expected.

'Don't thank me, you daft arse. It's not about thanks.'

'It is, because it's amazing you've asked me and I'm grateful and so, thank you.'

'Oh, right. This sounds fully ominous.'

Elliot stepped back.

'Elliot, I've thought about nothing else but how to be with you. But I'm staying here.'

'In the UK?'

'In Nottingham.' Edie said. 'I have my family here and I don't want to leave them again so soon, or my best friends. I have a job I can do remotely. I gave London some good years. It's time for a change.'

'I understand,' Elliot nodded. 'Then it's huge phone bills and flying back and forth for a few months and then we could look for a place.'

'Here?'

'Well, here and there. We'd figure it out.'

Edie shook her head.

'You know this isn't how it works. Successful actors don't commute to the Midlands from California. I'd have to go to America.'

Elliot made a face.

'Don't "successful actor" me, Edie, that's shit,' Elliot said. 'I'm offering you any compromise you want.' He paused and she could see he was really, really hurt, 'If it's a no it's a no, but don't hide behind the logistics.'

Edie put both her hands on his upper arms, as he dropped his chin and avoided her gaze.

'I'm not being ungrateful about what you're offering. Think

about it. You have to try America. And you said it yourself, you'll get a big job and you'll never be around. If we got a place together anywhere, my life would be on hold, waiting for you to come home every night. Trying not to hit the gin and pills thinking about what you'd been doing all day, some days.'

Elliot met her gaze and raised his eyebrows. 'Oh, it's *that*.'

'No it's not that. My point is we'd be unequal.'

Elliot opened his mouth to speak and stopped, paused and composed himself. Edie felt her chest compress.

'My mum said to me, *No sensible girl will want to commit to you now, it'll be like marrying Prince Harry*,' Elliot said with a taut, miserable smile. 'I laughed at her. It's true, isn't it? Here I am with one. And she doesn't.'

'It's not that stuff. I like you far too much to let any newspaper story put me off. It's because giving me what I want would make you unhappy, and me giving you what you want would make me unhappy.'

'It can be figured out.'

'It *can't*. You have to go. I have to stay. Trust me, I haven't been saying anything because I've been thinking about nothing else, hoping to find another answer. It's the hardest and simplest decision I've ever made, because it's so clear. I wish it wasn't.'

Elliot shook his head and looked completely agonised, yet Edie knew the one thing he wouldn't say – and she didn't want him to say – was that he'd stay. It wasn't his reality any more and it couldn't be, however much he loved her. He was passing through on his way somewhere else, as Margot had said. Edie would have to tag along and fit into his life, one way or another, and she wasn't prepared to make that sacrifice again, not even, she was astounded to find, for him. She wanted her own life. She'd finally learned to value it. She'd learned how to live it.

'Elliot,' Edie said, 'also. I'm thirty-six. You could have anyone you—'

Elliot looked outraged, so much so it startled her.

'Oh my God. Do not,' he cut across her, 'do NOT say that to me, for one single second. If you say that, all it tells me is you don't believe I feel for you what you feel for me, which is completely insulting.'

'I do believe you,' she said.

'But . . .?'

'But everything else I've said.'

'So, what? It's over?' Elliot said, and his eyes welled up.

Edie had to swallow hard. His tears were going to bring on her tears.

'Now's not the right time. That doesn't mean it won't ever be. But you're not on a promise, when you leave. You're free to do what you want,' Edie found that part hard to say. 'That's the point.'

'Is this a fidelity test? I'll pass it, but I don't see why I have to take it.'

'No, no, no. Absolutely not.'

'If you're building up to saying, "and if it's meant to be, it will be," I will buy you a dream catcher and tell you to sod off,' Elliot said, wiping under his now-streaming eyes. 'Relationships are choices, it's not about fate and karma and all that.'

'I know. None of this is because I don't love you enough to try something difficult. This is too precious for me to mess it up by doing something that every instinct I have tells me is wrong. It's taken me so long to get my life in order, Elliot. I can't throw it all away to sit around alone on the other side of the world, waiting for you to live your life and then find time for me. Can you see what I'm saying?'

Elliot took a shuddering breath.

'My head says maybe, sort of. My heart says no, this is stupid. We love each other. There has to be a way.'

'The way is to do the difficult thing, go our separate ways and see what happens.'

A silence where the only sounds were those of mutual stifled sobs, sniffing and throat clearing.

He looked at her with pink eyes. 'Why don't you just say it's over, for good?'

'Because I love you. Never say never.'

'You're really not going to change your mind? I'll be looking over my shoulder in Heathrow, you know. I know how this shit works. I've seen films.'

Edie laughed in relief and sadness and affection and was so glad he wasn't angry, pushing her away and saying *Oh well then, you don't care enough*. That would've broken her. Then again, it was another reminder of the size of person she was giving up.

'Please say you understand,' Edie said, holding him. 'It wasn't easy to think. Or say.'

'I do understand, I just hate it,' Elliot said. 'I think part of me knew it was coming. This is the most elegant and confusing dumping I've ever had.' Tears ran down Elliot's face. 'But I can see you mean it.'

He hugged Edie again so hard it momentarily squeezed the breath out of her. As their breathing became more even, he muttered into her hair.

'Don't marry some beard-having craft-ale-bore bicycle clips wanker and move to the street next to my parents and call your kids Victorian scullery maid names, OK? Don't break my heart twice over.'

Edie was laughing, as well as crying. She gulped and said: 'Don't marry a Victoria's Secret model called something like Varsity and move to Malibu and buy two ugly Boxer dogs and be in a shit side-project rock band. No one will tell you it's shit but it will be terrible.'

They held on to each other for a minute, eyes closed and arms thrown round each other, to record the feeling for posterity.

'This is goodbye though,' Elliot said, wiping at his eyes with his jacket sleeve. 'You know that? I can't stay awake all night staring at you and crying. I'll only spend the whole time pleading with you to change your mind.'

Edie nodded miserably, she had known that, which is why she had avoided it. 'Yes. I know.'

Elliot mumbled into her hair: 'How will I ever find anyone like you again? Tell me that, eh. OK. Fuck. Goodbye, Edie.'

Edie was glad she wasn't looking him in the eyes for those last words, or her resolve might've finally wavered.

'Goodbye, Elliot.'

They disentangled and looked at each other, both teary

messes, and Edie grabbed her bag from the floor. To make an elegant exit, she'd forego the toothbrush in the bathroom. Elliot kissed her hard on the top of her head, and reached down and held her left hand.

He wiped at his eyes again with his other hand, shook his head. Edie squeaked 'bye', and slipped through the door, closing it gently behind her.

As she fled down the carpeted stairs, making another emotional exit from a hotel, it was all she could do not to turn and run back up to Elliot, into his arms. She had to let him go.

In the time she'd known him, she'd found everything that mattered to her, and that was enough.

76

Edie and Meg scattered their mother's ashes at Lumsdale waterfall in the Derbyshire dales, a beautiful place in Matlock their dad told them she used to like walking with him, long ago, before either of them were born.

Their dad retrieved the urn from the back of the wardrobe. It was printed with her name, Isla Thompson, and a date, in small type, as if it was a doctor's prescription. It was strange looking at it, trying to comprehend some fragments of their long-lost mother were contained inside.

The spot was as wonderful as their dad had promised: damp emerald green, ferns and bracken underfoot, complete peace, apart from the sound of rushing water.

'She loved the waterfall,' their dad said, when Meg raised the contradiction that she'd died in the Trent. 'I promise, you she'd approve.'

They opened the urn and found a tiny cellophane bag inside, which had to be torn open. They took turns to lean over and shake the fine, silvery powder into the clear stream, all they had left of a precious human being who'd left their lives so long ago.

'Do we say goodbye?' Meg said, in tears, and their dad said: 'Say anything you like.'

'Bye, Mum. I wish I could remember you more,' Meg said, and Edie held her and their dad wept, and then they ended up wrapped round each other.

'Bye, Mum,' Edie whispered. 'Thank you.'

'I wish she could meet you both, as you are now,' their dad said. 'She'd think you were both wonderful.' Her dad's laugh broke through his tears. 'She always did have a soft spot for an eccentric.'

'I'm not an eccentric!' Edie said, and then they were all laughing and sobbing.

'She adored you both, you know. You were the apples of her eye. She thought you were better off without her. That's what I can't—' Her dad couldn't finish the sentence.

They simply stood for a while, letting the loveliness of the surroundings calm their spirits.

'The way I see it,' Edie said, holding both their hands, as they looked at the water rushing over the rocks, 'you get people who are important to you, for as long as you get them. You never know how long it will be. You have to accept it and make use of the time you have. We didn't have Mum very long. But that doesn't mean she didn't make a huge difference to us. We loved her and she loved us. We'll never forget her. We still love her.'

A plane passed high in the clouds overhead and Edie gazed up at it. She squeezed both their hands.

They drove to Matlock Bath and went for lunch in a pub with a flotilla of motorcycles outside it. They were deep in biker country.

'Isla is such a beautiful name,' Edie said. 'If I ever have a girl child, she'll have the middle name Isla.'

'If you still have a viable uterus,' Meg said, conversationally.

'Dependent on that,' Edie agreed. 'There's probably a family of moles living in there by now.'

'Good grief, Meg. Never get a job as a political speech writer,' their dad said.

'That reminds me. I've applied for a bunch of jobs,' Meg said. 'At care homes. I thought I could use the experience I've already got and get something with more hours.'

'That's great,' Edie said. 'Well done. Actually, I've been wondering,' she continued, as she plunked a piece of scampi in her pot of tartare sauce, 'if you'd like to live with me?'

Meg did a double take.

'What? Why?' she recovered, 'I mean, thanks. Really?'

'You don't have to,' Edie said. 'I thought it might be fun. I've been looking at houses in Carrington. I need a lodger, they might be big for me on my own. If Dad could spare you? It's only an idea. We'd be walking distance from Dad, obviously, too.'

'Dad, what do you think?' Meg said.

'I think it's a wonderful idea. You might, both, er, feel more comfortable to entertain young gentleman callers under Edie's roof. Can't stay as comforts to your father forever.'

'My squalid morals guarantee it will be naught more than a bonking shop, Dad. Are you finishing those chips?' Edie helped herself to one.

'I have one condition, however.'

'Yes?' Edie said.

'You take those bloody squawking budget parrots which I was completely hoodwinked into letting over the threshold. RSPB, my arse.'

77

Four months later

Edie and Meg had never catered Christmas lunch for guests before, and it'd be a lie to say the planning went off without a hitch or a cross word. The last few months living together in Edie's three-bed redbrick semi had gone extraordinarily well, but this hospitality tested the reborn sisterly harmony.

With some swearing and loss of temper, days before, she and Meg had assembled an IKEA side table on wheels, one that could accommodate the Meg spread, adjacent to and yet separate from the main meaty event. They drove there in Edie's new Mini, which had been purchased with the funds from her bestselling book.

The official Elliot Owen autobiography had sold an awful lot, way beyond expectations, netting Edie a hefty bonus. Whether it was simply the Elliot Owen effect, or the result of the publicity with Edie, no one was quite sure. As Richard relayed with evident pleasure: 'Failure is an orphan and success has many parents, and let me tell you, there's now so many parents of this project you'd think we were in a sex cult in Utah.'

Edie couldn't recommend having cardboard boxes full of hardback books bearing a stunning cover photograph of your beloved and much-missed ex-boyfriend around the house for your psychic calm, but the money had come in handy. She'd deliberately swerved knowing much about Jan's book, but the splash it made seemed to have been minimal, and the more diehard Owen fans had organised a boycott.

The dining room in Edie's house had doors that could be opened on to the front room, creating a bigger space, and they'd crammed in seven chairs round a table that was looking pretty cramped with this many place settings.

Edie's small galley kitchen was a chaotic scene, as one p.m. drew near: pans on every hob, cross-hatched Brussel sprouts waiting in a colander, the turkey resting while Meg blasted her somewhat fecal-looking nut loaf at the top setting. There was stuff *everywhere*. Edie felt if only she had a second kitchen, of equivalent size, her cooking would flourish and her angst would disappear.

Things eased when Meg made an executive decision to pop one of the cavas early: 'chef's privileges.'

Edie ran over to the CD player and moments later, they toasted the festive season and their culinary efforts to 'My Funny Valentine', background harmonies by Beryl and Meryl.

'It's our tradition we have Frank Sinatra during the making of lunch,' Edie said.

'Is it?' Meg said. 'Since when?'

'Since now. Traditions have to start somewhere. I'm starting one.'

Meg was unsure as Frank Sinatra represented a lot of patriarchal control and gangster capitalism, but Edie pointed out as a Sicilian-American he'd also done a lot for immigrants, so they agreed to overlook Ol' Blue Eyes more questionable qualities, for one day.

As Edie stirred the cranberry sauce, she wondered about absent friends. She had no idea where he was spending this day. Maybe on a beach. Maybe at a new girlfriend's. There had been no texts, tweets, emails, no 21st-century communications between them, whatsoever. They both had instinctively understood that not enough would be worse than nothing at all. Fraser had made an effort to stay in touch however, to let her know she was gone but not forgotten, and Edie was pleased.

'I have to tell you this so you don't ever think he's being ignorant or rude if you have any big personal news,' he said, in his first call. 'Elliot told me he didn't want to know, on pain of death, if you met anyone.'

Fraser clearly thought this was hard for Edie to hear but it comforted her, to know that was mutual.

'Likewise, if that's OK. I doubt the media will respect my wishes in this matter, mind you.'

'I think you're both being massive crywankers myself, you could just Skype. But what do I know.'

They had met for coffee a few weeks ago and Fraser said he knew that Elliot told Edie about the adoption.

In the long conversation that followed, Fraser said, 'You

realise what that meant, him telling you? That was well huge.'
Edie agreed it had been 'well huge', and at the time, she
hadn't realised.

The media definitely didn't get Edie's memo about Elliot,
far from it. And a few weeks ago, Edie couldn't avoid some
good news of his professional success, a major film role that
meant he was going to get even more famous, and he wasn't
coming back. It was possibly what prompted the postcard.

It was upstairs in Edie's bedroom, tucked in the mirror on
her night table: palm trees silhouetted against a Californian
sunset. It had only two sentences on it, the most reread
sentences in the history of sentences.

I notice, when you're not around. I think the word is 'saudade'.

Edie had allowed herself one bout of sobbing and fretting she
should've gone with him. Then looked around at her home, and
reminded herself why she hadn't. What happened between them
wasn't sad, it was wonderful. It would be with her forever.

Their guests arrived – first their dad, clutching his bottle
of port, then Hannah and Chloe, and Nick and Ros.

Ros, the blind date, had turned out to be batty in a good
way. Personally, Edie thought playing roller derby and having
a pet ferret was ace. She could take or leave the Reiki
healing.

Chloe turned out to be one of the loveliest, most serene
people that Edie had ever encountered, and had an effect on
Hannah she'd never seen before.

Meg found everyone a seat, and a hat – 'Oh God, what,

hats?' Nick said. 'Hats,' Meg affirmed, who was already in hers
– and pushed a drink into their hands.

Edie ran round panicking and chanting ROAST! ROAST?
at the parsnips.

'Right, this is a first time for Christmas lunch, so if there's
any bodges, forgive,' Edie said, when they were finally ready
to roll out. She thought the mash could've done with more
mashing, but other than that, she had to say it looked pretty
good.

As they got sat down, the doorbell went.

'I told Winnie and Kez they could bring their new dog in
to see us.' Meg jumped up, licking her fingers.

'As long as they know the dress code is "dressed". Oh
bugger, I forgot the pigs in blankets,' Edie said, getting up
too, and dashing into the kitchen.

They came back to the table at the same time, Edie holding
a roasting tray full of cocktail sausages, Meg looking more
excitable than the year she unwrapped a Sylvanian Families
Furbank Squirrel Family collection, which was saying something.

'Edie?'

Edie pushed the dish on to the table and wiped her sweating
forehead awkwardly, with one oven-gloved hand.

'Yeah?'

Meg looked at her with an expression of intense anticipation.

'It's someone for you.'

Acknowledgements

Gah, sorry for boring on here but the thank you list just gets longer each time. Every book is a group effort and I'm so grateful for the top level team I have around me. First of all, thanks to my editors Martha Ashby and Helen Huthwaite. Your hard work, humour, thoughtful notes and constant genuine care for the thing itself is hugely appreciated by your author. Further thanks to Kimberley Young and the whole HarperCollins family for their enthusiasm, creativity and excellent parties. Keshini Naidoo, Copy Editor Extraordinaire: gets laughs AND results, who can argue with that?

My agent Doug Kean, as ever, has gone beyond the call of duty and not only been a superb and supportive agent but consented to have the odd drink with me. Cheers to you, sir.

My first draft readers are indispensable and I'm more thankful to you all than you ever realise: my brother Ewan, Sean Hewitt, Tara de Cozar, Katie and Fraser (ta for the name,

Fraz), Kristy Berry, Jenny Howe, James Donaghy, Jennifer Whitehead and Mark Casarotto.

Also practical thanks to Jane Sturrock, who helped me on the logistics of ghost writing, and David Nolan, for pointers on penning autobiographies (you're NOT Jan, OK? Heh heh).

I wouldn't have been able to name the hero if my friend Elliot Elam hadn't generously lent me his, and equally I wouldn't have had one for the heroine without Julian Simpson and Jana Carpenter agreeing I could take their lovely daughter's name in vain. Speaking of Julian, thanks also for the odd hint, tip and a TV-world tale about a garden gnome. I never thought I'd meet someone who swore more than me. And thank you to the delightful beauty, Elizabeth Hampson, for letting me model artwork-Edie on you. It wasn't at all creepy when I asked to use your photos, right? Cool.

This is the first story I've set in my home city and it seems only right to thank everyone here for being so brilliant, sorry I can't name you all without this turning into a shopping list but you know who you are. This time I will just offer a special shout to my lovely in-laws Ray, Andrea and Sally, and their unwavering positivity. From the beginning of writing books, I've been bowled over by how much all my family has cheered me on, from Notts to Milton Keynes and up to Scotland: thank you all so much.

And thank you to Alex. None of it would be possible without you. Or it would, but not as good.